PRAISE FOR MARKO KLOOS

"Frontlines is earnest, optimistic, and fun, even as it deals with subject matter that's intrinsically grim. It's a story that strikes the perfect balance between escapism and serious reflection, and it's the perfect military sci-fi series to escape into for a week or two."

—The Verge

"Powered armor, nuclear warfare, and [a] bit of grand theft auto combine for a thrilling tale of battle in space."

—*Booklist*

"Marko Kloos's military science fiction Frontlines series is quickly becoming one of our favorites . . . Kloos is well on his way to becoming one of the genre's best assets."

—*io9*

"There is nobody who does [military SF] better than Marko Kloos. His Frontlines series is a worthy successor to such classics as *Starship Troopers*, *The Forever War*, and *We All Died at Breakaway Station*."

—George R. R. Martin

"Military science fiction is tricky because it either intends to lampoon the military industrial complex or paints it in such a way that you must really have to love guns to enjoy the work. *Terms of Enlistment* walks that fine line by showing a world where the military is one of the few viable options off a shattered Earth and intermixes it with a knowledge of military tactics and weapons that doesn't turn off the casual reader."

—Buzzfeed

CENTERS OF
GRAVITY

NAC

BY MARKO KLOOS

Frontlines

Terms of Enlistment

Lines of Departure

Angles of Attack

Chains of Command

Fields of Fire

Points of Impact

Orders of Battle

Measures of Absolution (A Frontlines Kindle novella)

"Lucky Thirteen" (A Frontlines Kindle short story)

The Palladium Wars

Aftershocks

Ballistic

Citadel

CENTERS OF GRAVITY

MARKO KLOOS

47NORTH

Published by 47North, Seattle

www.apub.com

Amazon, the Amazon logo, and 47North are trademarks of Amazon.com, Inc., or its affiliates.

ISBN-13: 9781542032810 (paperback)

ISBN-13: 9781542032803 (digital)

Cover design by Mike Heath

Cover image: © amgun / Shutterstock

Printed in the United States of America

*For all those who volunteer to go into dark places
to keep us safe from the monsters.*

CHAPTER 1

——————— FIRST LIGHT ———————

I thought I knew what darkness was before we got here, but I was wrong.

We are far out in the void between the stars, so far that the light from the sun closest to us has been traveling from its source since before I was born. The low-light gear on the Blackfly is state-of-the-art equipment, arrays of image intensifiers that can amplify that distant starlight by a factor of half a million, but through my helmet display, it still looks like I am trying to find my way through a pitch-dark building with only the feeble electroluminescent screen of my wrist chronograph for illumination. We have been flying recon missions in the Blackflies for the last two weeks, and whenever we return to NACS *Washington*, seeing the lights of the ship appearing in the dark on our return approach has become an almost religious experience to me. But the carrier is far behind us, coasting through the void a million kilometers away, and we are only beginning the recon run we were sent out to do.

"Coming up on the final nav marker in ten, Major Grayson," the pilot sends from the flight deck. I raise the visor of my helmet and look to my left, down the passageway to the cockpit. Inside the ship, the battle lights are red, to preserve our night vision, even though there isn't

anything to see with the naked eye outside, and even though we could all navigate the entire drop ship blindfolded by now.

"Copy that. What's the latest fix on the bogey?" I reply.

"Fifty thousand klicks off our starboard bow, still tracking on a reciprocal heading. No sign they have any clue we're here."

"We're just a tiny chunk of space debris," I say. "Don't mind us, Mr. Lanky."

Across the cargo hold from me, Sergeant Mills trains her sensor screen on the general area the pilot indicated. Even in the semidarkness of the hold, I can see the focused expression on her face.

"There he is," she says after a few moments. "The white ones are so much easier to spot."

"For relative values of *easy*," I reply. "We'd still be flying blind without the Wonderballs."

For the last couple of weeks, *Washington*'s drop ships have been seeding hundreds of Wonderballs, the experimental new optical drones, all over the neighborhood of the rogue planet. We are steadily building a web of optical trip wires that should be impossible to detect for the Lankies. The Wonderballs catalogue the way space *should* look around them, and whenever one of the Lanky seed ships in the system passes in front of another drone or a distant star and blocks its light momentarily, the drones get a fix and communicate the information down the chain to all the other ones with a light signal that takes less than a millisecond.

I get out of my chair and cross the cargo hold to grab the back of Mills's seat and look at her sensor screen. She is one of my combat controllers, the junior enlisted member of the section's third squad, and on her first combat deployment since she graduated from the CCT school. We've done three missions together now, and it took until halfway through the second one for her to stop ending every sentence with "sir." She's twenty-three but looks younger, and she makes me feel impossibly old even though I still have half a decade to go until forty.

"It helps when you know where to point the scope," she says. "Look at that thing, just tooling along."

I look at the outline of the seed ship that is taking up most of her screen. The new kind of ship we spotted for the first time a few weeks ago is not actually white according to the spectrometer readings, but rather various shades of dirty gray. Compared to the kind of seed ship we have known so far, however, it might as well be painted in blaze orange. Not only do the ship's hulls reflect the distant starlight instead of swallowing it, they also show up on infrared, which makes them a thousand times easier to track and target.

"Seventeen hundred meters," I read off the scale the computer superimposed on the bottom of the sensor screen. "That's a small one. The ones we've seen so far are usually almost twice as long."

"Maybe they have different ship classes, like we do," Mills says.

"A Lanky frigate," I say, and she chuckles softly. The seed ship on her screen is still almost three times as long as *Washington* and probably twice as massive, and thinking of it as a minor ship is darkly funny.

"Have you ever seen one from close-up?" Mills asks. I can tell she had to bite the "sir" off the end of the question with some effort, but it's coming easier to her now.

"More than one," I reply. "Back in '12, when we returned to the solar system on *Indy*, we popped out of the Alcubierre chute so close to one that we had to take evasive action. Could have just about stuck an arm out of the airlock and touched their hull."

"I read about that mission. When I was in tech school. I knew there was a combat controller with them. I didn't know that was you."

"I was a minor player," I say. "Colonel Campbell and his crew did all the heavy lifting."

"Everyone on that ship went above and beyond," she says. She shifts her attention from her screen and looks up at me. Then she shrugs.

"Not trying to suck up, sir. Just stating what the history books say."

"It didn't feel like it at the time. And some gave more than others."

Some of us are still alive, I think. The memory comes back with more impact than I had expected after all this time, that feeling of certainty the world was about to end. Then I realize that this young sergeant was fifteen when we battled the Lankies on Earth for the first time, and I decide to keep those thoughts to myself. On the screen in front of Staff Sergeant Mills, our alien nemesis continues its slow and steady journey away from the rogue planet and the moon we are about to survey. Since we arrived in this strange and hostile system, we have been mapping and cataloguing it, carrying a little light further into the darkness with every mission. The planet has four moons orbiting it, all bigger than Earth's moon and wildly different from each other as far as we can tell. Today will be our first close look at one of them. The recon drones showed that it's covered in ice, which could mean a solution to one of our pressing problems—a finite water supply that's slowly dwindling every day. But before we can send the engineer teams down to the surface to set up a mining outpost, we need to make sure that the place isn't already under hostile management.

On the screen, a readout shows the distance to the Lanky. I'm happy to see that the number's increasing at a good clip as the seed ship moves away from us: sixty, seventy, eighty thousand meters. I'll never get used to being this close to Lanky ships, even if the ones in this system have never shown any interest in our tiny little drop ships. It feels like how I imagine diving with sharks would feel, only without the benefit of a protective cage, and with sharks that are almost two kilometers long.

"Seven minutes to the final marker," I say to Sergeant Mills. "Let's warm up the birds and run one more check on the hardware."

"Affirmative," Mills replies. She switches screens to bring up the payload management page. Our Blackfly has six hardpoints, two under each wing and two on the belly of the ship. Each of them is weighed down with a missile-shaped seismic drone, a new development from the

4

R&D division. They've been tested in all sorts of different environments in the solar system before, but this is the first time they're going to be used in an operational setting.

I watch as she verifies the status of the drive systems, guidance modules, and sensor packages. Everything comes up green. We have a lot of new tech with us on this trip, and the new toys from R&D have worked flawlessly so far. The Wonderballs alone have been beyond invaluable. We are in a new environment, operating under conditions nobody has ever experienced or expected, but our technology has allowed us to start adapting to our predicament.

"If this works, we can take all the showers we want again," I say.

Mills groans wistfully. "I can't wait. I probably smell like a trash compactor by now."

"We all do, Mills. But it's like eating garlic. If everyone smells, nobody smells."

"Just think. Soap and shampoo. Fifteen or twenty minutes under steaming hot water."

"I'm a married man, Sergeant. I don't need to hear this kind of indecent talk," I reply.

She laughs and shakes her head.

"It's a pipe dream right now anyway. It'll take weeks before we see the first water from that moon." She finishes her checklist and glances up at me.

"Your wife's a pilot, isn't she?"

I nod. "Dragonfly jock. She's the squadron commander of ATS-13, on *Ottawa*."

"Military marriage," Mills says. "I never had the guts to even consider that. Seems like someone would always be on deployment."

"It's a little rough sometimes," I concede. "But we've made it work. It makes you much more mindful of how you spend the time you do get together."

5

"Makes sense, I suppose. My boyfriend is a civilian. No chance of him getting deployed while I am on leave. But there's stuff about my life that he just doesn't get. And there's no point trying to explain it."

"I know what you mean," I say.

Under normal circumstances, I would not be talking marriage and relationships with a junior subordinate, and she wouldn't be volunteering that information to me. But these are not normal circumstances. Since the initial shock of our situation has worn off just a little, the regular boundaries of military hierarchy have shifted, and the crew have been more egalitarian and less formal with each other across the ranks. It feels as if everyone is eager to share details of their lives and families back home to keep hope alive, to know that we are still connected to the rest of humanity even though we are separated from them by an almost unfathomable gulf of space and time. Halley may be nine hundred light-years away, but she is still my wife, and that will not change for me even if the distance between us remains forever.

"Launch window in five minutes," the pilot announces.

"Copy launch window in five," I acknowledge. "Anything other than that bogey in the neighborhood?"

"Negative," the pilot says. *"All dark and quiet out here."*

"Just the way we like it." I return to my seat to strap in for the launch and the orbital insert burn we will perform shortly after releasing our payload. Our mission profile calls for orbiting the moon and taking a direct look at the surface while the drones deploy to collect sensor data on the ground. The moon is so close now that it fills most of the view from the dorsal sensor array. It's the brightest thing in this system because of its frozen surface, but there's no sun here to illuminate it, and the light from the distant stars is barely enough to make the moon stand out from the background of deep space.

"We are go for launch on all six birds," Sergeant Mills says. "All systems green, guidance packages live and tracking."

"So far, so good," I reply. "It would suck to come all the way out here with a dead payload."

"Three days out, three days back. By the time they get together another mission package, that would be a week and a half down the drain, maybe two."

"So let's hope these things keep doing what the techies said they'll do. We can't afford two wasted weeks."

I lower my helmet visor and switch the display to DASS mode to get a look at our surroundings without bulkheads or armor plating obstructing the view. The Distributed Aperture Sensor System combines the inputs from all the camera lenses and sensor arrays on the hull and stitches them together into a seamless panoramic view of the space around us. The ice moon looms ahead and above the ship. It looks foreboding, cold and hostile, unwelcoming. The sight of it without the filter layer of a console screen makes me feel a primal trickle of fear that's creeping up my spine and seizing hold of some ancient part of my brain. I switch back out of DASS mode and raise my visor. The sight of the bulkheads and the hull plating in front of me makes the unnerving sensation abate. Our brains have allowed us to travel between the stars, but our instincts still make us want to crawl into little holes for safety whenever we sense danger approaching. The DASS is a fantastic tool for situational awareness inside an armored vehicle on firm ground. Using it in space always makes me feel unsettled, keenly aware of how tiny and fragile we humans are against the backdrop of infinity.

"May I ask you a question, sir?" Mills asks.

"Sure," I say. "What's on your mind?"

"You're the commanding officer of the special tactics team. You have a stable full of trained lieutenants and sergeants to send out on recon runs. We have four squads in the combat controller section alone. Why do you go on missions yourself? If you don't mind me asking."

"I'm not the type to sit in an office and push icons around on a screen all day," I say. "I'd go stir-crazy right now. And I wouldn't ask my team to do stuff I won't do myself. I guess I was an NCO for too long."

"I can respect that," Mills replies. "It's just a bit unusual for a field-grade officer, that's all."

"What, a major who gets his hands dirty?" I say.

"I didn't say *that*," she says, and I can hear the smile in her voice.

"Launch window in T-minus thirty seconds," the pilot updates from the cockpit.

"Copy launch window T-minus three-zero," I confirm. "Standing by on payload. All systems green."

Out of habit and paranoia, I check the location of the seed ship again even though I know that Mills and the pilot are tracking its course as well. There is no margin for error or sloppiness out here, in a place we have only started to figure out, where death can be around every corner we turn. The Lanky is still on the same heading and moving at the same speed, steadily receding into the darkness behind us.

"Ten seconds to launch threshold," Mills says. She's all business now, focused on her control screens, fingertips dancing across the input fields. When we reach the threshold, an alert tone chirps.

"Initiating launch sequence," Mills sends over the intercom. "Launching One."

The ship rocks just a little as the first of the recon drones detaches from its underwing pylon and shoots off toward the dark ice moon ahead. The drone's rocket drive burns for just a few seconds, then extinguishes again, just enough acceleration for the drone to make the orbital insertion trajectory.

"Bird One is away and tracking for orbital insert point. Ready on Bird Two. Three . . . two . . . one. Launching Two."

The second drone drops from a pylon on the other side of the ship and shoots off into the darkness to follow its predecessor. Mills launches the rest of the drones in ten-second intervals to keep them separated and spaced out. We've had the opportunity to run simulations of the launch a dozen times on the way here, and if Mills feels any nervousness at the live event, she doesn't show it one bit. After a minute, our drop ship's external ordnance pylons are empty, and half a dozen autonomous little spacecraft are rushing toward the surface of the ice moon.

"All birds are tracking in the green," Mills says and sits back in her chair with a slow exhalation. "Now the tricky part begins."

The drones make their way to six different insertion points in orbit, where they flip themselves around with brief bursts from their lateral thrusters to slow their descent to the surface with the lowest possible thermal signature. They are programmed to land on the ground a few kilometers apart in a hexagonal pattern that will allow quick and precise triangulation of seismic activity, whether from the moon's geological processes or from the movements of any Lankies that may be dwelling somewhere out of sight underground. It would be the first time we encounter them on a moon or a planet without an atmosphere, but this has been a month of many firsts, and we are not leaving anything to chance out here.

"Orbital insert burn in thirty seconds," the pilot sends.

I double-check my seat harness and connect the umbilical line that will feed my suit oxygen from the ship's supply in a depressurization emergency. If we have a major failure all the way out here, we will probably not be around by the time a rescue team arrives from *Washington*, but there is a certain comfort in safety routines when there is nothing else you can do.

The pilot brings the ship around, then lights the engines briefly to slow us down and nudge the Blackfly into orbit. The drones are racing down to the surface ahead of us, a little swarm of glowing dots on the infrared sensor that is barely visible against the much larger signature of the ice moon.

"First bird is past the horizon," Mills says. "There goes number two. And three."

We watch as the drones rush ahead and disappear beyond the curvature of the visible horizon from our view angle, already much closer to the ground than we will be unless our day takes a turn for the worse. The drones will touch down in another three minutes, and if they stick their landings, we will receive their light signals on our second orbit around the moon.

From far away, the surface of the ice moon looked as smooth as an eggshell. As we dip into our low orbit, I can see that the ground down there is irregular after all, dotted with little crater pockmarks and fissures that go on for kilometers. I've been all over the solar system and the settled part of our little backwater galaxy, but I've never seen a planet or moon that looked as alien and unwelcoming as this one, cold and hard and bathed in utter darkness. But if we can mine the ice down there without too much trouble, our water problem is solved, and before we send people to the surface, we need to make sure that ice crust isn't crawling with Lankies. It's not their preferred environment, but we know they can make themselves at home deep in solid ice.

"It looks cold as fuck," Sergeant Mills comments. "I don't envy the engineer teams that will have to go down there."

"They'll bring their own heat," I say. "Good old Mr. Fusion."

We hurtle around the curvature of the ice moon. Underneath the belly of the drop ship, the dark surface glides past at several kilometers per second. This one is the smallest of the four moons we have discovered around the rogue gas giant, but it still measures two thousand kilometers across, which makes it only a little smaller than Pluto.

A few minutes into our orbit, a bright little flare lights up the infrared sensor screen. Ten seconds later, another one follows, then a third. One by one, the drones are firing their rocket motors to slow down their descent to the surface.

"Four. Five. And six," Mills counts the thermal signatures. "We got positive retro on all the birds."

I check my chrono and compare it with the elapsed mission timer on my data screen.

"Touchdown in three minutes. Telemetry uplink in ten. *Hopefully*," I add.

The next few minutes are just a minuscule fraction of the time it took us to get here, but they seem to tick by much slower than the hours that came before. Once we are around the moon again, we will find out whether the experimental technology works as designed, or we have wasted a week of our time and a lot of precious fuel just to witness a brief firework show.

I watch the tactical plot on my console, where the little icon that represents our Blackfly is steadily crawling along the dotted line of our orbital trajectory at four kilometers per second. We are the loneliest humans in the universe right now, a million kilometers out in front of the carrier, circling a dark moon no human has ever orbited before. This is the sort of thing I had wished for when I left the PRC and joined the Corps, before the Lankies and all the death and hardship that came with them, and for just a little while I allow myself to take in the wonder of it all, the undeniable excitement of discovering something new, a place that wasn't on any stellar map before we saw it.

"We'll need to come up with names for these moons," I say to Sergeant Mills.

"We're the first ones here," she replies. "We ought to get to name this one at least."

"I'll stake your claim for you once we get back. No promises, though," I say.

"Ah, they probably already named it. Something boring, like Greek mythology. Or worse, just a bunch of numbers and letters."

I look at my screen, where the combined input from the ship's sensor array paints a composite image of the moon, the computer's best guess of what it would look like to our eyes if it had visible light from a nearby sun reflected on the surface. It looks as barren as the ice sheet on

Greenland, utterly bereft of any signs of life. Maybe a bunch of letters and numbers would be perfectly appropriate as a name for this frozen ball of ice spinning in eternal darkness.

On our third orbit, our consoles chirp with incoming transmission notifications from the optical comms array. Mills lets out a low cheer.

"We have telemetry uplink," she announces. "Counting one . . . two . . . three nodes. Wait, there's number four." She sits back in her chair and exhales sharply. "Four out of six. One more than we need. Looks like two didn't make it down in one piece."

The drones are designed to fire a probe into the surface of the moon and listen for vibrations, either from seismic activity or from Lankies moving around. The more sensors on the network, the faster and more accurate the triangulations, but the minimum of working probes for a detection network is three.

"Not perfect, but I'll take it," I say.

"We have a solid data link on optical. Man, these things work well in this darkness. Three gigabytes per second. I've never seen these do more than a gig and a half."

It takes us a few more minutes to get close to the spot where the drones have spread out on the surface. I watch the data rate increase steadily as we get closer until the throughput reads almost five gigabytes per second. The LED emitters in the drones are sending their data streams as light signals, the bits and bytes encoded in pulses and color shifts too fast for human eyes to see. We still don't know exactly how the Lankies sense the electromagnetic signatures of radio transmissions, but we do know that they are blind to visible wavelengths, and the Avenger-class carriers and all their drop ships have been built from the ground up for using free-space optical communication to take advantage of that blind spot. FSO is a very short-range way to talk on Lanky-controlled worlds with their cloud cover and high humidity, but out here in space, it works as well as radio signals, and it doesn't attract unwanted attention.

"There they are," Mills says. "First light on that rock in billions of years."

On the screen that shows the view ahead, four intensely bright pinpricks of light appear, forming an uneven diamond shape on the dark surface of the moon. In the utter blackness all around us, it looks like the little cluster of lights is rushing toward us, then passing underneath the ship and hurtling down our wake like tracer rounds from an autocannon. I switch the screen to the stern view and watch the lights recede into the distance, converging until they seem to touch each other before disappearing beyond the curve of the moon's horizon.

"All right, let's see what we can see." Mills taps the screen that shows the data stream from the drone network. I return my attention to my own console and set it to the same output. In just that single overhead pass, the FSO signal from the drones poured a few hundred gigabytes of data into the ship's computer, everything from environmental information to multispectral 360-degree video feeds from all four surviving drones. In the light from the high-powered LEDs of the transmitters, the landscape at the landing site looks hard as glass, with moderate variations and imperfections in the surface.

First light on that rock in billions of years. I repeat Mills's comment in my head as I look at the landscape. The drone LEDs are carving small islands of light out of the darkness, artificial campfires in the middle of a pitch-black frozen desert.

"Well, that worked like a charm," Mills says. "Surface temperature is minus 110 degrees. Surface composition is mostly water ice, some carbon dioxide, silicates, traces of organic compounds. Looks like the spectral analysis was pretty dead-on."

"That's a lot of water. And it's not sitting at the bottom of a gravity well. Should be easy enough to take. If there aren't any neighbors around who can object."

"We've never seen any Lankies on worlds without an atmosphere," Mills says. "Not once."

"That's true. But we've had a lot of firsts this month, Mills. The second we leave something to chance, we'll be in shit up to our eyebrows."

Sergeant Mills chuckles softly. "You mean we aren't already?"

"It can always get deeper. You've been in long enough to know that."

"Fair enough." Mills scrolls through her data screens. "We'll need to do a few more orbits to get the full picture for seismic activity. But there's nothing stirring down there right now. No Lanky signatures."

"We'll give it plenty of time," I say. "No reason to rush this."

We exchange smiles and settle in for our next orbit, with nothing else to do right now but keep an eye on the consoles and decide when we've extracted enough data to confirm that there aren't any Lankies tunneling through the ice crust out of sight. But so far it looks clean to the seismic probes, and in a month of things going violently sideways for us, I'll take all the wins I can get.

For the first few days after we arrived, despair came easily, and it was difficult not to give in to the feeling. But now that we all have things to do to assure our basic survival in this place, the overwhelming dread I felt in the beginning is diminished, a faint background current in my head that's easy enough to push aside with the immediacy and urgency of the basic survival tasks at hand. Find water, maybe find protein, keep an eye on our enemies, and then—hopefully—find a way out of here.

We are in the darkest place we've ever been, but we are not lonely. A million kilometers away, NACS *Washington* is waiting for our return, and we get to bring back word that our water supply isn't a problem anymore. However long our march home will be, we have just taken the first big step on the route, and we will keep putting one foot in front of the other, because that's what humans do. Even when the odds against us are stacked up sky-high, we are terrible at sitting down and giving up.

"It's kind of beautiful," Mills says when we see the cluster of lights on the horizon again on our next orbital pass. "Doesn't matter if it's dark and cold out here. We know how to bring our own light."

She swivels her chair around to face me.

14

"You think the Lankies have started to regret ever messing with us in the first place?"

I consider her question and find myself nodding in agreement.

"I think we got an upgrade from 'nuisance' to 'serious threat' the day we cracked one of their seed ships open for the first time," I say.

Mills smiles and turns back around. "Plucky little species, aren't we?"

We pass over the seismic probes' little island of light again and the console screen comes alive with the flow of incoming data. A month ago, we didn't know the place existed, and now we've brought heat, light, and a comms network to it in a single orbital pass.

Plucky little species indeed, I think. *And if we don't make it out of here, someone will know that we were here once, when the light from those probes reaches an optical telescope back home in nine hundred years.*

"Flight, mission," I send to the cockpit. "Give us five more orbits, and if the data are the same, let's get ready to head home. Looks like hot showers might be making a comeback."

The pilot chuckles as he replies.

"Copy that, and halle-frickin'-lujah."

CHAPTER 2

—————— SURVEY SAYS ——————

After a week spent in a vacsuit confined in the close quarters of a Blackfly cargo hold, it feels a little strange to walk around in regular fatigues on the decks of NACS *Washington* again. Even the meal I eat in the officer mess feels like an opulent indulgence compared to the emergency field rations that fed us on the trip out to the ice moon. But the nicest thing about being back on the ship is seeing other faces again.

"Good morning, Major Grayson. Good to see you back," Captain Harper says when I walk into the STT office. My team's second-in-command is the head of the SEAL section, and the most senior and experienced of my four captains.

"Is it morning? I didn't realize we're still tracking that sort of thing."

"Ship time is ship time, sir. I heard your field trip was a success."

"It was," I reply. "Found us a few trillion tons of water ice. But my back is still paying the mortgage on that. Six days in a Blackfly."

"That's rough." Harper winces in sympathy. "Glad it was you and not me, to be honest."

"Oh, I had plenty of time to question my decision, Captain. How is the team?"

"We are still one hundred percent combat ready. Had a bit of an issue with the supply division while you were gone, though."

"Oh?" I ask. "How so?"

"They're cutting back the rations for the crew. Including the grunts. Everyone's on eighteen hundred calories now. To stretch out the food stores until those new plants start producing beans, but that's going to be a while. Plants only grow as fast as they grow, no matter how much we need them. Had to take it all the way to the boss. I told him that I could either keep training my team or cut their calories by almost half, but not both."

"And how did that go?"

Harper shrugs. "I asked the colonel how much the calorie savings for one company-sized team would be worth to him in terms of combat readiness. Told him the STT needs to be on regular rations if he wants them to keep the edge honed. We spend three hours a day on PT and range time. He came around to seeing it my way. Full rations for special ops personnel until further notice."

"That's going to get us some resentment from the SI companies," I say. "I'm not sure I like the idea."

"If these boys and girls get their calories cut down like that, we can't do anything with them inside of a month because they'll start losing conditioning and muscle mass. And if there's ground action in our near future, the STT goes in first. They'll need us to stay sharp."

"I can't argue with that. As much as I don't want the SI grunts to think that we consider ourselves special."

"Well, we are," Harper says with a smirk. "It's right on the label. Special tactics team."

He walks over to the personnel status screen on the nearby bulkhead. I have sixty-four troops in the STT, all present and electronically accounted for, with location markers that show where each individual member is currently located on the ship. I'm happy to see that all the names are in green—no injuries or sick calls.

"The on-watch squads are down at the range right now, except for the two Force Recon squads. They're doing some running out on the silo track. Rest squads are in the rack and the off-watch squads are grabbing chow."

"I'm glad you've been keeping them busy, Captain," I say.

"Idle hands and all that. Oh, I got a notice from upstairs. Command crew meeting at 1100. You want me to take that one? You are probably looking forward to stretching your legs some after all that sitting."

I consider Captain Harper's suggestion. He was my stand-in during the week when I was cooped up in a Blackfly, but now that I'm back, I feel obliged to shoulder the team-leader burdens again, including the department head meetings.

"No, you go ahead and join the range squads if you want. I'll go see the bosses. They need an in-person briefing on that scouting run anyway."

"All right," Harper says. "Happy to let you take point again. I get anxious in a room full of colonels."

When I step into the flag briefing room at 1100 hours, there are more people gathered than just the four command-level officers usually present. Three people in civilian tech overalls are sitting on one side of the table, filling the room almost to capacity with their added presence. One of them is Dr. Elin Vandenberg, the ship's resident xenobiologist, who nods at me when our eyes meet.

"Major Grayson," Colonel Drake says. "Glad to have you back. And good work on the recon run."

"Thank you, sir. Glad to be back." I close the door to the briefing room behind me and claim the last free chair next to Lieutenant Colonel Campbell.

"We're joined by the Fleet Science Division today," Colonel Drake says. "You all know Dr. Vandenberg, our xenobiologist. This is Dr. Brotherton from the astro section. Major Grayson, our special tactics team lead."

We exchange courtesy nods as I sit down. The scientists of the astro section are technically commissioned officers, but the man sitting next to Elin Vandenberg is military personnel in the same peripheral way she is, as a highly trained specialist who got officer stars as an administrative courtesy to bestow the perks and pay of field-grade officers.

"All right. Command briefing is in progress," Lieutenant Colonel Campbell says. "Door is closed. All information is eyes-only and not for crew dissemination unless mission relevant. Go ahead, sir."

"Thank you, XO." Colonel Drake pulls up a tactical map on the bulkhead screen behind him. It shows the planetary constellation of the rogue system, a gas giant in the center and four moons orbiting it at various distances and velocities. The icon for NACS *Washington* is hanging in space between the orbits of the third and fourth moons, well away from any of the orange icons representing verified Lanky seed ships. I do a quick count and tally over a dozen enemy ships on the plot, most of them clustered between the gas giant and the second moon.

"*Situation*," Colonel Drake says. "We are in hostile space in a rogue planetary system in the Corvus constellation, surrounded by enemies and nine hundred light-years from our supply lines. We are on limited water, reactor fuel, ordnance, and food, and we don't have an obvious way out. That, to be blunt, is a terrible tactical position."

He rotates the map slowly to give us a view of the system from all angles.

"However, things are starting to look up. With the combined efforts of the assault transport squadrons and the logistics group, we have deployed more than a thousand Wonderballs over the last two weeks. Now we have a way to spot Lanky ships long before they get close to us. And with Major Grayson's successful survey of the ice moon, we now have a source of unlimited drinking water. Overall, we are much better off today than we were when we stumbled into this place two weeks ago. Now, the most critical issue is our food supply. Hydroponics has seeded thousands of new soybeans, but time is not on our side. We will be out of food stores before any of the new plants produces its first beans. Back in the PRC, the Basic Nutritional Allowance rations we got every week were said to be at least partly reconstituted human waste, but the ship lacks the technical facilities to recycle its sewage to reclaim calories."

On the map hologram, the four moons of the rogue system flash in turn, each in a different color: red, green, blue, yellow.

"I asked the astro division to join us this morning," Colonel Drake continues, "to share what they've learned from our surveillance." The commander of NACS *Washington* is tall and lean, and he speaks in a slow and deliberate cadence, with careful and clear enunciation. "They are going to brief us on the peculiarities of this system. And there are rather a lot of them."

He looks at the astronomer and gestures at the map.

"Your room, Dr. Brotherton."

Dr. Brotherton clears his throat and taps the controls for the holoscreen, and the rogue planet pops into existence over the table.

"That's our system center. Not a sun, but a planet. It doesn't orbit a star, it orbits the galactic center. We call this a rogue planet. Now, these things are all over the galaxy, but this is the first one anyone's ever observed directly," he says.

He decreases the display scale until the moons rejoin the planet in the projection. I remember what it looked like when we orbited it two weeks ago on our first recon run, a surface like swirling black ink. The representation looks friendlier than the actual thing, more abstract.

"It's very slightly bigger than Jupiter, but has only three-quarters of Jupiter's mass. It also has a lot fewer moons. So far we have only identified four. For ease of reference, we're going to assign them the names Red, Green, Blue, and Yellow."

He highlights the moon closest to the planet.

"This is Red, the first moon. Closest orbit, very close to the planet. We didn't run a survey mission to Red because it's pretty obvious that there's nothing there we could claim with the technology we brought along. It has no atmosphere, and the surface temperature is between five hundred and nine hundred degrees. It looks as bright as a decoy flare on infrared. We didn't bother sending probes because we'd lose them to thermal degradation or radiation. It's a really, really hostile environment. Lots of radiation from the rogue planet. If Lankies made their home down on Red somewhere, they can have it. But I very much doubt it. They're tough, but they're nowhere near tough enough to survive that place."

He zooms out the viewpoint until it shows the entire system again, then focuses on the moon in the outermost orbit, color-coded in yellow.

"Meet Yellow. That's the fourth moon, furthest out. Same story, different extremes. We didn't send a survey mission to Yellow either because it's an equally unfriendly place. It has a tenuous atmosphere of mostly nitrogen and methane. Not the best conditions for a field trip. Again, if the Lankies managed to put down roots there, I'd say they're welcome to it."

The viewpoint changes focus to the blue orb, the moon closest to *Washington*'s current position.

"Here we have Blue, moon number three. This is the one we just surveyed with the help of the STT. This one we like much better than Yellow or Red. It has no atmosphere to contend with, and the surface is mostly water ice. The seismic probes we dropped have confirmed the composition of the ice, and it's a form we can mine and turn into drinking water without much trouble. The gravity on Blue is only one-eighth of Earth's. That greatly simplifies the task of getting the H2O off the moon and back to the ship because we don't have to haul it out from the bottom of a gravity well. The process will be similar to New

Svalbard in the early days. We think it would be possible to inhabit this moon in the long term if we must, like we did there."

"What about Lanky presence? Are we sure there are none under the ice? We know they can survive in that sort of environment," Colonel Rigney says. The head of the ship's embarked SI regiment is a jowl-faced, stocky man with a graying buzzcut.

"We don't have any evidence yet that the Lankies can create their own atmosphere out of nothing," Elin Vandenberg replies. "At least not on a planetary scale. They've never shown any interest in planets or moons without an atmosphere. They seem to prefer shake-and-bake environments. Places where we have done most of the terraforming for them."

"In any case, the seismic probes show no evidence of Lanky movements," Dr. Brotherton says. "They do, however, show that the moon isn't completely inert. There's seismic activity down there. It's consistent with plate tectonics. Which leads us to believe that the surface ice is a crust that's floating on a subsurface ocean of liquid water. So far, the Lankies have only inhabited solid subsurface zones, not liquid zones."

"How much water are we talking about?" Colonel Pace asks. He's *Washington*'s CAG, the air/space group commander in charge of the attack and drop ship wings and all their ancillary support squadrons.

"The ice crust appears to be about a hundred kilometers thick, at least where we placed the probes. The depth of that ocean underneath is conjecture until we survey the place thoroughly and get an opportunity to drill down through the ice. But from the diameter of the moon and its gravity, it has a core of metal and rock. The water layer between that and the surface ice may be hundreds of kilometers deep, maybe thousands. That little moon probably has three or four times more water on it than Earth does."

Pace smiles curtly. "I guess our water troubles are over, then. If only a liter of water had more than zero calories."

"CAG, I want you to coordinate with Colonel Rigney and get an engineering task force together," Colonel Drake says to Pace. "Figure out how to get the combat engineers down there and start hauling water back to the ship."

"That's going to take all our resources," Rigney says. "I have one company of engineers. If we set up base down there and get a rotation going, they'll all be busy. If something else comes up, they won't be available for the regiment."

"Let's focus on one crisis at a time. Right now, our top priority is getting fresh water. Get a mission package together and give me a plan of action as soon as possible," Drake says.

"Aye, sir," Rigney replies and exchanges nods with Colonel Pace.

"Now that we've made sure the neighborhood is clear, we're going to move *Washington* closer to Blue, to shorten transit times for the ice mining ops," Colonel Drake continues. "Sorry for the interruption, Dr. Brotherton. Do carry on."

"Thank you, Colonel. So that is our water stop in this system," the astronomer continues. "The surface isn't a nice place to be. As I said, we should have no trouble settling in underground once we get some portable fusion power down there. It would not even be a bad place for a new colony—eventually. We've settled worse, right? Not that I have any particular interest in sticking around here."

"Nor do I," Colonel Drake says. He looks tired, and the wrinkles at the corners of his eyes seem to have gotten more pronounced since I left for my recon mission. Looking around the room, it strikes me how much older the other senior officers look than I know them to be. The colonels have fifteen years on me, which puts them all in their late forties, but Pace and Rigney, the career pilot and the infantry soldier, look ten years older than that.

I may look like that in another ten years, too, I think. *Should have turned in my stars and gone civilian with Halley years ago. But that ship has sailed well beyond the horizon now.*

"That leaves the second moon," Dr. Brotherton says. He changes the hologram to show the green orb on the stellar map, then zooms in on it.

"Meet Green. It's the biggest of the moons in this system. Half again the diameter of Red or Yellow, and three times the diameter of Blue. It has a magnetosphere and an atmosphere. That atmosphere is made up of nitrogen, carbon dioxide, and oxygen, with some helium and hydrogen in the mix. More CO_2 than oxygen, and at concentrations we can't tolerate for long without suits. Permanent cloud cover, surface temperature about forty degrees. Does that sound familiar to anyone?"

"It most certainly does," I reply.

"This is the one. If there are Lankies on the ground anywhere in this system, it's down there. It matches their preferred conditions exactly."

"This is also the only place in the system where we might find calories," Elin notes. "The Lankies are a carbon-based life-form, like us. So far, the specimens we've dissected have had local and terraformed fungi and some terraformed vegetation protein in their stomachs, so we guess their native foods might be, and this is a big *might be*, compatible with our needs, too. We have never found animal parts in their stomachs and nothing that we could identify as alien, but we've only had corpses from Mars and Earth. I didn't get a chance to gather plant specimens on Willoughby, which might be a great help to us right now, but I did note that the vegetation was profuse. This world has far less oxygen than Earth, so it stands to reason that the plant life, if any, will be somewhat different. How much different is the million-credits question."

"But we don't know for sure if the Lankies or their plants are down there," Colonel Rigney says.

"I would feel very comfortable with placing a very large bet on it," Dr. Brotherton replies. "But no, we don't know with certainty. We sent out several long-range drone missions, but the dense cloud cover kills our optical uplink. And without radio control or telemetry, we can't correct for circumstances once the birds are in the atmosphere. We lost four drones trying to get eyes on the ground from all the way out here. Nothing's for sure until we get confirmed eyeballs on it."

"That doesn't leave us many options." Colonel Pace frowns and folds his hands on the tabletop in front of him. "Low-level recon flight is out of the question. Not without ground-mapping radar."

"I agree." Colonel Drake folds his arms across his chest and looks around. When his gaze shifts to me and stops, I feel a little jolt of unpleasant anxiety.

"We can't send the strike fighters out there. They'd be flying blind, and we'd lose half the wing just trying to get a glimpse of the ground," he says.

"The Blackflies can feel their way in," I say. "They have much better low-light gear. And they can go slow enough to where it's actually useful."

"Are you volunteering the STT for that mission, Major?"

The hell I am, I think. But that sort of high-risk business is why the special tactics team exists, and I know I'll get the order anyway if the commander decides that it's worth the risk.

"We're the only ones who have the gear to even make it to the ground," I reply. "And if that's a Lanky world, with a Lanky atmosphere, whoever goes in will need bug suits. So we're also the only ones who have the gear to do anything useful when we're down there."

"That is one hell of a risk," Colonel Rigney says. "Are we sure we need to do this?"

"We don't know how long we're going to be here," the skipper says. "We still only have a rough idea what we're dealing with here. If there are Lankies down there, I'd sure like to know what we're up against. And we absolutely need to find a source of protein if we're going to last more than a few months out here."

Elin Vandenberg clears her throat.

"This may be one of their colonies," she says. "It may even be their home world. The place where they originated. Before they figured out how to get the hell out of this neighborhood and spread out."

"You serious?" Lieutenant Colonel Campbell smirks. "Lanky Prime? This little moon?"

Elin shrugs. "They had to come from somewhere. And think about it. They have no eyes, no way to see visible light. Wherever they evolved, it was likely a dark place where evolution didn't favor eyes as we know them. Just like species that evolved and live in subterranean places on Earth. Our naked eyes are pretty useless in this place," she says, pointing at the system map that's floating above the table between us.

"Here's your dark place. And if they came from here, if that is the place where it all started, we absolutely want the intel, not to mention the possible source of food. Whatever we find out down there could be life sustaining for us and war changing if we bring it home."

"*When* we bring it home," Colonel Drake says. "We have a long-term purpose. Let's talk and act like it. I have no desire to spend the rest of my life in this dark hellhole."

Elin nods with a curt smile.

"*When* we bring it home," she repeats.

"If that's a Lanky world, that'll be one hell of a field trip," Colonel Rigney says. "We tackled Mars with a few divisions. With armor elements and full air superiority. Strike wings from multiple carriers. We knew the ground, and we had full recon. And we managed to last less than forty-eight hours before they kicked us off. One regiment, dropping into an unknown place, with a single carrier in support? We'll get chewed up in an hour or two once they know we're there."

"And that's assuming that we can get the carrier close enough to the moon for a full space-to-ground assault without getting detected," Colonel Pace adds. "We'll have every seed ship in the system on our ass before we can even launch drop ships."

"I concur with both of you," Colonel Drake says. "This isn't something we can do with brute force. Not even with the new gear we have. The longer we avoid a stand-up fight, the longer we'll live out here. We need to find a way out of here. Not get into fights we can't win. When we leave this place, I want to take everyone with me who was on this ship when we got here."

"I agree as well," I say. "This calls for sneaking in through the basement window. Not kicking in the front door."

Colonel Rigney leans back in his chair and rubs his chin.

"This is your trade, Major Grayson," he says. "I just want the science team to be aware of the price tag we may have to pay for that intel."

"I don't relish the idea," I reply. "Not in the least. But we can pull it off. Like you said, Colonel, this is our trade. Get in quietly, gather possible food samples and information, get out. A few podheads draw much less attention than a heavy infantry company. And we're the only ones with the right equipment for this. But we can't bring back enough food in one trip to make that much difference, and the food is only a possibility."

The momentary silence at the table makes me feel like I just volunteered the STT for a spacewalk without EVA suits to free up some calories for the rest of the crew.

"I won't lie to you. On days like today, I wish I had stuck with my Neural Networks job instead of volunteering for the podhead track," I say. My remark is rewarded with a few smiles and chuckles from the senior officers.

"But this is exactly why there's a special tactics team on this ship. We can't send a whole regiment in there. And even if we could, it would make no sense to risk the SI grunts," I continue.

Colonel Drake looks at me and lightly taps his fingers on the table for a few moments.

"That is going to be a long haul for a recon mission," he says. "A very long haul. And there won't be any support if things go wrong. Only what you can bring along, which won't be much, and leaving space for what you might be bringing back."

"I am aware of that, sir. We're usually too far out for the cavalry to save us. It's the nature of the job."

"And you're sure you want to do this?"

"Oh, I'm sure I don't. But I am prepared to do it anyway," I say, and he flashes a curt smile.

"All right, Major. I am not giving the official go-ahead just yet. Maybe some alternative will come up before we must take that sort of risk. But you are hereby cleared to plan the recon mission to Green with your team. Pull in your section leads and coordinate your mission with the air/space group. Get me the final mission plan for approval by 1900. If I decide it's a go, Colonel Pace will make sure they give you all the resources you need."

"Aye, sir," I reply.

Above the tabletop, the hologram of the green moon rotates slowly between us, a computerized best guess of what it would look like if this system had the light of a nearby sun illuminating it. As Dr. Brotherton returns to his briefing, I study the projection, trying to divine something from it even though I know it's a representative model and not an accurate real-time image. Even without any intel from the lost drones that foundered in the atmosphere, I feel a sudden unshakeable certainty that this is the place we have been looking for all along—the source of my nightmares, the reason for all our hardships over the last thirteen years.

A world of monsters, I think. *And I just committed myself and forty other people to go down there among them.*

CHAPTER 3

- DOING SOMETHING WORTHWHILE -

When I leave the flag briefing room, someone quickly walks up behind me to catch up as I make my way down the passageway. From the sound of the footwear on the deck and the pace of the steps, I know who it is without having to look back.

"I have a good idea what you're about to ask," I say. "And the answer is 'absolutely not.'"

"I haven't even made my case yet," Elin Vandenberg says.

I stop midstride and turn to face her.

"All right. Give it your best shot."

Elin looks at the door to the briefing room we just left. The last one out of the room is Lieutenant Colonel Campbell, the ship's executive officer. She shoots us a questioning glance but doesn't say anything as she walks past.

"Can we talk in there? Just for a moment," Elin says.

"You're just going to keep on me about this otherwise, right?" I ask.

"That is correct."

I sigh and nod at the door.

"Fine. Try to make your case. And then I can tell you in great detail why it's a terrible idea."

I sit down in the chair I had just left a few moments ago. Elin doesn't bother to reclaim hers. Instead, she walks around the table and stands across from me, hands in the pockets of her overalls.

"I need to be on this mission," she says.

"You don't," I reply. "And be glad for that. Because you have absolutely no idea what you are trying to talk yourself into."

"I think I have a pretty good idea. You let me tag along on Willoughby."

"That was a smash-and-grab," I say. "We were in one spot, we had drop ships standing by for a quick dustoff, and we still almost got our tickets punched. This will be a long-range recon mission. It won't just be in and out in an hour, with a carrier ready to support us from overhead. There will be no place to retreat if something goes wrong. It's the most dangerous mission in the book."

Elin shrugs. "You told me you've done six hundred of these. And you're still here. Seems to me that I'll be fine if I stay close to you. It worked well on Willoughby. Look, can we just skip to the point where I wear you down and you say yes? Because we've already had this talk once."

I shake my head.

"This is different. This will be nothing like Willoughby. You don't want to be a part of this. You don't need to be. If we make it back, you'll have access to all the data from our suits."

"That's not the same as being there on the ground with you."

"It's a lot safer," I say. "I made it through six hundred drops because I trained for this stuff for years before I climbed into a pod for the first time. Plenty of guys have died on recon drops even with all that training. You're a scientist, not a soldier. You don't know the first thing about staying alive in a place like that. You told me yourself that you haven't even touched a rifle since Basic Training."

"I thought we weren't going down there to pick fights," Elin says.

"Yeah, well. Sometimes the fight comes and picks you."

"I think that if it comes down to whether or not I can hit anything with a rifle, the mission is well and truly fucked anyway," she says.

I laugh and shake my head.

"You got me there, I guess."

Elin grabs the chair next to her and turns it around. Then she swings her leg over the seat and sits down on it backward. She rests her arms on the backrest and takes a deep breath.

"Look," she says. "This is supposed to be a science mission, right? We're going down there to first"—she holds up a forefinger—"look for a source of food. And second"—she holds up another finger—"to see if there are Lankies on that moon. None of you have the knowledge to look for or identify potential food sources. I do. And if there are Lankies there, we're going to learn as much as we can about what they're doing and how they're doing it. Are these not the mission parameters?"

"They are. More or less."

"Well, that's what I am trained to do. Both parts. I know you've been fighting these things from the start. And I don't question your expertise when it comes to killing them. But I've studied them for years. I know more about Lankies than anyone else on this ship."

I fold my arms and lean back in my chair.

"Go on," I say.

"Now, if that's Lanky Prime down there, it makes no sense for me not to go with you. The one person who's on the ship just to gather intel on the Lankies. And if there's something I know about them that you don't, something that may tip the scales on that mission, I won't do you any good sitting in the medlab on a ship that's a million kilometers away. You heard the commander. You'll only have what you bring along. So bring me the hell along."

I let out a slow breath.

31

"This is going to be an all-hands-on-deck sort of mission for the STT," I say. "That's forty people I'll have to direct when I am down there. I won't be able to spare any bandwidth trying to keep you safe. And I won't have the personnel to give you a personal bodyguard or two."

Elin rolls her eyes a little.

"All the arguments you could have led with, and you pick the 'fragile girl' one?"

"Not at all," I say. "A quarter of my STT is female. But they're combat controllers, or Force Recon, or Spaceborne Rescue. They have the best combat and survival training in the Corps."

"I may not have the weapons training they do, but I'd wager that I am in good enough shape," Elin says. "I run marathons, remember? And I have to pass the same physical fitness test as the rest of the Corps every year. Obstacle course and all."

"What was your score on the last one you did?"

"Three hundred," she says. "Same as the one before."

"So you're fit enough for a perfect PT score. I don't doubt that. But you have no training as an infantry soldier. Or a recon scout. Or a combat medic."

"As I said, I'd bring essential knowledge to the party. No one knows what we're looking for better than I. And one more rifle isn't going to move the needle much."

She leans closer for emphasis and makes the back of her chair creak as she puts her body weight into the plastic.

"You know I'll be an asset. And there's just no way I'll sit this one out on the ship. We may never get to set foot on that world again."

"If we're lucky," I say. "Nobody in their right mind would want to go onto a Lanky world even once. There's a reason why the rest of the Fleet thinks we podheads all have a screw loose."

"I'm sure it'll be dangerous," Elin replies. "And I'm sure I'll be scared shitless. But this is the thing I've been working toward for the last ten years. Nobody else in my field will be able to do this."

"It may not matter in the long run. If we don't get out of here, that new knowledge will die with us. If we even get off that moon alive, that is."

Elin shrugs.

"This is what I want to do with the time I have left. Try to do something worthwhile. You volunteered yourself because you want to do your job, make a difference. Give me a chance to do the same, please."

There is a long moment of silence in the room as I think about what she has said. Outside, I can hear people walking down the passageway, but Elin doesn't look at them even though she is facing the door. Instead, she holds my gaze calmly.

We're all still doing our jobs because it's the only thing left to do, I think. *It's the only thing that keeps us all from going nuts. Who am I to keep her from doing hers?*

"Fine," I say. "Looks like I can't talk you out of it. I'll put you on the mission roster."

Elin nods. Then she closes her eyes, tilts her head back, and exhales sharply. When she looks at me again, she smiles.

"I am going to regret that, aren't I?"

"You can still decide to jump ship until the mission starts," I say. "No shame in getting cold feet."

"Thanks. I don't plan to take you up on that. But it's good to know that I can," she replies.

"I'll let you know the timeline once I've put together a mission plan with my section leaders. It all depends on how quickly we can get the resources together. But my best guess is that we will be skids-up within forty-eight hours. So if you want to ponder this some more, you don't have much time."

"I understand," Elin says. She gets up and puts her chair aside. "Thank you for letting me talk you into it. I mean that. I was afraid I was going to be luggage on this ship for the rest of my life."

33

She walks around the table and over to the door. When she is almost at the threshold, I clear my throat.

"Elin," I say, and she stops and turns around to look at me.

"I don't want to sound morbid," I continue. "And dying down there isn't exactly Plan A, of course. But you need to make your peace with the idea. I'm not just saying this to try and scare you off. It's reality. There is a chance that we won't come back from this."

She nods somberly.

"I'm okay with the odds. If I'm going to die soon either way, I'd rather go like that. Instead of waiting to starve on this ship."

I shake my head and smile. "Now you're talking like a podhead."

"See? I'll fit right in."

"But let's do our best to go ahead with Plan A first," I say.

"That would be my preference, too, believe me. I am not in a hurry to go."

"To that end, I want to send you down to the range with one of my STT sergeants before we head out," I add. "To get you familiar with a rifle again. Just in case."

"I thought we established that one more rifle won't move the needle much," Elin replies.

I get out of my chair and straighten out the front of my uniform blouse reflexively.

"Well," I say. "I've been at this for over a decade. There's not much that's for sure on a combat drop. But one thing that's certain is that nobody ever knows ahead of time how it's going to play out."

She considers my reply and nods.

"All right. I'll do a refresher. But I really hope this won't come down to my shooting skills. For all our sakes."

CHAPTER 4

— PLANNING A FIELD TRIP AGAIN —

The rank sleeves on the shoulders of my CDU blouse are only a few grams each, the same mass as the ones I used to wear as an enlisted soldier and then as a junior officer. They're just cloth formed into a flat loop, with some silver stitching on top. But as I walk into the secondary pilot briefing room near the hangar deck, the weight of those rank insignia seems to want to push me down toward the deck a little with every step. For the thousandth time since it happened, I find myself cursing the day I agreed to let them take my NCO stripes and replace them with officer stars.

"As you were, gentlemen," I say as I step across the threshold, before anyone else in the room can call everyone to attention. The briefing room is set up with four rows of seats arranged in stadium-style tiers, to give everyone an equally uncluttered view of the briefing lectern and the holographic screen behind it. Today, that seating arrangement is superfluous. My four section leaders, all captains in rank, are not enough in number to completely fill the front row. Sitting with them is Major Lynch, the operations officer of Carrier Space Wing 5.

I walk over to the lectern and log into the terminal that controls the holoscreen.

"Good morning," I say. "I hope everyone is rested up and ready to get some exercise. Because we are about to go on one hell of a field trip."

I call up the science briefing info and put Dr. Brotherton's survey data on the holoscreen behind me—the dark planet in the center of the plot, and the four color-coded moons orbiting at various distances. Our ship's icon, suspended at a point between the orbits of the little blue and yellow orbs, looks forlorn and out of place, the only human presence as far as scale of the hologram goes.

"The astro division has finished their system survey. They say there's lots and lots of smaller rocks in this place, but the ones that are relevant to us are these four moons. Red, Green, Blue, and Yellow." I point them out on the display in turn.

"We just did a close pass of Blue with a drop ship flyby and managed to stick some probes on the surface. It's a ball of ice, no enemy presence, and it has more water on it than we can drink in a lifetime. We just need to pry it off the surface and melt it. But that's a job for the combat engineers, not the STT. And now, we need food to go with that water."

I focus the display on the green moon and slowly zoom in until it takes up most of the screen.

"*That* is our job. Green. It's hot and humid and covered in clouds, and it's too far away to do a remote reconnaissance. The astro division tried to save us the legwork, but they burned up four of their long-range drones for no returns. And Green here is the only real possibility for food in this system other than our remaining stores. We are going to take a look. See if we can find something we can turn into edible calories. While we're there, we are going to look for neighbors."

"Guess we don't have to worry about losing our jobs to automation just yet," Captain Taylor says, and the other officers chuckle.

"What are the odds we're going to run into our friends down there?" Captain Harper, the SEAL section leader, asks.

"Let's see," I say. "Hypercapnic atmosphere. Forty degrees average temperature. Thick cloud cover. If I had to set up a Lanky exhibit in a zoo somewhere, that's exactly what it would look like. I'd say the odds are better than even that the joint is crawling with them."

"Pardon the negative vibes here, sir," Captain Lawson says. He's a tall, ruddy-faced man with a recruiting-poster buzzcut that's the color of rust. His Force Recon section is the Spaceborne Infantry component of our team, trained to blaze a path for the rest of the SI regiment. "But if we know the place is most likely full of Lankies, and we don't have the muscle for a full-scale invasion, wouldn't that be a good reason to avoid it?"

"That would be the sane thing to do," I agree. "Naturally, we're going to do something else instead because this is the Corps."

The subdued laughter from the other officers has a slightly grim edge to it.

"We need to find something to eat," I continue. "If we get down there and we have no Lankies to contend with, that would be fine with me. Command hopes that whatever we find down there will be worth the risk."

"Easy for them to make that judgment. They're not going to be down there in the muck with us," Captain Lawson says, leaving open whether he means the science division, the command officers, or both.

"That's not quite correct, Captain. One of the scientists has asked to be a part of the mission, so she *will* be down in the muck with us."

"The xenobiologist? Again?" Captain Harper's expression is suddenly sour. "I don't think that's a good idea at all, sir. She's practically a civilian. Even if she made it off Willoughby alive. Civvie scientists don't belong on pod drops. She has zero training for that."

"I tried to talk her out of it, but she made some good points," I say. "In any case, it won't be a pod drop anyway. We can't risk getting *Washington* close enough to Green to make a pod launch feasible. Too many Lanky ships in the neighborhood there. It's going to be a long-range stealth insert with the Blackflies."

"SEALs, then." Lawson exchanges a look with Captain Harper. "Who else is going?"

"Combat controllers, Spaceborne Rescue, one per team," I say. "We've all trained for ISTAR missions with mixed recon teams plenty of times. Well, this is pretty much the textbook definition of ISTAR in every way. Intelligence, surveillance, target acquisition, reconnaissance. The whole menu. I want to send out one squad of SEALS with each Blackfly, plus a combat controller and Spaceborne Rescueman each. That's eight troops per bird. Lots of space left for fuel and supplies."

"The transport and aerial logistics squadrons will be tied up for the water supply train," Major Lynch says. She taps the stylus of her PDP against the pilot wings on her flight suit. "I've got all my tankers committed to that run. That may be a bit too much of a stretch for Blackflies even half-empty and on external tanks. Unless you plan to coast ballistic most of the way. But you'll be en route for a month or more."

I shake my head.

"I just spent a week sitting on my ass in a Blackfly cargo hold. I have no desire to do a month that way. And I'm sure the rest of the team aren't wild about the idea, either. Not that we can spare a month of time."

"I can see if I can divert a pair of tankers for your mission," Major Lynch says.

I decrease the scale of the map on the holoscreen and point at a few of the orange icons clustered around the moon.

"That's some pretty heavy Lanky presence. We can get four Blackflies past that gathering. But our IR stealth goes to shit if we have tankers in the group."

"So what's your plan? You'll get there with mostly empty tanks. Even if you load all the hard points up with fuel."

"We've got four Blackflies and two spares. I want to take along the spares as fuel birds. Load them up with the full buddy tank arrangement. Bladders in the cargo holds, tanks on the wings."

"Just like we did at Arcadia," Captain Harper says.

"Exactly," I confirm.

"You use your spares as fuel mules, you'll have no redundancy if you have one of the mission ships fail," Major Lynch cautions. "And you're stretching your endurance to the max, even with two refueling ships."

"I've considered that," I say. "But I think the need for a low profile justifies the risk. The four troop birds will be half-full. We could lose two out of four and still have enough capacity to get everyone there and back. But I'd welcome any suggestions. This is your field. I just mostly run around on the ground and shoot things."

Major Lynch flashes a curt smile. She taps her stylus against her pilot wings a few more times in a rapid little I-am-busy-thinking staccato.

"Well, you need more fuel than you can carry with your Blackflies. But that doesn't mean you have to have tankers along all the way. We can probably spare two of the ships from the logistics squadron to come with you. They can top off the Blackflies halfway and then turn around and head home."

"That's a lot of eggs to juggle out in the middle of nowhere," Captain Lawson says.

I shrug.

"It's what we do, Captain. If it were easy, they wouldn't be sending the STT."

"That way you can burn for a good portion of the trip and still have plenty of fuel for surface ops and the trip back," Major Lynch says.

"Very well," I say. The look I exchange with Major Lynch tells me we both know that the "trip back" portion of the plan is anything but certain. We're already out on the end of a limb, but we are preparing to jump off and hoping we can bounce back onto the branch somehow. Every aspect of our presence here is uncharted territory, and adding a risk that would have seemed near suicidal under normal circumstances hardly seems to matter now. It feels as if we have moved beyond the reach of the fates.

"All right. I'll put in the task order and get those refuelers added to your mission package. Anything else you figure you'll want along for the ride?"

"What I want along for the ride is every Shrike on the ship with every nuke in the magazines loaded on the pylons," I say. "But that's probably not in the cards."

"Get us some recon on the ground and some target coordinates, and we can talk about it," Major Lynch says. "It's not like we're going to get any bonus pay for bringing all those tactical warheads back."

"Other than fuel, I think we're good. We'll have enough room in the Blackflies for supplies to last for the ride there and back. And it's an ISTAR run, not a search-and-destroy mission. If we fail for lack of ordnance, we went about it entirely the wrong way."

"I'll get you those tanker birds," Major Lynch says. "And take care out there. Those are thin margins you will be running."

"We all are," I reply. "Thank you, Major. I'll try to return them without a scratch."

Captain Harper raises a hand. "Question, sir?"

"Yes, Captain?"

"We're committing all the SEALs. But one combat controller and one Spaceborne Rescue trooper per ship, that's only a quarter of the combat controller or rescue sections."

I reach up with one hand and squeeze the back of my neck lightly.

"That's correct. If this doesn't go the way we want it to go, I don't want to leave the stores empty. There's still a full regiment of Spaceborne Infantry on this ship. If we don't come back, and they must move against a surface threat on the ice moon or anywhere else, I don't want to totally deprive them of STT capabilities. Captain Burns and Captain Taylor, you will pick the two squads from your sections that will come along. Captain Burns, you have seniority, so you'll be the STT lead in our absence, and Captain Taylor will be your second-in-command."

"Aye, sir," Burns says. His expression makes it clear that he's less than excited about the order to stay behind while a quarter of his team goes out on a mission. Captain Taylor's face is impassive as he sits and listens, his arms folded across his chest.

"We'll be in four ships," I continue. "That moon has a diameter of six thousand kilometers. It's half the size of Earth. There is no sunlight in this system, and we can't use active radar mapping because our enemies can sense EM radiation. We will have to go below the cloud cover and find our way around with passive sensors. Infrared, low-light magnification, everything we have in the toolbox that lets us keep a low profile. On the way in, our main concern will be to find a suitable LZ. Once we are on the ground, we can send out the recon drones to map out the immediate neighborhood and identify objectives for an eyes-on visit. Captain Lawson, how do you feel about the coverage?"

Captain Lawson rubs his chin as he considers my question.

"One mixed team of eight per ship. Each fire team gets a combat controller and a rescue trooper. Small enough to sneak through the tight spots. Capable enough to do a lot of things well. Versatile enough to be able to switch tasks without fucking the mission."

"You planning to keep the SEAL teams as a unit, sir?" Captain Harper asks.

"Affirmative. The four-man patrol is their natural order, anyway. I think we'll get a lot more use out of your boys that way instead of spreading them around. We'll give the SEAL patrols the juiciest recon targets, don't worry."

"I am more than fine with that," Harper says.

"Any thoughts or objections from the Spaceborne Rescue or combat controller sections?" I look at Taylor and Burns, who both shake their heads.

"That sounds as efficient as we can be with what we have," Captain Burns says. "Question, though—how are we deploying the ships? Are we staying close for mutual support? Or are we going for maximum coverage?"

I turn and look at the graphic representing the moon we've labeled Green, covered in clouds, with its secrets shrouded from us until we dare to get close and poke our heads under that shroud.

"We have no certainty what's under there," I say. "Just a really good idea. Let's maximize our coverage. We're limited to light comms anyway. Anything more than a hundred klicks between teams might as well be a thousand."

"Two ships on the northern hemisphere and two on the southern," Harper contributes. "Any ship that doesn't find a viable LZ makes orbit again and tries until they're bingo fuel. One of us is bound to find a landing spot."

"Agreed," I say. "Everyone finds their own place to put down. If there is no safe ground to be found, climb back into orbit and rendezvous with the tanker, top off, and head home. Each team lead uses their own discretion and sets their own schedule. We won't be able to talk to each other until we're in orbit again, and there's no way to know when everyone's going to show."

"The tanker Blackflies have a finite on-station time," Major Lynch cautions. "That's a hard time ceiling. Anyone who hasn't checked in and topped off before then is going to be on their own."

From the solemn nods my captains use to acknowledge the major's warning, I can tell they all know that anyone who doesn't make the rendezvous point in time is not likely to return to the ship at all.

I clear my throat, and all eyes in the room are on me again.

"We have a rough plan. Let's make it airtight. I want you to work out the assignments for your sections by 1600. Make sure you get any additional equipment requests in by then as well. This is a high-CO_2 world, so bug suits are going to be the fashion of the day. Kit your squads out for stealth and mobility, not firepower. You know the ISTAR rules of engagement. We look around, we take inventory, we report back, but we don't start pulling triggers unless it's necessary. The SEALs will remember how quickly we had the neighborhood coming down on us once we started making noise on the ground on Willoughby."

"Let's try to not do that again," Captain Harper says. "That was a close shave."

"Some of you fought at Mars back in '13," I continue. "Quite a few of your senior NCOs were there, too. But your lieutenants and your young corporals and sergeants? They have no idea yet what it's like on a Lanky world. That's nothing you can get from a battle sim, or a garrison tour above Mars. It's hot and it's crawling with these things, and it's going to be nothing we can shoot our way out of if we mess up. And if that's Lanky Prime, there's no telling just how many of them are down there. It may make Willoughby look like a RecFac. So make sure your teams have all their latches secured and their bolts tightened."

My captains nod and murmur their agreement.

"All right, people. Tend to your shops and let's get ready for showtime. Final readiness reports by 1600. Mission briefing with the squads at 1800. And then we wait for the go signal from upstairs. Dismissed."

The STT section leaders get up from their chairs and start to file out of the room. Captain Harper hangs back and lets everyone else through the door first. Then he turns and walks back to the lectern, where I am deactivating the holoscreen and logging out of the terminal.

"A quick word, Major Grayson?"

"What's on your mind, Captain?"

"I disagree with your decision to let the scientist come along again," Harper says. "I know it's your team, your decision. But I think she's a liability. She may get us all killed. You know as well as I do that there's no room for wrong steps in that kind of environment."

"Half the STT have never been on a Lanky world, either."

"But everyone in the STT has years of training."

43

"She has relevant training, too. Not when it comes to weapons or survival. But she knows more about Lankies and potential food than anyone else on this team, me included. She's coming along as a knowledge base."

"Permission to speak freely, sir."

"Nobody in this unit ever needs permission to speak freely, Captain. Say what's on your mind."

Harper lets out a long breath, and I can tell that he's taking the moment to calibrate his statement.

"It's your decision, sir. But I think it's reckless. In fact, I think it's borderline negligence. And I think it endangers my SEALs and the rest of the team."

"That is your prerogative. And it's your duty to let me know when you think I am making a bad call."

"Well, I think it's a bad call," Captain Harper says. "And I want to be on the record with that. Just in case this ends up badly."

"I'll make sure to log your objections," I reply. "But it's my prerogative to make the final decision. I think Dr. Vandenberg represents an intel asset we can't afford to leave behind."

Captain Harper holds my gaze for a moment. Then he exhales sharply and shrugs.

"You're the boss, Major. At least my conscience is clean on this."

Your conscience, I think. Harper was on the SEAL team that ran around and planted nukes on most of Arcadia's terraformers while my platoon played bait for the garrison to chase. I've tried to not let that memory taint my view of my second-in-command, but it galls me to hear someone who willingly took part in that deception talk about conscience. Still, I've served under too many officers who didn't take well to critical input from their subordinates, and not even Harper's association with Masoud and his cut-throat tactics will make me go back on my rule to never hold it against anyone under my command when they tell me I may be wrong.

"Thank you for your candor, Captain. If it's any consolation, I'll bear the brunt of the consequences if I am wrong. I am the team lead, so Dr. Vandenberg will be my responsibility."

Harper shrugs again.

"Aye-aye, sir. I just hope it's the right call."

"I do too, Captain," I reply. "Either way, it stands."

I wonder if Masoud ever had any doubts about the calls he made on Arcadia, I think as I watch Captain Harper walk out of the room. *I hope he did because that would mean the son of a bitch has a conscience after all.*

CHAPTER 5

— RUMORS AND HISTORIES —

I never sleep well before a mission. It's a kind of tradition for me to go
to Medical and draw a dose of no-go pills to knock myself out chemically and get at least eight hours of rack time before skids-up. But on
the night before the mission to Green, not even the industrial-strength
central nervous system depressants from the ship pharmacy are enough
to keep me down.

When I wake up and look around my darkened cabin, the time
projection on the bulkhead shows 0429 hours. Whatever sleep I've had
has been restless with unpleasant dreams I can only vaguely recall.

I try to go back to sleep for a few minutes before resigning myself
to the fact that I am wide awake now. The ballistic compression suit for
my armor is waiting for me on the ready rack of my equipment drawer,
but I don't put it on. Instead, I walk over to the bathroom nook, splash
some water on my face, and get into my Fleet-issued workout clothes.

With three watch cycles that constantly rotate with equal numbers
of crew, there's no true nighttime on the ship, and all the decks and passageways have the same ambient noise levels whenever I walk through
them. In space, the twenty-four-hour clock is entirely arbitrary, kept

around out of custom and habit, but the activities around me seem more subdued in the hours of the third watch cycle, the time span the civilian vestige of my brain still considers the middle of the night.

The officers' gym is almost deserted. Since the calorie allowance was reduced for the crew, few have a desire to burn up precious energy lifting weights and running on treadmills. When I walk in, there are only two other officers in the room. On one of the weight benches, a lieutenant from the strike fighter squadron is doing overhead presses with the computer-controlled resistance bar. In the back of the gym, where the SIMAP ring and the boxing bags are set up, Lieutenant Colonel Campbell is working the heavy bag by herself, landing deliberate and powerful combinations that make the fifty-kilo bag sway like a pendulum. From the sweat stain on the back of her shirt, I can tell that she has been at it for a while.

"I didn't know you had trouble sleeping as well," I say when I walk up and grab the bag to keep it in place for her.

Sophie Campbell, the ship XO and second-in-command of *Washington*, takes a moment to catch her breath at the interruption. We have been working out together almost every day since we made our truce down here in the gym a few weeks ago, and by now I know her well enough to know that she could probably kick my ass in the ring at least two out of five times if we went all out. She's just a little shorter than I am, and her build is all lean muscle, the kind that's a by-product of hard work, not the kind cultivated on a weight bench for appearance.

"I don't," she says when she has gotten her breath under control. "But I just had the deck in CIC for second watch. Eight hours of standing around, looking at plots, sitting in a chair, drinking coffee. I need to give my body something to do before I turn in."

She looks around in the gym. The lieutenant who had been working one of the weight benches has finished his sets. He wipes down the bench with his towel, shoots us a quick glance, and walks out.

"Almost everyone on this ship seems to have made their peace already," Sophie says. "Every time I come down here, there's only a handful of people around."

"Eighteen hundred calories a day," I say. "It's like being back in the PRC."

"Yeah, well. The people in the PRCs don't have a problem running around and killing each other on that calorie budget. The war was on hold for four years. A lot of people in the Corps got soft."

She raises her arms into a guard stance again and launches a combo into the bag as if to underline her point. I shift my own stance to keep her from pushing me back along with the bag I am holding.

We spend the next thirty minutes taking turns at the bag. I don't know how long Sophie has been working out before I got here, but she keeps pace with me, only stopping occasionally between sets to walk over to the water dispenser for a sip. Finally, we reach a point where we're both starting to drop our guards and throw slightly sloppy punches, and we both step away from the bag to recover and wind down.

"I don't usually keep up with the rumor mill," Lieutenant Colonel Campbell says as we pace around the bag to stretch. "Nobody gossips with the XO. But I should let you know that I've heard some rumors. And they've been going around quite a bit if they made it all the way to my ears."

"Rumors," I repeat. "What kind of rumors?"

"About you," Sophie says. "You and that scientist. Word has it that you keep green-lighting her as a ride-along on STT missions because you two have something going on."

"Are you kidding me?" I ask.

She unfastens the straps on her gloves with her teeth and pulls them off her hands.

"She is part of the science division. Science reports directly to the CO. That means she's not in your chain of command. It would not be against the regs if you two did have a thing. God knows half the ship is trying to hook up for one last fling before we all slide off into the abyss out here."

"We are not having a *thing*," I say. "I've got a million other concerns right now. And whoever is spreading that sort of bullshit just volunteered themselves to clean the enlisted head with a fucking toothbrush for the rest of their time on this ship."

"That's what I thought. You're not really the type."

I take my own gloves off with a feeling of reluctance. As tired as I am, the anger gives me some newfound energy, and I have an urge to direct it at the bag so I won't storm off and vent it on someone in my chain of command who doesn't deserve getting their ears torn off.

"I'm married," I say. "I made certain vows. And I remember clearly that they didn't have a distance limitation when I spoke them. So no, I don't have a thing with Dr. Vandenberg. Or anyone else. Even if I'm nine hundred light-years from my wife. And even if she'd never know because we'll probably never see each other again."

Lieutenant Colonel Campbell flashes her rare smile.

"See, that's the sort of thing married guys usually say to convince me that they're good and honorable. Right before they try to get me into bed. But I believe you. Like I said, you're not the type."

"How do you know I'm not?"

"We've been working out together for weeks down here, and I don't think you've looked at my ass even once," she says.

I have to laugh despite the anger I still feel, and she smiles again.

"Besides, the lance corporals aren't the only ones with an information network on this ship. The female officers and noncoms talk to each other, too, you know. We share intel as well. Names get passed around. Yours isn't on the list."

"I'm glad to hear that," I say.

"But it's still out there. I'm not saying you're running a loose shop. But someone on your team has a chip on their shoulder. Speaking as the XO and not your boxing partner, you need to come down on them like a kinetic strike. That sort of talk can sow doubt. And that's not good for the unit."

I put my gloves together and tuck them into the waistband of my workout sweats.

"We're going skids-up at 0800," I say. "Almost the entire STT except for two captains and four squads. I'll have to sort that one out after we get back."

"If you get back," Sophie replies. "And I hope you do. But you know you volunteered yourself for some serious Medal of Honor shit."

"I have no intention of earning one of those."

"Nobody does. Nobody in their right mind, anyway. I wouldn't go on a mission with someone who's craving one. Those things get handed out for surviving reckless stupidity against the odds."

"Your father got one," I say. It's the first time I've mentioned Colonel Campbell in her presence, and her subtle change in expression tells me that it's not a subject she likes to have brought up.

"I know. It's in a display case at my mother's house. Right next to the flag from his funeral."

"I was on his ship," I say. "The day he did what he did. It was bravery beyond measure. We won that battle because of him."

"It was brave," she replies. "It was also reckless and stupid. There was no guarantee it would work. He took a helmsman and his tactical officer with him. And he left a wife without a husband and a daughter without a father. It took me a very long time to come to terms with the fact that when he had to make that decision, he chose winning the battle over being around for his family. That medal gets a lot of respect. It got my mother a nice bonus on her survivor pension. But it's just a piece of gold on a ribbon. I can't hug it, or ask it for advice. Just some food for thought. I am sure that if your wife could pick between having you or having one of those medals in her living room, she wouldn't have to think about it for a second, pension bonus or not."

I don't have a reply for that, so I just watch as she dries her own gloves with a towel and tucks them away in the waistband at the small of her back when she is finished.

"See, I don't quite know what to make of you yet, Andrew Grayson. I can't decide whether you're too much like my father or not like him at all. But I do hope you make it back here. We don't know if we'll ever get to go home. But I think it's good policy to act as though we will. So try to pass up any chances for medals you may see popping up downrange."

"Yes, ma'am," I say. "If I see any glory somewhere, I'll be sure to steer clear."

"Good. Because no other senior officer on this tub knows how to throw a punch or hold a bag correctly. And I'd hate to switch my work-outs around at this point."

She nods at me and turns to walk out. I watch as she makes her way through the gym, past the empty rows of treadmills and weight machines, and realize that this is the closest the XO will ever come to wishing me good luck and saying her good-byes in case her wish doesn't come true.

CHAPTER 6

SKIDS-UP

In the military adventure vids I watched on the Networks when I was a kid, boarding a drop ship for a combat mission was always an exciting and hectic affair. Marines would grab their rifles out of the racks in a rush and head out to the ship at a run, egged along by the yelling of the hard-bitten veteran sergeants. The flight deck would be noisy and bustling with activity, and the marines would trash talk as they took their seats on the ship, ready to drop onto some SRA world and lay waste to the garrison there.

There's little that resembles its common fictional depiction less than a team getting ready for a drop. Nobody draws their rifle from the armory in a hurry, and there's no rushing around. Rushing leads to sloppy mistakes, and a forgotten fastener latch can kill you on the battlefield just as surely as a Lanky or an SRA fléchette. We all put on our armor in the assembly room very carefully and deliberately. Everyone has their gear double- and triple-checked by another teammate. We check out our weapons and load up our ammunition pouches, one magazine at a time, while speaking the ammo type out loud. The Jumbo, the Joint Modular Battle Rifle, can fire six different kinds of rounds, and stocking up on the correct loadout for the mission at hand is something nobody wants to do in a hurry or with someone else yelling at them.

"Armor-piercing delayed-explosive, silver with green tip, *one*," I say to myself, verifying the color-coded rounds in the disposable ammunition cassette before I slide it into a magazine holder. *"Two, three, four,"* I continue as I fill three more holders with the same kind of ammo. "High-explosive incendiary, yellow with red tip, *one*. Armor-piercing super-velocity sabot, black with silver tip, *one*."

When I have my full ammunition load for the rifle, seventy rounds, I secure the holders and step away to make space for the troopers behind me who are waiting to fill up their own pouches. I pass a rack of M109 pistols ready to be signed out, but I don't claim one. The sidearm is useless against Lankies and only adds nine hundred grams of dead mass to the armor, a weight budget that can be spent in a far more useful fashion. I used to take a pistol along all the time until I realized that it basically only served as a good-luck charm, a security blanket that made me feel I had last-ditch options.

Out on the flight deck, the Blackfly crews have been getting our birds mission-ready for the last few hours, a task that is also best done without yelling and excitement. The six mission ships are lined up side by side in their parking positions, each perfectly centered in the marker brackets painted on the deck in bright yellow. All the Blackflies have big fuel pods on each underwing pylon. We're in our customary semi-secluded corner of *Washington*'s massive flight deck, a little out of the way of the parking spots for the spacecraft of Carrier Space Wing 5 and their day-to-day ops. The Blackflies used to be a tightly guarded secret, but after seven years in service, they're just an interesting technical curiosity to the rest of the Fleet. Still, as I walk around the row of stealth drop ships, I can see that some of the nearby deck crew from other units are watching the proceedings in STT Country with interest. Every other combat craft on the deck is painted in the same pattern, titanium-white and orange, except for the Blackflies, whose matte-black hulls seem to suck in the light from the overhead fixtures. There's no practical reason why they're still in their original flat-black livery—Lankies can't see them either way, and we haven't been in a fight with the SRA in over eight years. But podheads like to keep a low profile on the battlefield, and a covert mission craft painted in a high-visibility color scheme would be institutional heresy.

Even with acceleration burns, the trip out to Green will take many hours, and I'll be spending most of the trip strapped into a seat, so I walk the deck for a bit to stretch my legs while the rest of the team draw their own gear and ammunition. The hangar decks on the Avengers are immense, half again as big as the ones on the old supercarriers, but it still feels a little claustrophobic to think about the fact that this deck is most likely the biggest air-filled open space in this entire system, and maybe light-years beyond.

When it looks like most of the team has gathered in front of the open tail ramps of the Blackflies, I make my way back to the drop ships. The four squads are standing in separate little groups, engaged in pep talk and low conversation. Some of them nod as I walk by. Once again, I am struck by how young most of them look. I know how they feel right now because I was a junior enlisted trooper once myself. But they have no idea how I feel, the person in charge of their fates, the one who will have to sign the casualty reports and find the contact information on record for the next of kin of those who won't come back. By now I am used to the conversations hushing when I walk past, but I know I am still an enlisted man at heart because it always bothers me to feel the wide gulf between our ranks.

When Elin Vandenberg comes out of the ready room and walks over to the STT area, she immediately looks out of place among the podheads. We're all wearing HEBA armor—bug suits—which are the same matte black as the drop ships when the polychromatic camouflage isn't activated. Elin's suit is white, with orange stripes running down the sides of the arms and legs. She's carrying her helmet under her arm, and

I see that it has a transparent visor, unlike the bug-suit helmets, which have eliminated that structural weak spot in favor of a sensor-fed internal display. There's a life support pack on her back that looks smaller and more streamlined than the ones on the HEBAs.

"Welcome to the party," I say when she walks up to me. "I see you dressed up for the event."

She looks down at her suit.

"Yeah, this is new. The science division's version of your bug suits. Minus the armor plating and the optical camouflage. But the IR suppression works as well as yours."

"That doesn't look like it will keep much out if things get hot down there," I say.

"It's made for field research, not for combat. But it's much tougher than it looks. Class-four spidersilk, Kevlar and carbon-nanofiber reinforced. I'll be fine unless someone starts firing armor-piercing rounds my way."

"These guys and girls are all pretty decent shots," I say. "They usually manage to hit what they're aiming at."

"I'm very glad to hear it." She looks around with a hint of anxiety on her face. "I've done this before. I should not be this nervous after Willoughby. But I am."

"You'd be out of your mind not to be. Every one of these podheads is nervous, too. Even if they'd rather gargle half a liter of drop ship fuel than admit it. Do you have all the gear you need to bring along?"

"I need to check and make sure they've loaded the equipment container I sent down earlier," Elin says. "Which one is our ride?"

I point at the Blackfly on the far left of the line.

"That one over there. Zero-five."

"Thank you. Excuse me for a moment."

She walks through the crowd of troopers. I notice quite a few of them turning their heads to look at her as she passes through the group in her pristine-looking suit and walks up the ramp of Blackfly 05.

"STT, listen up," I call out. "Stop the chitchat and gather 'round."

The squads walk over to where I am standing and form a rough semicircle. I wait until the chatter dies down completely and I have everyone's eyeballs on me.

"Time for the bullshit rah-rah speech from the brass," I say, and there's some laughter. I've done hundreds of briefings like this from both sides of the room, and I can almost smell the collective anxiety of the group, the controlled nervous energy of the inevitable and universal pre-mission jitters.

"All right," I say. "I have good news and bad news. The good news is that a bunch of you will finally get the chance to earn that combat device for your drop badges. The bad news is that you'll have to pay for it by pissing in a bug suit for about a week and a half."

There's another smattering of laughter. I like to joke a bit in my pre-mission pep talks to relieve the tension a little because I always appreciated that from my officers when I was listening to those speeches as an enlisted podhead.

"Yeah, nobody ever tells you about that in the recruiting center," I continue. "Join the Corps. Make new friends. Travel across the galaxy. Kill Lankies with large-caliber weapons. No recruiter ever goes into the details of body-waste management in airtight battle armor. Wonder why that is."

This one gets a good collective laugh from the group. Satisfied that I've dialed in the right degree of levity, I continue with the serious business of the day.

"I won't talk it up pretty because most of you have been around long enough to know when someone up the ladder is feeding you bullshit. Fact is that we're about to go to a dark and dangerous place. I've done combat drops since we first ran into these things twelve years ago, and I think this one is going to be right up there in the top three of pucker factors. But this is what we do. If anyone else could hack it, they wouldn't be sending us."

I nod toward the section leaders, Captains Harper and Lawson. "You've gotten the mission details from your leads. You know what's waiting for us out there. The science people use words like 'highly probable' and 'likely' because they don't do absolute statements without getting eyes on verified data. That's where we come in. This is a scouting and collection mission, not a search-and-destroy raid. Be always mindful of that. Do not pick any fights we won't be able to win. Support will be a long way off. We sneak in and we look around. If we find something that looks like it might be food or that's worth shooting or blowing up, we mark it and let the Fleet figure out how to gather it or bring the big guns to bear. But we do not get bonus points for Lanky kills. Remember that a perfect recon mission is one where you complete the task and bring all your ammo and info back home. Our xenobiologist has prepared a field guide of sorts on what to collect and what to avoid, and how to handle any samples safely. We'll have plenty of time on the ingress, so you're all ordered to read through her briefing on the way."

I look at the earnest faces all around me, and for a moment I find myself wondering how it ever came to pass that so many people look to me for guidance and listen to my advice.

I've come a very, very long way from PRC Boston-7, I think.

"All right," I say. "STT, saddle up. Sort by ship and do your final gear and equipment cross-checks. Section leads, report ready for drop when complete. Let's take it to them, people."

The troops bellow their customary motivational *oo-rah* shout and turn to walk to their assigned ships and prepare for the drop. I watch them as they sort themselves into sections and squads, moving with purpose and without idle chatter now, and I feel a fierce kind of pride at the sight of it. Many of them are kids, barely older than I was when I left the PRC for boot camp. Most of them have never been in a real battle, only garrison drops on Mars that were more enhanced live-fire training than serious combat. We are a long way from home and may never get back. But they are gearing up willingly to jump off into the unknown, to risk their lives for everyone else on this ship and maybe even for the rest of humanity, because they trust their training and their fellow troopers. In the PRC, most kids their age would be running the streets and hurting and killing each other over commissary vouchers, a few stim pills, a thousand extra calories for the day. They all live in constant survival mode, always looking to gain a little bit of an edge, in a place where almost everything is a zero-sum game to them. Of all the skills we need them to gain when they come to boot camp, the ability to trust and sacrifice are the ones that are hardest to impart, evolutionary disadvantages where only the strongest and meanest prosper. These troopers walking up the drop ship ramps in front of me are the ones who had enough of that capacity to carry them through years of training and hardship, the ones who will never again fit in back home because they have learned to give a shit about something other than themselves.

Elin comes down the ramp of Blackfly 05, walking against the stream of troopers going up into the cargo hold. She walks over to me and smiles apprehensively.

"Did they load all your stuff for you?" I ask.

"They did. It's just my field gear. Sample containers, sensor strips, that sort of thing."

"This is your last chance to back out," I say. "I won't think any less of you if you do. Once we're in the clamp and down in the drop hatch, there's no getting off the ride unless someone starts to bleed from the eyes."

"Oh, don't tempt me. I've had plenty of time to question my decision. And also all the ones that led me to the point of making that particular one."

"When we come back, you'll have access to every bit of data and helmet-cam footage from the entire team. And if we don't come back, you know you've made the smart call. It's a win-win situation, really."

Elin shakes her head.

"I need to be on that ship. I can't stay here and use up oxygen and calories if I back out of doing the one job I'm here to do. I don't want to be useless ballast."

She looks over her shoulder at the drop ship and lets out a long and shaky breath.

"Can we go ahead and do this now? While my resolve is still just a little bit stronger than my fear? Because that ratio is slipping with every minute right now."

I point to our designated Blackfly with an open hand.

"Let's go, then. After you, Doctor."

She marches off toward the ramp, and I follow her.

I don't turn around to take in the sights and sounds of the busy flight deck one more time the way I usually do before missions. We may not come back, but that has been true for every combat mission I have ever flown. I could have died on every one of those hundreds of drops, and it was only the luck of the draw that I came back when so many of my friends and comrades didn't. After all this time and all those deaths, it feels like the belief that we can load the dice in our favor just a little with the right kind of pre-mission ritual is more of a burden than a comfort.

When we are up in the Blackfly's cargo hold and the ramp closes slowly behind us, reducing the wedge of bright light inside the hold until it disappears into nothing, I don't look back.

CHAPTER 7

IN THE PIPE

"Bandit passing through three hundred by positive thirty-nine, distance now under ten klicks," the pilot updates. He's speaking in a lower volume than normal, as if the Lanky seed ship less than ten kilometers to our port is going to hear him if he's too loud.

The air in the cargo hold is filtered and temperature controlled as it has been for the entire ingress so far, but since we have started passing through Lanky patrols, it has felt hotter and stuffier somehow.

I'm at the command console at the front bulkhead of the cargo hold. Elin Vandenberg is in the jump seat next to me, and we are both watching the feed from the Blackfly's optical sensor array on every available console screen. The Lanky seed ship nearby is heading in a reciprocal direction slightly above and to the right of us. Ten kilometers is starting to get a little too close for comfort, but we are on a ballistic trajectory, and changing our course would mean lighting the engines and making ourselves obvious on infrared. The only thing we can do right now without giving ourselves away for sure is to sit still and trust the stealth properties of our Blackfly.

"Such a beast," Elin says next to me, in a tone that's almost reverent. "Look at the size of it. Two kilometers plus."

"Figure out what makes the dark ones invisible on infrared and radar, and they'll award you a shoebox full of medals," I say.

Our suits are plugged into the drop ship's environmental and communications networks, so we can talk to each other without having to speak up or using a radio link. In the twelve years since we met the Lankies, we've gradually improved our ability to function on the battlefield without emitting active radiation.

"That'll be really easy once we figure out why the light ones aren't," she replies.

"So simple. Should have thought of that."

I study the wavelike patterns on the hull of the seed ship, barely visible to the optical arrays even at this short range. We do know that no two seed ships look alike, but the reason for that is just one item on the very long list of things we don't know about them. I also know that if the seed ship less than ten kilometers away from our Blackfly senses our presence somehow and identifies us as a threat, it will blast a small cloud of penetrator quills in our direction that will go through the hull armor like a combat knife through a sheet of paper.

Behind us in the cargo hold, seven troopers are sitting in the two jump-seat rows on the inside walls of the hull. The Blackfly has space for twenty-five more, enough to transport a full platoon in full equipment, but the middle of the hold has equipment and supply pallets tied down between the rows of troopers, containing all the water, food, spare ammunition, and equipment we are bringing along. The usual headroom of the cargo hold is reduced by the flat Kevlar-lined fuel bags that stretch across the top of the compartment like big, padded blankets. The ship is loaded up to its maximum weight for atmospheric flight, and most of that weight is fuel, not ordnance or people.

"*Range is opening up,*" the pilot says. "*Two hundred seventy by positive twenty-two, distance fifteen klicks and increasing. We're clear of their port aspect. Forty-five minutes to aerobrake and orbital ingress.*"

On the tactical plot, the orange icon representing the seed ships moves off into our wake at a few hundred meters per second, a leisurely speed that indicates the Lanky is in no hurry. Behind us, the other Blackflies of the mission package are following our lead in thousand-kilometer intervals, spaced out far enough to react and change course if the lead ship attracts Lanky attention or trips any sort of unseen trap. We all topped off our fuel tanks from the tanker ships thirty-six hours ago, halfway to our destination, and the tankers are probably back on the deck of *Washington* by now.

"Dodged another one," I say to Elin.

"How close can we get before they notice us?"

"No idea," I reply. "Anyone who has found that out is no longer around. But this is as close as we've ever come with a Blackfly, I think."

"Fabulous," she says. "Happy to be part of that experiment."

"Hey, you wanted to collect data in the field."

Elin chuckles. "Guess I can't complain for getting exactly what I ordered."

Ahead of the ship, the moon we've labeled Green is looming on our sensors, a bright infrared flare against the coldness of the space behind and around it. The composite image from the low-light intensifiers is just indistinct enough to keep the moon alien and mysterious, vague hints of swirling atmospheric patterns churning in the near-total darkness.

I switch my comms line to the platoon channel and turn the seat around to face the troops in the cargo compartment.

"STT, listen up. Forty-five minutes to descent. Stretch those legs and shake off the sleep, people. We'll be on the deck in ninety," I say.

There's a general stirring in the hold as the troops straighten up in their seats and move their limbs to get the blood flowing again. We have been in this hold for over seventy hours, and even though I know everyone is apprehensive about what we will find on that moon once the ramp comes down, I know they all look forward to getting out of their harnesses and moving again because I feel the same way.

I turn my seat to face the console again. The Lanky ship is still widening the distance between our respective sterns. Its course is a few degrees offset from our reciprocal heading, so by the time the other three Blackflies pass it in the other direction, they'll have a few hundred kilometers of space between themselves and the seed ship, a far more comfortable margin than we got just now. The next closest Lanky ship tracked by the Wonderballs is twenty or thirty thousand kilometers above the north pole of the moon right now, moving into the system toward the gas giant and away from us.

"Do you ever wonder what they think about us?" Elin says next to me. When I glance at her, I see that she is watching my screen and tracking the distant seed ship as well.

"The Lankies?" I ask, and she nods.

"I'm not sure that they think at all," I say. "It seems to me they're mainly operating on instinct. Do ants think? Do wasps?"

"Maybe not the way we do," she says. "Almost certainly not the way we do. But they are a spacefaring species. They live in communal structures. They fight in large groups. They adapt to our tactics. There's a lot more going on there than just instinct."

"I've been fighting them for twelve years now. And I've never seen anything out of them that would make me think they have some sort of complex intellect. No culture. No communication. They're just mindlessly aggressive."

"You've only ever seen them in battle," Elin says. "They've only ever seen us in battle. They may have the same idea of us. Mindless aggression. I think our ways of talking are just so different from theirs that none of us have ever thought about the possibility that the other side can communicate."

I shake my head and smile. "Figuring that one out is going to have to stay your specialty, not mine. I've never had any particular inclination to try to have a talk with one of those things while it's trying to stomp me into paste."

"Of course not," she concedes. "Just thinking out loud here."

"But if you're looking to add xenolinguist to your job titles, I hope for you that we stumble across some sort of dictionary down there."

She shrugs with a little smile.

"Hey, you never know. Rosetta stones come in all kinds of forms and shapes."

"Well, whatever it is, you better hope it fits into this cargo hold, or it's staying right where it is," I say, and she laughs.

On the central console screen, the one that shows the feed from the forward-facing sensor array, the hot, cloud-covered moon looms larger with every passing minute. As I watch the indistinct atmospheric patterns, lightning flashes across a spot on the northern hemisphere, illuminating the dark, swirling clouds from below briefly, then again. For just a moment, it looks like the moon is flashing a hazard beacon, as if it's trying to warn us off: *Stay away, stay away.*

We need to slow down for the orbital insert, and whenever the mission profile doesn't allow for a deceleration burn or we want to save fuel, the only other way to scrub velocity is to use the atmospheric drag to do the job for us. It's called "aerobraking," and every time I am in a drop ship that must perform the maneuver, I turn off the external view and silently thank the designers of the current series of drop ships who decided that the cargo holds had no need for windows. Once, a very long time ago and hundreds of light-years away, I was in the cockpit of a Wasp next to my wife, Halley, when she did an aerobrake descent into the atmosphere of Willoughby, and the superheated plasma streaming past the cockpit windows made it look and feel like we were in the inside of a blast furnace. When I think of Halley, my heart feels like it is being yanked in two directions in my chest. Even though I would like nothing more than to have her nearby in the cockpit right now, I am glad that she isn't here.

The first part of the ride into the atmosphere is smooth, just a big light show as we use the friction of the upper layers of air to come to a reasonable speed for a surface descent. But when the pilot throttles up the engines again and dips into the denser air, the craft starts to bounce and shake with the atmospheric turbulences. I'm used to bad-weather descents—they're the default for combat landings on Lanky worlds—but I can tell by the way Elin grips her armrests that she isn't accustomed to having her teeth rattled in that fashion.

"How are you holding up over there?" I ask.

She doesn't turn her head as she replies, but she keeps her helmet firmly pressed against the padded headrest instead.

"Definitely having second thoughts at this point," she says.

In the cargo bay behind us, the STT troopers are swaying in their jump seats with every shake and bounce, and I can hear the occasional clatter of equipment getting knocked against seat frames and battle armor.

"*We're in the pipe,*" the pilot sends. "*Altitude fifty thousand, heading for the deck. We have some chop ahead, so sit tight. ETA to drop zone is thirteen minutes.*"

"Copy thirteen minutes to green light," I acknowledge. "How are we looking out there, Flight?"

"*We're looking great, sir,*" Captain Prince responds with a tinge of sarcasm in his voice that's just barely on the side of plausible deniability. "*Like a practice landing on a clear summer day. Nothing to it.*"

"Glad to hear it, Flight. Keep the cockpit pointing up and the skids pointing down, if possible."

"*You podheads, always with the special requests,*" Captain Prince says, and I grin. Levity is a common coping mechanism for stress among the STT, and it's comforting to know that our pilot in command still has the bandwidth for jokes because that means he's not feeling taxed to the limits of his abilities yet.

Now that we are in the atmosphere, I bring up the forward view on my console again. There's little to see yet except for swirling, indistinct darkness and streaks of raindrops slashing against the sensor array. I know the Blackfly pilots are the best drop ship jocks in the Fleet and that this sort of place is their natural habitat, but this phase of the mission is always the part I hate most because I have absolutely no control over anything while we are on the way to the surface.

"Hey, this is your second combat drop," I say to Elin. "Three more and you get the bronze drop badge."

"I thought that one was only for infantry," she says. The Blackfly jolts as it bounces off some unseen atmospheric swirl, and she squeezes her armrests a little harder.

"Any member of the Corps qualifies," I say. "Five drops under combat conditions. Whether you carry a rifle or a clipboard."

"I'm not sure the bragging rights would be worth having to do three more of these," she says.

"They're not," I reply. "You don't need the promotion points. And the badge is just a piece of tin in the end."

"Hey, a doctorate is just a piece of parchment in a frame and a few bytes of data in a file record somewhere. It's what you must do to get it that makes it precious. And let me tell you that I have an entirely new level of respect for anyone who has earned that piece of tin. Because this seems like a really rough way to make a living."

"I can't argue with that in any way," I say.

On the screen that shows the feed from the forward sensors, there's finally something coming into view more distinctive than just swirls of black and gray. The picture from the nose array of the Blackfly is a composite of the data from low-light magnification and long-wavelength infrared cleaned up for human eyes by the ship's computer. The resulting monochrome image always looks a little abstract in shades ranging from black to gray to white, but the surface emerging below the drop ship right now looks particularly alien to my eyes. As we descend through the clouds, the forward-looking passive array gradually reveals a rocky world full of vast plateaus crisscrossed by long, irregular crags and valleys and jagged rock formations that poke up through the sensor haze like the petrified teeth of some giant, long-dead beast. I have been to many inhospitable, barely terraformed moons before, but something about the geometry of this landscape makes me feel a deep sense of unease, as though the sight of it has triggered a long-dormant instinct from the ancient, collective memory of our species.

With every passing moment of the descent, the sensors yield a little more detail of the ground. The picture from the nose array has the information from the avionics superimposed on it, showing our speed and altitude as well as hash marks of the altitude indicator and the arrow-shaped wedges of the flight director computer that is guiding the pilot down our glide slope.

"Altitude nine thousand, looking good. ETA to drop zone five minutes," Captain Prince informs me over the intercom.

"Five minutes to drop zone, copy," I acknowledge and turn my chair to face the cargo hold.

"Five minutes to skids-down," I tell the troops. "Get that blood flowing again, people. You know your jobs. Secure that perimeter, place the seismic sensors, and get those drones unboxed and ready for flight. Anything comes our way, we want to spot it from a long way out."

I return my attention to the console behind me. The pilot has put the ship into a wide and gentle turn to port to follow the contours of a valley that spreads out for a hundred kilometers between two low mountain ranges. All over the sides of those craggy hills, there are large patches of ground that are just a little brighter on infrared than the rocks around them. As we descend into the valley, I see that the lighter spots follow the contours of the topography, dotting the moon's surface like an untidy camouflage pattern.

"Outside temperature thirty-seven degrees," Elin reads off the display in front of her. "It's a hothouse down there."

On our tactical plot, the other drop ships have faded into uncertainty, their icons now a pale blue shade surrounded by lozenge-shaped frames marking the range of possible locations based on the last positive contact we've had. Without using radios, all our comms are optical, and we lost our link the moment we dipped into the cloud cover of Green. The second ship in our formation should be entering the upper atmosphere above the southern hemisphere right about now, with the third and fourth following in ten-minute intervals.

"Tallyho," Captain Prince says from the cockpit. *"Got an IR visual on a possible Lanky structure at twenty-five degrees, distance thirty-nine."*

I sit up straight and lean closer to the display. There's an indistinct shape moving from the right side of the sensor screen into the center until the aiming crosshair sits right on top of it. It's barely visible against the background noise at this range, only the hint of an arch-like structure that looks just a little too regular to be a natural terrain feature.

"Copy that, Flight. I see it. Can you punch up the magnification?"

"We're at max zoom already. I can try for digital, but the resolution will turn to garbage. Not enough light for the image intensifiers under this cloud cover unless we get a lightning strike in the right spot."

"Understood. We'll send one of the drones over for a better look when we're on the ground."

"Can we get closer?" Elin asks.

"This ship is stealthy. It's not invisible. The stealth is for sneaking under SRA radar. If that's a Lanky settlement, I don't want to get too close and give us away with our IR signature. A drone is much smaller. And it won't have a dozen people on board to go down with it, if things go to shit."

"That is a good point," she says.

At the back of the cargo hold, the red LED array above the tail ramp starts blinking in a slow cadence.

"Three minutes to LZ," Captain Prince announces.

I turn my chair around and release the locks on the umbilical lines connecting me to the ship's air and power circuits.

"Three minutes," I tell the troops. "Lock and load. Let's get down to business, people."

CHAPTER 8

SKIDS-DOWN

Just before we touch down, the crew chief lowers the tail ramp, and a gust of rain blows into the cargo hold through the opening. Outside, it's utterly dark, and only the thump that goes through the hull when the skids contact the surface gives any sensory indication that we are not about to step out into nothingness. As soon as the ship is on the ground, the Force Recon sections rush out of the rear to take up perimeter security, followed by the SEALs and the combat controllers.

"Sit tight for a minute," I tell Elin Vandenberg. "I'll let you know when it's clear."

She nods and stays in her chair as I unbuckle my harness. I grab my rifle and follow the troops down the ramp.

The ground outside is coarse and gritty under the soles of my boots. The troopers with us have deployed in a circle around the ship, weapons at the ready and pointed into the darkness beyond. A strong wind is driving bands of rain across our landing site. The environmental alert system in my bug suit flashes a "HIGH CO2" warning across my field of vision. Even the advanced infrared and low-light magnification technology built into my bug suit only lets me see about a hundred meters into the rain-beaten landscape around the drop ship before the composite image from the sensors becomes indistinct.

The combat controller on our team, Staff Sergeant Mills, runs out to deploy the seismic probes we brought. A few minutes later, the three devices are set up in a triangular pattern around the landing zone, listening for the distinctive vibrations of Lanky footsteps.

"Probe uplink confirmed," Captain Prince sends. *"I show positive function on all devices. Neighborhood checks out clean. No seismic activity within twenty klicks."*

"All right," I reply. "Go ahead and wind her down."

Behind me, the engine noises of the Blackfly fade from a hoarse whine to a low whisper as Captain Prince shuts down the fuel-hungry main propulsion and switches the ship to standby mode. If the seismic sensors pick up any hostile traffic heading our way, we can be back in the air within sixty seconds even if only one of the two main engines starts up again. It's a calculated risk that leaves the ship a sitting duck for a minute, but we are so far away from our supply lines that every drop of fuel we save could be the one that gets us home in the end.

"We are clear for now," I send to my troopers. "Lieutenant Dean, keep up the perimeter watch. Mills and Martin, get those drones unpacked and ready for launch. And try to step lightly, everyone. We have no idea what's underfoot in this place."

I walk back to the ship and up the ramp into the cargo hold, now emptied of people except for Elin, who is still strapped into her seat by the forward bulkhead. I give her a thumbs-up, and she starts to undo her safety harness. Staff Sergeants Mills and Martin follow me up the ramp and unfasten one of the hardshell equipment containers from the tie-downs on the deck.

"It's a real vacation spot," I say to Elin when she is out of her seat.

"I hear the galaxy is full of those," she replies.

"Visibility sucks out there," I say. "Even with your low-light gear. Don't wander off. And if you hear the pilot yell 'emergency dustoff' on the general comms channel, you need to be back in this cargo hold in under sixty seconds."

"Got it."

"I'm serious," I say. "Less than sixty seconds. No matter what you're doing at the time. Don't stop for equipment or samples or anything else."

"I *got* it," she says. "Remember—fast runner."

"Right. Let's go, then."

We walk down the ramp together and step out into the darkness. Elin looks around for a few moments to get her bearings.

"Visibility does suck out here," she says. "Wonder if this is good or bad weather, relatively speaking."

She scrapes the ground with the toe of her boot. Then she goes down on one knee and turns on her helmet light, illuminating a little patch of the surface in front of her feet. Elin picks up a handful of the soil and looks at it under the light.

"This looks basaltic," she says. "Volcanic origin. If this place isn't seismically active, it sure was in the past at some point."

"All that heat has got to come from somewhere, I guess," I reply.

She gets up and dumps the handful of soil, then brushes off her gloves. With her helmet light on and her white suit standing out in the little pool of light, she looks even more out of place among the black-clad soldiers, standing in the darkness in front of a black drop ship.

Twenty meters beyond the end of the tail ramp, Mills and Martin are deploying the recon drones we brought along. They are using the upside-down lid of the transport container as a makeshift launch pad for the little devices, each no bigger than the length of a hand. I watch as they activate the drones and send them off into the sky as quickly as they can pick them up and throw them into the air. The drones whir off into the darkness, all but invisible to my helmet sensors once they are a few dozen meters off the ground.

"All drones deployed in local storage mode," Sergeant Mills reports when the last little swarm has taken off into the rain-streaked darkness.

"One hundred and twenty units, two per compass degree. Even if fifty percent of them drop in this weather, we should be able to get a pretty good picture of the area."

"What happens now?" Elin asks.

"Now we sit tight and check out the immediate neighborhood while the drones do their thing," I say. "You can start looking around a little. Just make sure you keep the drop ship in sight at all times."

"Sixty seconds or less," she recites.

"Affirmative."

Sergeant Mills's guess is not too far off the mark. The drones return one by one over the next hour and a half while we stake out our little base camp on the plateau. When the programmed time has passed for the last drone to return, Mills and Martin take stock as they place the units back in the charging-and-service case.

"That's seventy-one," Mills says when they are finished. "We may see another half dozen if their batteries hold out for whatever detour they had to take. This is a thirty-knot wind, gusting to fifty. Not the best weather for drone recon."

"Let's see if it was worth the expense," I say.

"Affirmative. Starting the upload now," Mills replies.

The drones did their runs in local storage mode, recording everything they saw on their internal memory units instead of broadcasting that information back to us over the usual encrypted radio links and laying an electromagnetic bread-crumb trail for any Lankies to follow. Now they are connecting to the control unit in the service case and uploading that information, which travels to the computers in our armor via line-of-sight optical data link.

"Section leads, gather 'round," I say. "TacLink update incoming. Let's see if there are any local attractions worth visiting."

The tactical map on my TacLink screen updates in splotches as the data from the individual drones gets added to the big picture. There are some empty sections on the map where the assigned drone for that bearing got blown out of the sky or higher up into the atmosphere by the weather and didn't have the thrust or the battery juice to make the trip back. We're in the middle of a wide, shallow valley between two low mountain ridges thirty kilometers to our east and west. There's a river flowing out into the valley from the western mountain ridge and taking a northward bend a dozen kilometers to our north. On the infrared image from the drones, the banks of the river are lined with wide patches of brighter spots that are slightly warmer than the surface. The irregular heat signatures follow the length of the river until it passes out of the extent of our drone sensor coverage.

"What do you think we have here?" I ask the SEAL team leader.

"Looks like vegetation to me," Lieutenant Dean says. "Follows the water, doesn't move, coverage thins out the more it gets away from the river."

"That's the first area of interest," I say. "The second one is the structure we spotted from the drop ship. The drones closest to it didn't come back, but we got some lateral views from some of the other units."

I bring up the sensor image and isolate it at maximum magnification, then share it around. Not quite thirty kilometers away, something juts from a low hillside that looks vaguely familiar, a cluster of interconnected arches that form an elongated dome of sorts. I've seen something like it many times on Lanky-occupied worlds. We used to call them "Lanky towns," but it was only when we got to see some of them up close on Mars that we learned the Lankies don't really use them as shelter, at least not in the way humans use structures. Whatever significance they have still eludes us. The one on the sensors looks different—denser somehow, less sprawling, and more regular in its geometry.

"That's local attraction number two," I say. "The river and the vegetation are natural features as far as we know. This here is almost certainly not. We know who builds stuff that looks like that. So that place is a priority for a visit."

"There's a coverage blind spot about ten klicks south of there in those foothills," Lieutenant Rogers points out. "The nearest drone got some blips on IR, but nothing distinct. Whatever it is, it's in a ditch below the line of sight from the drone."

"And there we have location number three," I say. "Now we just need to figure out who goes where."

"I want to take the SEAL section over there to number three, sir," Lieutenant Dean volunteers. "The blind spot. It's the biggest unknown on the list."

"You don't want Sergeant Mills along for combat controller business?"

Dean shakes his head.

"We can do the basic CC stuff if we need to. Not that we're here for a fight. I don't intend to kick anything off that requires us to call in close air support."

"Very well," I say. "You get attraction number three. Take your team out there, get eyeballs and sensors on whatever you find, and come back to the LZ by dust-off time. Twenty-four hours from fifteen minutes ago."

"Aye, sir."

"And remember—weapons hold unless it's immediate self-defense. And even then you want to think twice about whether it's going to help or hurt the mission if you start pulling triggers."

"Aye, sir," Dean says again, this time with a slightly impatient tinge in his voice.

"I know your guys are all pros. But you know what it's like when one of those things gets close to you and you don't know whether you've been made or not," I continue.

"We'll keep our cool," Dean says. I realize that I have no idea whether he was a team member already the last time we went into a stand-up fight against the Lankies, seven years ago on Mars, and conclude that he almost certainly wasn't. As quickly as podhead officers get promoted, Dean is a first lieutenant, which means he got his commission four years ago at the most, and he is too young to have made his way up through the enlisted ranks.

"I know you will," I reply. "Godspeed, Lieutenant. See you in twenty-four hours."

He nods and turns to walk to his team. The four SEALs confer among themselves briefly, then do their final gear checks and walk off on their patrol, taking long strides enabled by the power assist of their bug suits. Soon, they are just indistinct blobs on my helmet sensor, and when they activate their polychromatic camouflage and IR suppression gear, the four-man patrol disappears from my field of vision completely even though they're only two hundred meters away in a light rainsquall.

"All right," I say to the rest of the team. "Do we go to the river, or do we visit the structure?"

"I would like to go out to the structure," Elin says. "I really want to get a close-up look of that. Maybe we can swing by the river on the way back. But if that's Lanky architecture in those hills, I'd say it has intel priority."

I consider her request and nod.

"All right. The structure it is. We have twenty-four hours. If we don't dawdle, we can probably make both," I say.

"Flight, we are walking out," I send to Captain Prince, who is monitoring comms and sensor screens back in his drop ship. For the next twenty-four hours, he will trade shifts with his copilot and the crew chief while they wait for us to return.

"Copy that, Mission," Prince replies. *"Everything is still quiet on seismic. The place is silent as a tomb."*

"I'd be fine with it if it stays that way. Keep those ears to the ground, Flight. We'll see you in twenty-four hours."

"Affirmative. Good hunting, Major."

Nearby, my little team has assembled, made up of Elin, Staff Sergeant Mills, and Staff Sergeant Martin, the Spaceborne Rescue medic. All of them are new to combat—this sort of combat, sneaking around on Lanky worlds without a carrier overhead or an armored column nearby. Mills and Martin represent the most highly trained and best-equipped members of the Corps, the sharp edge of the spear. But none of them have ever stared down their sights at a charging Lanky in real life, and I know that no amount of training can fully prepare someone for that moment. All I can do now, beyond hoping that the place is a long-abandoned piece of inert rock, is trust that the people I am leading will do as they were trained, and that they'll do whatever they can to not let their squad mates down.

"We have a destination," I say to the squad when I walk up to the semicircle. "Does everyone have a lunch packed?"

"Good old battle sludge, full of essential vitamins and nutrients," Sergeant Martin says and pats the supply module on his armor lightly. Our armor will provide liquid calories and water through sipping tubes while we're sealed into the bug suits. The suit's autodoc measures our vital data and keeps up a steady stream of stimulants and appetite suppressants to make sure nobody is tired or distracted by hunger.

"Let's move out," I say. "Martin, you take point for now. You know the dance. Patrol spacing, staggered formation, watch your sectors. Be prepared to become part of the scenery at all times. Lead on, Staff Sergeant."

"Aye, sir." Martin lifts his rifle into low ready position and walks off on our target bearing. The rest of us follow in ten-meter intervals.

"Ready for that field trip?" I ask Elin. She is carrying no weapon, just her suit's supply pack and two smaller equipment bags suspended from a load-bearing harness. She doesn't have to tell me that she's nervous because I can see the obvious tension on her face through her clear visor even in the near-total darkness.

"As ready as I will ever be," she says. "Let's get on with it before I run back into the cargo hold to hide under a thermal blanket for the next twenty-four hours."

"After you," I say and gesture toward our bearing. "I'm right behind you. Staff Sergeant Mills will bring up the rear."

Elin shrugs to adjust her harness and shifts the weight of the containers she is carrying, then follows Staff Sergeant Martin with the same firm and deliberate strides he uses. I check the status of my rifle and take my place in the formation. A few dozen steps along, I turn around to take a last look at the drop ship, its squat shape already almost invisible in the darkness and rain except for the red battle illumination from the forward bulkhead shining through the gap of the tail ramp.

Overhead, lightning flashes silently, cutting a searingly bright swath across the sky for a second, the only natural illumination I have seen on this moon since we landed. It lights up the whole valley for the fraction of a second. The thunder follows a few moments later, rolling across the valley and reverberating from the mountains like a drumroll, a moody orchestral opening to our mission.

CHAPTER 9

RELIC

The valley floor gets rockier the closer we get to the mountain ridge. When we're three hours away from the drop ship, the volcanic gravel under our boots gradually starts to morph into fields of larger basaltic chunks and little rain-slick ledges. I know that the Blackfly is still in line of sight to our patrol because we're steadily moving up higher ground, and I get TacLink updates from the drop ship, but whenever I turn and try to spot it nested on the valley floor below, I can't make it out at all.

Elin is keeping pace between Sergeant Martin and me. I can tell that she really is in excellent shape because she's barely breathing hard. With their weapons and ammunition, the STT troopers have much bigger loads to haul up this slight incline, but the bug suits have power assist servos to compensate for the weight of the equipment. Her science division suit doesn't have those boosters, but that lack doesn't seem to slow her down.

A few hours into our ascent, the rain stops and the winds slack off a bit. The cloud cover overhead is still complete, stretching from horizon to horizon, blocking out whatever little light this place receives from the distant stars. Despite the darkness that shrouds our patrol, I feel exposed on these wind-swept gravel fields, where there are no ground features big enough to hide us if we come across Lankies, and I am relieved when we cross the first shallow ravine winding its way down into the valley, signaling more rugged and varied terrain ahead. There's a small stream of rainwater burbling down the middle of the ditch, just enough to wet the soles of our boots and splash up to our ankles. I can't see all the way up the ravine, but I can gauge the path it's taking down the gentle slope by the infrared signature of the steam that's rising from the water at its bottom.

"Got some weather coming in from the south," Sergeant Mills says.

In the valley to our right, a squall line is advancing, visible on infrared mostly through the way the rain gradually reduces our line of sight as it moves toward our patrol. We stop and watch the scenery for a few moments. There's an undeniable beauty to this harsh and hostile landscape. If this moon got any daylight, the valley and the low mountain ridges framing it on either side would probably look a lot like our training grounds on Iceland.

Underneath our feet, the ground shifts with a barely perceptible rumble. It's not the slow, rhythmic vibration that is generated by the footsteps of a Lanky, but a continuous tremor that seems to swell in intensity just a little before it fades away a few seconds later.

"Guess that answers the question whether this place is still seismically active," Elin says.

"Let's hope it won't do too much of that while we're here," I reply.

The wind picks up again, and the squall line passes over us a few minutes later, soaking us with rain that is coming down in sheets. From one moment to the next, our visibility is reduced to a little bubble just a few dozen meters around us. Then the torrential downpour slacks off again as suddenly as it had started, leaving a comparatively gentle rain in its wake that's coming down sideways, driven by forty-klick winds.

"Temp is down to thirty-four Celsius," Elin says. "Guess that was what passes for a refreshing cooldown here."

"A real vacation paradise," Staff Sergeant Martin says from the front. "You know the Corps would build a RecFac on this rock without blinking."

"Everyone who goes to one of those stays indoors and gets plastered all day long anyway, Martin," I say. "Don't tell me you remember the weather on your last RecFac leave."

"No, sir, I do not," Staff Sergeant Martin says matter-of-factly. "I don't remember much of anything about that leave, to be honest."

"I rest my case." I check my map display. "Target is twelve klicks ahead. Let's make sure we don't drift off our bearing in this weather. I don't have a strong desire for long detours today."

"I hear that," Martin says. "We don't get paid by the hour, right? Except maybe our scientist here."

"You mean you people actually get paid for this?" Elin says.

"We do. They pay us in beer and shiny buttons," Martin replies. "But now they've cut off the beer on the ship, so I think I'm gonna quit. Just the buttons aren't cutting it for me. We grunts aren't idiots, you know."

I grin and shake my head.

"All right," I say. "Back to it and watch your bearing. Let's see if we can get this climb done in less than three hours."

When we finally crest the ridge that marks the edge of the valley, our target is immediately obvious in the distance even through the wind-whipped rain. It rises out of the haze a little more than a kilometer away from where we are gathering ourselves after the long climb, an elongated dome-like edifice that is at least twenty meters tall at its highest point.

"Someone explain to me why we didn't just have the drop ship get us up here," Elin says. "I mean, not that I mind the exercise. Or taking the scenic route."

81

"Drop ship makes too much noise," Sergeant Mills answers. "Draws the wrong sort of attention when you have a twenty-ton craft putting down skids in the neighborhood. Best for them to stay put and keep a low profile where they can see trouble coming."

"Saves fuel, too," I add. "And it doesn't alert anyone to every spot where we're dropping off a recon squad."

"That makes sense. I guess I'm still not used to having to sneak around."

"That's pretty much all we do. The guns only come out as a last resort," I say.

We are standing on a plateau that extends as far as our sensors can see. The wind is blowing more fiercely up here than in the valley, but the earlier downpour has slacked off to barely more than a drizzle.

"Nothing moving up here but the rain," Staff Sergeant Martin says.

"Let's tiptoe our way in," I say. "Keep up the column, space it out a few extra meters. If we have contact, we do a center peel to disengage and fall back to the ridge. Everyone copy?"

"Affirmative," Martin and Mills reply.

"What do I do if that happens?" Elin asks.

"Turn around and run down the centerline of the column until you're back at the ridge. Don't stray to the left or right so you don't block anyone's line of fire. Once you're over the ridge, find cover and make yourself small. And don't lose your head."

"Got it," she says in a tense voice.

We move out onto the plateau, weapons at the ready, scanning the darkness at the edge of our sensors for movement. I know that there aren't any Lankies moving around in the immediate vicinity because I don't feel the ground vibrating with the distinctive tremors caused by their walk, three hundred tons of mass moving on three-toed feet. But Lankies can cover a lot of ground very quickly when they're stirred up and in a hurry, and I've been in situations that went from dead calm to a fierce, close-quarters battle in just a minute or two.

Its size makes the dome seem much closer to the edge of the plateau than it is. With our cautious advance, it takes us fifteen minutes to cross the open space until the structure looms directly above us, almost as high as a Lanky is tall.

"The fuck is this thing," Staff Sergeant Martin says. "Ever see this anywhere before, sir?"

"Negative," I say.

The outer wall of the dome is a tightly woven latticework that doesn't look like anything I've ever seen on any Lanky world. The interconnected weaves of the Lanky edifices we know have irregular spacing and look like they were strung together randomly to cover as large an area as quickly as possible. The outer wall in front of us is regular and precise, strands of perfectly spaced arches interspersed with perforations of roughly equal size and width.

"What do you make of this?" I ask Elin.

"I have no idea yet," she says. "It sort of looks familiar. But it's nothing I can place right now. Let's get a little closer."

"All right. But watch your step. You spot anything even slightly weird, you step away."

"Goes without saying."

I follow her at a few paces distance as she walks down the length of the object for a hundred meters, pausing occasionally to look at specific features.

"Think I can use a light? I would like to see what this looks like with photons bouncing off it."

"I don't see why not," I reply.

She turns on her helmet light and pans it across the structure. Whatever it is, there's a certain sense of order and beauty to it. The regular holes in between the long, thin strakes of material form a lattice pattern that looks almost like lace or filigree. In the beam of Elin's helmet light, the structure looks severely weathered, streaked by gouges and pockmarks of corrosion. Rainwater runs down the side of it and drips from every protrusion. Elin steps close to one of the latticework sections and shines her light inside.

"Nothing in there," she proclaims after a few moments. "I'm going to take a quick look around inside."

She starts to climb across a knee-high strand of the lattice-like material, and I rush up to her and hold her back.

"Wait up," I say. "Let me go first. Just in case."

"All right."

"Mills and Martin, wait outside and keep perimeter watch," I say.

I shuffle through the opening, which is wide enough to admit a bug-suited trooper sideways. Inside, I keep my weapon at low ready and scan for threats. I cycle through all my sensor filters in rapid succession, but none of them show anything other than a vast, empty cavity. The ground under my boots is the same volcanic gravel we've been walking on since we landed here, unmarked by Lanky footprints or any other signs of life.

"All right, come on in," I tell Elin.

She steps through the opening and walks into the structure, slowly turning her head to take in the surroundings in the beam of her helmet light. Now that we're inside the edifice, we can see that it's not a dome but a stretched-out half-tube shape reminiscent of an aircraft hangar or colonial shelter. I turn on my own helmet light and look at the ceiling. Water is dripping down everywhere from the many rows of latticework sections, collecting in hundreds of puddles on the ground.

"Cozy," I say. "Question remains—what the hell is it?"

"Whatever it is, there hasn't been anything going on here in a long time, I think." Elin aims her helmet light at the ground. "No vegetation. No Lanky footprints. Just rocks and puddles."

She walks to the center of the structure until she stands underneath the highest point of the dome.

"It's derelict," she says. "I wonder how far down it goes. Wish we had some ground-penetrating radar, though. I'd love to see how far down this goes."

"That would be the worst possible thing to turn on if there are Lankies around," I say. "Like turning on a big neon sign that says *'Humans Are Here, Come as You Are.'*"

"Yeah, I know. But I have some suspicions I would like to confirm."

"Like what?" I ask.

"The structure reminds me of something. This weave-like pattern. I remember where I've seen something similar before. Back in biology. Ever see a picture of a sea sponge?"

"I vaguely remember that," I say. "Biology class was a very long time ago."

"They used to be all over the oceans until we turned them into acid soup. Sea sponges, sea cucumbers, all kinds of filter- and flow-feeders. A lot of them had really complex hydrostatic internal structures."

I look at the elaborate mesh structure of the ceiling and follow the curve of it with my light. The parallel strakes of alternating solid and latticework material twist in a gentle corkscrew pattern, maybe half a turn in a hundred meters. The precise elegance combined with the sheer scale of the dome makes it feel a little like we are standing in a cathedral.

"What are you saying?" I ask.

"I'm saying it looks like it was grown, not built."

"Grown out of what?" I look down and scuff the dirt with the toe of my armored boot. "You saying we're standing in the middle of a giant *plant*?"

"Not exactly," Elin says. "Now I really wish we had a way to set up a ground-penetrating radar. I bet this isn't a dome at all. It's a tube. And half of it is buried in the ground."

"Not grown out of something. Grown inside of something," I say, and Elin nods.

"Pretty sure we're standing in a hydrostatic skeleton," she says. "I want to try and bring back some samples. Whatever it is, it's not just calcium carbonate or it would have been long gone in this climate. Maybe I'm wrong and it's something entirely different."

"What would have a skeleton this big?" I say. "It would make a Lanky look tiny."

Elin looks at me and shrugs.

"You're thinking our Lanky-eating friend from Willoughby, maybe?" I ask.

"It would fit, wouldn't it?" She gestures from one end of the dome to the other. "Just this part we can see is—what, thirty meters wide and a hundred long? And that's just what's above ground. We have no idea if there's another hundred meters stuck in the dirt on either end."

I look up at the vault above our heads again and try to imagine the sort of creature that would be wrapped around a bone tube of this size. Unbidden, my brain serves up the memory from the grab-and-snatch attack on the Lankies we saw from a distance on Willoughby, when something large and immensely strong came up from the ground and took several Lankies back down with it in just a few seconds.

"That was at Capella," I say. "Nine hundred light-years away. If this is the same creature, that would mean it can travel through Alcubierre just like the Lankies."

"Or they bring it with them somehow," Elin says.

"Why would they do that? Why would they haul lifeforms around that prey on them?"

She shrugs again.

"Maybe it's not voluntary cargo. A parasite of some kind. Or maybe it's a natural predator that follows them through space wherever they settle. I am just spitballing here."

She walks over to the nearest wall and runs her glove along the rain-slick surface. In the light of her helmet lamp, the material looks like dirty ivory.

"But whatever this used to be, it's long dead and it's not going anywhere. I want to collect a few souvenirs and then look around some more. Maybe we'll find an answer to that question around here somewhere."

"All right," I say. "First tourist attraction checked off. Let's do a walk-around and get it from all sides and carry on with our day."

I walk over to the wall where Elin is standing to give the light transmitter a clear line of sight to the troopers outside.

"Sergeant Martin, we're coming out. Nobody's home and everything looks inert in here."

"Copy that, sir. Good timing. Mills just picked up something on infrared a few klicks out."

CHAPTER 10

THE CABBAGE PATCH

"Got something on infrared at ten o'clock," Sergeant Mills clarifies when I am out of the structure and on my way to her position fifty meters away. "Not a Lanky. Something stationary, low to the ground."

Elin steps out behind me, and I motion for her to follow me.

"What do we have?" I ask Mills when we're next to her.

"Check that bearing," she says and points into the darkness. "It's barely popping through the clutter from the heat that's rising from those puddles all over the place."

I dial in on the heading Mills has indicated and crank up my sensor magnification. There's a shimmer of thermal bloom on the surface of the slope a few kilometers to the south of the structure we just surveyed. It looks irregular and spread out over a larger area, a patch of ground that is just a little brighter on infrared than its surroundings.

"It's stationary and it's not giving off vapor, so it's not water," I say. "And it's not very hot. Just a degree or two over ambient. Any thoughts, Doctor?"

Elin Vandenberg looks at the distant anomaly through her own helmet sensors for a few moments.

"I'd guess it's some sort of vegetation. It looks like the ground coverage we saw from the air, up at the riverbed."

"What in the hell even grows in a place like that?" Sergeant Mills asks.

"Lots of stuff can grow without sunlight," Elin replies. "Even on Earth. Look at fungi."

"You're saying we're looking at a mushroom field," Martin says.

"Something like it, sure. But I'd like to make a little detour and check it out if we can. Get a closer look. Some fungi are edible."

I look at the tactical map overlay and gauge the distance to the patch of ground under scrutiny.

"Five kilometers, give or take. An hour and a half on this terrain. That's if there aren't a bunch of deep ravines to cross between here and there. What do you think, Sergeant Martin?" I ask the Spaceborne Rescue trooper, my ranking second-in-command on this patrol.

"We can do it," Martin replies after a few moments of deliberation. "If we don't linger there for hours. Ground gets too rough, we can always turn around and go back to our original track."

"I concur. Worst outcome, we get a little bonus exercise," I say. "All right, Doctor. We'll take the scenic route just for you."

Our squad formation deviates from our planned easterly path and heads north toward the warm patches on our infrared sensors. There are more shallow ditches and ravines as we make our way along the elevation line, and now we must traverse them because most of them run downhill in an east-to-west direction. After an hour of walking down into ravines and back out on the far sides, even these shallow inclines start adding up, and I am grateful for the power assist from the bug suit's servos. Before I went out with *Washington* on the Capella mission a few weeks ago, I hadn't been on a real mission in a long time. Now I am starting to feel the drawbacks of sitting behind a desk much of the day even though I never skipped PT and joined every STT training march I could back on Iceland.

"Well, I'll be damned," Sergeant Martin says when we climb out of yet another shallow ditch. We finally have a clear line of sight to our new target, now just a few hundred meters away. "It is a fucking cabbage field."

The surface of the slope ahead doesn't precisely look like it's covered in cabbages, but I find that the analogy is close enough. Some form of growth is clinging to the rocks and the soil between, a vast field of irregular half spheres that glow faintly in the composite image from the infrared sensors. As we get closer, I see that the largest of them are no more than maybe hip high, and the space between the bigger ones is interspersed with clusters of smaller blobs. There are thousands of them, stretching out on an irregular patch that's at least half a kilometer wide on each side.

"What do you make of that?" I ask Elin.

"That definitely looks fungal to me," she replies. "Ever see anything like this on any of your missions?"

"Can't say I have."

"I'd love to get closer and take a few samples. I know some mycologists who would lose their shit if they could be here right now."

"I don't know if that's a great idea. That stuff might be benign. Or it could be wildly toxic. You may wipe out the whole drop ship with a handful of spores before we can all get decontaminated."

"You don't think the xenobiology division has come up with safe ways to get field samples?" Elin says. "Like I'm just going to pick up some alien fungus and lick it?"

I laugh for what feels like the first time since before we left for the mission.

"Sorry. I am sure you know your occupational hazards much better than I do."

"That is a safe assumption. I've probably spent more time in a hazmat suit in the last five years than you have in that battle armor of yours."

"We'll take a closer look," I say. "I'll leave it up to you if you think it's safe enough to sample. But we don't have a lot of time to stop and pick mushrooms. The clock is ticking."

"I'll be quick."

We're a hundred meters from the first patches of whatever low growth is covering the rock slope when Sergeant Martin in the lead stops and raises his right fist to the level of his head.

"Movement front," he sends. Then he gets down to one knee and raises his weapon.

Sergeant Mills and I do likewise, orienting our guns to cover our frontal arc. Elin Vandenberg crouches down a few meters to my right without delay or hesitation.

I check the terrain in front of us, but all I see is the patchy field of bulbous plants and the warm fog rising from the puddles left behind by the earlier rain.

"I don't have a visual," I send to Sergeant Martin. He's focused on a spot somewhere in the area he called the cabbage patch. A few seconds later, he activates the IR laser of his rifle's sighting system, and a bright beam reaches out into the darkness to a spot in the middle of the patch.

"On my mark," he says.

"I have eyes on it as well," Sergeant Mills says.

In the cabbage patch, some of the fungal domes are moving slightly. The movement is going across the field in a slow ripple, as if something is passing through the patch just barely above the ground, nudging the irregular spheres a little as it goes.

"Yeah, I see it." I turn up the magnification on my sensor and track the ground disturbance. It moves at the pace of a slow walk, visible only through the soil it displaces underneath the fungus caps. My suit's computer is linked to those of the squad, and the image on my display gets sharper and more defined as the others get eyes on the rippling patch of ground and the sensors all share data through the optical link between us. Still, we are in complete darkness, and at this distance, it's hard to make out any details with just the coarse imagery from the infrared and thermal sensors.

"Question is, what the hell are we looking at here?" Sergeant Martin says.

"Hopefully something we can turn into stew and steaks," I reply. "The wind's died down enough for drones, I think. Sergeant Mills, send up some gnats and see if we can get a closer look."

"Aye, sir," Mills replies.

She activates her personal suit drones. The gnats are short-range recon units, each no bigger than a thumb. Their batteries are small and their propulsion rotors feeble compared to the regular drones we used right after we landed, but they are tiny and almost impossible to spot from more than a few dozen meters away. They also have enough range to peek over obstacles a few kilometers away without risk to the recon team.

When the gnats leave their charging docks in Sergeant Mills's armor, I call up their sensor feed and watch myself through the drone optics from the overhead perspective. Even from just fifteen meters up and fifty meters away, we are all just the vaguest of outlines against the warm ground in our IR-camouflaged bug suits. The gnats head out toward the cabbage patch, and our squad recedes into darkness on the tiny sensors of the micro-drones. The wind and rain have slacked off again, but I can tell from the shaky stabilized drone imagery that the lightweight units are having to fight the air currents that are whipping them around.

"Units one through four are live and tracking," Sergeant Mills says. "Let's see what's bumping through the cabbage out there."

The drones level out at fifty meters above the ground and line up in a box formation, with their sensor ranges just barely overlapping for maximum coverage of the ground below. On my helmet display, the gravel-strewn landscape scrolls by at thirty kilometers per hour. Dozens of puddles are shimmering on the infrared sensors, radiating warm spots up at the drones as they pass overhead.

A minute later, the front of the drone formation crosses over the edge of the cabbage patch and the fungal structures start showing up on the screen, first alone or in small clusters, then in bigger patches, until the ground is almost entirely covered with irregular tubes and orbs of various sizes.

"Twenty degrees to the left, eighty meters," I direct Sergeant Mills.

The drones follow the input and veer off to one side of the cabbage patch. A few moments later, they are above the slow-moving disturbance that is jostling the fungal caps from below.

"Mark that movement, match speed and track," I say.

The drones keep pace with the moving ground. Whatever is causing the fungal growth to move is slowly pushing its way through the patch just barely underneath the ground, shifting the volcanic gravel under the mushrooms to the left and right along its line of travel. Every few moments, it changes course slightly in a leisurely zigzag, a few degrees left, then right, then left again, a pattern that looks very much organic in its randomness.

"Got ourselves some local wildlife here," I say.

"Looks that way," Elin says. Her eyes behind the see-through visor of her helmet are fully focused on the screen projection that shows the drone feed. "And we've only just started looking around. This place isn't as empty as it looks at first glance."

"Drop those drones down to twenty meters," I send to Mills. "Nice and slow. Try for a close-up."

The tiny personal drones are limited in their sensor capabilities, and the lack of visible light makes them only half as useful as they would be if we had stars for illumination overhead. Whatever is moving the soil doesn't offer much of a contrast on passive infrared. But as the drones get closer to the ground, I can see occasional glimpses of a smooth shape underneath the fine gravel, something long and streamlined that can easily bend its way around the occasional small clusters of rocks that are littering the cabbage patch.

"I'd say two, three meters long," Elin says. "A quarter of a meter wide, maybe a bit less."

"That would be one hell of a sample to bring home for the collection," I say.

"Whatever that is, it's strong enough to dig through this soil at half a meter per second," she replies. "I don't think I want to go near that while it's alive."

"There's another one," Sergeant Martin says. "Mills, pan ninety degrees right with one of your units. It's moving off to the side laterally."

Mills follows the order, and the feed on my helmet display splits, one large image following our original target and a smaller one veering off to the side. After a few moments, she has zeroed in on the second target, which is moving in a different direction but in the same winding manner, twisting itself around rocks and pushing aside fungal clusters. As we watch, the second creature pauses its forward motion, and a small mushroom cluster in front of it disappears below the surface in a few quick, jerky motions.

"They're feeding," Elin says with incredulity in her voice. "Whatever they are, they're feeding on the fungal growth out there. That's amazing."

"If they can eat it, maybe we can, too," I say.

"Or them," Sergeant Martin adds.

"If their protein molecules are the right kind, sure. I'd try the mushrooms first, though. They're probably easier to harvest," Elin says.

"Considering our recent luck?" Martin says. "We've probably just discovered the most toxic plant life in the universe."

"Those things eat it, don't they? It's much more likely that we just can't digest it," she replies. "But there's a way to find out."

There's a slight vibration under my feet that makes me stop in the middle of formulating my next sentence. I hold up a hand for attention and look at the ground. After a few seconds, there's another one, just as faint, little more than a shifting of the gravel under my weight.

"Anyone feel that?"

I've felt the seismic concussions from Lanky footsteps so often in my career that I sometimes feel them on leave in Vermont where there are no Lankies within fifty light-years, phantom sensations caused by stress and an overactive brain. But when I feel the fourth little tremor, I know these are not imaginary, and when the command channel on my comms set comes to life, I already know what I am about to hear.

"Dagger One-Niner, this is Flight. Do you read?"

"Flight, One-Niner. Affirmative. Are you LOS to the patrol right now?"

"Uh, negative, sir. We sent up a relay drone. Got some major hits on seismic. Computer says there are five-plus likely LHOs headed in your direction from due south, moving along the ridgeline. Distance eight thousand and closing at fifteen meters per second."

I feel the old, familiar pre-battle surge of adrenaline flooding my system and blowing way every bit of fatigue or levity, setting my nerves on edge like an electric current.

I guess that takes care of the other half of our reason for being here, I think.

"Copy five-plus Lankies inbound," I send. "We'll get in position, lay low, and receive incoming."

"We are standing by for close air support. We can intercept and hose 'em down before they can get close."

"Negative, Flight. If you take off and start lighting them up with cannon fire, they'll know for sure we're around. We can handle five or six if it comes down to that. Stand by and give me position updates. I'll call you if we need CAS and a quick exit."

"*Copy that, One-Niner. Standing by for hot exfil. Flight out.*"

I take a deep breath and turn toward the other troopers.

"Look alive, people. We have company on the way. Five-plus Lankies inbound from the south, eight klicks out."

"Coming for us?" Sergeant Mills asks. "Did we stir them up somehow?"

"I hope not. They're moving at fifteen meters per second. Means they're in no great hurry. We've got seven or eight minutes to get as far out of their way as we can. But if they come to pick a fight, we'll give them one."

I check the topographical map on my display, where the data link from the drop ship has just added a small gaggle of orange icons eight kilometers to our south, surrounded by small uncertainty zones. I scroll away from the Lankies and magnify the terrain around us. The cabbage patch is between us and the valley ridge, and we'd never make it a meaningful distance into the valley even if we were foolhardy enough to risk cutting through the patch and stirring up whatever creatures are churning it up in search of dinner right now.

"There's a small ridge to the east. Six hundred meters." I mark the spot on our shared tactical map for everyone to see. "Let's go, troops."

Nobody needs a special invitation to hurry. We leave the cabbage patch behind us and run toward the ridge and the virtual marker I just placed on the map. Somewhere to our south, the Lankies are walking along the ridge and toward our patrol, and even though I know they're too far away for me to hear the concussion of their footsteps, my brain has no problem remembering those thundering sounds and serving up ominous phantom sensations.

CHAPTER 11

—— DARK HARVEST ——

The ridge is merely an irregular shallow ledge that's barely knee high, but it's the only cover in reach on this side of the cabbage patch. We drop down on the ground behind the ledge and set up a defensive line.

"Mind your spacing," I send to the squad. "Thirty meters between positions."

"What do I do?" Elin asks.

"If they get close, hunker down and stay low. Keep still and let them pass. You can't outrun them."

"I know," she says. "I read an article on these things once."

"We'll be okay. We can handle a few of them if they come for us. The drop ship is standing by. If you get separated from the squad, break radio silence and contact them to pick you up. If we get to that point, it won't matter if the Lankies hear you."

My heart is thumping in my chest while I scan the horizon for the incoming Lankies, and I know that it's not just from the three-hundred-meter dash to cover we just made. The last time I was on a Lanky world with a recon patrol was many years ago, before we tried to retake Mars, and I find that I have not missed this feeling of isolation and low-level dread. It's one thing to be on a battle line against them, with drop ships and armor in support and orbital firepower on call. It's a different game altogether when it's just you and your little squad and whatever you carried in, and the next piece of hardware that could make a difference in a fight is too far away to be of any use if things go sideways.

"*Tallyho,*" Sergeant Mills says. "Here they come. Eleven o'clock, range seven hundred."

He marks the spot on the tactical display, and I look at the marker that appears on my helmet display. There's a low ridgeline at that bearing and distance, barely visible through the rain and fog, and several huge shapes are moving through the haze like specters. As usual, they are all but invisible on infrared, but in this weather, they show up on our sensors because of the disturbance their bodies leave in the semi-regular shimmering patterns made by the rain.

"Good eyes," I tell Mills.

We watch the indistinct shapes in the distance as they advance through the squall lines that are lashing the plateau. They're too far away and too hidden by the haze to get an accurate count yet, but it looks like a group of at least three or four. Looking at their IR echoes, I realize that I haven't seen so many Lankies moving around out in the open without hurry in a very long time. We were never able to fully claim Mars back from them, but we flew constant combat patrols above the surface and launched rockets at everything that moved until they stopped coming out of their underground burrows. From the way this group moves, I know they've never been in a place where death can come out of the sky onto their heads without warning.

"Changing bearing, decreasing range," Sergeant Mills says. "*Very slowly* decreasing range. They're not coming for us. Looks like they're headed for that cabbage patch."

The Lanky shapes move laterally across our front, becoming more defined with every meter closer they get to us. As big as they are, the sensors in my bug suit must pool all their input sources to make the creatures visible to my feeble human eyes in this suffocating darkness.

Lankies are scary to begin with, but something about the scene in front of me gives the primitive part of my brain an extra jolt of fear: huge monsters, lurking in the dark just beyond the reach of our artificial little campfires, ready to drag us off and eat us if they find us. Then they are close enough for us to start feeling the concussions of their footsteps: *thrum-thrum-thrum,* tiny earthquakes that mark their progress across the plateau.

"Over there," Elin Vandenberg says. "Look."

I glance at her and she nods toward the cabbage patch, where the movements underneath the surface have increased. There's activity all over the patch now, fungal caps and soil getting stirred up from below in random directions.

"Distance five hundred," Sergeant Mills announces. "They're definitely headed for the patch. Head count is five—make that six—individuals."

I gauge the distance between the edge of the cabbage patch and the little ledge where we are hiding. If the Lankies sense our presence and start coming our way, we won't have much time or space to get the drop on them.

"Marking targets," I say as I place designators on the helmet display for the squad to see. "If they get frisky, two rifles to a target, and keep it up until they go down. Center-mass shots, semi-auto. Burst fire only if they get inside a hundred meters."

When the lead Lanky finally steps out of the nearest squall line and becomes fully visible to my helmet sensors, it feels eerily like the first time I ever saw one of them, back on Willoughby many years ago when it appeared out of the rain in the same way. It shakes its massive head slowly and flings water off its cranial shield. Behind it, another one appears, then another, specters made solid by proximity and a changing wind.

"Four hundred," Mills counts off.

"Weapons *hold*," I remind the squad. "They're still moving off to the side. Let 'em pass."

It's strange to be this close to Lankies again that aren't on the attack, that aren't even aware of my presence. I watch the group of twenty-meter creatures as they stride toward the cabbage patch in a staggered line, splashing wet gravel and rainwater with every step they take. Even from four hundred meters away, their sheer size and weight is intimidating.

It's amazing that we managed to hang on against them this long, I think.

Just before they reach the outer edge of the patch, the lead Lanky drops to its forelimbs into a quadrupedal stance. One by one, the others follow suit until all of them are crouching low above the ground, almost perfectly still except for their heads, which are slowly moving from side to side in an unmistakably surveying motion. Next to me, Elin Vandenberg is so intensely focused on what's going on in front of us that half her upper body is above the rock ledge, and I reach over and grab the back of her suit to pull her back a little.

"What the shit are they *doing*?" Sergeant Martin asks in a low voice.

"Harvesting," Elin replies. "They're on the hunt, I think."

"I guess it's *their* cabbage patch," Sergeant Mills says.

I know without asking Elin that nobody alive has ever witnessed what we are seeing right now. The Lankies move out into the cabbage patch on all fours, slowly and deliberately, placing their limbs so carefully that I can't sense the slightest impact shock through the ground underneath me. It's an obviously planned action, without the hint of any overt coordination from the Lankies, vocalized or otherwise.

The subterranean turmoil their approach has caused is still going on as the Lankies advance into the patch. I can see the soil and the fungal domes heaving and shuddering in many spots. Reflexively, I look at the ground beneath us, half expecting it to shift beneath me as some unseen creature passes below. But the surface of the ledge and the little ravine right behind it seem to be solid rock covered by a thin layer of volcanic gravel, so I ignore the primal instinct and return my attention to what's playing out in the cabbage patch in front of us.

The Lankies spread out as they advance across the fungus field until the line formed by the six creatures is spanning almost the entire width of the patch. Then the Lanky at the far end of the line rises from its crouch and assumes its bipedal posture again. It starts walking across the end of the field in slow, weighty steps.

"I'll be damned," Sergeant Martin says. "It's a drive."

"A *what*?" Mills asks.

"A hunt," Martin replies. "He's driving the prey toward the others. Making noise to scare it up and flush it out."

"You gotta be kidding me," Mills says.

"Just watch. You'll see."

The upright Lanky walks in what seems like a random pattern, changing directions a little every few strides but moving slowly toward the middle of the patch, kicking up gravel and chunks of fungus with every step. Then one of the crouching Lankies lunges and plows both its front appendages into the ground a few meters ahead. When it withdraws, there's something squirming violently in the grasp of its front claws, something long and bristly and multi-segmented that has a nightmarish number of legs. The thing twists and rotates in the Lanky's grip for a few moments, clearly struggling to get free. It makes a sound like nothing I've ever heard, an enraged high-pitched squeal that cuts through my audio filters and makes the hair on my arms stand on edge.

As strong and agile as the creature seems to be, it's no match for the Lanky, which slams it into the ground a few times with blows so powerful that I can feel them shake the ground a little from more than four hundred meters away. By now, two of the other Lankies have pounced on targets of their own, and they yank them out of the gravel and subdue them in a similarly violent fashion. The rest of the group join in one by one, some coming out of their crouch and dashing a few dozen meters to where they've spotted their quarry. It has been a very long time since I have seen firsthand just how strong and fast Lankies really are, and how hopelessly our species is physically outmatched by them in every way.

"Whoa," Sergeant Mills breathes. One of the Lankies is chasing its quarry across the patch directly toward us, cutting the distance between us by twenty meters or more with each long stride it takes. On my helmet display, I see aiming markers appear on the creature's midsection as the members of the team bring their rifles to bear.

"Weapons *hold,*" I say again. "Mind those trigger fingers. We start shooting, we're done here, one way or another."

The Lanky skids to a halt just before it reaches the edge of the cabbage patch. It drops to its four-legged stance and digs into the gravel in front of it, shoving fungus caps aside in huge clumps and spraying gravel into the air that rains back down and bounces off the Lanky's cranial shield. After a few moments, it pulls one of the hidden creatures from the ground with a few violent tugs.

The thing in its grasp struggles against the capture. It's wrapping itself around the arms of the Lanky and lashing out with one of its ends in a whipping motion. We watch as the Lanky briefly struggles with the creature, which looks like a fever dream of a millipede. Then the Lanky jerks its head forward and snaps its prey in half with a crack of its jaws that sounds like a rifle shot even from this far away. The halves of the wormlike creature twitch and tighten their grip on the Lanky's arms in what looks like death throes, then go slack, and the Lanky shifts its grip to hold on to the pieces. The Lanky gets up on two legs again and walks back toward the middle of the patch, carrying half of the creature it just killed in each claw.

"Holy shit," Sergeant Mills says. "Holy. Fucking. *Shit.*"

"I'm going to have to agree," Elin replies.

The Lanky ambush is over almost as quickly as it began. Every one of the Lankies in the cabbage patch now has one of the subterranean wormlike creatures in its claws. The unearthly squealing has died away, but I feel like I can hear the fading echoes of those screams coming from the mountains behind us.

The Lankies gather in the rough center of the cabbage patch, which now looks like it has been worked over by an artillery barrage. Near the edges, I can see some more movement just under the disturbed soil, but the Lankies seem to have caught their fill, and they pay no more attention to it. Instead, they walk away the patch, forming a widely spaced single column as they make their way back in the direction they came from.

I let my breath out slowly.

"Was that close enough for you, Doctor?" I ask Elin.

"The scientist part of my brain says no," she replies. "The rest of my brain was screaming at me to run away for the last ten minutes."

"Good work on weapons discipline. Everyone's undersuits still dry?" I ask the squad. Mills and Martin have never been this close to a Lanky, if they have ever seen one in the wild at all. It's one thing to experience them in the safe environment of a holographic sim, and a whole other experience to see one in the flesh, with the knowledge that those three-toed feet digging up the soil with every step can crush an armored transport and all the grunts in the back like a ration box and then kick the mangled wreck fifty meters.

"That was something else," Sergeant Mills says.

"That's one way to put it," Sergeant Martin grunts. He's a sergeant first class, so he's been in the Corps long enough to have been at the Battle of Mars, but even there we had lots of combined arms support on call. Here on this pitch-dark moon, millions of kilometers from our carrier and nine hundred light-years from the rest of humanity, it feels like being in a forest at midnight and trying to hide from the bears and the wolves with only a flashlight and a pocketknife.

We track the Lankies as they march off into the rain again, each clutching their grisly spoils. With every meter of distance that opens between us and them, my heart rate goes down a little, and my anxiety slowly releases the hold it has had on my brain for the last half hour.

"That field has got to be full of tissue samples," Elin says. "I want to collect some now that they've done all the disassembly work."

Sergeant Martin makes a retching sound.

"You really want to walk out there and pick up chunks?" he says. "We have no idea how many of those things are still under the soil. You may end up in pieces, too."

"I'm going to use a remote unit," Elin replies. "I have no particular desire to die for my research."

"Flight, this is Dagger One-Niner. Do you still have your relay bird up?" I send to the drop ship.

"One-Niner, Flight. Affirmative. Twenty minutes of flight time left on the drone. We show the Lankies moving away from your position."

"Yeah, they stopped by for dinner. Luckily we weren't on the menu."

"Glad to hear it, One-Niner. Still standing by for an evac."

"That's a negative, Flight. I want you to stay on the seismic and track our friends. Once that relay bird is RTB, swap it out with a new one and keep the link running as long as the weather permits. I want to make sure they don't turn and double back onto us once we follow."

"Say again. You're going to follow *the Lankies?"*

"Affirmative. They just whacked a bunch of local wildlife and carried it off. I want to see where they're going with it. If there's a burrow in the neighborhood, we're going to find it and mark it for follow-ups."

"Whacked a bunch of local wildlife," the pilot repeats. *"That'll be an interesting debriefing. Copy seismic sensor updates via TacLink as long as we can keep drones in the air. Be advised that we may lose our link at any time."*

"We will deal with it then," I reply. "Just keep feeding us their position. One-Niner out."

On the tactical display, the orange icons representing the Lankies are now a kilometer from our position and moving off at what is a leisurely pace for them. On my helmet display, they're already only vague outlines in the rain again as they slip back into the weather.

"All right, listen up," I send on the squad channel. "Get ready to move out. We are going to tail them back to their place. The ship is tracking them on seismic for us."

"Copy that," Sergeant Martin says.

"Do I have time to get some samples?" Elin Vandenberg asks.

"I want to avoid that patch entirely," I reply. "But you have fifteen minutes to send off your remote unit and grab what you can. We're going to pass that spot five hundred meters to the left. You can probably meet up with your remote as we pass."

"Got it," she says and unfastens one of her equipment containers. I watch as she takes the drone out of its storage case and quickly readies it for flight. It's white and orange and somewhere in size between our gnats and the regular recon drones. She unfolds the shrouded rotor assemblies and activates the device, which flashes a series of diagnostic lights that change from orange to green and then to white. A minute later, the science drone is on the way to the cabbage patch on nearly silent rotors, bouncing and shaking on the strong winds.

"That's not going to hold a lot of samples," I say.

"It doesn't need to. I just need a few grams, not fifty kilos. Although a whole specimen would be even better."

I shudder at the thought of spending a multiday ride back to the carrier while sharing the cargo hold with a bristly three-meter millipede from hell.

"There's absolutely no way," I say. "Even if we could carry one back to the ship. No space, and we're already maxed out with extra fuel weight."

"Oh, I know, I know. But it would be fun to just plop one of those things down on the flight deck when we get back. Imagine the reactions."

I laugh at the mental image. "We'd spend a month in decontamination with that monster. No, thank you."

"Mills, you take the lead this time," Sergeant Martin says. "Stay sharp. Who the fuck knows what else is under that gravel."

We leave the cover of the rock ledge and walk back out onto the plateau, following Sergeant Mills's lead. Elin trots up behind me to take her position in the formation, her eyes focused on the drone controls that are projected on a little screen inside her visor.

"This has been an awesome day so far," she says. "Found a skeleton of a new species, found a live new species. Got to watch a bunch of Lankies hunt that new species. And now we're actually hunting *them*."

Staff Sergeant Martin, who's in formation behind Elin, shakes his head and chuckles.

"With all due respect, ma'am," he says, "but you have a really fucking weird definition of 'awesome.'"

CHAPTER 12

——— STERN CHASE ———

The Lankies have a head start, and even when they aren't in a hurry, they move much faster than any of us can hope to march. But the ground up here on the plateau is covered in coarse volcanic gravel, interspersed by low rock formations, and it's not difficult to follow the path of our quarry because their feet leave knee-deep prints that are several meters long.

After an hour of fast marching on increasingly rugged terrain, the group of Lankies is a little more than five klicks ahead of us, still walking in a single-file formation. The weather on this moon is extremely volatile. In the hour since we started to give chase, the winds have gone from thirty- or forty-klick gusts and heavy rain to almost still air and over a kilometer of visibility and then back to shit weather several times. We've gradually moved away from the edge of the valley and into a more challenging landscape, craggy and filled with spiky rock formations and deep ravines. The Lankies are still unwittingly showing us the way with their tracks, which stick to the gravel flats between the rock formations and cross ravines at shallow spots that aren't difficult for us to traverse.

"This place is a hellhole," Sergeant Martin mutters after he slips on a wet rock ledge and has to go to one knee to keep his balance. "Never been anywhere with weather this shitty."

"Then you've never been to New Svalbard in the cold season," I say. "Eighty degrees below, and two-hundred-klick winds."

"Oh, yeah, I've been there. I'll take that over this place, though. Hot and humid and dark as the inside of a latrine. On New Svalbard, at least you could take your helmet off. Get some fresh fucking air now and then."

I grunt in agreement. New Svalbard is an ice moon in the Fomalhaut system. It was one of our watering holes in the settled galaxy and was home to the last human colony in Fomalhaut until the Lankies took it over. Now it's an irradiated relic. We had to evacuate all colonists and dropped a twenty-megaton nuke onto the main settlement. It was cold and desolate and barren, and there was nothing to do but drink in the underground bar on the main mercantile loop of the town, but Sergeant Martin has it right. You could take your helmet off and get fresh air, and the air on New Svalbard was the cleanest I've ever breathed. It occurs to me that my lungs have had nothing but recycled and filtered starship or bug suit air since I gave in to General Masoud and left Iceland to join STT 500 on *Washington* well over a month ago. Corps grunts and Fleet personnel are used to living in filtered atmo for months at a time on deployment, of course, but this system has no terraformed moons or planets, and for the first time in my life I find myself thinking that I will probably never breathe fresh air again. I think of the last hike I took with Halley up in the mountains around Liberty Falls, but as soon as I unearth the memory of that day, I shake it off again and focus on my tactical screen so the sudden spark of despair I am feeling won't flare up and overwhelm me.

On my tactical display, one of the orange Lanky icons fades from the map, then another. One by one, the bright orange icons turn into weak faded ones, signifying a contact that is no longer up-to-date information. I punch up the optical link to the drop ship on comms.

"Flight, Dagger One-Niner. Do you read?"

"One-Niner, Flight. Affirmative," Captain Prince sends from the distant drop ship, now ten kilometers away on its spot on the valley floor to our right.

"We just lost the Lankies on Tactical. Did the seismic crap out?"

"Negative. But you're close to the edge of coverage range. Things get fuzzy from ten klicks out."

"Understood. How are you doing on relay drones?"

"We have lost one to weather so far. We're rotating the other three as they run out of juice in turn."

"Keep the link going as long as you have units. And stay on the seismic. If these things have decided to double back and check their tracks, I want to have early warning. Visibility is shit up here right now, and we won't see them until they're on top of us."

"Copy that. We are keeping ears on the ground and birds in the air."

"Counting on you, Flight. One-Niner out."

I switch the comms to our local squad link.

"Looks like they either dropped out of range or went stationary again. Flight's going to warn us if they're coming our way. Let's push on and see what's going on."

"How much longer do you want to give chase, sir?" Sergeant Martin asks.

I check the mission timer. We are just a little over ten hours into our patrol, and the route back to the drop ship will take six hours from where we are right now, with some slack built in because the Blackfly can always take off and pick us up along the way in a dire emergency.

"Bingo point is in eight hours. I'd say we keep looking around for six before we start making our way back to the bird."

"That sounds reasonable, sir," Martin replies. "I suggest we take ten to get our hydration sorted, and then we'll wrap up this self-guided tour."

The Lanky tracks take an increasingly meandering route through the foothills of a small mountain ridge that runs parallel to the valley where our drop ship is waiting. We follow the tracks uphill, through ravines, and across vast gravel fields that are steaming with evaporation from the copious rainwater. The seismic sensors from the ship are still feeding us updates, but even though they aren't showing Lankies on our path ahead, I still order the squad to send up a steady traffic pattern of personal drones to scout the next thousand meters in front of us, to make sure nothing is lying in wait.

Overhead, the ever-present cloud cover swirls and roils like a living thing, occasionally backlit by a lightning bolt arcing across the sky and illuminating the clouds from above. Without a Lanky presence, this would be the most suitable place for human habitation in this godforsaken nightmare of a system, but even with all the might of the Corps and the assets of the colonial administration, it would take twenty years to turn this moon into something habitable, and those are resources and time we don't have.

When we are a little more than a kilometer away from the spot where the seismic sensors last spotted a moving Lanky, the gnats fly low over a hillside that's blocking our direct line of sight ahead. When they reorient their sensors and show us what's beyond the crest of the hill, I give the squad the signal to halt and cover. They all spread out into cover formation, twenty meters between each trooper, making use of whatever cover the nearby rocks offer.

"Will you look at that," Sergeant Mills says when the feed from the gnats pops up on our helmet displays.

The area behind the hill in front of us is a long downslope ravine between two ridges. The incline is at least ten degrees steep and interspersed by dozens of little rivulets that carry rainwater downhill. At the bottom of the ravine, two hundred meters down, there's a cave mouth that looks big enough to be a drop ship shelter, easily ten meters high and thirty meters wide. In the IR sensor feed from the gnats, I can see the outlines of hundreds of Lanky footprints in the gravel of the ravine, both leading into the cave mouth and coming out of it.

"That's a burrow," I say to Elin. "You know what that means."

"There's never only one," she says. "Means the place is full of 'em. Could be one of those holes every fifty klicks all over this moon."

"Every fifty klicks if we're lucky," I reply.

"That's a pretty old hole, too," she says. "Look at the erosion around the edges. They've been here for a good long while."

"Look at that slope," Sergeant Martin says. "It's like a ramp. Fleet could roll a nuke down there and give 'em one hell of a knock on the door."

"That never worked on Mars," I say. "We tried that one a lot. They dig those tunnels with lots of angles. We'd launch a fifteen-kiloton tactical nuke into the burrow mouth, and all it would do was to collapse the entry and spray around a bunch of irradiated rock. They'd just write it off and dig another exit half a klick away."

"Well, someone should have gone down with a nuke on a handcart or something. Right into the middle of the burrow," Sergeant Mills says. "Boom, done."

"You volunteering, Mills? I think we have a dolly on the drop ship," Sergeant Martin says. "I mean, that would really be taking one for the team. I'd put you in for a medal."

"Sergeant Mills knows good and damn well that we didn't bring any nukes along for the ride, anyway," I say. "All right, let's get overwatch from the top of that ridge and get a better visual. But be prepared to drop out of sight in a hot nanosecond."

111

We take up position right behind the hillcrest. The sensors on our bug suits are much better than the ones on the gnats, and it's much easier to pick out details without having to tell someone to steer a drone to a different spot. The ravine lies dark and almost silent, with only the gurgling of the rainwater in the rivulets audible over the wind.

The mouth of the cave is indistinct even with all the light amplification and infrared magic my bug suit can conjure up from its neural processors. It's just a dark, foreboding arch that gives no clue what lies beyond it. Just the sight of it makes me feel like someone has fastened a steel clamp around my chest and is slowly tightening it.

"What's that right there?" Elin says. I look over at her and then toward the spot she is pointing at.

"Mark it on your display," I say.

She does, and a moment later, the marker appears on my helmet display as well. There's a faint IR glow at the right side of the cave mouth, maybe half a meter in. It's circular and emits only a hint of infrared radiation.

"Someone set a bread crumb," Sergeant Martin says. "Looks like the SEALs are already here."

"What's a bread crumb?" Elin asks.

"New tech," I explain. "We came up with it to have comms down in Lanky burrows. The rocks block radio signals, but you wouldn't want those signals down there anyway. Instead, if you stick a bread crumb on every turn in the tunnel, you have a light-based relay."

"And the Lankies can't sense it?"

"Well, that's the thing," Sergeant Mills contributes. "In theory, no. But we haven't exactly had a lot of opportunities to field-test them. In a live environment, that is."

I switch the light comms to the mission channel.

"SEAL team leader, this is Dagger One-Niner. Do you copy?"

There's nothing but dead silence on the light comms channel. I try the challenge two more times with the same result.

"Maybe they didn't bring enough bread crumbs," Sergeant Mills says.

"Or maybe shit don't work as advertised," Martin offers.

"Whatever is going on, we're going to have to figure it out," I say and toggle the transmit switch on the inside of my left index finger.

"Flight, Dagger One-Niner. You still with us?"

"Affirmative, but I don't know for how much longer. We lost another relay drone to high winds, and one of the remaining ones refuses to charge. You have an hour and a half of direct line comms left unless we can fix the second unit."

"Understood. We're at the mouth of a Lanky burrow, and it's marked with a bread crumb. Any word from the SEAL team?"

"That's a negative, One-Niner. They've been silent on comms since they left."

Fucking Tier One prima donnas, I think. *Half of them don't know that the last "T" in STT stands for team.*

"I'm getting zip on light comms from the bread crumbs. We're going to go after them to see what's up."

"That's a big risk, Major," Captain Prince says. *"You're the boss, but I suggest you tread lightly. You'll have no contact with us while you're down there."*

"We won't be long. Just a quick dash inside to see what's going on. And what's holding up the SEALs. See if you can get that second comms drone charging again. We'll make contact when we're out. Otherwise, wait for the other teams and dust off at skids-up time as planned. That is an order. Don't hang around. This place is lousy with Lankies and god knows what else."

"Affirmative, One-Niner. We are out of here and RTB in twelve hours, eleven minutes. Just be sure you catch the ride, sir."

"I have no intention of spending my retirement in this hellhole, Captain. Dagger One-Niner out."

I terminate the comms with the drop ship and look down at the cave mouth again. It's the most inhospitable sight I have ever seen. Even the Lanky tunnels on Greenland had some light to them, trickling in through cracks and gaps in the ice, reflecting off the surfaces. This one is dark and grim as a tomb.

"You sure you want to do this, Major?" Sergeant Martin says. As the most senior NCO in the group, he is supposed to be my adviser and backup conscience, the person who tells me when I have made a mistake or am about to make one. I give him the same reply I gave Colonel Drake when he asked me if I was certain about wanting to volunteer the STT for this recon mission.

"I'm sure I don't want to do this, Martin. But we're going to do it anyway. We're here to do recon, so let's do recon. And if we can help a bunch of cocky SEALs out of a tight spot, it'll be worth it."

"They'll never get over it," Martin says. "All right, let's earn those paychecks. Mills, send your gnats in as far as you can. It'd be really nice to know what we're walking into before we do."

I turn to Elin.

"I've been in Lanky burrows before. They're not fun places. I've been on sleeping meds ever since the last one. And that was seven years ago."

"I am not going to throw in the towel at this point," Elin says. "Not a chance. I may never get an opportunity to go into one of these again."

I shrug and shake my head.

"All right, Doctor. *Captain.* From now on I will avoid paternalistic attempts at safeguarding our only science officer. You have a commission and a doctorate. Know that you have the privilege to tap out of any military ops, but I will not bring it up again."

Elin turns her head toward me and smirks behind the clear face shield of her helmet.

"All right, *Major*. I acknowledge the privilege and the option. If I ever choose to exercise both, I will let you know. And I appreciate your promise that you will shut up about it now forever."

"I don't believe I used those terms."

She taps the side of her helmet.

"What? I think we have a bad comms link."

For once I am glad for the opaque nature of the bug suit helmets because that means she can't see my smile behind it.

"Fine," I say. "Welcome to the special tactics team."

I toggle back into the squad channel.

"Form up and head down. Martin and Mills, you hug the right side of the ravine. I'll take the left side with Dr. Vandenberg. I'll cover your descent; you cover ours when you're down. Lankies show up, everyone freeze and make like an inconspicuous rock. Understood?"

"Affirmative," they both send back.

Sergeant Martin checks his rifle and looks over at Mills.

"All right," he says. "Let's go spelunking."

CHAPTER 13

BREAD CRUMBS

Elin and I watch Mills and Martin descend the steep sides of the ravine as quickly as they can. This is the most dangerous part of the entry. When a bunch of armored troopers are in a gravity-assisted motion, they can't stop on a dime if a Lanky shows up in that cave mouth. The two sergeants take five seconds to slide down the steep slope, but it feels a lot longer from up on the ridge while I have my weapon aimed at the entrance of the burrow. The first section reaches the bottom of the ravine and rushes into cover positions.

"Covering," Martin sends when they are in place. "Go, go, go."

Elin and I haul ourselves over the rim of the ravine and slide to the bottom. When we cross the gulch to the other side, we hop across numerous Lanky footprints and ankle-deep rainwater rivulets. The ravine is only about three meters deep in this spot, but I instantly feel trapped here, all my instincts rebelling against going into a place that's hemmed in by rock walls on two sides, with a looming darkness nearby and only one difficult route of escape. Then we're in position on the far side of the ravine, and I aim my weapon at the cave mouth.

"Gnats show nothing but rock wall for the first fifty meters at least," Mills reports. "There's a bend to the left that's clear as well. Bread crumb on the tunnel wall before the next bend. Nothing moving except water."

"Advance, nice and easy," I say.

We work our way down the slope toward the tunnel entrance, each section sticking close to the walls of the ravine on the left and right. The lower we descend into the ravine, the higher those walls get. Halfway down the slope, the edges of the ravine are at least ten meters above our heads.

"If we have to engage, watch your firing angles," I say. "Lotta hard rock all around us."

"No worries. We'll be shooting upward at this range anyway," Martin replies.

Without the constant noise from the wind, it's ghostly quiet down here except for the trickling water. My own footsteps seem unnaturally loud to me even though I am placing my boots carefully and deliberately.

I hear the Lankies coming up the tunnel long before they come into sight, a slow shuffling and muffled scraping that drifts up from the mouth of the burrow and gets just a little louder with every second. Paradoxically, all my anxiety falls away as the adrenaline surge washes it out of my brain in an instant.

"Hold position," Martin says. "Everyone freeze."

"Weapons hold," I add in the squad channel. There's a little outcropping in front of me, laughably inadequate for either concealment or protection, but I crouch down behind it anyway because it's the only cover within ten steps. Elin quickly follows suit.

The Lanky that appears in the tunnel mouth a few moments later is clearly visible against the backdrop of darkness, an indistinct outline against the warmth of the cave mouth. Only the slight temperature difference between the creature and the air from the tunnel behind it makes the outline visible. It comes out of the burrow entrance bent over in what is almost a quadrupedal stance. Once it steps out into the ravine, it straightens itself up to its full height and continues to walk on without pause, a nightmare taking form in front of me. The cave entrance is a hundred meters ahead of our lead troopers now, and the Lanky will cover that distance in just a few seconds at a slow walk. I have a few heartbeats to decide whether to engage the threat or hope it passes by without noticing us.

"Hold your fire," I say.

The Lanky stomps up the center of the ravine. Behind it, another emerges from the cave mouth and follows the first creature. I don't even dare to track them with my rifle for fear of catching their attention somehow even though I know they have no eyes. If anything gives me away, it will be my infrared signature, and I can only hope that the bug suit shields it well enough even at very close range.

Seventy meters. Fifty. Thirty.

The moment passes when we could have engaged them with some room to spare. Now they're almost on top of us, and if we open fire, they'll be able to stomp half the squad. They're so tall that the walls of the ravine are only reaching up to the level of their midsections. I watch the feet of the closest one as it comes toward us, three toes splaying out in the wet basaltic gravel with every step, leaving deep divots with its claws. I've not been this close to a Lanky in a very long time, but the old feeling of primal terror comes back with ease, that fear of imminent, awful death—getting stomped flat and crushed, or picked up and torn in half, or thrown a hundred meters and getting dashed against the rocks like an annoying insect.

The Lankies pass between us with slow, weighty steps that make the ground shake slightly. From this perspective, and with so little distance between us, they look even more immense than I had remembered them, towering monsters with spindly arms and legs, and heads that are the size of armored vehicles. One of them passes close enough to Elin and me that we get splashed with rainwater from the puddle it steps into as it passes by. They are quickly past the squad and fifty meters upslope from us, and I give myself permission to start breathing again. Nobody moves until the Lankies are at the top of the slope and have started to disappear from our point of view.

"That," Elin says, "may have been a bit too close after all."

"They had no idea we were here," Sergeant Mills says.

"We don't exist in their world yet," Elin replies. "There's never been a human on this moon. They have no reason to look for us."

"Then let's do what we can to keep it that way," I say. "Keep to the corners, freeze, let them pass. Don't even think about firing until that's the last thing you can do."

I look over at Sergeant Martin and raise my hand for a thumbs-up. Mills and Martin just had their first real-life close encounter with Lankies, and as well as they have been trained before today, this is the sort of battlefield stress that serves as the ultimate test of a soldier's ability to keep their shit together under pressure, to control their fear enough to keep it from unraveling their mind. I'm as shaken and full of adrenaline as they are, but I have done this hundreds of times, and I know the junior enlisted are looking to me for guidance, to assure them there's no reason to panic. But I also know there's a certain thrill to an encounter like this, to come face-to-face with a terror and then walk away from it. If we make it back, these two sergeants will swap their stories from this patrol in the mess hall for a long time to come.

I get up from my crouching position and make the hand signal to advance. The sergeants get to their feet again and continue the descent toward the cave mouth. Behind me, Elin keeps pace, and not for the first time on this mission, I find myself thinking that she is the toughest one of us, doing everything we're doing but without armor or a weapon.

———

Just inside the cave mouth, the bread-crumb relay placed by the SEALs earlier is stuck to the rock at head height, emitting a barely visible glow on infrared. We advance into the tunnel beyond. The floor of the tunnel is smooth and even, and when I examine the ground, I see that the rivulets from the outside have been funneled into many parallel channels in the rock, far too clean and regular to be a random erosion feature. The channels are running in pairs, and they follow the course of the tunnel down the center. They're just wide enough for a human to jump over them, but I am not adventurous enough to stick my leg into one to try to gauge the depth.

"Irrigation," Elin says behind me. "Damn. They have plumbing down here."

"The awesome day keeps getting more awesome?"

"Something like that." She squats in front of one of the channel pairs and observes the rainwater rushing downslope in it. "Wonder what they used to make these parallel cuts in solid rock. The edges are too sharp for this to be erosion."

The tunnel curves to the left and then makes a hard right turn after fifty meters. On the wall right at the turn, there's another bread-crumb relay stuck to the rock. I bring up my comms controls and press the send button.

"Trident, this is Dagger section, Dagger One-Niner. Do you read?"

There's no answer coming back from the relay, and I give it ten seconds before I try again.

"Trident, Dagger One-Niner. We are at the cave mouth, making ingress. What's your status and location?"

My second attempt at contact doesn't yield anything but silence on the optical comms channel. I verify that my own transmitter works properly and give it one more try.

"Trident, this is Dagger. We are going to advance into the burrow and attempt to link up. If you can hear us but aren't able to respond, hang tight. We are on the way down."

"What the hell are they doing down there?" Sergeant Martin says.

"Same thing we are about to do, I suppose," I reply. "Take a look around, get a whiff of the local culture."

Elin Vandenberg has finished her examination of the water channels and moved over to the wall of the tunnel. Now she's removing something from one of her equipment containers and applying it to the rock.

"What do you have there?" I ask.

She turns and shows me what she's holding. It's a stubby wand-like cylinder with a slightly pointed end that has a different texture from the rest of the device. She turns and drags it across the rock wall, and a faintly glowing line appears. She draws the line about the length of an arm and caps one end with a chevron, forming an arrow that is pointing the way to the cave entrance.

"It's a marker," she says. "Weakly bioluminescent paint, mixed with adhesive. Can't use it for bouncing light signals. But it works without a power source. And it'll stay on the wall unless someone paints over it."

I step next to her and look at the waypoint marker she made. It's a low-tech solution but undeniably effective in this kind of environment.

"Not quite a big ball of yarn, but I figure it's the next best thing. As a backup. Just in case we run out of bread crumbs," she says.

"I guess it can't hurt," I say. "Redundancy is good."

We form our squad up again and continue our descent down the tunnel toward the faint glow of the second bread crumb. When we have almost reached the turn, I look back at the arrow Elin painted on the tunnel wall. The faint glow of the symbol is clearly visible on the image intensifier sensor, and the sight of it pointing at the way out of here is a strange little primitive comfort in all this hostile darkness.

The Lanky tunnel takes random turns at equally random distances—a left turn after forty meters, then two right turns with over a hundred meters between them, then left at sixty and left again almost right away—but the trajectory is always down. We see bread-crumb relays from the SEALs at every bend in the tunnel, but every time I try to contact the SEAL team via optical comms, there is only silence in response. Three times, we are passed by individual Lankies making their way up the tunnel to the exit. They all pass through us without so much as turning their heads toward the tunnel walls where we crouch and hold our breaths as they pass. The rainwater channels are still following the exact center of the tunnel, and most of the time the burbling water in the stone channels is the only sound we hear. There's a tomb-like silence down here that feels like a physical weight on my ears even through the audio filters of my helmet. An hour later, my suit's computer says we've covered a kilometer and a half of absolute distance at a steady 3 percent downhill incline, and that we are now fifty meters below the level of the burrow entrance.

No wonder we couldn't touch them even with nukes, I think. *Nothing we have goes through fifty meters of solid rock, and we're not even at the bottom yet.* The Lankies on Mars eventually learned not to show themselves on the surface, but if their burrows there are as deep as the one on this moon, we probably didn't even make a dent in their numbers.

"I sure hope you didn't skip leg day too often," Elin says during one of our brief rest-and-listen breaks. "That hike back up is going to be a bitch."

"I have servo assists in my armor," I reply. "How about you?"

She smiles and shakes her head. Through the transparent face shield of her helmet, I can see the sheen of sweat on her face and the hair that is plastered to her forehead. The environmental display shows forty-three degrees Celsius, and it seems to get warmer the deeper we descend.

The humidity down here is so high that the rock is dripping with condensation.

"There's a lot more CO_2 down here than on the surface," Elin says. "They sure like it warm and wet."

"So much heat for a place that doesn't have a sun," Sergeant Mills says.

"Tidal flexing," Elin replies. "All that gravitational pushing and pulling with that rogue planet and the other moons. Squishes the core around constantly. You can be sure we probably have a few billion tons of magma under our feet."

"That's comforting," Mills says. She looks at her boots as if she's expecting a volcanic crack to open in front of her on the spot.

A few hundred meters further into the den, the tunnel takes a slight right turn and then levels out. We advance even more cautiously than before, everyone mindful to place their boots as silently as possible. It feels like we're breaking into someone's dark house at midnight and sneaking around to look for the bedroom.

"Think we reached rock bottom?" Mills asks.

"There's always a way further down, Mills," Sergeant Martin replies. "You know that."

In front of us, the already enormous tunnel opens into a void that is all just complete blackness on my sensors at first. As we continue down the tunnel a careful meter at a time, the helmet computer starts to make sense of the limited input and combines all the data into visuals my brain can understand.

The cavern at the end of the tunnel is huge. At first, it feels like we are walking out into the open again because the ceiling is so high that I can't even make it out. I can't gauge just how wide the cave is because my sensors can't reach into the darkness far enough, but it's many hundreds of meters across. There are massive pillars between the cave floor and the ceiling, much too evenly shaped and regularly spaced to be natural rock formations. They resemble the trunks of huge trees at first glance, but when I focus on the closest one, I can make out the familiar structure of Lanky edifices, the strong and lightweight latticework material I've seen in many settlement valleys and burrows that looks like someone weaved a bunch of immense tree roots into a mesh.

"Fuck me," Sergeant Mills mutters in a reverent tone of voice. I'm too overwhelmed by the sight to voice the same sentiment.

"Clear the doorway," Sergeant Martin says. "Thirty meters to the right at least. Let's stay out of their traffic pattern."

We file along the cave wall and take whatever cover we can find in the many nooks and crannies. Out in the cave, there are Lankies moving around, but they are far off and indistinct as they pass between those pillars in the distance.

Along the floor and walls of the burrow, I see infrared heat signatures that contrast clearly with darker sections of floor, wall, and ceiling. On the floor, the heat sections look like trails. There are patterns on the walls, both geometric and flowing, with deeper heat in some places. Some areas are just dots or splatters, like a starry night sky. They are beautiful and comforting in a weird way—maybe because my brain is seeing the IR patterns as light, or because they could be art in a museum at home from an abstract period. The heat markings extend ahead of us unabated as far as I can see, varying in shapes I can distinguish but don't recognize as meaningful.

"Are you seeing this?" I ask Elin.

"Am I ever," she says. "This is unbelievable."

"What do you make of it?"

"This is all deliberate. Those are geometric shapes over there. Right angles, there and there, on that wall. There's a set of spirals. This is art, or language. Maybe both."

"Language," Sergeant Martin repeats in a mildly skeptical tone.

"Based on infrared," Elin says. "I know a bunch of xenolinguists who will absolutely lose their minds when they see the data from our suits. We've never figured out how these things communicate with each other. Whatever this is, it's a piece of the code."

The nearest set of shapes and lines is just a few dozen meters ahead of us on our side of the cave. As we pass the faint heat glow of the markings, Elin runs her glove over a part she can reach and looks at her fingers. Her fingertips are now showing up on our infrared sensors as five little warm spots, like the faint echo of an afterglow. She gets a scraping tool from a pouch on her harness and reaches up again to scrape a sample off the wall. When she is finished, she sticks the tool into a storage container and detaches the tip with the sample to let it drop into the collector.

"We still have a squad of SEALs to find down here," Sergeant Martin says. "Let's take stock of the local art scene on the way out maybe."

"Mills, send your gnats out," I say. "All the ones you have left. Link 'em for a wide pattern. Let's see how deep this rabbit hole goes."

The personal drones fan out and proceed to map the interior of the burrow, which is so large that it would take us hours to do the same on foot even without having to dodge Lankies along the way. Gradually, the data coming back from the gnats shows that we're at the edge of a roughly circular cave that is almost a kilometer across. The pillars in the cave are set in a pattern that can't be anything other than deliberate design, a hundred meters apart in concentric half circles that decrease in radius toward the center, as mathematically and structurally precise as anything ever planned and built by humans. The heat markings are everywhere on the walls, clustered more tightly together in some areas and widely spaced out in others. On the outer perimeter of the cave, there are more tunnels dug into the rock at irregular intervals, fifty meters between some and several hundred between others, each entrance large enough for a crouching Lanky. The floor is interspersed with the water channels that are coming in from the entrance tunnel and spreading out in various directions.

"Look at those patterns," Elin says in wonder. "That's a forty-five-degree angle. And a right angle. It's an irrigation network. This is amazing."

"Irrigating what, though?" I ask.

"Set one of those drones to follow this pair of channels right here." She marks the spot on the video feed.

"Mills, have that gnat follow that double ditch and see where it goes," I order. "Don't hit any locals."

"On it." Sergeant Mills takes manual control of her gnat and steers it around to follow the course Elin requested. The water channels go straight toward the center of the burrow for a few hundred meters, where they split up and continue on either side of a triangular section of ground that looks familiar in the image returned from the infrared camera. The patch between the water channels is lined with rows and rows of fungal caps of various shapes and sizes.

"Son of a bitch," Elin says. "They're doing agriculture down here."

"There's more on the other side of that," Sergeant Mills says. "They're sort of stacked into each other. With walkways in between. It's like a little mushroom farm or something."

"That's exactly what it is," Elin replies.

We watch the feed from Mills's gnat as she pulls it into a silent hover above the mushroom patch. Underneath the drone, a Lanky walks along one of the pathways between the patches, its cranial shield seemingly only a few meters below the gnat's camera and infrared lenses. It passes through the drone's limited field of vision in just a moment, but the sudden appearance makes me want to flinch away from the screen, nonetheless. I can't quite consolidate the Lankies in my head—vicious, relentless, destructive, and single-mindedly aggressive whenever we encounter them—with the idea of a species that practices a form of organized agriculture.

"Got another bread crumb in sight," Sergeant Martin says.

"Where?" I tap into his drone feed. "Show me."

He marks the location on our shared tactical map. "Three hundred meters to our right. There's another cave entrance. We can't see it from here because there's a pillar between here and there, but the drone has line of sight."

I move up along the cave wall, passing my troopers in turn, until I am at the far right of our squad. A dozen meters further along the wall, I'm at an angle that lets me spot the faint glow from the bread-crumb relay on the inside of the tunnel mouth.

"Trident, this is Dagger One-Niner. Do you read?"

This time, I get a reply almost right away.

"Dagger One-Niner, Trident," Lieutenant Dean's voice sounds in my headset. *"I hear you loud and clear, sir."*

"What's your status, Trident?"

"We found a Lanky burrow and we are well inside," Dean sends. *"Be advised that it's a long-ass climb down."*

"We're already there," I reply. "We followed your bread crumbs down. I've tried to make contact for the last hour."

"Shit," the SEAL section leader says. *"That didn't work as planned. Setting up a line-of-sight network is a bitch down here. Lots of obstacles. What's your location?"*

"We are down in the main chamber, fifty meters to the right of the end of the tunnel you marked. I'm looking at another bread crumb at a tunnel entrance about three-zero-zero meters ahead and further to the right of us."

"Copy that. We are inside that tunnel, a hundred meters in."

"Understood. We'll regroup with you at that cave mouth in five."

"Uh, sir . . . you may want to come down here and join us. Because I think you'll want to see what we are looking at right now."

CHAPTER 14

BEHEMOTH

We descend into the tunnel the SEALs marked with their bread-crumb relay. When we reach the end, it opens onto a wide rock ledge that's overlooking an area even more vast and spacious than the cave we just left. Unlike the cave, which was carved out of the rock with clear intent and by design, the chasm in front of us is clearly a natural formation, all irregular and with the chaotic geometry of geological processes. The ledge we're on is a roughly semicircular promontory that juts out from the rough rock wall of the gulch. One of the SEALs is waiting for us at the tunnel mouth. The other three have taken up observation positions at various spots near the rim of the ledge. Lieutenant Dean turns around when we arrive and waves me over.

"Don't lose your step, sir. It's a freaking long way down. And these things don't believe in safety rails."

When I step close to the rim and crouch down next to Lieutenant Dean, my brain doesn't quite want to process what the helmet sensors are showing. The gorge in front of us is a deep rock cleft that's at least half a kilometer long and several hundred meters wide. The ledge we're on is roughly halfway up the rock wall. I can only guess how far down the bottom of the gorge is because most of it is occupied by a huge, dark shape that somehow looks familiar and utterly alien at the same time. It's long and cigar shaped, and I've seen it in my nightmares a thousand times, but never like this, and never at this scale. Seed ships are several kilometers long, and the seedpods they drop are only fifty meters in length. The thing in the gorge below us is much too small for a seed ship but far too big for a pod. I let the suit computer measure the length of it, and it returns an estimate of three hundred fifty meters length and forty meters width.

"What the shit," I say quietly.

"That was my first reaction, too," Dean says. "Interesting, isn't it?"

"Doctor, you may want to come over here and look. I think this qualifies as awesome in your classification system," I comment to Elin.

She leaves the nook where she has been crouching next to the tunnel entrance and comes rushing across the ledge to join us.

"Easy, watch your step," I caution as she reaches us. I don't need to point out what I want her to see. She sucks in a sharp breath and lets it out very slowly.

"It does. It really does," she says. "Look at the size of that thing."

"Three hundred fifty meters," I say. "That's big, but it's no seed ship."

"Maybe it's the keel for one," Lieutenant Dean offers. "Who the fuck knows how they build those things."

"What's the status on the gnats?" I ask Sergeant Mills.

"Two are missing in action, three at low power levels and still recharging, three ready to go."

"Bring up the ready ones right now. One to either end of this place. One overhead right above us as high as it can go."

"Aye, sir."

The drones take off and disappear in the darkness. I bring up the drone feed and monitor all three at once. At this point, I am so used to seeing everything in the vague, diffuse black-and-white imagery from the passive sensors that it feels like there's no color left in the universe at all.

As the drones progress through the gulch, I see that our little promontory isn't the only one sticking out of the rock walls. There are dozens more passageways and platforms, both above and below our vantage point, some connected to each other or clustered together.

"That's a lot of tunnels," Elin says. "If each of them leads back to some other burrow like the one we just came out of . . ."

"Then it's like an ant hive," I reply. "Hundreds of chambers. Dozens of exits. Thousands of Lankies. Maybe tens of thousands."

"That's a cheerful thought," Lieutenant Dean says. "Well, we can't say we didn't find what we came to look for."

"I want to look around just a little more," Elin says. "How long before we have to think about making the climb back up?"

I check the mission timer.

"We have five and a half hours until the halfway mark. It's four hours from the burrow entrance to the drop ship, but that's a downhill trek, so we should be able to shave off some time there. With a safety margin, I'd say we have about four more hours to look around here. I do not want to come anywhere near to cutting it close on this one."

"I know it sounds nuts but I wish I could spend a week in here," Elin says. "We'll probably never be able to make that trip again."

"No offense, but I really hope you're right about that," Lieutenant Dean says.

The drones map out the gulch below us in rough strokes, limited by their small infrared and thermal sensors. From above, the gulch looks very much like a natural feature, a ragged fissure that cuts through the volcanic rock like a giant scar, inflicted on the moon's surface during some geological event when the crust cooled or some nearby volcano went dormant. From fifty meters up, the hull of the seed ship–like shape at the bottom of the fissure looks smooth and even, but something about it changes when the second drone reaches the end of the object and adjusts its altitude for the return leg.

"Whoa," Sergeant Mills says. "Did you see that?"

"Drive that bird down the hull about thirty meters and hold it there," I say. Mills complies, and I watch the footage from the drone reverse direction.

"Right there. What do you make of that, Doctor?"

On the feed from the drone, there's an obvious line on the hull where the IR signature drops dramatically on the sensor. It looks like someone drew an unsteady line along the bottom of the hull, and everything below that line is all but invisible on infrared.

"Think we can risk just a smidgen of light again for the optical gear?" Elin asks. "I want to take a closer look at that."

Mills looks over at me, and I nod.

"Make it short. Half a second, freeze-frame it at max magnification. If they sense it somehow, it's three hundred meters downrange right now."

"Got it," Mills says.

Out in the distance, a weak light flashes for half a second and goes out again, but in the utter darkness down here, it leaves a bright spot on our image intensifiers even from over a quarter kilometer away.

"There's your beauty shot," Mills says to Elin and sends the still image over our optical links.

The part of the hull that's clearly visible on infrared has the same eggshell color as Lanky skin. The transition zone where the IR signature starts to drop off is a splotchy white, and everything below the white line is a fuzzy black.

"Looks like mold to me," I say.

"That's exactly what it looks like," she says. "Like a mold spot on a petri dish. And what's mold?"

"A kind of fungus," I offer.

"You paid attention in biology," she says. "It's all that grows down here. No sunlight, no photosynthesis. But fungi don't need sunlight. Just a place where it's warm and wet."

"Like a dark, hot moon where it rains all the time," I say.

"That's right. And they don't necessarily need that environment to survive. Just to grow."

"Mills, see if you can get that gnat close to the ground. See what that thing is sitting on," I order.

"Copy that. Going down."

The gnat descends vertically alongside the hull, which is now just the hint of an IR echo in front of the drone.

"Use just a bit of light again," I say. "Just enough for the image intensifiers."

"Got it. Dialing it up a lumen or two."

The image greatly improves as the lens of the night-vision camera on the gnat finally has some photons to convert into electrons. The hull looks pebbly and uneven in texture, and now that I have an idea what I am looking at, it's hard to miss the subtle bloom-like patterns that seem to radiate out from certain spots and then overlap.

As the ground comes into view, it's clear that it's not the same volcanic rock we're standing on. It looks like the gulch is carpeted with the same rough black texture that's stuck to the bottom half of that strange hull. Then Mills stops the vertical movement of the drone and pans the sensor array in a semicircle.

"Looks like it's stuck in the ground, sir. The whole bottom quarter."

Where the hull of the unknown ship meets the ground, there's no displaced gravel, no disruption of any kind an object of this size and weight should be making in volcanic soil. Instead, the ground seems to rise to meet it, forming a near-vertical transition before flowing into the shape of the hull a few meters up. In the amplified image from the night-vision optics, it looks fuzzy and indistinct, but as the drone gets a little closer, it comes into focus until the mass looks like a curtain of countless fine threads, too many of them to begin to count, even though the sensor image only shows a square meter at most at its current magnification.

"That's not the ground," Elin says. "That's what's covering the ground."

"And what the shit is it?" Sergeant Martin asks.

"It's a mycelium colony. A fungus forest."

"You're joking," Lieutenant Dean says.

"Not even a little." Elin takes one of her equipment containers off the carrier harness around her waist and opens it to get out her own drone. "I really, really need to get a sample of that stuff."

"A fungus forest," Mills repeats. "That thing is sitting on a mushroom carpet."

"It is," Elin says without taking her eyes off her drone as she preps it for flight. "And that fungus down there may be how the Lankies hide themselves from infrared."

She looks up at me and flashes a wild grin.

"And that would absolutely qualify as awesome. Because if it does, and we can figure out how it does what it does—"

"Then we can figure out how to undo it," I finish her sentence.

"Exactly." She unseals a sample cylinder and inserts it into the bottom of the drone with a firm twist. "Think of the most expensive substance you know. Whatever I can get into this thing is going to be a billion times more valuable per gram."

I think of the implications of her statement as I watch her unfold the drone's rotors and activate its sensor package. If we can figure out how to break Lanky stealth, we would never have to fear any seed ships again. We would be able to see them on infrared and radar from billions of kilometers away and send out an Orion welcoming salvo long before they could be a danger to Earth or any of our colonies again. It wouldn't get them off the colonies they took or undo the rapid terraforming they've done to those worlds, but it would stop their free movement between systems and their sneak attacks, give us the ability to isolate them effectively, and scrape them off our old colonies one world at a time.

"I have to admit, I didn't have 'mushrooms' on my list of war-winning technologies," I say.

"Then you didn't pay too much attention in biology after all," Elin replies with a chuckle. "Remember penicillin? Lowly little mold, ended up saving millions of lives."

Elin sets the drone down onto the rock in front of her and sends it off with a tap on the control terminal in her hand. It lifts off silently and soars over the edge of the promontory, then dips downward into the chasm.

"That fungus down there may save the entire human race," she says.

CHAPTER 15

OVERWATCH

"I don't want to spoil the festivities," Staff Sergeant Martin says from his overwatch position at the tunnel mouth behind us. "But we should get moving soon. Things are stirring in there."

Next to me, Elin is securing the second sample container the drone hauled up from the bottom of the chasm. She puts the cylinder into her leg pouch and pulls a new clean one from the storage container in front of her to insert it into the bottom of her drone.

"We're too exposed out here," Lieutenant Dean agrees. "No cover on this ledge. We've been out here in one spot for twenty minutes. That's asking for trouble, sir."

"One more and I'm done," Elin says. Her reluctant tone tells me that she's not done by a long shot, but there's a certain hum to the activity in the burrow behind us that wasn't there before, and I know that the tension in the voices of my troopers is getting through to her and beginning to override her excited focus.

"Major," Martin cautions. "We should really pack it up and get to cover."

The drone zips off and dives toward the fungus field again. The previous sample runs have taken about five minutes each, and Elin is working with speed and efficiency, but standing out on this rock ledge makes five minutes feel like an hour every time.

"Last run," I say. "Then we scram. Lieutenant Dean, take your section back through the tunnel and set up overwatch on the other side. We're right behind you. Four minutes."

"Copy that," Dean says. "SEALs, on me. Don't be long, Major."

The SEALs line up behind their lieutenant and head back into the tunnel toward the burrow. With the four of them gone, the rock ledge seems a lot emptier than before, and I am acutely aware just how few we are, how utterly lonely and cut off from the rest of our species, clutching our little rifles for safety in the middle of a hive full of creatures that are fifty times our size and a thousand times our weight. The possibility of my impending death has been on my mind many times since I joined the Corps, but it has never been as strong as the premonition I am feeling right now. I watch Elin as she works the controls of her drone, intensely focused on the task in front of her, and I wish I could speed the little machine along just by force of will.

"Trident is in position," Lieutenant Dean sends a minute and a half later. "You want to expedite, Dagger. There's quite a bit of foot traffic out here now."

"Copy that," I reply. "Map us a way through the pattern to the exit. We'll be right out."

Over by the edge of the promontory, Elin does a little fist pump.

"Got it," she says. "Give me a minute and I'm ready to go."

"Those samples will only do us any good if we get them home," I say.

"I know, I know. But we won't get another shot at this."

I look down into the chasm at the huge shape stretching out at the bottom for hundreds of meters. There are no Lankies around it, and nothing has changed down there since we first arrived, but now I feel a sense of danger and malice radiating from it, a deeply unsettling primal feeling that I can't just shake off as a stress reaction.

We shouldn't be here, I think. *We shouldn't be anywhere near here.*

"Drone's on auto-return," Elin says. "Forty-five seconds."

She tucks away the control unit and opens the drone's storage container.

"Dagger, we have possible incoming," Lieutenant Dean sends. "One individual, heading for the tunnel to your position."

"Elin, *now*," I say. "We need to move."

"Seventy meters out," Dean says. "Do you want us to engage?"

"Dagger squad, take cover," I tell my troopers. "Hug the wall."

I dash over to Elin and pull her away from the ledge of the promontory.

"Lanky on the way," I shout. "Get to the rock and make yourself small."

"Fifty meters," Lieutenant Dean says with urgency. "Do we engage?"

"Negative," I reply. Elin is now sprinting toward cover with the appropriate urgency, and she is pulling slightly ahead of me despite the servo assist of my bug suit that is operating at maximum power, automatically triggered by my adrenaline spike. "Weapons hold. Let it pass through. We'll deal with it on this end."

"Goddammit," Dean replies.

"You shoot it now, you stir them all up. If it spots us, we'll deal with it out here."

"I hope you're right. Thirty meters. Ten. It's past us and in the tunnel. Fuck."

I can hear the Lanky before I see it, just like the ones we saw emerging from the burrow entrance, a shuffling and scraping sound from long, hard-armored limbs scraping on rock as the creature makes its way through the passage in a low crouch. We reach the rock wall and squat down just a few seconds before the Lanky emerges from the tunnel and stands upright again, barely fifty meters to our right. In each clawed hand, it's carrying something—not the millipede-like creatures we saw them harvest in the cabbage patch earlier, but something organic, torn and bloody and shapeless.

You're not here for us, I think. *Just do your thing and leave.*

The Lanky walks over to the edge of the promontory and throws the bloody chunks into the chasm in a motion that looks unhurried and almost casual. It turns its head to the left, then to the right and back again. Just as the Lanky is turning around, Elin's drone comes whirring out of the dark only ten meters to the left of its head. The drone continues its automated path, smart enough to see obstacles but too dumb to recognize danger, and it tilts its rotors and steers for the location of its operator, who is crouching a few meters to my right.

For a moment, it looks like the Lanky takes no notice of the object near its head. Then it continues its turn, swings a long, spindly arm, and swats the science drone out of the air. The drone shatters under the blow, and the pieces continue their motion and smash against the rock wall right above our heads. Against my instincts, which are screaming at me to bring up my rifle and empty a magazine into the Lanky's chest and blow it off the ledge, I remain as still as a landscape feature as the giant head swings toward me. Next to me, Elin follows my cue and stays in her stock-still crouch even as pieces of her own drone are raining down on us. Then my chance for a relatively certain kill is gone as the Lanky drops on its forelimbs and turns its head again, looking strangely like a dog trying to locate the source of an unfamiliar sound. Now all I have to aim at is the thick skull and the massive cranial shield, which will deflect even the armor-piercing high-density sabot rounds from an autocannon, much less my weaker rifle.

We face each other for a long moment. Even though the Lanky has no visible eyes, I know that it's trying to sniff me out somehow on whatever wavelength their sensory input operates, infrared or ultraviolet or both or maybe none of it at all. My bug suit is designed to mask my body heat and camouflage me perfectly against my background environment, the computer taking measure of all relevant values and adjusting the thermal profile five hundred times per second, but I've never tried to hide from a Lanky that was facing me head-on from only thirty meters away. Then it shifts its head to my right ever so slightly, and I know that the hostile environment suits of the science division aren't as well camouflaged as the military bug suits.

I bring up my rifle just as the Lanky sets itself in motion toward the spot where Elin Vandenberg is crouching. My thumb flicks the fire selector all the way to its bottom position, full-auto fire at maximum cadence. But the gunfire that erupts doesn't come from my muzzle. The tracers are streaking in from my right and slamming into the Lanky's unprotected side. It stumbles in midstride and turns toward the threat, lowering its head to meet the storm of armor-piercing rounds. Fifty meters to my right, Sergeants Mills and Martin are shooting on the move, raking the Lanky with bursts from their rifles as they walk back out onto the rock promontory from the relative safety of their cover. Now that the Lanky is facing my troopers, I have a clear shot at its left flank, and I hold down the trigger and shoot a burst into its side. It wails, a dreadful sound that drowns out our gunfire with ease, and falls over on its side. I hear Lieutenant Dean shout something on the squad channel, but it's all just meaningless noise in the moment amid the screaming Lanky and the muzzle blasts from our automatic rifles. My weapon's bolt locks back on an expended ammunition block, and my hand reaches for a reload and slams the new ammo pack into the gun, my body running purely on muscle memory.

Just when it looks like we have beaten it down to the ground with our concentrated barrage, the Lanky raises itself up on one forelimb and lunges forward. I pour another burst into its flank and see the rounds smacking into its skin, tearing loose chunks of matter with the detonations of the high-explosive payloads behind the kinetic penetrators, but the Lanky has worked up a last bit of forward momentum that can't be deflected even by a few thousand joules of impact energy driving tungsten darts from one side of its body to the other. It lashes out with one arm just as it collapses again and slides forward, catching Sergeant Mills with one of its claws and sweeping her off the edge of the promontory. She disappears into the darkness without a noise, and the Lanky slides off the ledge and follows her into the abyss with another ear-splitting wail.

I don't realize that I've run all the way to the spot where Mills disappeared until I am already at the edge, screaming out my shock and rage. The sergeant has disappeared in the mycelium thicket at the bottom of the gorge, but the Lanky is still squirming around among the fungus strands, too large to be completely submerged in the layers of thin black threads. I aim my rifle and empty the rest of my magazine at the creature. Then Sergeant Martin is by my side and pulls me back from the ledge.

"We need to fucking leave," Martin shouts at me. I reach for another ammo pack, but Martin yanks the rifle out of my hands and pushes me backward.

"Move," he shouts. "Let's go. Get your shit together, sir."

He drags me with him until we're twenty meters from the ledge. Martin reloads my rifle and smacks it against my chest armor in a present-arms position, and I take my weapon back reflexively.

"You good?" Martin shouts, and I nod even though I am anything but good right now.

Elin is still couching behind her inadequate little cover, and Martin pulls her to her feet as well. We dash into the tunnel and emerge on the other side at a run.

"That stirred up the whole fucking place," Lieutenant Dean says when we join him behind the Lanky pillar where he has taken cover with his SEALs. "There's a bunch of noise coming from those side tunnels. Hope that third sample was really worth it."

I glance at Elin, who is crouching next to Staff Sergeant Martin and looking around wide-eyed. She appears to be in the middle of a thorough reassessment of the quality of this day.

"Fucking Lanky smashed the drone. It popped up right in front of the fucker," I say.

"That's fabulous," Dean says. "Tripped the burglar alarm for absolutely nothing, I guess."

"We hosed it down but it took out Mills," I say. "She went over the edge. She's gone."

"Shit." Dean tightens his grip on his rifle. "Goddammit."

"We got the other samples. We need to get her topside and back to the ship."

"Copy that. Let's go, then. Exit is three hundred meters that way." He points to our left. "We can use these pillars as cover, bounce from one to the next."

"All right," I say. "SEALs, take the lead. Weapons tight, last resort only. We won't last long in here if we get into another fight."

I look over at the tunnel mouth Lieutenant Dean indicated. To our right, in the middle of the burrow, several tall shapes are moving through the darkness toward us. Right now we have to hope that they are merely investigating the gunfire and the screams from the Lanky we killed, because if they already know where we are, we'll never make the three hundred meters to the exit tunnel before they cut us off and stomp us into the ground. I have already burned through twenty of my seventy rifle rounds, and we've only managed to kill one of their number.

We form up behind the SEALs and follow them into the darkness toward the nearest pillar to our left. The pillars are the only cover on this side of the burrow except for the little crevices and ledges on the rock wall. As tiny as we are compared to them, right now I am thankful that the Lankies are as big as they are because they can't sneak up on us in the dark.

The SEALs reach the pillar first and take up covering position. The rest of us get there a few moments later, and we huddle behind the cover. Sergeant Martin still has Elin next to him. Even in her bulky hostile environment suit, she looks tiny next to the Spaceborne Rescue sergeant in his battle armor.

"You get her topside, no matter what happens," I tell him. "Once you're outside, call the drop ship for immediate emergency dustoff. You stay with her and get her on that bird."

"Affirmative," Sergeant Martin says. "But don't be planning to get your name on the Wall, sir."

The Wall is the memorial in the staff building at Combat Controller School back home, engraved with the names of all combat controllers who have died on the job. It has a lot of names on it for an occupational specialty that trains maybe fifty new members every year. I recall that Lieutenant Colonel Campbell said something remarkably similar before I left, telling me to avoid Medal of Honor heroics.

"I'm not craving that, Martin," I tell him. "Not even a little. But do what you have to do to get her on that ship in one piece."

He nods, and I pat his shoulder twice with my armored glove.

"Next pillar, fifty meters," Lieutenant Dean calls out. "Trident, cover. Dagger, *go, go, go.*"

Now it's our turn to make the dash deeper into the darkness while the SEALs cover our run. Our sections leapfrog across the outer edge of the Lanky burrow fifty meters at the time, pillar by pillar, and each run feels like a twenty-minute event even though we only need twenty seconds for the dash. As big as this cave is, it feels as through the walls are coming together a little every time a new Lanky appears out of one of the side tunnels. There's at least a dozen of them moving in the burrow in the detection range of our sensors now, far too many for us to take on with the limited firepower we brought along. The closest one is a hundred meters to our right, moving the way we came, turning its head from side to side in an unmistakable searching pattern but giving no indication that it has spotted us. In front of me, Martin has reached the cover of the next pillar with Elin, and he crouches down with her, keeping his body in the line of sight between her and the Lanky as it moves off. I join them and cover our little perimeter to our rear. I look back toward the entrance of the tunnel that leads out to the promontory above the gorge. One of the newcomer Lankies is stooping down to step through the passage, and another one follows. I know that there's no way Sergeant Mills could have survived that blow from the Lanky or the fall from the ledge, but I still feel a burning, helpless anger at the thought of having to leave her out there in the darkness with these things.

We gather ourselves and make the final dash to the mouth of the exit tunnel. The SEALs line up on the left tunnel wall as they go in. Staff Sergeant Martin leads us to the other side of the tunnel and follows the SEAL section. For a moment, I am firmly convinced that the inertial guidance systems in our suits have lost our track, that we're going up the wrong tunnel in this maze of pillars and passages, but then I see one of Elin's bioluminescent paint arrows on the wall of the tunnel, glowing faintly in the dark about thirty meters in. I look back at the tunnel mouth and the cavern beyond, where the number of Lankies seems to have doubled since we started our retreat.

"Clear in front," Lieutenant Dean sends from the front of our formation. He's already at the next bend in the tunnel and scanning ahead.

"Our six is clear as well," I reply. "For now. Let's get the hell out."

"Affirmative," Dean says and moves around the corner, his rifle ready and at eye level. Behind him, his SEAL section follows with smooth precision, a well-practiced tactical stack right out of a special-operations textbook. We follow the SEALs around the bend and into the dark. Before I turn the corner, I look over my shoulder again. From this angle, I can't see the Lankies moving around in the cavern anymore, but not being able to see them is worse than having them in my line of sight because now the monsters can pop out of the dark behind me without warning.

"Staff Sergeant Martin," I call out. "Bring any grenades?"

"I did," Martin replies.

"Take rear guard and set up a hi-ex behind us. Trip-wire fuse."

"Aye, sir," Martin replies. He turns and rushes back down the tunnel toward me.

Martin runs past and skids to a stop five meters down the tunnel from me. He unclips one of the multipurpose grenades he's carrying on his bug suit's load harness and puts it down on the tunnel floor right next to the wall. He pops off the safety cap of the grenade and turns the fuse to trip-wire mode. The guide laser shines in the darkness like a sharp little sunray for a moment as he orients the device. Then it turns off again, and Martin gets up from his crouch and rushes back to us.

"Trip wire is set. Five seconds," he announces.

We follow the SEALs up the tunnel at a run. Behind us, the high-explosive grenade is now arming silently, activating a proximity sensor and an infrared laser that forms an invisible wire across the floor of the tunnel. The grenade isn't likely to kill a Lanky outright unless the creature somehow picks it up and swallows it before it can go off, but it has enough punch to hurt it and give it pause, and the noise will let us know if something is coming up the tunnel behind us. Still, when I follow my squad up the slope of the tunnel as fast as the servo assist in my suit will boost my strides, I feel a lot like I did when I was a kid in the PRC, running up the stairwell to our floor in the dark in the middle of a disciplinary blackout, convinced that if I didn't make the door fast enough, something would drag me back down and eat me alive.

We pause at every bend in the tunnel while the SEALs check the next stretch. Every time they do, I expect them to open fire as our luck runs out and we run head-on into Lankies coming down the tunnel from the outside. But we negotiate turn after turn without contact as we pass Elin's glowing markers on the way up. The rainwater in the irrigation channels at the center of the tunnel is burbling downhill into the burrow and masking most of the sounds of our footsteps.

We're only half a dozen bends up the tunnel, a few hundred meters at best, when the sound of the high-explosive detonation of the trip-wire mines arrives from below at the same time as the shock wave from the overpressure. It knocks me down midstep, and I crash to the tunnel floor. My helmet bounces off the rock, jarring my skull and rattling my teeth even through the built-in cushioning and shock-absorbent layer. I get back to my feet and check my rifle. From the tunnel below, there's a loud and angry wail that washes over us like a second, weaker shock wave.

"Fuck," Martin says. "I was hoping it would take them a little longer than that."

"Me too," I reply. "Got any more hi-ex?"

"No, sir."

"Trident, we may have company coming up behind us," I tell the SEAL section.

"We can't outrun them," Lieutenant Dean says. *"It's still five hundred meters to the exit."*

"I know," I reply. "We can play turtle and hope they go straight past us."

"They weren't looking for us before. They sure as shit are now."

"We have two minutes, tops."

"Fucking hell. Coming down."

Ahead of me, Dean and his SEALs run down the tunnel back toward us.

"Never should have set foot in that recruiting office," he says when he's next to me. "Go up and get some distance. Get the doctor out of here. We will hold them off."

"The fuck you will, Lieutenant," I say. "You'll last thirty seconds if they crowd you."

"We have two rifles with launchers and half a dozen thermobaric rounds if it comes down to that," Dean replies. "We can hold them for a lot longer than that. Now get going. We'll catch up when we've plugged the gap. *Go,*" he adds with urgency. He joins his SEALs, who have already taken up covering positions at the next bend down, without waiting for my reply. I suppress the reflex to try to order him into compliance because I know it would be a futile waste of precious time. As I turn to lead the rest of the squad up the tunnel, the despair I am feeling makes me nauseated.

"Let's go," I shout to Staff Sergeant Martin and Elin and run up to the bend the SEALs vacated a few moments ago. The tunnel behind the turn is still dark and silent, a straight and level stretch of a hundred meters. In the distance, the faint glow of a paint arrow on the tunnel wall points to the right, marking our next turn. I run toward the arrow to reach the bend as fast as I can and secure the corner for the rest of the team, keenly aware that I am leaving half my troopers behind. I want to turn around and join them so we can all make a stand together, add our firepower to theirs, and dish out as much as we can give. But I know that if I give in to that urge, I'll volunteer everyone for a certain last stand, and I don't have a right to invalidate Lieutenant Dean's decision like that.

I crash to one knee at the tunnel bend and look down the next segment with my weapon up and ready. Nothing is moving in the range of my sensors except for the flowing water in the drainage channels. The tunnel ahead goes straight for fifty meters on an upward incline before the next turn, this one slightly to the left. I give the "all clear" and signal the squad to catch up.

Gunfire rolls up from the lower tunnel and reverberates in the confines of the passages. Several rifles are firing single shots in rapid succession as the SEALs are engaging whatever is coming up the tunnel after us. I know there are only four people in the SEAL section, but it sounds like an entire platoon at the firing range, the muzzle blasts amplified and multiplied by the echoes bouncing off the rock walls all around us. Next to me, Martin slides to a stop and aims his weapon down the next stretch as well. I signal an advance to the next bend at double-time.

"Fifty meters, let's go," I shout against the noise of the gunfire that threatens to overwhelm the audio filters of my helmet comms.

Martin and I start to run up the incline. We are barely ten meters into this tunnel section when something comes around the bend ahead and blots out the faint glow from Elin's little waypoint marker as it passes in front of it. The Lanky is hunched over a little but it's still tall enough for its cranial shield to almost scrape the ceiling as it turns toward us.

This time, I am not willing to risk my life on a game of hide-and-seek. I bring up my rifle and start firing single shots into the Lanky's midsection before it has a chance to drop to all fours and put its heavily armored head in front of its body. Next to me, Martin joins in with his own rifle. The storm of armor-piercing bullets takes the Lanky seemingly by surprise. It stumbles from side to side in the tunnel, which suddenly looks much narrower than just a few moments ago when it was empty. When it slams into the tunnel wall, I can feel the impact shake the ground. For a moment, the Lanky seems unsure whether to advance or retreat around the bend. Then it gathers itself and takes two big steps toward us. I aim for the front of its legs and squeeze off three rounds in rapid succession. They tear into the leg and blow big holes into it that send bits of organic matter flying. It's all but impossible to miss the hulking creature at this range and in the tight quarters of this tunnel, and this one doesn't have the space to move around like the one on the promontory did.

The Lanky makes it another step before it succumbs to our rapid and accurate fire. It crashes to the tunnel floor and slides toward us on the downward incline. When it comes to a stop, its head is only ten meters away from where we have formed our firing line.

"Hostile down," Martin says with more than a little elation in his voice.

"Damn fucking straight," I reply.

I reload my rifle with another ammo pack from my harness, then count the rest of my magazines. With one full pack in the rifle and four on the harness, I have fifty rounds left. If we had more time and space to engage the Lankies, we could coordinate our fire better and drop them with fewer rounds, but in the confines of this burrow, I am emptying a magazine every time I open fire while wishing they held a hundred rounds each instead of just ten. It's their home turf, an environment that maximizes their strengths and minimizes ours. I feel like the world's biggest fuckup for having led my team down here and into a close-quarters battle under these conditions. Down in the lower tunnel, the SEALs are keeping up their own fusillade, a steady drumroll of rifle fire.

"We're clear," I send to Elin. "Move on up."

Elin comes around the corner. The scientist's eyes widen when she sees the Lanky on the ground in front of us. It's not big enough to completely block the tunnel, but we have to switch to single-file formation to make it past the splayed-out body and further up the tunnel.

"You all right?" I ask Elin when she passes. She just nods, but I can tell that she is so full of adrenaline that she could probably lift a drop ship off its skids.

"You're doing fine for a nongrunt," Staff Sergeant Martin tells her. She rewards the assessment with a strained smile.

I stay at the end of the choke point between the tunnel wall and the dead Lanky to provide cover while the staff sergeant rushes up the tunnel with Elin. The gunfire a few bends down is still thundering in the darkness, but it sounds a little less frenetic, as if at least one rifle has dropped out of the firing line or run out of ammo.

"Clear ahead, eighty meters," Martin sends from the tunnel bend. *"Moving up to the next leg."*

"Keep going until you're at the exit," I reply.

"Copy that."

I turn around to catch up with them, but part of me still wants to go back down to where the SEALs are continuing their rifle fire.

"Trident, fall back by pairs if you can. There's a dead Lanky three bends up from you that's blocking most of the tunnel," I send on the squad channel through the optical link.

When no reply comes, I look back and see that my line of sight to the next bread-crumb relay is blocked by the mass of the Lanky we killed. I turn, intending to run back to the body and get a clear angle to let my message to the SEALs get through on the optical relay link.

The sound of the explosion below reaches my ears just as a shock wave blasts up from the tunnel and hits me midturn. It feels like I just got drop-kicked by a Lanky. The force doesn't just knock me off my feet, it rips the rifle from my grasp and flings me into the tunnel. When I slam into the rock with my right shoulder and the side of my head, there's a blinding burst of bright-electric shock, like the worst punch I've ever taken in the ring magnified a hundred times, such sudden and massive force that I don't have time to feel even a spark of fear before my consciousness blinks out.

CHAPTER 16

——— DARKNESS ———

The pain I feel when I come to again is a relief of sorts because it tells me that I am still alive.

I try to move my head and see which way is up, but a white-hot jolt of agony stabs through the general fire that has set the nerves on the right side of my body alight. And I have the worst headache I've ever experienced. There isn't enough air in my lungs for a scream. It feels like I have the bow skid of a Blackfly parked on my chest.

The familiar sting of the autodoc's injectors is barely noticeable, but the effects are instant, the characteristic momentary light-headedness of strong anesthetics entering the brain via the short trip from the injection site on my shoulder. I ride out the feeling, eager for the relief I know will follow in a few seconds. The pain recedes quickly until it's just tolerable background noise instead of an overwhelming orchestra.

My vision is distorted and somehow diminished, and my right eye hurts deeply despite the medications. The right side of my face feels wet and sticky. When I try to raise my right arm to check for damage to the suit, there's another sharp stab of pain and another quick wave of light-headed nausea as the autodoc dutifully compensates with another dose of pain meds. My mouth goes completely dry in response. My helmet's display is flickering. It's scrolling a long list of alerts and system warnings that I can't read because I can't focus. I know the helmet isn't breached because I'd be dead if it were, suffocated in the minute or so I was unconscious in this lethally high CO_2 atmosphere.

My right eye sees only darkness, like something is covering it, but the left one is focused enough for me to be able to read my helmet display. The suit is as broken as I've ever managed to break one. I scroll through the system messages and status diagrams to find that the helmet was indeed breached but that the automatic sealing function patched it up with liquid polymer matrix before I could lose all the air to the outside. Still, the breach has taken a toll on my breathing air. When we walked into the burrow, I was at 80 percent, and now the level in my tanks is at 29 percent. One of the two breathing-air units in the suit got damaged too much for the suit to patch it up before it bled all its contents out into the tunnel.

The autodoc's assessment of the state of my body isn't any more positive than the suit computer's diagnostics of the state of the hardware. I have a dislocated shoulder and a blunt impact injury to the right side of my head. The force that broke the helmet was strong enough to crack my skull, despite the shock-absorbing layer and the internal cushioning. My right eye isn't working because it was cut or punctured, but I can't figure out which from the display. I'm a wreck, my bug suit is a wreck, and the only reason I can do anything except lie here and wince in pain is the medication in my bloodstream that won't last forever.

I move my left arm and my legs, with some success. There's a layer of rocks and rubble on top of me that is weighing me down but doesn't feel immovable. I start kicking rocks aside and shoving them off me with my good arm, and the pressure on my body lessens gradually. When I feel that I am mostly free, I roll onto my uninjured side and use my left arm to prop myself up. The motions send fire through my right side again, but it's muted fire thanks to the autodoc and adrenaline.

Beyond the graphics on my helmet display, I see nothing all around me. Where before I had an image of my surroundings that was a slightly abstract composite of the infrared, thermal, and image-intensifier sensors of my bug suit, now there's only impenetrable darkness. I check my status display again and discover that the sensor package of my helmet is offline. My high-tech eyesight is reduced to the lens of the little daylight camera in the top part of the bug suit's helmet. It's there for exactly this emergency, a total failure of the main array, but it has no image-intensifying capabilities so it's almost useless down here.

I get to my feet and find with relief that my right leg seems to be working. But without a visual reference, I can't even begin to tell where I am and where I'm going. The formerly smooth tunnel floor is now littered with stone rubble, and I can't even reliably tell which way the ground is slanting. The anesthetic tamps down the pain, but it makes my head feel fuzzy. Still, I have to move; my time is running out. I stumble ahead and feel only emptiness with my left arm. When I contact the nearest rock wall, it's with my right arm, and the pain that shoots through my arm pierces the heavy dose of painkillers and make me cry out. The sudden light-headedness and nausea I feel drops me to my knees with another painful jolt.

"This is Dagger One-Niner," I mumble into the comms link, my dry tongue feeling way too big and heavy for my mouth. "If anyone can hear me, I am down and my optics are out."

There's no reply on the optical link, which means there's nobody in my line of sight who can talk to me. Elin and Sergeant Martin went around the bend just before the explosion, so they probably didn't get hit quite as hard as I did. I am blind, lame, in a damaged suit that's low on air, and hundreds of meters from the mouth of the tunnel, without a weapon to defend myself if more Lankies show up.

This may be the end of the road at last. I'll be part of this place forever just like Sergeant Mills and the SEAL team. The thought should scare me, but right now I just feel a nearly overwhelming sense of sadness and loss.

The best thing I can hope for at this point is that Elin and Martin will get back to the drop ship with the protein and fungus samples she collected. If they make it all the way home one day, they'll tell the Corps where we're buried and how we ended up there. And then someone will pass the news to Halley and give her closure instead of keeping her in limbo for the rest of her life, never knowing what happened to me and where I am. I dwell on Halley and memories of Liberty Falls for a moment and comfort myself with the knowledge that she's safe and far away from this.

I consider overriding the autodoc's safety protocol and telling it to inject me with every cubic centimeter of sedatives and painkillers it has in its dispenser. It would be a painless death, and more pleasant than running out of oxygen or getting crushed into mush by a Lanky.

That can wait until my oxygen drops to 5 percent or I feel Lankies coming.

I gather myself for another attempt to get to my feet. It's a little easier now, maybe because the drugs have had a little more time to work. One thing the bug suit has left in abundance is battery power, so I juice up the leg servos and let the armor help me with the walking. A few meters into my new attempt, I stumble over a pile of rubble and fall to my knees again, reaching out reflexively with my right arm to stop my fall. Fresh pain breaks through the medication. I've hardly moved from the spot where I dug myself out, but I am already out of breath and getting light-headed again.

I hear a rock skitter in the tunnel and look around futilely for the source. And suddenly, there's a light. It's moving toward me in the darkness, a crescent-shaped sliver of brightness that bobs up and down a little on its way. I get to my feet and reflexively fumble for my rifle with my left hand, but the weapon isn't there anymore. My addled brain takes longer than it should to realize the light can only be a human coming my way. Hope flares in me. A moment more and Elin Vandenberg materializes out of the darkness in front of me. The light is a bright beacon atop her helmet, and the sight of her face behind her transparent visor makes me groan with relief. Next to her, Staff Sergeant Martin moves in the periphery of Elin's helmet illumination, his bug suit seemingly absorbing the light.

"Are you all right?" Elin says. I shake my head in response and regret it.

"Holy shit, your gear took a beating," Sergeant Martin says. My knees buckle and he grabs my right arm which is immobilized, fixed by the joints the autodoc locked in place with the suit's servos to turn the sleeve into a provisional splint. At the same time, Elin reaches for the left arm.

"Don't," I slur. "It's out of its socket."

Elin lets go instantly.

"Right one's dislocated," I clarify, and Martin moves to my left side with a quick "Sorry."

Now that there are other humans with me again, I wish the autodoc had been a little less aggressive with the painkillers because it feels like I am moving underwater, performing every action with great effort and against a lot of resistance.

"Sensors on my helmet are fucked," I say to Martin. "Can't see a thing. All I have left is basic optical. No low-light gear."

"Got it. We need to get you out of here," he replies. "The doctor here insisted on doubling back to look for you."

"I ordered you not to stop for anything," I say, even though I am profoundly glad they did. I won't die alone in the dark.

"I didn't leave him a choice," Elin says. "Pulled rank on him. You weren't around, so I was ranking officer."

"The only officer," Martin says. "What the fuck happened?"

"Thermobaric grenade," I mumble. "Lieutenant Dean said they had a few. They must have gotten swamped. Lit them all up at once."

"If he wanted to make sure they couldn't come after us, he did all right," Sergeant Martin says. "Took down the tunnel ceiling. All the way up to the bend. Knocked us all right on our asses."

"Did a little more than that," I say.

"Let's sort all that shit out on the way home," Martin says. "Let's make the most of what they did. How's the walking, Major?"

"I can walk," I say. "Servos are still working. Just can't see shit."

"Just hang on to me and we'll get you out of here. I'll be able to fix you up on the ship."

He locks my left arm in place over his shoulder with his own. I dial the servos up to full power assist for the legs so the suit will do most of the walking for me. As we start to make our way up the rubble-strewn tunnel in tandem, the knowledge that the bodies of more than half my team are buried in the darkness behind us weighs on my conscious mind like a physical presence, a deep and powerful pain that the anesthetics can't touch.

———

My legs are working but my head isn't along for the ride much of the time. Without Sergeant Martin to guide and direct me, I would be walking in circles and running into walls because I keep getting light-headed to the point of almost passing out. The autodoc is maintaining its valiant efforts to keep me on my feet. I'm so full of painkillers, adrenaline, stimulants, and synthetic boosters that I suspect one vial from a single blood draw right now could give a great buzz to an entire boot camp platoon. But there's a limit to what the bug suit's built-in medical assistant can do, and the farther we make it up the tunnel, the more pain burns through the chemical shield of the anesthetics.

Between the medication fog and the inability to see, I have no spatial or temporal orientation as we go up through the tunnel, taking an indeterminate number of left and right turns, until I am so lost that I might as well be floating in outer space. I don't know how much time has passed since the explosion, or since Elin and Sergeant Martin found me, and when I try to read the mission clock on my helmet display, I can see the numbers, but my brain can't make sense of them, much less perform simple addition or subtraction.

"We run into a Lanky, you ditch me and go," I say.

"We run into a Lanky, we're probably fucked either way," Sergeant Martin replies without breaking stride. "Now stop talking nonsense, sir. With all due respect."

"Insolent fucking NCOs," I mumble and get a chuckle from Martin in return.

———————

"Tunnel exit is clear, fifty meters ahead," Sergeant Martin says an indeterminate amount of time later. I try to shake off the thick fog that has settled on my brain and attempt to make out the tunnel mouth in front of us. Without the low-light gear and the infrared sensor from my helmet, it's almost invisible, and I would have missed it without being told where it is. Just the act of raising my head is enough to make the pain flare up on the right side of my skull and reminds me of the strong headache suppressed by the drug cocktail. I suck in some air and clench my teeth with a groan.

"How are you holding up, Major?"

"I've been better," I admit.

"We're almost out. We'll have you back on the ship before too long."

I know he's trying to keep me alert and prop up my spirits like any good medic would, but I lack the emotional control to suppress the tiny glimmer of hope I feel, anyway. Even if I die on the way to the ship, anything is better than being down in that tunnel for the rest of my life.

We leave the tunnel mouth and work our way up the slope of the ravine. The rain has picked up again outside, and the rainwater streaming past us is now flowing downhill in small brooks instead of thin rivulets. I'm still almost blind with just the emergency backup camera from the helmet to show me my surroundings, but at least now it's just various patterns of black and almost-black instead of the absolute nothingness of the tunnel. As we get higher and the walls of the ravine recede on either side of us, I can tell sky from ground again thanks to the lightning.

"Help me with the major," Sergeant Martin says when we've reached the edge of the ravine at a point where the ledge is only chest-high. Together, Elin and Martin help me up over the edge and onto the flat ground below. A fresh spike of pain lances through my body when I hit the ground, and I bite off a groan.

Unseen hands help me to my feet; Sergeant Martin is by my left side.

"One klick to the ledge, and then it's all downhill from there," he says to me. "You can do it, sir. One foot in front of the other, right?"

"Right," I agree even though I don't share the sergeant's optimism. It took us three hours to get from the drop ship to the plateau. Even if the return trip is downhill, it will take more time and effort than I think my body has left to give right now. But the alternative is to stay behind and wait for death by hypoxia, synthetic morphine overdose, or Lanky attention.

"Where's the doctor?" I ask between shallow breaths.

"I'm right here," Elin Vandenberg says. "Five meters to your right."

"How you holding up?"

"Okay," she replies. "Scared shitless, but I'm okay. You don't look like you are."

"I've had worse days," I lie.

"I can't imagine how," she chuckles.

Even though I can barely see my surroundings, it feels less claustrophobic to know that we are moving out in the open. The rain that is coming down on us is welcome evidence to me that I am now underneath a dark sky instead of a million tons of rock. I move just like Staff Sergeant Martin prompts, one foot in front of the other, as fast as my bug suit will boost my movements. Several times, we stop and crouch behind low cover as Lankies walk past us through the squalls somewhere nearby. Every time I must get back up, it takes a bit more effort and leaves me in a little more pain. The autodoc advises that I am at the maximum safe dosage for the anesthetic, and I don't dare to override the computer because I don't want to become dead weight for Sergeant Martin or stop breathing altogether. I know I am holding the squad back from moving as quickly as they could, and the heroic thing to do would be to order them to leave me behind. But I also know that Sergeant Martin would flat-out refuse the directive again, and the truth is that I don't want to be left behind. I don't want to die yet. I want to get off this toxic, hostile moon and live a little longer in light and air among other people, even if it's only for a few more days or weeks.

Before we even reach the edge of the plateau, I lose consciousness again. Martin is helping me along when I feel that nauseating light-headedness once more, but this time it doesn't come in a wave that ebbs and flows. The wooziness just keeps getting worse until I pass out.

When I come to again, I am on my back on the rocky ground, with Staff Sergeant Martin leaning over me. My helmet display is scrolling through information that's beyond my ability to parse at this point. I try to tell Martin that I am all right, but the sound coming out of my mouth is little more than a muffled groan.

"He's not gonna last. It's over ten klicks to the ship. He can't make it that far," Martin says to Elin. I don't want to turn my head because the pain in my skull is intense again.

"Can you give him *something*?" Elin asks.

"Negative. He's already maxed out on everything I can give him out in the field. If I dose him again, I might stop his heart and lungs. He's got a skull fracture and a slow brain bleed. It's slowed thanks to the meds, but I shouldn't have him walking anymore. It just makes it worse. If I don't get him medevaced out of here in the next thirty minutes, he's done."

"Call the bird," Elin says. "Call 'em on regular comms."

"If we break radio silence, we'll have every Lanky on the moon on our ass before too long," Martin replies.

"It's a few half-second transmissions. It's not like we'll be chitchatting with them for a while."

"We'll be breaking EMCON. There's no telling who will hear that signal, Doctor. You know the mission regs."

In my helmet headset, their voices are distant, like they're coming from the bottom of a Lanky tunnel. I want to speak up, but I am in no condition to take charge. I've never felt so helpless in my life, so utterly aware that my existence depends on someone else. Whatever consensus they achieve will decide whether I live or die in the next half hour.

"Call the ship over," Elin says. "I am the ranking officer right now. I'm telling you to call it in."

"With all due respect, ma'am, you're not in the military chain of command," Staff Sergeant Martin tells her. "Even if you outrank me. Lieutenant Dean is gone. Major Grayson is out. That puts me in charge of this mission until we get back to the ship."

"Just call the fucking evac, Sergeant," Elin says. "I'm not leaving him here. He'll die on the way if we try to walk him out. And the Lankies are stirred up already."

"Goddammit." I hear Staff Sergeant Martin stomp off a few yards, then return.

"Fine," he says. "Don't blame me if we all get kicked into orbit in a few minutes."

He toggles his comms to the emergency mission frequency.

"Flight, this is Dagger Two. Do you read?"

"Dagger Two, Flight. Loud and clear."

"Flight, we need immediate evacuation and dustoff at our location. Dagger Actual is down, and we lost Trident. All of them."

"Copy that," Captain Prince replies from the distant drop ship. *"Engines are going hot. ETA four minutes."*

"We'll find some flat ground and put down an IR beacon. Dagger out."
Martin ends the transmission and shakes his head.

"It's done," he says. "Let's find a pickup spot and light a bread crumb. And hope the ship gets to us before the nearest Lanky does."

I drift on the edge of consciousness, and each time I become aware of my surroundings again, the sounds and sensations feel a little more distant. I hear gunfire and shouts, and the feeling of getting jostled around with rapid movement. The pain is all-pervasive now, if dull. I feel disconnected from the pain, as if I am experiencing it all through an abstraction layer, like observing the sun through heavily filtered optics. A Lanky wails nearby, a sound so intense I feel it in my bones.

Then there's a new sound overhead, a low roar that drowns out the sounds of the falling rain and whipping winds that have been a constant and somehow soothing background noise since we came out of the burrow. The roar is followed by the rapid concussions of heavy autocannon fire. Each time the guns go off, I feel the slap from the pressure waves of the muzzle blasts as they displace the air around them. Then I'm on my back again, somewhere in a mental zone that is somehow both entirely pain and none at all. When I try to focus on the helmet display, I see a huge shadow directly overhead, just a vague outline against the roiling dark clouds above it. The front of the shape lights up in concert with the thunderclaps of the gunfire, muzzle blasts that reach out for meters in front of the Blackfly's bow. The spent casings from the cannon shells are raining down nearby, splashing into puddles and careening off rocks with dull metallic sounds. As damaged and pain-soaked as my head is right now, my old memories are intact because I instantly remember being on my back on the street in Detroit in the same way over twelve years ago, hurt and waiting for help, with the empty shells from another drop ship coming down on me and my squad like a brass-and-steel

160

shower. The memory is so strong that I can smell the scents from that night again, the hot asphalt and the burned caseless propellant from our rifles, the dirty air of the city, all enhanced by the stifling humidity of that long-ago summer night. The loud, drawn-out death wail of a Lanky pulls me back to the moment.

Several pairs of arms grab my armor and lift me off the ground. Suddenly I am in motion again, bounced around by the quick and out-of-sync steps of a small group of people at a run, and I close my eyes as a new wave of nausea blooms inside me. More small-arms fire bellows, close enough to us that it sounds like the gun is going off almost next to my head. I hear yelling and recognize voices, but I can't make out what they are shouting.

The next time I open my eyes, the world is bathed in the red battle light of a drop ship's cargo bay, and I am suddenly filled with a sense of relief. Someone is carrying me through the Blackfly's hold and up into the EVA lock between the armory and the cockpit. They place me on a gel-cushioned surface, and Staff Sergeant Martin appears next to me again.

"Got you on the pod base," he says to me. "You're still with me, right?"

I grunt an affirmative.

"You got a real beating down there. I can't do much more for you with what we have on this little boat, so I'll have to put you in medical stasis for the trip back. We have to pick up the other team, then we're bound for *Washington*," he says.

When the Blackfly takes off, I can feel the upward acceleration as the deck seems to rise and push into my back. The drop ship's guns are hammering out short bursts again, but now the sound is muffled by the armored stealth hull and overlapping the howl from the engines.

"Dustoff complete," the drop ship's pilot sends over our command channel. *"Twenty minutes to orbit."*

"We got what we came for," Staff Sergeant Martin replies. "And then some."

"Glad to hear it because our EMCON went all to hell. Seismic's got movement all over the place now," Captain Prince says.

"Couldn't be helped," Martin says. He closes the intercom and looks down at me again.

"Now comes the not-so-fun part," he says. "I need to remove your armor before the autodoc can do its work for the trip back. But you should be feeling comfortable now, sir."

I manage a small nod in response.

He connects his medical handheld to my suit's computer and runs an emergency override on the safety latches. It takes him several minutes to remove my armor one piece at a time, and every time he removes a segment on my right side or arm, I can feel how weak and raw it is, but Martin has done a great job. I just ride it out and distract myself with pleasant thoughts of Halley and our dreams for our future, even though I doubt they may ever come true now. Still, I want those dreams, and I want to take those thoughts into stasis with me, so I try to stay positive. The floating cloud that is my mind right now makes dwelling on pleasantries a little easier.

Martin lets out a low whistle as he sets my helmet down. "Okay, that was the last piece. I don't think I've ever seen a helmet take this kind of damage yet stay airtight. You are one lucky man."

After Martin adjusts me, the sides of the pod arc up and create a trough that reminds me too much of the capsules we use for burials in space. I feel a needle prick my left arm and see Martin install a saline and then a blood bag in the pod.

"I'm going to close the lid now and let the autodoc take over. I'll see you back on the ship after we get home. All right. Here we go," Martin says.

The pod slowly closes above me. The lid that lowers itself onto the medical cradle has a large polyplast window in it, and I am glad that it isn't opaque, because even in my current state I don't want to be in the dark again. When the lid locks into place, it cuts off all the sound from the drop ship's interior, but I can still see through the window and make out the bulkheads and ceiling of the EVA compartment. I can feel the vibrations of the Blackfly's hull as it makes its way out of the atmosphere and back into space, away from this dark and steamy hell that swallowed up five of our comrades forever.

I feel the coolness of an injection being released into my bloodstream, and I let the meds pull me into unconsciousness.

CHAPTER 17

———— GROUNDED ————

I'm not dreaming, but my mind isn't at rest, either.

Sometimes I think I can hear familiar things, but the sounds that reach my ears are vague and distant, and they bleed into each other much of the time. I feel and hear the thrumming of engines at full burn, and the sound of voices, but it's all faint and ephemeral, like catching snippets of a noisy Network show from the neighbor's unit through two sets of walls in the bedroom of my old PRC apartment. When I do see images in my mind's eye, they're as indistinct as the sounds: flashing red beacons in the shadows, darkness trading places with diffused light, faces that are little more than blurry avatars. I sense that my body is still in pain, but the sensation is distant as well, locked away behind a thick shield of anesthetics and chemically distorted perception.

I don't know how long I have been floating in the void like this when I open my eyes again.

The pain that was all consuming is now a blunt ache, unpleasant but infinitely more tolerable. I move my head a little, wincing inwardly in anticipation of the white-hot flare of agony lighting the right side of my head on fire. It hurts only a little and I sigh heavily, releasing my anticipated tension. I look around and see that I'm still in a pod, but this one isn't the little foldout one shoehorned into the EVA lock of the drop ship. It's a full-sized medical cradle, which means I am back on *Washington*. The room I'm in is darkened, with only the red battle light for illumination, a mercy to my light-starved eyes, though I can't open my right eye. The red lights are a source of concern because I know that the lighting only switches to battle mode when the ship is at combat stations, and I have no idea what's going on.

There's nobody else in here with me. I turn my head to see two empty pods on either side of me, and an electronic status board on the bulkhead on the other side of the room. It's scrolling through updates that I can't make out. If I am on *Washington*, I've been out for the better part of a week because that's how long the flight back to the carrier would have taken.

I feel something shaking the deck below me a little, the familiar low vibration of a missile launch. We're at battle stations and engaging something with the heavy ordnance from our missile silos. I try to raise my arms to sit up and get out of this pod, but the restraints keep me from doing more than lifting a finger. I want to call for help but my throat is bone dry, and when I make the attempt, I can't get a sound out. When I exhale in frustration, I realize that I am wearing a respirator mask. The right side of my face and head are devoid of sensation, numb as a piece of deck lining.

I close my eyes and try to concentrate on my breathing. I can tell that the autodoc just added something to the intravenous feed on my left arm because I feel the medication surge through my bloodstream and flood my brain, bringing with it relief and pleasant drowsiness. I drift off again, and the concern I felt at the realization that the ship is in combat while I am strapped into a pod is quickly replaced by a drug-induced indifference.

When I wake up some indeterminate amount of time later, the lights in the medical suite are back to normal mode, and the brightness of the overhead illumination hurts when I open my left eye; my right eye is still impeded. The sounds of distant battle are gone, and the compartment is quiet except for the soft beeping of various medical monitors and the general background hum of the ship's environmental systems. There's someone else in the room, a blurry figure that comes into focus as I blink to get rid of the reflexive tears. I clear my throat to get attention but the noise I make is more air than voice. My throat feels raw. The respirator mask is gone, replaced by a nasal cannula.

"Oh, hey. You're awake," the other person says. It's a young male voice I don't recognize. The speaker is wearing the shipboard uniform but without the blouse, just the undershirt. When I shift my gaze, I can see that he's also wearing a vacsuit from the waist down, with the upper part of it secured around his middle using the sleeves as a belt. He leans over the control screen of my pod and taps a few data fields.

"Your vitals are good, all things considered. I'm going to go fetch the doctor. Hang tight," he says before I can even try to ask a question. It's a pointless directive because my arms and legs are still secured in restraints, and I can't move.

All things considered, I think with some dread. *What the hell is that supposed to mean?*

I close my eyes and wait, suppressing an almost irresistible desire to drift off to sleep again.

A little while later, someone else comes to my pod, and I recognize one of the ship's doctors, a passingly familiar face from the officers' wardroom. He checks my pod's data panel as well.

"Hello, Major Grayson. Glad you could rejoin us. How are you feeling?"

"Like shit," I croak and wince at the rawness of my throat as I produce the sounds.

"I would be shocked if you didn't," he says. "I'm Dr. Kelly, the attending on this watch. I was also the one on watch when they brought you in."

"What happened?" I mouth at just above a whisper. There's a lot more I want to know than only that, but speaking is painful enough to keep my words to a minimum.

"What happened?" he repeats. "You got hurt. We put you back together. Now you're healing up."

"You can be a little more specific," I rasp in a voice that isn't my own. The inside of my mouth feels like it has been lined with sandpaper.

"Well, I can't tell you how you got hurt the way you did. But when they brought you in and dropped you on my OR table, you had a cracked skull, a swollen brain, broken bones, and a little more besides."

"Huh," I reply. "I had a feeling."

"You got hit hard by something," the Fleet surgeon continues. "On the side of the head, right here." He draws a line on his own head with his index finger to illustrate, from the center of his right eyebrow all the way to an area above his right ear. "Cracked your skull in several spots."

"What about my eye?" I ask, dreading the answer.

"When your helmet broke, a piece of it sliced the side of your face open and damaged your eye. We fixed what we could. However, you may have lost some or all your eyesight in your right eye, so be prepared for that possibility. We won't know until the patch comes off and we can check. But," he pauses, "we can't rush ahead faster than your body can heal itself beyond the rushed healing I already forced your tissue to do. On Earth, this process would go faster and you would have more options; here, we do the best we can with what we've got."

I rub my left thumb over the prosthetic fingers, recalling a similar predicament. "How long was I under?" I ask.

He glances at the data panel.

"You're on day thirteen today."

I feel an unpleasant jolt of disbelief. "I've been out for almost *two weeks?*"

"You've been here in *med bay* for almost two weeks," the surgeon says. "You were in medical stasis for six days before that."

"Three weeks, then." I feel a bit of light-headedness that I'm sure isn't coming from any medication. I've lost three weeks of whatever time I have left, and my team has been without its leader all this time, right after losing an entire squad of SEALs and the team's junior member.

"You're extremely lucky to be awake and lucid again after only three weeks, Major. You came in so broken that we barely managed to piece you back together."

"How long until I can get out of here and rejoin my unit?"

He shakes his head. *Fucking idiot grunts,* his expression says.

"Major Grayson," he says. "We put you back together, but this is a med bay on a warship, not a Level 1 trauma center. There's only so much we can do here. We don't restore you to factory new. We fix you up enough to make it back to the nearest proper medical facility on shore. You need a lot more fixing. And then you'll be needing rehab for a long time. You're not going to hop out of that pod and get back to business as usual."

"We're a long way from any med centers," I say.

"Yes, we are."

"We're all on borrowed time out here. I'm not going to spend the rest of my life slurping applesauce in a med bay, Doctor."

"God, I keep forgetting how reckless you podheads are," Dr. Kelly says. "It's like they excise your sense of self-preservation in tech school."

He taps the medical insignia on his collar. Like the orderly I saw when I woke up, the Fleet surgeon is wearing his vacsuit halfway, with the sleeves tied around his waist, but he's wearing full shipboard uniform underneath.

"You'll be out of here soon if that's what you want," he says. "Take another day or two to get your bearings and let your bones knit themselves together a little more. Then sign yourself out. It's a med bay, not the brig. But I am not going to clear you for any more combat duty on this deployment. If we were back on Earth right now, you'd almost certainly be looking at medical retirement."

I nod at his half-tied vacsuit.

"First time I woke up, the ship was at combat stations. Unless that was a dream. What's happening?"

He shrugs. "I don't know what's going on in CIC. I'm just a flight surgeon. But we've had a Combat Stations alert every day for at least a week now. And we've splashed a seed ship. The XO made the announcement when it happened. That was, uh . . . three days ago, I think?"

The news that the ship has been in combat while I was out greatly amplifies my already strong desire to get out of this pod and go back to the STT. I don't want to be just a passenger while the command crew are planning missions and maybe even sending out my podheads into harm's way.

"So I can sign myself out of med bay?" I ask.

"Yes," Dr. Kelly says. "You can sign yourself out of med bay. Hell, you could hop off the table in the middle of surgery and take your leave if that's what you choose to do. I can tell you it's a bad idea. I can't keep you here at gunpoint."

He taps another control on my pod, and the restraint straps around my arms and legs retract. I raise my left arm and slowly make a fist to make sure my fingers are working the way they should.

"But I don't have to clear you for duty, so I won't," he adds. "And not even the skipper can override that."

Three weeks. That may have been most of the rest of my life. Then I remind myself that it damn near *was* the rest of my life in its entirety, and that I am only here because a lot of people did their best to keep me breathing.

"Thanks for putting me back together, Doctor," I say. "I don't want it to sound like I'm disrespecting your professional skills. Or your judgment."

The surgeon nods. "Thank you, Major."

"But if this ship is going into battle, I need to be with my troopers," I continue. "Even if I can't put on a bug suit again."

"I understand completely," Dr. Kelly says.

He looks at my data screen again and purses his lips in thought. Then he sighs and shakes his head.

"Stay in the pod for another twenty-four hours. Get used to your new physical limitations. If you continue to improve and your values don't dip, I'll release you for restricted duty after that. No combat, no strenuous activity. Nothing that requires putting on armor. Not even the firing range. But you'll at least be able to hold briefings and sit behind a command console."

I don't have to think long about that proposal.

"Deal," I say. "But if we go to combat stations again, all bets are off."

"Like hell," the flight surgeon says. "If we go to combat stations, the best thing for you to do is to stay in that pod, safely restrained, with your own oxygen supply. Because I am not about to have someone deliver you a vac suit in here."

Now it's my turn to shake my head with a sigh.

"Fine. Twenty-four hours," I concede.

"Thank you," he says again. "But for the record, my professional judgment still says it's a boneheaded move and a terrible idea. So don't come complaining when you collapse out there or break something else and they have to bring you back here again."

"It's the latest in a very long chain of boneheaded moves, Doctor," I respond, and he chuckles.

"Well, try to make sure it won't be the last, Major."

CHAPTER 18

OUT OF PHASE

When I leave the med bay twenty-four hours later, my first port of call is my berth in Officer Country. It's a bit of a walk from the medical ward to the deck that houses the ship's field officers, and it's much more movement than my body has had to do in weeks. After negotiating the fifth or sixth ladderwell, I am feeling achy and tired, and I'm starting to wonder whether I am in fact a complete idiot for going against the flight surgeon's advice.

As I walk down the ship's passageways, the troops who pass me shoot me glances that range from surprise to shock to concern. I am dressed in the light-blue medical garb they put on patients, which doesn't have any rank insignia or identifiers on it, and only the troops who recognize me mumble a greeting as they pass. After a while, I feel my own level of concern climbing because almost nobody I encounter has a normal reaction to the sight of one of the ship's field officers walking by.

I get to the door to my quarters and unlock it with my biometrics. The berth is cool and dark, and as I step over the threshold, I turn on the lights. After three weeks away, the sight of my few possessions and the sparse decorations on the bulkhead above my little desk is strangely unfamiliar, a glimpse into a different time and place altogether.

When I step into the little wet cell and peek into the stainless steel mirror on the bulkhead for the first time since I left the ship, I recoil in shock and surprise. The person staring back at me looks nothing like me. I am haggard, lean, with hollow cheeks and prominent cheekbones. My head is almost completely bare. Just a few millimeters of uneven fuzz cover my skull, and even that sparse coverage is interrupted by a series of vivid red scars on the right side of my head. I look like I've lost at least twenty kilos, and those were kilos I didn't really have to spare. The right side of my face is black and purple, covered in a splotchy bruise that runs from my hairline to my jaw. I look at the unfamiliar face in the mirror for a while, trying to reconcile reality with memory. My right eye is covered by a patch that sits on a layer of medical gauze, an arrangement that doesn't look rakish in the least. It just looks like a crude retention mechanism to keep my eyeball from falling out of my head.

I splash the unbruised side of my face with some water and dry it slowly and carefully. What I want more than anything is to take a long shower to wash the smell of sweat and med bay off my body. But the control panel of my wet cell's shower capsule shows a red status light for shower water availability. Instead, I do a quick cleanup with the meager water ration allocated by the sink's faucet timer.

The uniform I take out of my under-bed drawer is much too loose on me when I put it on, and I mess with the internal adjustment straps for a while to take some slack out of the fabric. My right arm still hurts when I put it to use, but it's a diffuse and dull sort of pain, unpleasant neural echoes of the repaired bone fractures. When I am dressed, I look at myself in the mirror again. The uniform is an improvement, but I still look diminished and out of place somehow, as if the uniform belongs to someone else and I am wearing it without authorization.

I use my left hand to touch the bandage pad and the gauze over my right eye. In the dim light of the wet cell, I can see the difference in skin tone and texture between the real fingers and the prosthetic ones. It's subtle, but it's there, the way the artificial skin reflects and absorbs the light just a little differently from the natural skin next to it. When I flex my fingers a little, I can see that the back of my hand now has a lot of wrinkles that are not matched by the synthetic skin.

It's because those wrinkles weren't there when they put that prosthetic on eight years ago. The rest of me has aged much more quickly than the bionic replacement parts did. I find myself wondering what my hand will look like when I am seventy before I remember where we are and what is happening, and that the cosmetic mismatch is the absolute least of my worries.

When I am finished in the wet cell, I sit down at my little desk for a moment to log on to the MilNet terminal. I am not expecting any messages from Earth, of course, and the long list of administrative ship alerts and command missives that have piled up since I left for the Lanky moon hold no urgency for me. Instead, I go into my personal files and select the most-opened item in that list, a picture of Halley.

The photo is an outdoor candid one I took on one of our hikes in the mountains around Liberty Falls when we were on leave together a year or two ago. The hike had taken us longer than expected, but Halley wanted to keep pushing, and we made it to the top right in time to watch the sun setting beyond Lake Champlain and the Adirondacks in the distance. I shot the photo in that fortuitous split second between the time she turned her head toward me and her realization that I was taking a picture of her. In the photo, she is looking up at me from the rock she's sitting on, and her expression is all affection and contentment, someone who is completely happy with her company and her place in time and space at that moment. It's my favorite picture of my wife, and I look at it every time I open my terminal. I want to etch it into my brain because if the time comes when I know I am about to die, I want to recall that image so it will be the last thing I see.

I look at Halley's face until it feels like the yearning and the sadness will pull my heart out of my chest if I don't stop. I gently close the terminal screen and leave my berth.

The tension on the ship is so thick that it basically radiates from every grunt and crew member I pass on the way to the STT module. Most of the people who greet me as they walk past sound stressed and anxious, and I recognize the cumulative fatigue that comes from staying alert for too long and having too many watch cycles interrupted by Combat Stations alerts. Above all, I know that the mood on the ship has turned grimmer since I left because I hear very little of the usual levity, people joking with each other or talking about trivialities in the passageways and open compartments I walk past. But it feels so good to be walking on well-lit decks and seeing the faces of other humans again that I find myself wanting to take detours for an hour just to keep moving.

In the company office, two troopers in battle fatigues are standing by the front counter and having a conversation in low voices. When I step across the threshold, they both turn their heads, and from the way they recoil a little, I can tell that my appearance is as unsettling to them as it was to me when I saw myself in the mirror. They both straighten up to stand at attention.

"As you were," I say. "Good morning, gentlemen. Or good evening. What the hell is the time right now, anyway?"

"It's 1445, sir," First Sergeant Gallegos says. My company senior noncom seems to have more gray in his hair than I remember, and the lines on his face are deeper than I recall as well. "Didn't know you were already out of the med bay. They said you'd be in there another week at least."

"If I left it up to them, I would be," I reply.

Next to Sergeant Gallegos, Sergeant First Class Jordan clears his throat.

"Good morning, sir. Good to see you back on your feet."

"Jordan is the new SNCO for the SEAL section, sir," Gallegos says. "I gather Staff Sergeant Martin has filled you in on what went down."

"There were lots of debriefings," Sergeant Jordan says. "And we've all seen the data from the suits."

"We had plenty of time to go over it," Gallegos adds. "Not much use for the STT at the moment. They have us parked on hold just like all the SI grunts down in mud leg country."

"Those SEALs held the line," I say. "The rest of my team wouldn't have made it out otherwise."

Gallegos and Jordan nod solemnly. Both the sergeants are SEALs as well, and of all the fraternities inside the already insular STT, the Fleet's elite commandos are probably the most tightly knit. Lieutenant Dean's squad represented a quarter of the STT's entire SEAL components, and that kind of loss can shatter a team's morale.

"I don't know shit about anything from the time the ship lifted off that moon," I say. "Tell me everyone else made it out."

The two sergeants exchange looks.

Gallegos is visibly uncomfortable. "I'm not sure we should be the ones to tell you, sir. I think Captain Harper was going to do that."

"Spit it out, First Sergeant. Please. That's my team. My responsibility."

Gallegos trades looks with Jordan again. Then he shrugs and shakes his head.

"Your patrol lost five. Blackfly 03 and 07 returned with no enemy contact and no losses. But Blackfly 09 didn't make it back. We think they never even made orbit again. No crash beacon, no emergency message. Just gone."

I feel a wave of nauseating dizziness that isn't unlike the ones from the autodoc's anesthetic injections.

"Blackfly 09," I reply. "Who was on that ship?"

"From the SEALs, all of Second Squad. Lieutenant Cameron, Sergeant Clarke, Sergeant Bellini, Sergeant Tindall," Jordan says, and each name hits me like a slap. "Combat controller, Lieutenant Ellis. Spaceborne Rescue, Staff Sergeant Booth."

They've clearly had enough time to process the loss and begin to come to terms with the reality of it. But I've had no preparation for the news that six more of my troopers and two pilots are gone, lost forever on that toxic hothouse of a moon. It's not the first time I have lost people in combat, but this hits harder than anything else I've had to process, and the magnitude of it threatens to squeeze the breath from my lungs.

"What about search and rescue?"

Gallegos shakes his head.

"Blackfly 03 remained on station to look for them until they were at bingo fuel. Dodged a seed ship or two along the way. They got back to the ship on fumes, last ones in. No sign of 09 anywhere. They're long beyond their endurance limit now."

I take a deep breath and focus on exhaling it slowly. The two sergeants are watching me with concern.

"This was never going to be a milk run," Gallegos says. "We all knew that."

I've always been on uneasy terms with the stars on my shoulder boards, but now I hate them outright. After the initial surge of emotions passes, I take a few more deep breaths until it feels like I'll be able to talk again without screaming out my anger and thoroughly freaking out my sergeants.

"We held our farewell ceremony for them last week," Sergeant Jordan says. "Out on the hangar deck, in our regular spot. Said our good-byes in the usual way. Ship ran out of booze, but we sourced some engineering moonshine from the jarhead regiment. They gave it up for free when they heard what it was for."

"I'm sorry I couldn't be there," I say.

"Of course, sir," Jordan replies.

"Who took charge while I was out?"

"Captain Burns was CO while you were on the mission. Captain Harper took over when he got back in."

I look past Jordan and Gallegos down the compartment's central passageway. The door of the CO's office—my office—is standing open and the desk inside has nobody behind it right now.

"Any idea where Captain Harper might be at the moment?" I ask.

First Sergeant Gallegos walks behind the counter and checks the electronic duty roster.

"There's a command meeting at 1500. He's up there, most likely."

"I think I'll go join him," I say. "Carry on. I'll want to sit down with you when I'm done up there, First Sergeant. I need you to bring me up to speed on the team."

"Yes, sir," Gallegos replies. "I'll be right here."

I turn around to leave the STT compartment, but as I walk out and take a left turn onto the passageway outside, I see the two sergeants out of the corner of my good eye exchanging looks with each other again.

I've been out for three weeks, and they've muddled on and buried their friends without me, and now I am waltzing back in and taking charge again. The talk with my senior sergeants has given me the strangest sensation—that we're out of phase now, that I am three weeks behind everyone else and in a different reality altogether, and that nothing I can do right now will get me in sync with them again.

CHAPTER 19

—————— PATTERNS ——————

The door to the flag briefing room is closed when I walk up, and two SI troopers in soft armor are standing on either side of it, both wearing helmets and armed with PDWs that are slung across their chests. They both eye me as I approach.

"Major Grayson, here for the command meeting. I'm the STT commander."

One of the troopers taps his headset.

"Sir, I have Major Grayson out here requesting access to the flag briefing room for the command meeting."

He listens for a second, then nods.

"You're good to go, sir."

He activates the security pad on the door and opens it for me. I nod and step across the threshold. Inside, the command section is already assembled around the briefing room table. Every set of eyes in the room is on me as I walk in, and the staff officers are only slightly better at hiding their surprise at the sight of me than the NCOs and enlisted I've met so far.

"Major Grayson," Colonel Drake says. He has dark rings under his eyes, and his beard is a regulation-defying red stubble that hasn't seen a shaving implement in several days. "I was sure we wouldn't see you for at least another week. How are you feeling?"

"A little rough, sir. But I'm all right."

From the other side of the briefing table, Captain Harper gives me a curt smile and a nod. Colonel Rigney, the commanding officer of the SI regiment, looks like he can't quite make up his mind about whether to be impressed or horrified by my appearance, which I know is rough indeed. The CAG, Colonel Pace, looks more irritated at the interruption than anything else. Lieutenant Colonel Campbell, the ship's XO, is unreadable, as always, wearing her typical expression of cool detachment. Dr. Brotherton, the lead fleet astronomer, looks as out of place as usual. It seems that the science division is on short rations as well because the doctor has lost almost all the extra padding he had been carrying at the beginning of the trip.

"Mind if I join you, Captain?" I say to Harper. "You're the STT lead right now, but I would like to stay on top of things."

"By all means, sir," Harper says and gestures to the empty chair next to his own. I move around the table and sit down, stifling the little groan that threatens to well up when the sudden change in posture sends an ache up my leg and into my hip. I know everyone is a little shocked at my sudden appearance, in my current condition, but the rest of the command council gives the impression that it has not been smooth sailing since our mission departed for the Lanky moon. Everyone looks haggard to various degrees, and they've all lost quite a bit of weight in the last few weeks.

"Let's go back to the start," Colonel Drake says. "For Major Grayson's benefit."

"Sorry," I say. "I've been out of the loop for a bit."

"No worries, Major. We were just getting started, anyway."

He resets the holoscreen behind him, which briefly cycles back to the NACDC logo before switching to a strategic map of the rogue system. Right away, I am alarmed by the number of blaze-orange icons on the map. There are at least two dozen Lanky ships scattered all over the system, and some of them are uncomfortably close to the blue lozenge shape that represents NACS *Washington*.

"Situation," Colonel Drake says. "We are still on the run. We've had to reposition twice in the last twenty-four hours. Every time we light our engines, we are hanging out a blinking billboard. But if we don't move when we have a seed ship in the neighborhood, we are sitting ducks. Fact is that without the Wonderballs, we would have been dead two weeks ago already. Whoever invented those things should be awarded a box full of medals and made president for life as far as I'm concerned. The good news is that the last evasive course change put us in the clear for a bit, relatively speaking. The nearest seed ship is three million klicks away but no longer CBDR. Let's hope this little break lasts for a bit longer."

He zooms the map in on *Washington* and the immediate space around it until only our ship and the nearest Lanky are visible.

"Logistics," he continues. "We are running on empty in almost all categories across the board. We expended one Orion and scored a hard kill on a seed ship seven days ago, but now we're down to three Orions. We are starting to get low on water again because we had to suspend the ferry ops from the ice moon before STS-55 could get them into full swing. Food stores are down to seventy-five percent after only a month out here even with the calorie restrictions we put in place, which have kicked morale right in the crotch. And all the evasive maneuvering is chewing through our reactor fuel at five times the expected rate."

"How long have we been on the run?" I ask. Once again, every pair of eyes in the room is on me. "Sorry, but I am clearly not up to date on current events. When did this happen?"

"About halfway through your recon mission," Colonel Pace says. "Like someone flicked a switch. Every moon has seed ships in orbit now. And half the ships in the inner system have changed course to join them."

"Something tipped them off that we are here," the CO adds. "Could be something that happened while you were on that moon. Could be just random coincidence, or plain bad luck. Maybe they picked up a whiff of our IR signature or a bit of RF noise. Doesn't matter now. The fact is that they are no longer unaware. And there are only so many spots in this system where we can hide behind something. Sooner or later we'll run out of reactor fuel, or water, or food, or luck," he adds. "We're rolling the dice every day out here. And they'll come up with our number on it eventually. We need to get out of this place now because we have no alternatives left other than slow starvation. And the hounds are trying to flush us out of the thicket."

"So where are we going?" Colonel Rigney asks.

"The astro division has some ideas," Colonel Drake says. "Dr. Brotherton, want to jump in?"

"Absolutely," Brotherton says. He no longer has the jovial air about him that I remember from the last briefing with the Fleet astronomers. Now he's as subdued and tired-looking as the rest of us. He picks up the pointer for the holotable and takes over the display.

"All right. We've spent the last two weeks sifting through the incoming surveillance data from the Wonderballs. We have 1,024 units on station, and we've been able to keep a pretty good eye on the neighborhood. Now that the network has been online for a while, we have been able to identify trends and patterns."

He highlights the space between the rogue planet and the Lanky moon.

"The Lankies have been moving all over the system since we got here, but they're not just randomly flitting about. We have noted several travel patterns among the seed ships. One major highway is this one."

He draws a line with his light pen that starts with a swirl around the rogue planet, then to the Lanky moon, and all the way back until the line has formed a closed loop that looks like a stretched-out racetrack.

"Seed ships leave the orbit of the gas giant at a rate of one every two to three days. They go out to Green and make several orbits where they go so low that they dip into the upper atmosphere. Then they return to the gas giant and resume their orbit there. We don't know if it's always a new ship or whether they all make that trip repeatedly every few days in turn. But the weird thing is that it's only the light-colored seed ships, the ones we can track on passive IR."

He rotates the map and plays back the sensor data from the last few days. The orange icons leave the rogue planet in irregular intervals, sometimes days apart, sometimes so close together that they almost seem to be traveling in formation.

"But there's a different pattern. This one took a lot longer to figure out because only the stealth seed ships do that particular run, and it takes them so far outside the Wonderball sphere that the sensors have a hard time picking them up again after a while."

We watch the seed ship icons move across the system in seemingly random excursions, but when Dr. Brotherton resets the timeline and plays it back at much higher speed, another pattern reveals itself. The stealth seed ships patrol the space between the moons seemingly at random, but every now and then, a Lanky icon appears at the moon we called Green and heads toward the outer regions of the system, past the orbits of the rogue planet's moons, and out of sight of the Wonderball sensors.

"Where the hell are they going?" Colonel Pace wonders.

"I can't tell you that with absolute certainty, Colonel," Dr. Brotherton says. "But—"

He draws a line away from the Lanky moon to follow the widely spaced procession of stealth seed ship icons.

"If you extend this line all the way out of our surveillance range, it ends up pointing right here."

He does just that, running the line through all the Lanky ship icons in sequence. When he crosses the last verified and marked Lanky position, he keeps drawing in a straight line until he reaches the edge of the holographic orb. It neatly bisects the oval blue icon that marks the point where we entered the system—the exit point of the Lanky Alcubierre chute.

"You're kidding me," Colonel Pace says. "That's where they're going?"

"That's the inbound," I say. "That's the way we came in after the Lanky dragged us along."

"Yes, it is, Major."

"So why are all these seed ships heading that way?"

"Well," Dr. Brotherton says. "If we assume they're not just having some big gathering out of sensor range, it seems logical that their outbound transit point is very near the inbound one. Maybe they're even the same thing. We've never taken their network using our drive, just our networks—that we built."

"It doesn't work that way," Colonel Pace says. "It's a one-way street every time."

"For us it is," Dr. Brotherton replies. "But we also can't go nine hundred light-years in thirty-three minutes on our network."

The statement lingers in the room for a moment as we all digest this information.

"And you are sure they're not leaving this system from any other point?" Colonel Drake asks.

"No, I am not sure. We're in a place with no sunlight. We can't use active sensors. And our enemy doesn't show on infrared. I can only give you my best guess based on the data. And according to the data, no Lanky ship has crossed into or out of Wonderball detection range at any other point in space since the optical network went live. Add to that the fact that we're looking at what is pretty much the direct route from Green to the transition point, and I'm as sure as I can be with what I have."

Colonel Drake looks at the holotable and studies the markers Dr. Brotherton drew on it. He scrubs through the timeline, going forward and backward in time, reversing and advancing the steady flow of orange icons. Now that we know what to look for, the pattern is obvious. Only the newest data, the time stamps from the last few days, show a gradual dispersion of the orange icons from the area around the Lanky moon to the other moons in the system, but the stream from the Lanky moon to the area around the Alcubierre entry node remains as steady as before.

"We can't go to ground anymore," he says. "They're combing all the hiding spots around the moons. We need to get out of here one way or the other. And if that's the way to the exit, I'd say it's as good a heading as any."

"Even if we find the exit node out there, we can't use it," Colonel Pace says. "Unless one of the seed ships lets us tag along."

"That may be an option," Colonel Drake says. The CAG chuckles, but his smile fades when he realizes that the commander is serious.

"How are we going to do that? Bribe it? Appeal to its better nature?"

"We just need to be in the same space at the same time," the XO says. "Just like the first time. Doesn't mean they have to be aware of us. We can let the computer calculate an intercept that will get us to an exact point in space at a precise time. Down to the cubic meter and the millisecond."

"We don't have a precise point," Pace objects.

"Yet," Colonel Drake says. "We'll get a better picture as we get closer. But if the opportunity presents itself, we must be able to seize it. If we stay here, we're just waiting to get discovered again."

"Do we have a backup plan if we end up missing our shot?"

Colonel Drake considers the CAG's question for a moment. But it's Lieutenant Colonel Campbell who replies first.

"If we don't make the chute out of here, I'd say we point this ship toward Earth and run the engines at full thrust until our reactor fuel is gone," she says.

"We'll run out of food and water hundreds of years before we make it home," Colonel Pace says.

"I know," the XO says. "But if we miss the chute, we're dead anyway, and soon. I don't know about you, Colonel. But I'd rather die tomorrow trying to get home than in a few weeks or months while playing hide-and-seek with these things in this hellhole of a system. I'm ready to leave. One way or another."

I can't suppress a grin at her bristly insouciance, and I look down at the tabletop to not be obvious, but she sees it anyway and gives me the tiniest of smirks along with a little twitch of her eyebrow.

"Well," Colonel Pace says after a moment. He looks around at the rest of the people gathered around the table.

"Is that the general consensus?"

There's no objection coming from anyone, and Pace sighs and leans back in his chair far enough to make the backrest creak in protest.

"Well, then. Let's plot a course and get the hell out of here."

Colonel Drake restores the map view to the strategic picture of the system, then centers the map on the ice moon and zooms in again until *Washington*'s icon is just at the edge of the map. Two orange icons are circling the moon, where a single blue rectangle marks our tiny little surface outpost in this system.

"We have one little snag here. Twenty-one hours ago, two seed ships moved into orbit around Blue and took up station there. That's a problem that needs solving before we can be on our way."

"Have they attacked the outpost?" Colonel Rigney asks.

Colonel Drake shakes his head. "We're still getting updates from them every four hours as the moon's rotation gets them into our line of sight. So far, they haven't been touched. The Lanky orbits aren't anywhere near the station. But while there are Lankies overhead, we can't send a pickup mission. And I don't think they'll do us the favor of clearing the neighborhood again any time soon."

Colonel Pace sits up and looks at the holotable as if he's seeing the tactical map on it for the first time.

"You want to go in with *Washington*, guns blazing."

"It's too far for the drop ships. And it would be a suicide run for them. They may make it in without being seen. But they'll never make it back out."

"Are we sure we can't just let the engineers lay low for a while? Ride it out until we're in a better spot to do a pickup?" Colonel Pace asks. "They have supplies, and all the water they need."

"I'm not comfortable with that gamble. There are at least three more seed ships heading in the general direction of that moon. I have a feeling that this is the best set of odds we'll get. We can scrape two out of orbit. We can't deal with five or six."

"We have three Orions left," Pace says. "We'd need to use up two of them for those bogeys, and that's the best-case scenario. How many engineers are on that moon right now?"

"Sixty-four," Colonel Rigney replies. "Two platoons of my combat engineers, working shifts."

"Sixty-four," Pace repeats. "There are over five thousand people on this ship. We'll risk all their lives and burn through most of our remaining ordnance. To retrieve sixty-four."

Colonel Drake looks at the CAG for a moment, and I can see his facial muscles tightening a little as he clenches his jaw.

"That's not an equation I am prepared to make," he says. "Not now, not later. Not while I am in command of this ship."

"I'm not saying we shouldn't get them off that moon," Colonel Pace says. "I'm saying we don't have to take on two seed ships and risk the carrier to do that. They are set up down there. They can weather this until the tactical situation overhead changes."

Lieutenant Colonel Campbell takes control of the holotable and changes the scale of the map from tactical back to strategic. There's a distinct new traffic pattern in the Lanky movements of the last twenty-four hours, small clusters of seed ships heading from the core of the system out to the moons in their various orbits. She highlights the line of orange icons that is reaching out toward Blue.

"The skipper doesn't believe that the tactical situation overhead will change to our advantage. And I agree with him. In another ninety-six hours or so, that neighborhood is going to be crawling with bad guys. If we want to get our people out of there and leave for the transit point, we need to do it now."

"If anyone is strongly opposed to that plan, voice your objections now," Colonel Drake says. "I will consider them and make sure they are logged. Otherwise, let's get a mission plan together."

"No objections from my end," Colonel Rigney says. "Let's go get our people and go home."

I almost speak up for the STT before I remember that Captain Harper is sitting next to me, and that he's speaking for the team right now. The SEAL captain looks at Colonel Drake and shakes his head.

"No objections from special tactics," he says.

Colonel Pace sighs and leans back in his chair.

"No objections from the CAG. But I still think there's a good chance we'll all end up stardust over this. I don't like the odds. Three missiles for two seed ships. That's too thin a margin."

"I don't care much for the odds, either," Colonel Drake replies. "In an ideal world, we'd have a full load of Orions and another Avenger nearby for backup. But this is what we have, so it'll have to do."

He swaps the strategic map on the holotable for the standard mission planning template.

"And if we all do get turned to stardust, there's no shame in it," Lieutenant Colonel Campbell says. The XO's face looks like she also lost a bunch of weight she couldn't afford to lose, and her cheekbones are even more prominent than usual. We're all slowly fading out here, and that thought is scarier to me than the prospect of a quick death by explosive hull decompression.

"No, there isn't," Colonel Drake says. "Shameful would be to leave sixty-four people behind just to save our own hides. And I'll have this ship go head-to-head against a hundred of those things before I let that happen on my watch."

CHAPTER 20

──── ODDS AND ENDS ────

When we leave the briefing room almost an hour later, I wait in the passageway outside for Captain Harper to catch up. He sees me waiting for him, and something about the subtle change in his expression tells me that he's not entirely happy to have to deal with me right now.

"Good to see you back on your feet, Major. I heard it was touch and go there for a while."

"That's what they tell me. I was out entirely, so I'll have to take their word for it. Sorry to have stuck you with the team by yourself for so long."

"From the mission report, it sounds like you almost stuck me with the team for good, sir."

We start walking down the passageway toward the ladderwell that will take us back down to the STT module.

"I haven't had a chance to go over the mission reports yet," I say. "I hear your patrol had no contact."

"Not much to tell. We walked for twenty-four hours and then got back on the bus and left," he says. "Nothing but gravel and rocks at our landing site. Totally dead on seismic. Not even a scrap of vegetation.

We did see an active volcano about a hundred klicks away. That was it for local sights, though. Waste of fuel and time."

"I wish ours had been less eventful," I say.

"Yeah. I've had a few weeks to go over the reports and the data from the suits. You're damn lucky any of your team made it out at all."

"Only thanks to your SEALs," I reply. "I know it's not worth much right now, but when we get back home, I am putting Lieutenant Dean and the rest of his squad in for the Medal of Honor. Every one of them."

Harper glances at me and looks ahead again, and I can see the line of his mouth thinning a little.

"Something you want to get off your chest, Captain?" I ask.

He stops and turns to face me.

"Look," he says. "People die in war. SEALs sure as shit know what we signed up for. Life can be a bitch for podheads. Usually is. I don't blame you for what happened to the squad."

"I sense a *but* coming," I say.

Captain Harper hesitates for a moment. I can see the anger flickering in his eyes, but I know that he's holding back because he doesn't want to have to regret it later in the brig. I know that because I've had the same look in my eyes before when talking to superiors I would have just as soon slugged in the face than addressed as 'sir.' Seven years ago, at a place called Arcadia, I only barely managed not to land myself in the brig when I unloaded on Major Masoud, the man in command of our costly mission there. Harper was there as well, as a young second lieutenant, sneaking around the moon with Masoud and the SEAL team and planting nukes on terraformers while my platoon got chewed up as bait for the planetary garrison.

"You got something you want to say, spit it out, Harper," I say. "Forget about the rank."

I can see that he's trying to decide whether I am baiting him. Then he shakes his head, an angry little flick of a gesture that looks like he's shooing a fly off his face.

"I told you from the beginning that taking the doctor along was a bad idea. And I was right."

"What are you talking about? The scientist had nothing to do with that. We stirred up the hive because we had to pop a Lanky. The SEALs held them off in the tunnel so the rest of us could get out."

"As I said, I've had a few weeks to look at the data from the suits," he says. "You were out on that ledge for too long. She just *had* to go back for more samples, and you *let* her. You were in that spot for over *seven minutes*. Stationary, in the middle of a Lanky burrow. If she hadn't done that extra run with the drone, you wouldn't have had to shoot that Lanky. That's what killed my team, Major. Those extra two minutes you gave her."

"We got invaluable intel because we brought the doctor along. They didn't lay down their lives for nothing, Captain. Don't do this to yourself. Don't play these 'what if' games. Trust me on this."

He smiles without humor and shakes his head again.

"I lost half my team a week ago. I went to SEAL school with some of those people. Forgive me if I process that in whatever way I choose. You weren't here for any of that. You didn't have to update the company roster. You didn't have to close out your friends' personnel files. Or pack up their stuff and clean out their lockers. So I respectfully request that you withhold your advice."

I don't tell him that I know all those feelings too well, that I have done those same things before, and that the memory of them still visits me almost every day. He's hurting, and I know how that particular sort of pain makes you want to lash out and put the blame on someone or something so it doesn't burn a smoking hole in your heart. But I also know that right now there would be no point in telling him that because the wound is too raw. I am here, and I was in charge on the ground, and he is venting his anger the only way he can right now.

"Now if you'll excuse me, I still have a team to run," he says. He walks briskly down the passageway without looking back, a deliberate insubordination that I choose to ignore.

Now you know how I felt after Arcadia, I think.

The ship's medical lab is just as I remember it, but it still looks strange and different from the rest of the ship, like a little slice of the civilian world that got wedged into the austere and no-frills environment of a modern warship by accident. It's the only spot on the ship where people don't walk around in uniform or color-coded deckhand overalls. As I walk in, I spot something that is different from the last time I was here almost a month ago. Every workstation pod has a vacsuit hanging on a ready rack nearby.

Elin is in her own pod, her impressive array of terminal screens fanned out in front of her. She is scrolling through some data readouts and cross-referencing them with the stream on another screen, highlighting lines as she goes. There's a mug sitting next to her right hand, and as I walk up to her pod, she picks it up and absentmindedly takes a sip from it only to make a face.

"They're still serving coffee?" I say. She startles and turns toward me. Her eyes widen when she takes in my appearance, and I can see her shock despite her efforts to keep a neutral expression.

"No, they're not," she says. "This is some instant powder I found in the science galley. Soy and binders with some flavoring. How are you, Andrew?"

"I've been better," I admit. "Been worse, too. But not by much."

"You looked bad when they carried you into the drop ship. If it hadn't been for the vitals screen on the pod, I would have thought you were dead."

"Almost was," I say. "But the autodoc can work miracles. How are you doing?"

"I'm all right," she says. "Haven't slept through a night since we left that moon, though."

"I tried my best to warn you," I reply.

"Yes, you did. And I should have listened. But I'm historically bad at that."

"I owe you thanks. For coming back with Sergeant Martin into that tunnel. I would have died down there without your help. So—*thank you.*"

"I just had this nagging feeling in my gut. Maybe I heard you without realizing it."

"Gut feelings aren't a very scientific basis for decisions."

"No, they aren't. But I am glad I listened," she says.

Elin inclines her head toward the pod next to hers, which is empty.

"Why don't you grab that chair and sit down for a minute? If you have the time, that is."

"I'm still grounded, I think. So yeah, I think I have the time."

I walk over to the other pod and drag the chair from it to Elin's space.

"I hear the protein you sampled is edible," I say.

"It is," she says. "We can break it down and use it for calories. It just needs a lot of processing before we can use it as food. The mushrooms in that cabbage patch are inedible. To us, anyway. Those crawlies eat them, and when they metabolize them, it turns their tissue mildly toxic. It's like that basking shark they eat on Iceland. Ever heard of those?"

"Hákarl," I say. "Our special ops training base is on Iceland. The locals used to serve that stuff to newcomers as a practical joke. Or a rite of passage, maybe. Worst stuff I've ever put in my mouth, and I grew up on BNA rations."

"This may taste worse. But it would keep us alive. From what I hear, the point is moot now, anyway."

"Yeah, nobody's going to make that trip again. Not that I was wild about the idea of going back there and dragging those things out of the ground."

"For what it's worth, I have all the protein samples in stasis in the lab. The xenobiologists back home are going to go nuts when they see what I am bringing back. If we ever get back."

"If we don't, you're still the one who discovered them. You'll have naming rights. Unless you plan to stick with 'crawlies.'"

Elin smiles. "I'll think of something good and proper in Latin. But man, coming up with an entire new taxonomic hierarchy is going to be a lot of damn work."

She nods at the array of screens behind her.

"Now the other samples, those are the real prize."

"The mycelium and the wall scrapings from the cave," I say, and she nods.

"My equipment here is a little limited. This is a medical lab, not a bioresearch facility. I couldn't bring much specialized kit with me when I got on board because everything was so last minute, and they'd only let me bring ten kilos of gear. But I've done a bit of testing with some of the samples, and they're remarkable. The stuff on the walls is a sort of simple fungus-based heat paint. But the mycelium? That's the opposite. Much more complex. Any organic material it touches, the infrared signature goes down by ninety-eight percent. It's like a natural stealth coating. And it's easily as good as anything we've ever put on our own stealth ships. Better, in a lot of ways. It applies itself. *Repairs* itself."

"A living stealth paint," I say. "The biotech people are going to be all over that."

"The *weapons division* is going to be all over that," she says. "Everyone's going to want to get their hands on this stuff."

"As long as we use it against the Lankies somehow. Not as a new edge against each other. Imagine if the NAC and the Euros could put full IR stealth on their ships and the SRA couldn't. It wouldn't take long before some hothead decides that now's the time for winnable wars again."

She frowns and looks back at her screens.

"That's not a cheerful thought. I don't want to think we went through all that just to bring back some new profits for the defense industry."

"I don't want to think that, either. We paid a lot for those samples. You decide what happens next."

"This is what I wanted to do since I was in school," she says. "Go out into space and discover new species. Exploration and wonder. Something to add to the sum of human knowledge. And now we're in a war, and everything I do is valued by whether it will help us kill better. It's enough to sap the sense of wonder right out of you."

"The sense of wonder will come back, I think. We just need to survive first."

"We will. That's what we do. As a species, I mean. We always find a way. We're like galactic cockroaches. Think about how pissed the Lankies are when they come to a new moon and they take it over, and they *just can't get rid of us.* Always underfoot somehow. Scurrying everywhere. Ruining the nice new place."

I laugh at the visual even if it's probably a little too close to reality.

"We're not going to make it, are we?" she asks. "I mean us, personally. Not the species. We're not going to get out of here."

"There's a plan in the works. But a lot of it depends on an unlikely shit-ton of dumb luck. I'm sure that's not what you want to hear."

"If it's the truth, I am fine with it. Even if it's not comforting. Reality is what it is. Not going to lie, though. I was hoping I'd make it quite a bit longer than my thirties."

"Me too," I say. "But I wouldn't trade any of it for dying at seventy-five back home in the PRC."

"Which one was yours?"

"Boston-7. You?"

"Philly-28," she replies.

"Good times," I say, and she laughs.

"No, not really. I imagine yours weren't, either."

"It wasn't living," I say. "It was just existing. That's only good enough if you've never seen anything else. When I joined up, I got to make friends. Fall in love. Get married. Have a purpose. I don't want to die just yet. But I'm fine with getting only thirty-four years. Some of them were good years. And even the bad ones had their moments."

"That's not a bad perspective," Elin says. "I can get on board with that."

"There's always hope. Even if it's just because we're terrible at math when it comes to judging odds. But we may get home."

"What are they planning up there?"

"Well, the command briefings are classified. I can't give you the details. But we're leaving soon, and we're going to try to catch a ride out of here."

"Catch a ride," she repeats. "You mean, the way we came in?"

"I can neither confirm nor deny," I say. "But you can probably figure that one out."

"That sounds like we're making a Hail Mary pass," she says.

"The textbook definition of a Hail Mary pass. Split-second timing, low chance of success, no backup plan, and it's all fueled by desperation."

"But there is a chance of success."

"It's not a set of odds I'd choose to go all in on if I had the choice. But we're all out of choices at this point," I say. "And it wasn't mine to make, anyway."

Elin leans back in her chair and clasps her hands behind her head. She looks around the lab and exhales a slow breath.

"I don't know how you do it," she says. "You combat troops, I mean. How long have you been doing this again?"

"Thirteen years," I say.

"You've done this for thirteen years. I've gone on two missions with your team, and now I have the jitters so badly that I jump a foot in the air whenever someone slams a hatch or drops a coffee mug on the deck. I have absolutely no idea how you can still walk around and function."

"With a carefully calibrated mix of psychotropic drugs and stubborn spite," I say, and she laughs again.

"I'm only half joking about that. It took me forever to concede that my brain wasn't right anymore," I continue. "Grunts have a hard time with admitting weakness. Especially podheads. But my wife is about five times smarter than I am, and she wasn't having any of my bullshit anymore. She had me go and see the Fleet shrink. If you want some help with that sleep issue, you should go see them, too. I don't know how many more nights we're going to get. But it would be nice to be able to sleep through them, right?"

"Right. I'd hate to die tired."

Elin smiles and does her slow, almost meditative exhalation again.

"Well, Andrew. I don't have any combat stations job on this ship. So I'll keep doing my work down here and assume that the Hail Mary pass is going to score. And if it doesn't, I hope it's all over so fast that I'll never know. But however it goes, I'm glad to have met you."

"Likewise," I say. "And however it goes, I'll see you on the other side. Wherever that is."

We smile at each other, and I get up to leave her to her business.

"Andrew," she says when I am at the door, and I turn around.

"Take it from a scientist," she says. "Math isn't everything. Fuck the odds."

"I'll see if I can talk the XO into painting that on our bow, in letters twenty meters tall," I say, and Elin laughs. I rap my knuckles against the doorframe and walk out into the passageway with a smile.

CHAPTER 21

BLUE TEAM

Washington is on the offensive again, and it feels good.

I'm in my seat in the CIC, strapped in securely with the five-point harness, and wearing a vacsuit instead of battle armor. There's nothing to do for the STT on this assault, but I have elected to man the special ops station anyway. If this goes badly, I want to see death in the eye instead of meeting it in my berth with nothing to do but listen to the ship disintegrate around me. To my right, the holotable shows the tactical plot—*Washington* at the center, hurtling toward the blue orb representing the ice moon, and the two orange icons that represent our targets. I'm scared as always before the start of battle, but I'm also buoyed by a sort of exhilaration. We are the predator once more, on the attack instead of running away and hiding.

"Blue Station will be in line of sight for comms in thirty seconds," Lieutenant Cole announces. "Distance to bogey Lima-1 is now under a million. We're coming in like a freight train. Approaching first launch point in seven minutes."

"Weapons, give me a status, please," Colonel Drake says from his command chair.

"Green light on Orion tubes six through eight. Particle mounts Alpha and Beta are energized and on standby," Lieutenant Lawrence reports.

"We're as ready as we're going to get," Lieutenant Commander Campbell says. She's ahead and to the left of me, strapped in and fully vacsuited like the rest of the CIC crew. "Recovery drop ships are in the clamps with hot engines. Once we have those seed ships out of the way, we'll be in and out of there in forty minutes."

"No course or speed change on Lima-1 since we started tracking him with the targeting computer. He's just chugging along. No idea he's about to get smacked into puree," Lieutenant Lawrence says.

"Give me the time for line of sight on Lima-2 and put it on the screen," the CO orders.

"Aye, sir." Captain Steadman checks his tactical station and adds the projection to the situational orb on the holotable. "They'll be coming around the bend over the northern pole in thirteen minutes, thirty seconds."

"If he doesn't notice that we've blown up his buddy," Lieutenant Colonel Campbell says wryly.

"The bulk of the moon will be between us and him when that happens. Unless that Orion goes wide and goes past the moon, he shouldn't notice a thing until it's too late."

The Lanky ships on the tactical plot are on vastly different orbits. Over the last half hour, I've watched the tactical orb for lack of something better to do on our approach, and the movement of the seed ships has been kind of mesmerizing, like watching one of those perpetual-motion toys where a bunch of steel balls are spinning around a common center without ever contacting each other. Lima-1, the ship we have locked up with our targeting system, is orbiting the moon around its equator. Lima-2 is going around across the poles, so the dotted lines of their movement projections are at ninety-degree angles to each other. Their orbits are almost perfectly timed to avoid being on the same hemisphere together at the same time. I've seen that sort of timed precision from the seed ships before, and I still have no idea whether it's just a highly developed instinct or an alien intellect consciously using mathematics. But their orbital pattern means that we must engage them separately and in turn because the Orions are just giant nuclear-propelled cinder blocks, not guided missiles.

"Blue Station is now in comms range, sir," Lieutenant Cole says. "We have line of sight to their optical transmitter."

"Establish a comms link," Colonel Drake orders.

"Aye, sir. You are go for optical to Blue Station."

"Blue Station, this is *Washington* Actual. Do you read?"

"*Washington, Blue Station. You're coming in loud and clear.*"

"We are inbound and about to engage the enemy as planned. Proceed with the evacuation and stand ready to receive drop ship pickup."

"*Understood, Washington. We are all packed up and standing by. Good luck.*"

"We'll update you with an ETA when we've cleared house above your heads. If you don't hear from us again, it was an honor and a privilege to serve with you."

"*Likewise, Washington. Whatever happens, we gave as good as we took. No regrets. Good luck and kick some ass, sir. Blue Station out.*"

"That is our intent. We will see you up here soon. *Washington* Actual out."

"Launch point in six minutes," Lieutenant Cole says.

"Stand by on silos. Let's not get hasty and whiff that shot," Colonel Drake says.

The orange icon labeled "LIMA-1" glides along the dotted line around the moon's equator. There's a cone-shaped field projected in front of *Washington*'s icon that represents the optimal engagement range for the Orions to secure a kill, and the outside of the cone creeps closer to the orbiting Lanky with every passing minute.

"We're close enough for a visual now," Lieutenant Cole says.

"Let's see it," Colonel Drake says. "Bring it up as a quarter overlay."

A new viewing window appears in one quadrant of the tactical orb. It shows the outline of the ice moon, faintly glowing with infrared radiation against the absolute zero of the space behind it. The Lanky ship is a familiar dark shape in the middle of the moon, visible only by the infrared glow missing from that spot.

"Does that look like he's trailing debris?" I ask. "Look at the wake."

"See if you can get some more zoom dialed in," the XO says to Lieutenant Cole.

"I can get closer but the resolution goes to shit on passive. Hang on."

The viewing window changes to isolate the area around the Lanky ship, then the rear half of it. With the ship a mere shadow in front of the moon, the sensor is constantly trying to focus and sharpen the details, but it's still just a shadow in front of a shadow. We are approaching the moon at thousands of meters per second, and with the decreasing distance, the picture gradually sharpens until I see clearly what I had just glimpsed a few moments earlier.

"There," I say and point at the projection. Something is leaving the stern section of the Lanky ship at regular intervals, too regular for it to be random debris.

"Is he . . . dispensing something?" Captain Steadman asks.

"He's laying a fucking minefield, that's what he's doing," Lieutenant Commander Campbell says. "Those nasty proximity dispensers. Haven't run into any of those in a long while."

"Well," Colonel Drake says. "That explains why they're in such divergent orbits."

"They're putting in a security system," the XO says. "Now that they know there are burglars in the neighborhood."

"Send word to the transport squadron," the commander orders. "And start mapping and tagging those mines for the missiles. We're going to go active on the ballistic defense grid. Once we light that

Orion, there'll be plenty of EM noise. Everyone on this side of the moon will know we're here anyway. I'm not risking the drop ships by sending them through a minefield. We're going to punch a hole in it once we've taken out those seed ships."

"We'll be drawing every Lanky in the system to this moon," Captain Steadman says.

"And we'll be gone by the time they get here. The next group of seed ships is seventy hours away. That's a good head start."

"We're committed now," the XO says. "No turning around at this point. Might as well really rattle some cages."

"Launch point coming up in three minutes," Lieutenant Cole says.

Colonel Drake puts his hands together in front of his helmet and taps his index fingers against his lips as he's watching the distance numbers on the display count down rapidly.

"Weapons, open doors on Orion tubes six and seven," he says.

"Aye, sir. Opening silos six and seven," Lieutenant Lawrence acknowledges and turns the hardware switches on the weapons console clockwise. I know that deep underneath us, along the ventral edge of the ship, the silo covers are retracting from the huge tubes that hold the ship's long-range Lanky interceptors, two thousand tons of dense kinetic penetrator sitting on top of five hundred nuclear charges.

As time elapses much faster when I am on leave, it seems to slow down to a syrupy trickle whenever I watch a Lanky ship on the tactical plot as we creep up on it to get into firing range for the Orions. In theory, the missiles have practically unlimited range because they'll keep going at fractional light-speed velocity once their nuclear propellant charges are used up. But there's no way to guide them, and every second of flight time between our ship and the target increases the chance for a miss. As big as the Lanky ships are, they're still moving targets, and they've shown that they can make course changes very quickly. There will be a time when they will have adapted to the Orions and come up with countermeasures, and every time I'm in a ship that launches one at a Lanky, I expect for fate to choose that day for them to figure it out.

"Tube six, ready for launch. Tube seven, ready for launch. Confirm fire mission," Lieutenant Lawrence announces.

"Release of kinetic weapons is authorized. Weapons hot. You have fire control."

"Weapons hot. I have fire control, aye." Lieutenant Lawrence is now fully focused on his weapons console.

With nothing else to do except grab the armrests of my chair, I watch the tactical display as the Orion's engagement cone eats up the distance between its outer edge and the orange seed ship icon. Then the arc of the cone crosses the Lanky and moves beyond it. The weapons officer flips the safety cover off the launch button.

"Target aspect unchanged. We have a green firing solution. Launching in five . . . four . . . three . . . two . . . one. *Firing Six.*"

Lieutenant Lawrence punches the launch button. The Orion ejects from the launch tube and leaps ahead of the ship. On the tactical display, it shows up as a blue V shape with a dot in it. The little blue V rapidly opens the distance between itself and the blue lozenge shape representing *Washington*.

"Missile away," Lawrence reports. "Clean separation."

"Here come the fireworks," the XO says.

On the screen that shows the Lanky seed ship moving along the moon's equator, a bright pinprick of light appears that grows to wash out the sensor image completely. I know that the first atomic propellant charge just exploded right behind the Orion's ablative pusher plate to give the missile its first mighty kick toward its target. Nothing we have ever put into space can accelerate like something that rides the plasma debris of a thermonuclear detonation. Every second, the missile drops another quarter-kiloton nuke in its own wake and ignites it, and with every exploding nuke, the Orion accelerates more, building up the kinetic energy needed to punch through a seed ship's hull. The new

Orions are smaller than the first model, but they have been designed to detonate the unused propellant nukes a few microseconds after the kinetic warhead has punched through the hull to add their destructive power to the inside of the seed ship.

"Nine minutes, twenty-seven seconds to intercept," Captain Steadman says from his tactical station. "Missile is tracking true. No changes in aspect or speed from the Lanky."

"Keep that heading for just a little while longer," the XO says to the orange icon on the situation orb in a low voice. "It'll all be over before you know it."

"Weapons, get ready for a follow-up with tube seven," Colonel Drake says.

"Aye, sir," Lawrence replies. "Standing by on tube seven."

There's the familiar eerie silence in the CIC as we all watch the missile icon race toward the Lanky icon on the tactical screen. The forward view from the optical sensors is useless because it keeps getting washed out by the nuclear explosions that are going off in one-second intervals.

"You do realize that if this missile hits, we'll be the first Fleet ace, right?" Lieutenant Colonel Campbell says.

"I think that's an air-to-air thing, not a capital ship metric," I reply.

"We have four and a half kills right now. That first Lanky in Capella only counts as half because we scored the hit simultaneously with *Johannesburg*," she says. "We splash this one, we're at five and a half. Five kills get us ace status."

"Ace or not, this ship has killed more Lankies than any other ship in the Fleet," Colonel Drake contributes. "And I promise that once we get home, I will strong-arm Fleet command into painting all those kill marks onto our hull. But let's not count our chickens before they're hatched."

"Two minutes to intercept," Captain Steadman says. "Missile is still tracking true. Coming in for a broadside hit."

The nuclear fireballs on the feed from the forward optical array are getting smaller with every explosion as the missile hurtles along thousands of kilometers every time. Now we see the outline of the moon again, and the vague silhouette of the Lanky ship that is still plodding along on its orbital trajectory, leaving mine pods in its wake in a steady stream. The seed ship is now presenting us with a perfect side view, more obliging than any target drone in a missile exercise would be.

"One minute to intercept. Switching to terminal phase."

"God, I wish there was a way to put a camera into the nose of that warhead. Be nice to be able to watch it home in," the XO says.

I watch the counter next to the missile that's labeled "TIME TO TARGET," the rapidly decreasing life span of the Lanky ship.

I wonder if they're as aware of their own mortality as we are. We have faced them on the ground in attacks that have seemed suicidal in their execution, waves of Lankies throwing themselves at our defensive positions even as they had to crawl over the dead bodies of their own. If they have a sense of self-preservation at all, it's almost entirely subsumed by the survival of the group, like bees sacrificing themselves for the hive. I make a mental note to save that subject for a future discussion with Elin, who is doubtlessly far more knowledgeable on the subject than I am.

If I ever see her again, that is.

"Time to target, ten seconds," Captain Steadman announces. "Nine. Eight. Seven. Six . . ."

The numbers counting down next to the missile icon turn from white to red. The blue V and the orange lozenge icon on our tactical display are now almost overlapping and merge completely just before the counter reaches zero.

The visual of the Lanky ship washes out in a brilliant flare of nuclear fire that expands like a tiny star in front of the ice moon. It blooms into a sphere of terrible beauty, plasma heated to millions of degrees, so hot and energetic that the sensor feed gets overwhelmed in a blinding wash of white light again.

"*Splash one,*" Captain Steadman says with deep satisfaction. "That is a hard kill on Lima-1."

There isn't any of the usual cheering that follows a confirmed Lanky kill, just a grim sort of collective exhalation.

"Nice shooting," Colonel Drake says. "Get ready on tube seven and let's greet his buddy when he comes around the north pole."

"Estimated time to engagement is now four minutes and forty seconds," Captain Steadman says. "If he maintains course and speed."

"We're going to reach minimum launch distance for the Orions in thirteen minutes," Lieutenant Lawrence says.

"That's eight and a half minutes of cushion. It'll have to do. Let's hope he's not slowing down for sightseeing along the way."

"We can still launch inside the minimum," Steadman suggests. "It just may not be enough to crack the hull. But it'll rattle their cage, maybe score a mission kill."

Colonel Drake shakes his head.

"We have two Orions left. I want to save those for sure kills. We don't know what's going to happen on the way to that exit node. We may end up short just that one missile we would need to clear the way. If push comes to shove, we go in for CQB and use the particle mount."

"Aye, sir," Captain Steadman says.

Colonel Drake turns to Lieutenant Colonel Campbell and smiles curtly.

"There's your ace status, XO. Five and a half kills for six missiles expended. A clean sweep so far."

"I wish we had three times as many silos," she replies. "We could clean this place out. Imagine what we could do if we rolled in here with all six of the Mark I Avengers in a task force."

"That day may come, and it'll be a great time to be in the Corps." Colonel Drake flashes another one of his abbreviated smiles. "Unfortunately, it is not this day. Today, we hit and we run."

"Three minutes until projected engagement," Captain Steadman warns.

"All right. Let's prepare to receive number two so we can get our people and get the hell out of this place." Colonel Drake leans back and rubs his hand across the stubble on his chin. Nobody in the CIC looks like they've shaved or gotten more than a few hours of sleep in the last several days. It's not just the ship that's starting to run low on resources.

Once again, I watch a countdown on the tactical map that won't speed up no matter how much I try to will it along. The CIC usually has a dozen people in it, but it can feel like the loneliest place on the ship when everyone is alone with their own thoughts while we bridge the enormous distances and time spans involved in space combat. Even with all the hardships I have had to endure, I am glad that I switched to the podhead track when I did instead of spending my career behind a neural networks console and looking at screens all day long for years on end.

When the counter reads zero, it starts flashing.

"Projected engagement time is now," Captain Steadman says. "No visual yet."

"Keep your eyes peeled. You know how hard these things can be to spot," Colonel Drake says. "He'll pop up as soon as he starts the downward orbit. We should be able to get a juicy center-mass shot on his dorsal."

A minute passes, then another, without a new orange icon appearing on the tactical orb. The zeroes of the countdown are still flashing, like a mocking or a warning. The feeling of grim excitement that had welled up in me when we killed the first seed ship dissipates more as every second ticks away without our quarry materializing. *Washington* barrels on toward Blue, a quarter-million tons of warship in motion that can't be stopped or turned around without a stern-first deceleration, a massive energy expenditure that would also entail the temporary loss of all our defensive capabilities.

"Still no eyes on target," Steadman says. "They should be long out and over the pole."

"Why did you change your orbit?" Colonel Drake muses. "Did something tip you off? Or are you just spreading out your minefield coverage?"

"We're going to be at projected minimums for the Orion soon, sir."

"I'm aware of that. Stand by on the launch button, Lieutenant Lawrence."

"There's a lot of radiation noise from the nukes now, sir. He may have caught a whiff."

"If he was where the computer says he was, he couldn't have noticed. Not with a few thousand kilometers of rock and ice between him and the explosion," Lieutenant Colonel Campbell says. The XO is looking at the tactical display with a furrowed brow and slightly pursed lips, as if she's mildly irritated at the lack of cooperation from the other seed ship's willingness to aid in its own destruction.

"Steady as she goes," Colonel Drake orders. "If he's hiding behind the moon, we're going to lock him up when we swing around for our orbital insert. But we have some time left on the clock for the Orion."

The engagement cone in front of our ship's icon now extends well beyond the moon, and the narrow end marking the minimum effective range is creeping closer to it with every passing minute. I know the capabilities of this ship, but I still can't suppress the feeling that we're heading into an ambush somehow, something that will turn out to be too much for us to handle. I shake it off as a case of grunt jitters, professional paranoia, but the little voice in the back of my head refuses to be quieted all the way.

"Crossing beyond minimum engagement range now," Captain Steadman says from the tactical station a few minutes later.

"Up close and personal it is, then," Colonel Drake says. "Weapons, secure tube seven. Weapons hold on kinetic ordnance."

"Weapons hold on kinetic ordnance, aye," Lieutenant Lawrence acknowledges. "Closing silo door. Tube seven secured, sir."

"Helm, thread us in for orbital insertion. He'll pop up in front of us sooner or later. And if he decided to run, it won't break my heart."

The minutes tick by, and the sphere on the forward sensor view grows gradually to fill more and more of our field of view as we approach the moon. As dark as it is, it's the brightest thing in this system because of the ice that reflects the faint light from the distant stars, and it merely looks cold and lifeless instead of hostile and menacing like the Lanky moon. I remember my survey run with Sergeant Mills, firing seismic probes into the surface ice to check for Lanky presence underneath, and finding that this place is too rough and unwelcoming even for Lankies.

And yet we managed to get a foothold down there. *We really are the galaxy's cockroaches,* I think, recalling the last conversation I had with Elin, who is sitting in her office pod right now and doing her work while we make life-and-death decisions that could kill us all in a blink.

"Sensors are starting to cut through some of the radiation noise from the nukes now," Lieutenant Cole, the astrogator, says from his station on the other side of the command pit.

"New contact," Captain Steadman announces. "Lanky seed ship at three-oh-three by positive nine degrees, range eighteen thousand kilometers and coming around the bend in a hurry."

The orange icon that pops up on the display between the moon and our ship is coming in from the moon's horizon halfway between the pole and the equator, far from where we had expected it to appear.

"Sneaky little shit," Lieutenant Colonel Campbell says in a tone that almost sounds like grudging respect.

"Tell me that is Lima-2 and we're not about to get jumped by three more of those," Colonel Drake says.

"That is Lima-2, sir. Optical profile is a match. And the nearest inbound seed ship is seventy hours away."

Captain Steadman replies. "Aspect change on Lima-2. He's departing his orbit, now coming around to three-ten by positive six. Bogey is now on intercept heading with us, sir. Closing in at fifty kilometers per second."

"He really wants to close the distance," the XO says. "Wonder if word got around about the Orions."

"Let's save him some time and meet him halfway," Colonel Drake says. "Lieutenant Cole, bring the ship about to three-ten and match his approach angle. Bring the reactors to full power. We're going to take him head-on with the forward mount."

"What the hell is he planning to do?" I ask.

"Make a close pass and give us a broadside," Lieutenant Colonel Campbell says. "Or he's decided to take a page out of our Violence Through Applied Physics book and just ram us."

"We can't get into a dogfight with him because he can out-turn us. And we can only shoot straight ahead right now. He's doing us a favor by coming in for a head-on attack. Lieutenant Lawrence," Colonel Drake says.

"Yes, sir."

"I won't tell you 'no pressure.' We get two shots, so make them count. We won't have the time for another charge of those coils before he's on top of us."

"Aye, sir. My board is green. Reactor output is at one hundred percent. Mounts are energized."

"Weapons free."

"Weapons free, aye." Lieutenant Lawrence grasps the control stick for the particle mounts and flips the trigger from the safe to the live-fire position.

I watch the orange icon rapidly leave the moon's orbit and hurtle itself toward us like a million-ton homing missile. With our combined velocities, a head-to-head collision may even hurt the Lanky, but there's no doubt that it will obliterate *Washington* like a rock smashing a housefly.

"Lieutenant Cole, take over the helm. Once we get our shots off, hit the topside and starboard bow thrusters for maximum deflection. We want to clear the debris cloud we're about to make. But if it's not quite enough, we'll let the hard stuff hit the dorsal armor saddle."

"Aye, sir," Lieutenant Cole says.

"Thirty seconds to outer engagement range," Captain Steadman says. "He is really, really booking it, sir. Still accelerating, now at seventy kilometers per second."

The XO picks up the handset for the 1MC and toggles the transmit button.

"Now hear this: We are about to engage in CQB. All hands, prepare for possible debris impact."

I check my seat's safety harness. The nylon-weave straps will do nothing if we have a head-on collision with a seed ship, but it gives my hands something to do while I watch the orange and blue icons race toward each other on the plot, each intent on extinguishing the other.

"Ten seconds to outer engagement range," Captain Steadman says.

On the tactical orb, the narrow forward-facing cone originating at *Washington*'s icon creeps up to the orange seed ship icon. When the Lanky crosses into the cone, the tactical display chirps a brief alarm and flashes the outline of the cone.

"Target in range," Captain Steadman announces.

"Fire when ready, Lieutenant," Colonel Drake says.

"Target is locked. Firing Alpha."

He presses the trigger, but the lights in the CIC don't dim briefly, and the environmental controls don't change their pitch momentarily the way they usually do when the particle cannon monopolizes all the output from the reactors for the fraction of a second. The Lanky on the viewscreen is not disintegrating in a white-hot fireball, and the orange icon on the tactical orb keeps up its rush toward us.

"I have negative function on the Alpha mount, sir. Red light on the electrostatic lens assembly. Coil charge is dropping."

"Oh, god," Captain Steadman says.

"Switch to Beta mount. Don't rush that shot. You're fine," Colonel Drake says.

"Aye, sir. Switching to Beta."

He takes a deep breath and focuses on his firing controls again. Then he puts his hand on the stick in a careful, almost gentle motion, and I hold my breath as he presses the trigger.

The red battle lights flicker, and the humming from the air-conditioning system cuts out. There's a deep, resonant thrumming coming up from deep inside the ship's hull, the familiar sound of the particle accelerator pumping out a stream of hydrogen atoms at the speed of light.

The fireball on the optical sensor screen that takes up a quarter of the tactical orb makes the Orion detonation from earlier look like a mediocre fireworks show in comparison. The Lanky ship disappears in the middle of a white-hot new sun that expands rapidly and illuminates the surface of the nearby moon.

"Splash two," Captain Steadman says. His voice is much less controlled than it was when he announced the first Lanky kill earlier. "Hard kill on Lima-2."

This time, there's loud cheering in the CIC, and I join in. The tension and anxiety that have been squeezing my chest for the last few minutes dissipate so quickly that it feels like the rush of a drug high.

"Evasive action now," Colonel Drake orders. "On the thrusters, Lieutenant."

"Aye, sir." Lieutenant Cole works the controls of the helm station, and the immense mass of the carrier starts to slowly change its bearing and nudge itself away from the still-expanding fireball we're rapidly approaching.

"Good shooting," Colonel Drake says. "Cycle the Beta mount. And let's figure out what happened with Alpha. We need that gun. We've got no redundancy left with only one."

He looks around in the CIC.

"Good work, people. That was a nasty surprise. But it turned out a little nastier for them than for us."

He rubs his face with both hands, and I can hear the scraping of his beard stubble against his palms.

"Bring us back into an orbital insertion heading and give me a link to Blue Station, please."

"We're still line of sight to the station. Bringing up the link," Lieutenant Cole says. He continues to grin from the post-kill elation that swept the CIC. "You are go for optical link to Blue Station."

"Blue Station, *Washington* Actual. I am happy to report that we got rid of the unsavory elements in the neighborhood. We will be in orbit and sending down your pickup in two hours."

When the reply from Blue Station comes, there's cheering in the background.

"Washington, Blue Station. Affirmative. We are standing by and ready to leave. Thank you for that cleanup job. We're pretty relieved down here."

"So are we. It has been a good day so far. We will see you all in a few hours. *Washington* out."

Colonel Drake unbuckles his harness and slumps down in his chair a little with a soft groan.

"I feel like that just stripped a year off my life," he says. "Let's get into orbit and get our people off that clump of ice. And then we're getting out of here. We have a seventy-hour head start on the Lankies, and I don't want to waste a second of it."

The activity in the CIC picks up again, everyone returning to their tasks with renewed energy. I unbuckle my own harness and look over to Lieutenant Colonel Campbell, who is stretching her back.

"We may yet make it out of this alive," I say.

She turns her head to look at me and smiles wryly.

"I've learned to temper my hopes, Major," she says. "It cuts down on the disappointments. Right now, I am just satisfied that we probably won't die *today*."

CHAPTER 22

MIDDLE WATCH

I wake up in total darkness with my own scream echoing in my ears.

The terror that grips my chest and threatens to make my heart burst out of my rib cage is the strongest fear I've ever felt. It's debilitating in its totality and intensity, and it makes me sob in abject desperation.

My hand finds the little safety rail at the edge of my bunk, but even this anchor back to reality doesn't help at first. I sit up and put my other hand on my chest, and I am convinced something horrific is about to happen, some faceless danger that will leap out of the darkness and drag me back with it.

I fumble for the light switch sensor and slap it blindly in desperation. The light in my berth comes on, and I suck in air in deep breaths, trying to get my heartbeat under control. In my dream, I was underground again, in utter darkness, with walls closing in all around me and some unseen thing approaching. I know that I won't be going back to bed tonight, just like every night since I woke up in the med bay. Something dark and sinister has firmly embedded itself in my memories, something that bares its fangs and uncoils when I am asleep, and not even the sedatives I got from the ship's pharmacy can keep it at bay.

I swing my legs over the bed's safety rail and stand up. My knees are shaking, and I have to steady myself on the overhang of my bunk for a moment. When the jitters have finally passed, I walk over to the wet cell on unsteady feet to splash some water on my face. I dry off without looking in the mirror because I don't want to see that I look as awful as I feel. Now that the panic and fear of the nightmare are slowly fading from my brain, I feel drained and spent despite the sleep I got.

Of all the privileges that come with my rank, I've always enjoyed the private berth the most, and I usually find the tight quarters comforting and cozy, a small capsule of privacy. Now it suddenly feels confining and claustrophobic, and the bulkheads seem closer together than I remember them. It feels like a coffin instead of the safe cocoon it was before.

I get dressed and leave my berth. In the passageway outside, there is no foot traffic, and all I can hear is the hum of the environmental system. For a moment, I am somehow certain that I am the last living soul on this ship, that something strange and terrible has happened while I was asleep that erased all my shipmates and comrades from existence and left me behind as some sort of cosmic punishment. Then someone walks through the next intersection ahead and briefly glances my way before disappearing down the port-to-starboard passageway. I let out a slow breath as the feeling dissipates.

I don't really want to be among people right now, but I also don't want to be alone in my berth, not even with the lights on, so I just wander the decks for a while with no specific destination in mind.

The officers' gym at the front of the running-track loop is empty when I pass it, so I walk inside. Nobody is on the weight benches, and all the machines are dark and silent. I walk past the rows of computer-controlled treadmills and resistance-training equipment to the back of the gym, where the SIMAP ring and the punching bags are set up in their own little area.

When I walk in, someone is already here. Lieutenant Colonel Campbell is sitting with her back against the rear bulkhead. She's in her uniform, not her workout clothes, the first time I've seen her in here without boxing attire or wrapped hands.

"Sorry," I say. "Didn't know you were in here."

"Don't worry about it," she says in a tired drawl. Her forearms are resting on her knees, and her right hand is idly dangling a steel flask in front of her leg. "Didn't think I'd see a soul all night. Nobody's burning extra calories on exercise anymore."

"Even if I had the calories to spare, I think my boxing days are over," I say. "Flight surgeon says I need to avoid blows to the head if I want to keep being able to count past ten with my shoes on."

She nods at the floor next to her.

"Have a seat while you're here. Help me finish off this flask."

I sit down with a little groan and look at the flask she is holding. It has a ship's crest on it but I can't see the name or hull number that's engraved on the polished stainless steel.

"What is this?" I ask.

"It's bourbon," she replies. "Almost certainly the last bit of it on this ship. I've been carrying that flask around for the last eight years. Figured now's a good time to drink it. I'll be damned if I'm going to waste it by letting it get turned to plasma with the rest of the ship."

"You're the XO," I say. "You're not supposed to be negative. You're supposed to keep up crew morale."

"I'm off duty. I'm allowed my own private pessimism."

She takes a sip from the flask and hands it to me. I take it and turn it in my hand so I can see the engraving: **NACS SARNIA FF-308**.

"That was my father's first command," Sophie Campbell says. "Shitty little frigate, even older than that Treaty-class frigate he served on with you."

"*Versailles*," I say, and she nods.

"That's the one. *Sarnia* was a downgrade from that. But he was in the big chair. God, he loved that piece of junk. They say your first command is always your favorite. No matter how great and shiny the next one is."

"You're almost there," I say. "You'll get your own piece of junk after this."

She huffs a little laugh.

"You think there'll be an 'after this'? We're going to try and hitch a piggyback ride on a seed ship. The odds are really not in our favor on this one."

"Math isn't everything," I say, repeating what Elin Vandenberg told me in the science lab earlier. "Fuck the odds."

I sniff the mouth of the flask. The smell is strong and biting, but not unpleasant. I take a small sip and let it wash around on my tongue. It's like nothing I've ever tasted before, malty and rich, hints of flavor my PRC-raised palate can't identify. When I swallow the sip, it lightly burns my throat and warms my esophagus as it goes down.

"That's not synthetic," I say.

The XO shakes her head.

"Hell, no. That's barrel-aged Kentucky bourbon. A hundred years old. That stuff was distilled before there was an NAC."

"Damn." I savor the aftertaste.

"My mother went all in and bought a bottle for him when he got that first command star. Took him seven or eight years to drink it. One little glass of bourbon, two fingers, after each deployment. The last bit he put into that flask. Kept it on the shelf at home. To be enjoyed when he retired."

I hold the flask out for her to take back, suddenly very mindful of the value of the item and its contents.

"Have some more," she says. "He wouldn't mind. You served with him, after all."

I take another sip and hand it back to her to forestall the temptation of taking a third. She takes it and sips from it again.

"I got it off the shelf after he died, before some asshole relative could claim it and chug it like it's engineering moonshine. It has been with me on every deployment after that. Against the regs, but nobody ever gave me any shit about it. They all knew the story. The big hero of the Battle of Earth. This thing is practically a religious relic. Like the finger bone of some saint."

She shakes the flask lightly and sloshes the rest of the bourbon around.

"You know how I know that I am not a good person? If it had been up to me, I wouldn't have traded him for the rest of humanity that day. I'd rather we had all died together than to go on without him for the rest of my life. Not very altruistic of me, is it?"

"We're all broken," I say. "Every fucking one of us. No matter how much someone looks like they have their shit together. Took me a long time to learn that everyone is fucked up in their own way, no exceptions."

"Your father bail on you, too?"

I shake my head.

"Nah, my mom bailed on him. Left him when I was fourteen. He was a mean, violent asshole. Drank himself to death and died of cancer right after I shipped out to Basic. Never saw him again. Never even thought about him until my mother told me he'd died. I didn't feel a thing when I read that. Turns out that the opposite of love isn't hate. It's not giving a shit."

She chuckles and takes another sip from her flask.

"Major, I swear to you that if you tell anyone about our little therapy session down here, I am going to give you the beatdown of your life."

"That wouldn't be hard to do right now," I say. "You could probably kill me with a stale loaf of bread to the side of the skull."

We sit in silence for a little while, passing the flask back and forth. I try to gauge the dwindling supply of priceless bourbon to make sure I won't be the one taking the last sip from the flask. At one point, the motion-controlled light in the room turns off, and I quickly turn it on again with a wave of my hand.

"I like that you still have optimism," she says. "I've lost all of mine years ago. You really do think we might make it, don't you?"

"There's an antique M17 service pistol with three loaded magazines in my personal locker in my berth," I say. "It's against the regs so don't tell the XO. If I didn't think there was even the slightest chance we may pull this off and I will get to see my wife again, I would have splattered my brains all over the bulkhead already."

Lieutenant Colonel Campbell shakes her head with the first broad grin I've ever seen on her face.

"Goddammit, Grayson. You really are still a junior NCO at heart."

She upends the flask to let the rest of the contents trickle into her mouth and screws it shut with an air of finality.

"I guess I still have some hope left after all," she says. "Because I am not even a little tempted to borrow that gun."

Overhead, the 1MC announcement tone sounds.

"All hands, this is the CO. Mess call, mess call," Colonel Drake's voice says. *"The mess will stay open for the next twelve hours, with no calorie restrictions. Announcement ends."*

Lieutenant Colonel Campbell and I look at each other in surprise.

"How about that," I say. "Guess the skipper doesn't want to let the good stuff go to waste, either."

The XO tucks her flask away and gets to her feet.

"Come on, Major. Let's go and see what's on the menu. Might as well go out with a full stomach."

I accept the hand she holds out and let her pull me up.

"But if it's that chipped-beef-on-toast garbage, I may ask to borrow that pistol of yours after all," she says as we walk out of the boxing nook of the gym. "I loathe that stuff. No way in hell will I have shit on a shingle for my last meal."

CHAPTER 23

HAIL MARY PASS

"It seems like a waste to leave all that hardware behind," Lieutenant Rogers says. I've just come up to CIC to relieve him for the next watch, and he is gathering his coffee mug and resetting the console. "That's a thousand Wonderballs out there."

"They were never meant to be reusable, anyway," Lieutenant Colonel Campbell says from her station. She has a coffee mug in her hand as well. The scent of coffee has been absent from the CIC for so long that it's a little strange to walk in here and smell it again. The kitchen has released much of the remaining fresh food stores to put the crew back on full calories, and while it feels a little like the last meal of a death-row inmate, nobody on the ship has turned down the opportunity to catch up on some enjoyments.

"But they're still there," she continues and nods at the tactical orb. "If we ever get back there, we'll already have a surveillance system to tap into. Those internal batteries are supposed to last ten years."

We are far outside the coverage range of the Wonderball sphere now, tens of millions of kilometers from the rogue planet and its satellites, coasting through deep space on the way back to the spot where the Lankies pulled us with them into this system. Tens of thousands of kilometers in front of us, two Lanky seed ships are on the same heading, with a gap of ninety minutes between them. We locked onto them when they passed the outer edge of the Wonderball network, and *Washington*'s entire Battlespace Control squadron of surveillance and command ships have been flying continuous racetrack pattern patrols in front and behind the carrier to make sure we don't lose sight of the Lankies as they move away from our optical trip-wire network.

If we ever get back here, I hope I'm not along for that ride, I think. *Not even if it's an all-out assault with every warship in all the fleets of Earth.*

"You're relieved, Lieutenant," I tell Rogers as he gets up and clears the station for me. "Go get some chow and rack time."

"I stand relieved," Lieutenant Rogers replies. "Hope there's something left in the wardroom other than baloney sandwiches."

"There's plenty left. They've been putting out hot meals all watch long."

I watch him make a beeline to the officer's wardroom from the CIC. He's a freshly minted officer, on his first deployment after graduating from Combat Controller School and receiving his commission, and he's in charge of Fourth Squad, which is always led by the most junior officer backed up by the most experienced NCO. As far as first deployments go, this has been a grindingly difficult one. Yet all the new lieutenants and junior NCOs have done their jobs in exemplary fashion despite knowing how high the odds are stacked against us.

The new kids are all right. Maybe there's hope for the future yet. It's weird to think of Lieutenant Rogers as a kid because I only have thirteen years on him. But many of those thirteen years were rough ones, a relentless stream of deployments and battles and dead friends. Now it feels like I've done this for half a century and not just since Rogers was in elementary school.

I log into the combat controller station and set up my screens. My headache has been constant since I got back to the ship, but the meds keep it down to an unpleasant background nuisance, and coming up

223

here to give my brain something to do makes it easier to ignore the aches and pains I still feel all over the right side of my body. Captain Harper is in nominal charge of the STT right now. While I could overrule his decisions, I didn't get any argument from him when I put myself on the roster for manning the watch in CIC, and I suspect he's glad to be running his own show and not have to deal with me.

———————

Lima-8 and Lima-9, the seed ships we are tailing as close as we dare to get, are steadily crawling along the dotted line of their computer-projected course toward the spot on the tactical map where we transitioned into the system a few weeks ago. It's marked with the symbol for an NAC Alcubierre node even though it's not part of any network known to our ship's computer. Nobody ever thought of programming a tactical icon to represent a Lanky node because nobody knew such a thing existed until a few weeks ago.

"Wonder what would happen if we just turned on our own drive and tried to go through their node alone," Lieutenant Cole says.

"Probably nothing," Lieutenant Lawrence replies.

"Or maybe we'll just get pulled apart into our component molecules," Lieutenant Colonel Campbell says. "Or get swept another thousand light-years deeper into the galaxy. We have no idea how they do it. All we know is that their stuff is much more efficient than ours. It's like we're dropping our canoes into a lazy little brook. And they drop theirs in a raging river and shoot the rapids."

"And their river can reverse flow and take the canoes the other way, too," I say.

"At least we hope so," Colonel Drake says. "Because if these two are just heading out there to pick up some visiting relatives from the inbound transit station, we're kind of screwed."

I look at the tactical orb, which just barely shows the rogue planet and the cluster of moons in its orbit at this point. Since we left for the node, the number of orange icons tallied by the Wonderballs in the inner system has at least doubled, and each moon has multiple seed ships in orbit now. There's no ground to go to anymore, no rocks to hide behind. If this isn't the way out after all, there's nothing left for us to do but run until we exhaust our supplies or stand and fight until we go out in a blaze of defiance.

"Lima-9's time to target for the transition point is now three hours, eleven minutes," Captain Steadman says. "Lima-8 is ninety minutes behind."

"Time to get the birds back to the barn," Colonel Drake says. "Tell BCS-55 to release their recon drones and head back to the ship."

"Aye, sir." Steadman turns toward his comms screen and opens an optical link. "*Washington* to all battlespace control units. Release the payload and return to the ship. I repeat, launch drones and come on home."

On the tactical display, the command-and-control ships launch the reconnaissance drones they've been carrying on their underwing pylons. Then the ships break out of their racetrack patterns one by one and start their return trips to the carrier. The drones are now our advance eyes and ears, and while their sensors are less powerful than those on the battlespace control craft, we can afford to leave them behind if we manage to transition out of this system behind the Lanky ship.

"Drones away. Advance screen units are on the way back to the deck. Twenty-five minutes to retrieval."

"Very well," Colonel Drake acknowledges. "Lieutenant Cole, make very sure you have all your decimal points in the right place for that acceleration burn. If Lima-9 goes through and verifies it really is a two-way door for them, we have ninety minutes to catch up to Lima-8."

"Ninety minutes, thirteen seconds, sir. We're calculating trajectory updates every fifty milliseconds," Lieutenant Cole replies. "We'll be within five hundred meters of Lima-8 when he transitions, and just a little above him. Same conditions we had on the ride in."

"If he doesn't notice us coasting in behind him," the XO says.

"Let's hope their ships have blind spots in their wakes just like ours do," Colonel Drake replies. "Once we finish the burn and we're coasting ballistic, I want this ship on maximum EMCON. We're shutting down all nonessential systems. I don't even want anyone to chew loudly."

He looks at the tactical plot and scratches the back of his head as he contemplates the information on the display. The battlespace control squadron is now well on its way back to the ship. The drones are forging ahead, spreading out on their computer-controlled course to maximize sensor coverage.

"This is like that old game where you throw a horseshoe at a peg," he says. "Only we're throwing that horseshoe ninety thousand kilometers, and we have to hit the peg at just the right second for the score to count."

"Sneaking up on a Lanky ship, on purpose," Lieutenant Colonel Campbell says. "That's another first I gladly could have done without."

I know I ought to spend what could be the last few hours of my life differently. I should be down in my berth, looking at pictures of Halley or taking enough meds to sleep through the end of my world. It would be easier not to have a warning when it happens, instead of sitting in a place where I can see death approaching with a precise counter. When I was doing pod drops, I used to do just that. I used to turn off my heads-up display and the sensor feed whenever my pod passed through a Lanky minefield because I wanted to stay ignorant of how close I was getting to the mines. But once I became a platoon and then a company leader, I lost that luxury because I always needed to be aware of the big picture for my troopers. Now I find that I prefer the awareness, even if it only gives me the illusion of agency. So I remain in my seat in the CIC, watching the situational display, sipping coffee, listening to the low-key banter between the people around me, and savoring all the sights and sounds and sensations consciously, even the headache that hasn't left me in days. And when the moment draws near the point of no return, I find that I want this chase to go on for just a little while longer.

"Lima-9 is now five minutes from the calculated transition point," Captain Steadman reports. "Bearing, heading, and speed all unchanged."

"All right," Colonel Drake says and sits up straight in his command chair. "Let's get ready for the main event. Go to combat stations."

The XO picks up the 1MC handset, and the all-hands announcement tone sounds.

"General quarters, general quarters. All hands, man your combat stations. Set material condition Zebra throughout the ship. This is not a drill."

I buckle into my safety harness and put on my helmet. It's a pre-battle ritual that my hands have performed countless times on autopilot, but now I do every movement with slow, conscious deliberation. The helmet liner is tight enough to secure a solid fit that doesn't allow for the skull to bounce around inside, and the pressure on the injured side of my head makes the pain flare up sharply. I sit back and take a few slow, controlled breaths until the pain disappears into the general background of discomfort I've lived with since I got out of my med pod.

"The board is green, sir. All departments report ready for action," Lieutenant Colonel Campbell says.

On the tactical display, the orange icon labeled "LIMA-9" is moving toward the transit node's larger ellipse-shaped symbol in tiny stuttering steps, one display refresh per second. The ellipse icon is pale in color and surrounded by a very small lozenge-shaped outline representing the uncertainty zone. With every refresh of the display, the Lanky creeps closer to the blue outline of the node, one tiny blip of movement at a time.

"Helm, stand by on engines. Prepare for acceleration burn," Colonel Drake says.

I usually find myself trying to will the numbers on the tactical display to tick by faster, but right now I want to slow them down, delay the point at which we hurl ourselves into our intercept trajectory and lock us into the maneuver. But just as I never had the power to make things happen faster, I can't hold back the flow of time, either. The numbers next to the Lanky icon count down the time to target with a merciless precision to the millisecond. When the counter is down to one minute, Captain Steadman calls out the remaining range in ten-second intervals.

Fifty. Forty. Thirty. Twenty.

I take a deep breath and let it out gradually, trying to slow the heartbeat that is pounding in my ears underneath the helmet.

"Ten seconds," Captain Steadman says.

"Open sesame," the XO says under her breath.

When the counter reaches four, the Lanky icon disappears from the tactical map in a blink. I hold my breath for two or three refresh cycles of the holographic display, but the seed ship does not materialize on the plot again.

"Lima-9 is off the sensors. Passive EM sensors just spiked with a transition signature. Lima-9 has left the system," Captain Steadman says. He looks up from his screen with a grin. "It is a two-way door."

"Execute intercept burn for Lima-8," Colonel Drake orders.

"Executing intercept burn, aye," Lieutenant Cole replies. "Recalculated trajectory is laid in. All ahead flank."

A low vibration goes through the ship's hull as the eight massive engines on the stern go to their maximum power output. Even with the artificial gravity compensating for the acceleration within a few milliseconds, it still feels like someone gave us a giant shove from behind.

"The computer was off by only eighty kilometers," Captain Steadman says.

"Not bad at all," Colonel Drake says. "Now let's make sure we hit that bull's-eye."

"So we found the exit," Lieutenant Colonel Campbell says. "Gonna have to buy the astronomers a bottle of the good stuff. That was one hell of a hunch."

"Lima-8 is now ninety minutes, forty-five seconds from the updated transition point," Captain Steadman says. "Time to intercept is ninety minutes, thirty-nine seconds." The grin has faded from his face, and he is all focus again. There are no expressions of levity in the CIC like when we finally killed the second Lanky ship above Blue Station. Finding the door was only the start, and now we are committed to the far more dangerous second part of the equation.

The time readout on the tactical display changes to a new clock, this one showing the countdown for our intercept. A little more than a minute later, the vibration of the hull fades away into the background hum of the ship.

"Acceleration burn complete. Time to target now eighty minutes, ten seconds," Lieutenant Cole says.

"Lima-8 is now CBDR, sir," Captain Steadman says. "Trundling into the transit node slow and steady. Looks like he didn't notice the IR flare we just lit."

"That is fine by me, Captain," the CO says.

The distance between the blue and the orange icon in the center of the tactical display shrinks gradually. But the seed ship doesn't change course or alter its speed even as we catch up to within fifty thousand, then forty thousand kilometers of him.

"Get a visual up on Tactical," Colonel Drake orders.

A moment later, Captain Steadman opens a new window on the situational orb. The Lanky is an irregular dark shadow on the image from the optical lenses. We're directly behind him, so we have a perfect stern view of the seed ship that gets a little sharper and more distinct the closer we get. The cross section is roughly circular, with the top and bottom very slightly flattened and the sides bulging just a little. There's no visible plume from a propulsion system that could obscure our view of the Lanky's stern.

For the next few minutes, I watch as the Lanky ship grows larger on the display and the camera keeps readjusting its magnification. The seed ship's stern comes to a blunt end, and the slope of it reminds me strongly of the shape of the thing we saw in the Lanky burrow, the proto-ship or pod that was sitting in a slowly encroaching bed of mycelium strands. The ship in front of us has the same cigar shape, the same not-quite-round cross section, as any seed ship we've ever spotted, and the thing in the gulch deep under the surface was merely a smaller version, almost identical to the ship in front of us in every metric but size and weight.

What if they don't build them at all? What if that thing in the mycelium just wasn't done growing yet?

It's a deeply unsettling thought, and I try to push it away as I watch us draw closer to the Lanky with every passing minute, but now the idea has taken hold, and I know I'll never be able to look at one of these ships again without imagining that it started deep underground as a smaller nucleus, growing to its final size in years or maybe decades, nurtured by the fungi all around it and the protein the Lankies collect and provide. It's a bunch of new puzzle pieces that click perfectly into some of the empty spots of my knowledge. I wish I could rush down to the science lab and hear Elin Vandenberg's thoughts, but we're a few minutes away from the transit point now, and I'll either have time once we are through on the other side, or none of this will matter anymore.

"Crossing inside five thousand kilometers now," Captain Steadman says.

"Steady as she goes," Colonel Drake replies. "Ninety seconds to intercept and transition."

"Such a nice, fat target," Lieutenant Lawrence says. The weapons officer has his hands resting on the console in front of him next to the firing controls for the particle-gun mounts, which have their safety levers firmly in place over the triggers again. "A perfect stern shot, right down the center axis."

"You'll get your chance, Lieutenant. Once he gets us through the door with his hall pass, he's all yours," the XO says.

On maximum magnification, the Lanky's stern fills out the entire sensor window on the tactical display now. We're close enough that I can see the little ridges and bumps on the hull, the surface patterns that are slightly different from seed ship to seed ship. The size of it is awe-inspiring, even from this angle. It feels like we're a minnow chasing after a shark.

"Sixty seconds," Captain Steadman says.

On the tactical display, one of the numbers next to the orange icon flashes red, and a short, unpleasant alert sounds in sync with the pulse.

"*Lima-8 is decelerating,*" Steadman shouts. I didn't think my adrenaline levels could go any higher, but I feel a new spike jolting my system.

"He's dropped to two kilometers per second. Now one point five. We're going to overshoot him," Lieutenant Cole says.

"If we're lucky and he doesn't make us rear-end him," Colonel Drake says.

"Fifty seconds to transition point. Twenty-five seconds to intercept. Now twenty," Captain Steadman says, his voice just short of a shout now. "Incoming ordnance. He's launching kinetics."

On the visual feed, something fast and indistinct leaves the stern of the ship and rushes toward the optical lens, streaking out of focus and beyond the sensor frame in the fraction of a second. I seize the armrests of my chair, and my still-recovering right arm sends a jolt of pain up into my shoulder.

"All hands, brace for impact," the XO shouts into the 1MC.

The small cloud of penetrators from the seed ship's stern streaks toward us at thousands of meters per second. The passive sensors do their best to spot them, but there are too many and they're moving too fast for the computer to predict any trajectories. In any case, there isn't enough time to do anything about it. We can't dodge what's being thrown into our path, and we can't knock it out of space, either.

A few seconds later, the impacts of the Lanky rods on the bow armor reverberate through the entire ship, ringing like hammer blows on a metal roof. Then, as quickly as the hail of kinetic penetrators began, it stops even as the ship shudders with the energy it just absorbed. Over on the damage control panel next to the XO, red text starts popping up.

"Ten seconds to intercept. He's going to pass below us with less than a hundred meters' clearance," Steadman calls out.

I know that we're hurtling toward the Lanky, not the other way around, because we have a speed advantage and he merely put on the brakes. But looking at the rapidly closing stern coming toward us on the optical feed, it looks like he's the one rushing toward us.

"Five seconds. Now eighty meters projected clearance."

"Come on . . . ," Colonel Drake says through gritted teeth.

"Three. Two. One."

I close my eyes and conjure up the picture of Halley.

Our ships seemingly pass each other in opposite directions as we overshoot the Lanky. At our speed difference, we are past the seed ship in the fraction of a second, but in that moment, the ship rocks again with the impact of more kinetic darts, and all the alert sounds in the CIC seem to go off at once.

"Multiple hull breaches on the ventral armor," Lieutenant Colonel Campbell shouts. "We've got compartments open to space from bow to stern."

"That was a well-timed broadside," Colonel Drake says with something like grudging respect in his voice. "Gave us a parting gift on the way by, right where our armor is thinnest."

"Twenty seconds to transition point. What are your orders, sir?" Captain Steadman asks.

"Steady as she goes. Get me a fix on that Lanky," Colonel Drake replies.

"Lima-8 is now at one hundred eighty by negative one, eight hundred klicks. He is accelerating again. Closing the gap," Steadman says and shifts his gaze from the tactical console to the CO.

"Coming back to finish the job," the XO says.

"Fifteen seconds to transition point. Lima-8 is accelerating hard. Intercept in twenty seconds."

"Power up the Alcubierre drive," Colonel Drake says.

"We can't make that trip with our gear, sir," Lieutenant Cole says.

"Just power it up, Lieutenant. Don't activate it. We have no numbers to feed it anyway. But he'll notice the EM spike. Maybe he'll follow suit."

"Ten seconds to transition point. Twelve seconds to intercept. He's gaining on us hard," Captain Steadman calls out.

"Do it *now*," Colonel Drake says, in a voice that's the closest I've ever heard him come to a shout.

"Aye, sir. Energizing Alcubierre drive," Lieutenant Cole replies. His fingers dance across the control panel in front of him. "Drive is charging up."

"Five seconds to transit point. Seven seconds to intercept. He's closing in for a ram."

Behind us, the Lanky comes rushing out of the dark, its bullet-shaped bow aimed right at the back of our ship. I want to look away but the sight is mesmerizing, one of the monsters from my nightmares about to swallow us whole. It closes inexorably with every second, until it takes up the entire field of view of the rear sensor lens array with just the upper half of its bow.

Ready on Alcubierre, Lieutenant Cole shouts.

The vibration that shakes the ship feels like some giant pair of hands has grabbed both ends and is now twisting them in opposite directions. All the consoles in CIC shut off in a blink, and the tactical orb disappears as the holotable goes dark as well. The sensation that follows is one I've experienced many times, but this is the first time I've welcomed it. A familiar electric sour taste settles on my tongue, and I know even without looking at Lieutenant Cole's station that we are in Alcubierre again.

For a few moments, all I can hear is heavy breathing all over the CIC as we are all processing the last fifteen seconds in our own ways.

"Restart the CIC systems," Colonel Drake finally says. "Get me a navigation fix and a damage report as soon as everything is back up."

"Well," Lieutenant Colonel Campbell says. "That was a bit of a nail-biter, wasn't it?"

I have a sudden onset of nausea that makes me feel like I must puke, but I can't stifle a grin at the XO's nonchalant understatement.

"We're through the door," Captain Steadman says with a tinge of disbelief.

"It looks like his hall pass worked," Colonel Pace agrees. "But it certainly didn't go as planned. Let's see what the sensors say. If we have any left that are working."

The CIC systems come back on one by one. When the XO turns her damage control screen toward her seat, most of the data fields on it are blinking yellow or red.

"Front and aft sensor arrays are offline," Lieutenant Cole says. "Astrogation computer has no reference points for a navigation fix. I can't be entirely sure until the sensor arrays are back on the network. But all signs point to the fact that we are in Alcubierre."

"That and the fact that we're not splashed across the bow of that seed ship right now," Lieutenant Colonel Campbell says. She thumbs through the alerts on her screen.

"We took a real beating. The bow armor deflected most of the stuff from the front. That's a steep armor angle for penetrations. Our underside is a different story."

She brings up a ship diagram on the tactical orb that has restored itself above the holotable. The ventral side of our hull is peppered with blinking red dots, and entire sections in the stern of the ship are red as well.

"He gave us a nice, juicy broadside when he passed us. Of course, he had to go under instead of above, or the dorsal armor saddle would have caught most of it. As it is, we have nineteen compartments open to space. Also at least half a dozen penetrations in the hangar bay. All the ventral engine pods are holed, so we have four working engines left. And we're down to six reactors. Number four and seven went into emergency shutdown."

"Damn." Colonel Drake leans back in his chair. He looks like he's aged another five years in the last half hour. "That was an expensive passing maneuver."

I look at the diagram to find the area of the ship where the STT is quartered. We are near the hangars so we can be ready quickly for missions without having to traverse half the ship. The STT section is forward of the hangar bay, and most of the impact damage is concentrated in the aft section and the hangar itself. But once those Lanky penetrators punch their way through a ship's armor, they can go through a lot of interior compartments with the energy they have left, and there's no telling how much ancillary damage the ship has suffered.

"All that damage in less than a second," Colonel Drake muses. "A single close-range broadside to our belly, and this ship is combat ineffective. This is what CQB with a seed ship looks like. If any of you ever get your own command, try to keep this day in your memory. For when you're tempted to let yourself get into a knife fight with a Lanky."

"Forward sensor array is back online, sir," Lieutenant Cole says.

"Optical feed, on the forward bulkhead, if you would."

"Aye, sir." Lieutenant Cole opens a new screen on the bulkhead as ordered to show the view from the front of the ship. We're in the Alcubierre stream, red and purple streaks and flares, flowing past us like a raging river.

"We're in an Alcubierre bubble," Lieutenant Cole says. "And it's not ours because our drive powered down as soon as we entered."

The junior officers let out cheers, and Captain Steadman pumps his fist and high-fives Lieutenant Cole, whose station is closest to him. Even Lieutenant Colonel Campbell raises both fists and shakes them at the tactical display in triumph.

"It was a long shot," Colonel Drake says. "These things seem to run on instinct, from what we can tell. So . . . I figured we could make him chase us through if he thought we were getting away. Like a dog chasing a deer. Or maybe it was just a sympathetic response. Doesn't matter. It seems it worked, because this is Alcubierre. But I think we may have just postponed the inevitable a little bit."

"The question is, where are we going this time?" the XO says.

Colonel Drake looks at the tactical display. It's empty except for the blue icon with the label "CVB-63 WASHINGTON" in the center.

"Hopefully, back to the Capella system, Willoughby space. How long were we in Alcubierre when we got dragged in with the first one?"

"Thirty-three minutes and fifteen seconds, sir," Lieutenant Cole replies.

"Subtract the time that's elapsed since we started this run. Then put a shot clock on the bulkhead."

"Aye, sir," Cole says. A few moments later, a counter appears on the forward bulkhead—00:28:29—counting down to zero.

"Let's assume that this is all the time we have before we pop out on the other end of this particular two-way chute," Colonel Drake says. "How far away was the Lanky before we transitioned?"

"He was almost on top of us," Captain Steadman says. He scrubs back through the tactical data from the situation display. "Six point three seconds to impact, coming in from one eighty to negative two."

The CO points at the shot clock on the bulkhead.

"When that counter goes to zero and the Alcubierre bubble collapses, we will have a seed ship right on our stern, and he's going to rear-end us a little over six seconds later. Even if we had all our engines working, and we went all ahead flank the second we come out of the node, it wouldn't be enough to make up the speed advantage he has over us."

I look at the ship's diagram on the tactical screen. Four of the eight engines are blinking red. The four that are still working are the dorsal ones on the top of the stern.

"Can we turn out of his way with what's left?" I ask.

Colonel Drake and the XO turn around and look at me as though they had forgotten that I was still sitting behind them in the CIC, making me keenly aware that I am talking out of turn in an area that is not my field of expertise.

"No," Lieutenant Colonel Campbell says. "This ship is a quarter-million tons of mass, Major. That's a lot of inertia to overcome in two seconds."

"We're not going to get out of his way. The bow thrusters don't have the pop to get us more than half a degree of rotation per second. There's just no scenario where we can work up enough thrust to match or exceed his speed. Or turn out of his path," Captain Steadman says.

"We can at least turn some," Lieutenant Cole says. He gets out of his chair and walks over to the holotable, where he starts marking the ship diagram with a light pen.

"We lost half our thrust, so we can't out-accelerate him," he says. "Not with the speed advantage he has. But the dorsal engines still work.

We can go asymmetric on the thrust and go full power on the two starboard ones. We'll start yawing around our center of mass."

He marks the axis that goes through the middle of the ship between its dorsal and ventral sides.

"Best we can do is make the physics work for us as much as possible, right?" he says.

Lieutenant Commander Campbell nods when she catches on. "Kick that yaw into high burn. Not bad, Lieutenant."

"We still won't get out of the way in time," Captain Steadman cautions.

"No, but we may get a glancing hit instead of a full rear-ending," Colonel Drake says. "He'll wreck our stern, probably. But if he rams us directly from behind, he'll split us lengthwise like a rotten log."

"We burn the two starboard engines the moment we drop out of Alcubierre," Lieutenant Cole continues. "That turns us to port and moves us ahead a little. And we use the starboard bow thrusters to help with the rotation."

"We've had power grid overload and momentary shutdown the last time we dropped out of the transition with the Lanky. If that happens again, we'll need to restart everything from scratch," the XO says. "We won't have engine control. Or reactor power."

Colonel Drake ponders her statement for a moment.

"That's true. We won't have time to wait for a reactor restart."

He looks at the schematic of the ship that's still on the tactical screen.

"We decouple the two remaining engine pods from the main power grid and isolate them on their own network with the reactors. Switch the rest of the ship to emergency backup power. No sense in waiting for it to kick in after the transition," he says.

"You want to run the *entire ship* on tertiary backup power?" Lieutenant Colonel Campbell asks.

"Just for a few minutes. Once we make our evasive burn, we'll switch back to the reactors."

Colonel Drake looks at the shot clock on the bulkhead, which has ticked down to 00:25:49.

"This plan still involves us getting hit in the ass by a million tons of seed ship," he says. "I am not crazy about it. But we're short on options and time. I say we go ahead with it and hope our dumb luck holds today."

CHAPTER 24

—— TECHNICAL KNOCKOUT ——

"All personnel present and accounted for," Captain Harper says from the STT compartment, via my comms link. *"Just a few bruises and cuts from getting bumped around. But we can hear the decompression alarms going off over by the flight deck."*

"We got shotgunned by that seed ship from nose to stern," I reply. "Finish patching up anyone who needs it and make sure everyone's strapped in. Things may get very bumpy in a hurry."

"Affirmative. Good luck up there, Major. We will hang tight and ride it out."

"See you on the other side, Captain."

I terminate the link and say a silent prayer of thanks to whatever gods are taking calls right now that my team has suffered no casualties from the Lanky broadside. The damage reports are still rolling in at Lieutenant Colonel Campbell's station, department after department calling in casualty numbers and system malfunctions. Everyone on the ship is in a vacsuit and connected to an independent oxygen supply, so the breached compartments losing air won't directly kill anyone whose suit hasn't malfunctioned somehow. But the Lanky penetrator quills are almost a meter in diameter, and whenever they intersect with a human body at high speed, they leave nothing but a cloud of fine organic mist behind. Our casualties are in the dozens and climbing with every new report. I feel a little guilty for my gratitude that none of my people are among that number, but I remind myself that the STT has bled plenty already.

"Attention, all hands," the XO says on the 1MC. "All personnel to the aft of frame 350 are ordered to move forward and upward to the exercise track immediately for emergency overflow seating. Set your stations to automated control and seal and secure all compartments. Repeat, all personnel aft of frame 350 will move to the track immediately. Seal and secure all breached compartments. Announcement ends."

She puts the handset back into the console and gives me a grim look. "If there's anything left to fix in fifteen minutes, we'll get to it then."

The elation I felt earlier when it was clear we were in Alcubierre has disappeared entirely. I have no education in warship design, and while I know that the Avengers are the toughest ships we've ever put in space, I have no idea whether we can take the hit we're about to receive without disintegrating under the blow. From the looks the rest of the CIC crew exchange now and then, I can tell that they don't know for sure, either.

"Lieutenant Cole," Colonel Drake calls out.

"Yes, sir," Cole replies.

"Bring the remaining online reactors to full power. When that counter on the bulkhead over there reads ten seconds, start throttling up the two starboard dorsal engines. When we drop out of Alcubierre, you will initiate a full burn and maximum starboard bow thrusters. Understood?"

"Aye, sir. Throttle up in time to initiate full burn at shot clock zero, maximum bow thrusters," Cole repeats.

"Very well," Colonel Drake says.

I watch the seconds count down on the shot clock.

Another countdown to my possible death, I think. *How many of those can someone endure without losing their mind?*

———————

"We've emptied out the stern section," the XO says to Colonel Drake ten minutes later. "Track reports all personnel secured and strapped in. Bulkhead doors are sealed, compartment is ready for action."

"Well done," Colonel Drake replies. "I guess we are as ready as we're going to get."

I look at the ship diagram, where the kilometer-long racetrack is now divided into fifty compartments by airtight bulkhead doors, each with its own air supply and emergency power. Four years ago, I was on another Avenger when we evacuated the colony of New Svalbard under Lanky attack, and the racetrack served as temporary berthing for two thousand colonists on the trip back to Earth. It's not the most comfortable space, especially when it's crowded, but it's the safest area on the ship other than the CIC because it's next to the armored silos for the nukes, and right underneath the thick dorsal armor saddle.

"Four minutes, thirty seconds to projected transition," Captain Steadman announces.

We watch the numbers on the counter tick down in silence. All around us, the hull pops and creaks with the stress of the transition in ways I've never heard on our self-powered trips through our own network. Even the unpleasant sensations are different this time, more intense and disconcerting. My teeth, which usually hurt a little during Alcubierre journeys, now feel sensitive to the point where even the air I'm breathing in through my mouth sets my nerves on edge. My joints always ache during transitions, but now they feel like someone is trying to pull them out of their sockets in very slow motion.

Three minutes. Two minutes. One minute.

"Decouple the power grid and switch to emergency backup," Colonel Drake orders. "Execute pre-burn sequence."

"Aye, sir. Switching power to tertiary," Lieutenant Cole says. The battle lights flicker for the fraction of a second when he makes the switch on his console screen.

"Execute pre-burn sequence," Colonel Drake says at the thirty-second mark. "Throttle up engines five and seven. Stand by on starboard bow thrusters."

At the ten-second mark, I close my eyes to perform my private little just-in-case ritual, recalling a loving smile and a beautiful mountain sunset instead of staring at a bulkhead that may not be there anymore in a few seconds.

"All hands, brace for impact," the XO announces on the 1MC.

"Three. Two. One," Captain Steadman counts along with the timer.

The transition back into normal space hits me like a slap on the chest, but I know that we're through on the far side because all the discomfort falls away at once, and the metallic taste in my mouth fades with it.

"Punch it," Colonel Drake orders even as I feel the remaining engine pods kick in and send a low rumble through the hull.

"All ahead flank, full bow thrusters," Lieutenant Cole shouts.

I can sense the sudden shift in thrust that starts nudging the bow of *Washington* to port. When I open my eyes, the console in front of me flickers in synchronicity with the red battle lighting. The tactical orb above the holotable blinks out and comes back to life a second later, still showing nothing but the icon for our own ship. A heartbeat or two later, an orange icon pops up right on our stern, already overlapping the blue one as it starts to merge with it completely.

"Three seconds," Captain Steadman shouts.

"Come on, swing around," Colonel Drake mutters.

The position grid on the tactical display rotates through five degrees, ten, then fifteen. Then the hull gets jolted so hard that it drives me back into my seat as if someone had taken a running start and jump kicked me in the chest. The sound that rolls across the ship is the worst thing I've ever heard, far more terrifying than even the Lanky wails from my dreams. It's a tortured metallic shriek that drowns out all other noises, all the alarms going off and the voices shouting out in the CIC, and it sounds like the ship is getting twisted in half behind us. It goes on for what feels like half a minute, but when it dies down again, I look at the shot clock and see that only ten seconds have passed since we transitioned in.

Over on the tactical orb, the position grid is spinning much faster now, thirty or forty degrees per second, a rate of turn I've never seen any ship do.

"We're in a horizontal spin," Lieutenant Colonel Campbell shouts over the din of the alarms going off all around us.

"Cut the power on main engines," Colonel Drake orders. "Full port bow thrusters. Get us out of this spin."

"Aye, sir. Cutting propulsion, full port bow thrusters."

"Our emergency power levels are dropping like a rock," the XO says. "Get the main power grid back online."

I feel out of place and useless while everyone around me is doing something to get the ship back under control. All I can do is stay strapped in and hope we didn't get damaged beyond recovery.

The spin rate of the tactical grid slows gradually. With the ship spinning on its vertical axis, it looks like the Lanky is circling us as the icon constantly changes relative bearing to our sensor arrays. There's a little bit of space between those icons now, and as I watch the orange lozenge shape circling the blue one, it looks like the range between us is slowly increasing.

"Get me a bearing on that bastard," Colonel Drake says. "He may come around for seconds."

"Aye, sir," Captain Steadman replies. "Range to Lima-8 is one hundred kilometers and increasing. Bearing ninety-eight by positive eleven. Now one hundred ten by positive eleven."

"Get this spin under control already," the XO says.

"Trying, ma'am. Port thrusters are at full power. He gave us one hell of a bump."

It takes another minute for the thrusters to arrest the ship's spin to port. When the orange icon on the tactical screen stops circling ours, the distance has opened to over five hundred kilometers, but the seed ship is slowing down and drawing a curved trajectory on our map.

"He's turning and burning. Coming around for another pass," Captain Steadman says.

"He can slow down in a hurry, but he can't turn well. No better than we can. Lieutenant Lawrence, status report on the particle mounts."

"Alpha is still offline. I've got a green light on Beta. Targeting computer is offline, sir."

"Energize the mount. Weapons free. Take manual control and bore-sight him."

"Weapons free, aye. Energizing Beta mount. I have the helm for manual aim."

"You have the helm," the XO confirms.

I can see the sweat running down the weapons officer's face as he grasps the control stick for the carrier's particle-gun mount and moves the hat switch on top with his thumb to activate the bow thrusters. The particle gun is mounted along our centerline in the bow of the ship, and aiming it requires the entire carrier to adjust its heading in two dimensions. I am not a cap-ship space warfare specialist, but I know that under normal circumstances, the weapons officer would let the computer control the bow thrusters and the firing of the gun, and Lieutenant Lawrence would just hold down the trigger to allow the computer to fire when the target crosses the centerline of the light-speed weapon's bore. With the computer out of the equation, he has to dial the bore in on the target manually, using only high-powered optics and his thumb on the directional switch for the thrusters.

"He's definitely coming around for a second helping," Captain Steadman says. "Turning into us at just under a thousand klicks. Bearing now sixty to positive five."

"All yours, Lawrence. Blow that piece of shit into plasma," Colonel Drake says.

"Aye, sir," Lieutenant Lawrence replies without taking his eyes off his targeting screen.

Captain Steadman puts the visual from the targeting camera up on the tactical display. A distance of a thousand kilometers is trivial for the optics, and the particle gun fires its stream of atoms at near light speed. The Lanky ship is starting to turn its bow to us on its parabolic trajectory to intercept. Whatever damage the seed ship caused to *Washington*, the Lanky's front seems unmarred even through the high magnification of the gun optics. As we all watch, Lieutenant Lawrence puts the targeting marker on the center of the Lanky's hull and gives the bow thrusters a little burst with his thumb to match the seed ship's turn rate. From deep below and in front of us, the humming of the charging particle gun resonates through the hull.

"Should have run away, you dumbshit," Lawrence says and squeezes the trigger.

The image from the optics goes white with the intensity of the fireball that follows. We cheer as we watch the glowing orb of superheated plasma expand and then begin to dissipate slowly. When the optics cut through all the intense brightness again, I sit up in my chair with a jolt. There's still a torpedo shape on the screen, but something is different about it now. It's spinning until it's bow on to *Washington* and continues the turn in an obviously uncontrolled fashion. When the back end comes into view, we see that the entire back third of the Lanky is gone, and the seed ship is trailing brilliant sparks and streams of bright plasma. The edge of the hull is glowing white-hot in the darkness of space where the particle beam from our cannon amputated the aft section of the ship and turned it into superheated gas.

"That's a kill," Captain Steadman announces to cheers.

"Hit him a little further aft than I meant to," Lieutenant Lawrence says. He sits up straight and wipes the sweat from his eyebrows with the sleeve of his vacsuit.

"Doesn't matter, Lieutenant," Colonel Drake says. "Good shooting. He's a mission kill. There's nothing left alive on that thing."

A red data field starts flashing on the weapons console in front of Lawrence. He looks down and bites off a curse.

"The Beta mount just went offline, sir. The coil is de-energizing."

"Fantastic," the XO says. "At least it held out for another shot."

"See if you can figure out what ails it. In the meantime, let's figure out where we are and how badly we got hurt," Colonel Drake says.

"We're in *slightly* better shape than that Lanky," Lieutenant Colonel Campbell says.

She scrolls through the cascade of diagrams on her screen. Everything that pops up seems to be blinking orange or red.

"Stern sensor array is offline. Tactical, bring up the dorsal and give me a stern view."

"Aye, ma'am." Captain Steadman opens a new screen on the holotable and displays the external view of *Washington*'s stern.

"Holy shit." The XO voices my thoughts.

Our stern section is a mess of shattered armor plate and severed hoses and cable trunks. I can only see one of our dorsal drive pods where there should be four. We're trailing a long comet of frozen air and debris.

"We almost got out of his way. *Almost*," the XO says. She is alternating her attention between the image from the dorsal cameras and the damage control screen in front of her. "Looks like he clipped our rear port quarter from slightly below. All the ventral drive pods are gone, and most of the dorsal ones are, too. Everything from frame 371 aft is open to space on the portside. We've lost half a million cubic meters of hull space, and we have two working reactors left. And I would wager a bet that there isn't a single straight bulkhead beyond frame 300. We're damn lucky that we're still breathing air."

"Well, that's less than ideal," Colonel Drake says. "But I suppose it could have been worse. Lieutenant Cole, do you have a fix on our position?"

"Aye, sir. Galactic Positioning System triangulation says we are in the Auriga constellation." He slaps his console with a grin. "We're back in the Capella system, sir. Right where we started. An hour out from Willoughby at full burn."

Even the colonel contributes to the cheer that goes up in the CIC at the news. The visceral joy I feel exploding in the center of my chest isn't quite enough to wash away all the anxiety and fear I felt in the last few hours, but it's more than enough to dilute them into mere background worry for a few minutes. As damaged as we are, we have made it out of the death trap of the rogue system. The Hail Mary pass worked, and we probably used up all our collective luck for the rest of our lives.

"All right, settle down," Colonel Drake says after a few moments of unbridled levity. "We're still a long way from home, and we're still in a bad state. Let's get back to the work at hand."

He picks up the comms handset.

"All hands, this is the CO. The good news first—we made it through. We are out of Alcubierre, and the ship is back in the Capella system. And we just splashed the Lanky that took us along for the ride."

He pauses for a moment to let the cheers pass that are undoubtedly filling the air in every compartment of the ship that can still hear 1MC announcements.

"Now the bad news," he continues. "The Lanky rammed our stern and disabled our ship. We need to get propulsion back and restore whatever systems we can. Stand to your posts. Damage control crews, to your stations. We are not out of the woods yet. But we're only one hop away from home now. CO out."

Lieutenant Colonel Campbell is still going through the malfunctioning and disabled ship systems on her damage control panel. She looks up when Colonel Drake finishes his announcement and shakes her head lightly.

"What's the matter, XO?" Colonel Drake asks.

"That was good for them to hear. But that one hop might as well be twenty right now. The Alcubierre drive is out. I can't even get a system status."

"Oh, that's fantastic." Colonel Drake frowns. He looks over at the image from the external cameras.

"Get on comms with flight ops. See if they've patched things up enough down there to get a drop ship into the clamps. We need some external visuals from our stern. See what we can fix and what we have to write off."

"Aye, sir," the XO says and picks up the handset again.

I unbuckle my harness and lean forward in my chair, trying to stretch my aching and sweat-soaked back. Suddenly I am aware of my empty stomach growling. It's as if my biological functions have been on hold for the last few hours and are reasserting themselves now that death no longer seems imminent.

"I think I've come to the conclusion that space travel really isn't for me," I say.

Lieutenant Colonel Campbell looks over from her damage control station and shakes her head with a sparing smile.

"I'd say that realization is coming a little late, Major Grayson," she says.

CHAPTER 25

—— UNSAFE HARBOR ——

"Well, that doesn't look promising," Colonel Drake says.

We're all out of our seats and enjoying the opportunity to stretch our limbs after the many hours we spent strapped in. The command crew are standing in the holotable pit at the center of the CIC, observing the feed from the drop ship that is circling *Washington*'s hull. Seeing the damage from that perspective is much more unsettling than the abbreviated glimpse we got from the dorsal array. There is a hole in the ship that's two hundred meters long and goes from the top of the ship all the way to the bottom. It's a giant, ugly wound of mangled bulkheads and deck plating, and it looks like a huge shark took a bite out of the ship and chewed off most of our stern section. The drop ship pilot is shining his searchlights into the mess as he slowly works his way around the port quarter. It's strange to be able to see the inside of compartments and passageways that should be shielded by a meter and a half of composite armor plating. It's stranger still to see sunlight reflecting off the hull again after so much time spent in utter darkness.

"The dry dock supervisor is going to have a stroke when he sees what we're bringing back," Lieutenant Colonel Campbell says, and the CO chuckles.

"If we make it back with this ship, they won't bother with the dry dock. She's going straight to the breakers. That's the most structural damage I've ever seen on a ship that still had air inside of it," he says.

The drop ship finishes its survey of the destroyed aft starboard quarter and moves around the stern, which is more than halfway gone. I'm amazed to see that we still have three drive pods on the starboard side of the stern, two at the top and one at the bottom, but the lower pod has gaping holes in it, and the armor cladding is buckled and cracked in a dozen places.

"Rear sensor array gone." The XO tallies up the defects that come into view. "Pods one through four gone. Pod six gone. Pod eight looks like it's hanging on by three bolts and a lucky weld seam. If we get even one of the remaining ones lit up again, I'll be amazed."

She taps the side of her headset.

"Flight, XO. Give me a slow starboard-to-port pass underneath the stern, please."

The angle of the sensor image changes as the pilot complies and uses his thrusters to maneuver around the remaining starboard drive pods to map the damage to the underside of the ship. It's clear that the Lanky came from slightly below the stern and pushed us up a little because the damage to the underside looks even more catastrophic than the portside. Whatever isn't torn off the lower stern is smashed and pushed in by unimaginable forces, an impact the ship was never designed to withstand.

"And that's it," Lieutenant Colonel Campbell proclaims with finality when the drop ship has finished its pass. "He crushed a hundred and fifty meters of hull down there. Our Alcubierre drive components are now the world's biggest engineering puzzle. A million pieces, some assembly required."

She looks at the CO.

"This ship is never going to make a transition again," she says. "She's in Capella for good."

"Drone seven launched. All remaining drones away," Captain Steadman says. On the tactical display, there's now a short chain of inverted V shapes rushing away from the ship and fanning out in an arc. At the edge of the display, another inverted V is on a different course, heading off the map and toward the NAC transition point—the ship's crash buoy, our Alcubierre-equipped messenger in a bottle that will hopefully reach our solar system and let the Fleet know that we are back and in need of help.

"Those were the last recon drones. We're starting to scrape the bottom of the barrel," Lieutenant Colonel Campbell says. For the last hour and a half, she has been collecting damage reports and directing engineering crews, and her mood has darkened progressively.

"No point holding anything back now," Colonel Drake replies. "Still no sign of the Lanky that transitioned into Capella ninety minutes before we did?"

"Negative, sir," Lieutenant Cole replies. "Nothing from the task force, either. No passive relays, no radio chatter. The neighborhood is empty."

"I wasn't expecting them to stick around in hostile space for a month and a half, but you never know," the CO says. "Would have been nice to transition back in and find a welcoming committee."

He leans on the rail that surrounds the holotable pit and sighs heavily.

"All right, let's take stock again. We have no propulsion. And even if we did, we wouldn't be able to leave the system because our Alcubierre drive is trashed. The particle mount is down, so we can't defend ourselves if another Lanky closes in. At least one seed ship is present with us in this system already, and more could come out of that transition point behind us at any time. That doesn't exactly leave us with an abundance of options."

"The engineering chief whose crew is working on the number seven pod says they may have it back up and running in another hour or two. He says the fuel line is still undamaged, and they're running a new network connection to the pod through the undamaged bulkheads."

"Well, that's some good news. We need to get some distance from this spot as soon as we can."

"And where are we limping on one drive pod, sir?" the XO asks.

Colonel Drake turns toward the tactical orb again and touches the controls to alter the scale of the display until it shows the blue orb representing Willoughby, our old colony moon that has been Lanky territory for thirteen years now.

"That's the only port of call I see," he says.

"You want to go back there?" Lieutenant Colonel Campbell says. "It's crawling with Lankies."

"We're sitting ducks out here. The next Lanky that comes through that transition point is going to finish us off. And we don't know how much longer this ship is going to hold together. We go to Willoughby while we still can. And we get everyone off the ship and to the surface."

"I don't know how long we'll last down there against the Lankies," I say, and the other officers in the CIC turn their heads to look at me. "You saw how quickly they were on us in Willoughby City. The moment they know we're there, we'll have every Lanky in the neighborhood converging on our location."

"We'll last a lot longer down there than up here," Colonel Drake says. "Maybe we'll even hold out until a rescue force arrives. That'll depend on the Spaceborne Infantry and the air wing."

"I think we need to involve the rest of the command council for that decision," Lieutenant Colonel Campbell says. "I'm not a grunt. I'm out of my depth when it comes to ground combat."

"All right. Call in Colonel Rigney and the CAG. Flag briefing room, thirty minutes," the CO says.

"Aye, sir." She picks up the comms handset for the 1MC. "Command personnel, report to the flag briefing room in thirty minutes. I repeat, command personnel to the flag briefing room in thirty minutes."

She puts down the handset and nods at me.

"Come on, Major. Let's go bet against the odds some more."

"A full-scale regimental assault drop," Colonel Rigney says. "We haven't done a real one since Mars."

"Are you still up to it?" Colonel Drake asks. "I know the regiment was on reduced rations for a while. Is it your assessment that you're still fully combat ready?"

The commanding officer of the Spaceborne Infantry regiment folds his arms across his chest and shrugs.

"Truth be told, the grunts have been cooped up with nothing to do for so long that they'll be eager to see some action. Morale really takes a hit when you feel like you're just ballast. They'll all jump at the chance to do something useful."

"We have to get every living soul off this ship and onto the surface," Lieutenant Colonel Campbell says. "It's not really something we usually have to consider when we war-game our planetary assaults. It's going to make your jobs a lot harder."

"If it were easy, nobody would need to send the SI," Colonel Rigney replies. "We can handle it. This is our bread and butter."

"This will not be an offensive mission. We're not going in like we did on Mars," Colonel Drake says. "We have to establish a defensive perimeter and hold it, then shuttle the rest of the crew down."

Colonel Rigney looks at the overview map of Willoughby that's slowly turning on the holoscreen projection in front of the bulkhead.

"They wrecked all our terraforming stations down there many years ago already, or I'd split up and distribute the regiment down there by platoons or companies. That would have been ideal. We could have kept a lower profile and dispersed a bit."

He uses the control screen set into the briefing table in front of him to bring up the overhead image of Willoughby City.

"As things stand right now, this is the only spot that makes sense. We land in force down in the city. There's an air and space field with hardened shelters that are still standing. And we can use the existing infrastructure for shelter and defense. Especially that main administration building. We may even get some of their systems back online once we hook up our portable power units. Heck, there may even be fuel left in the underground tanks at the airfield."

He marks an oval on the map that encompasses the admin building on one end and the airfield on the other.

"That's going to be our initial perimeter. First battalion goes in and secures this zone. Once the second battalion is on the ground, we push the perimeter out. Until we have as much of the place covered as we can without stretching the line too thin."

"The STT has four platoons you can use to stretch the line," I say. "The Force Recon platoon and the SEALs have each lost a squad. But we still have fourteen combat-ready squads to add to the perimeter."

Colonel Rigney nods.

"I'll never turn down extra rifles, Major. Your people are force multipliers. I don't want to use them piecemeal in the main offensive line, though. I'd rather have you as a fire brigade. To reinforce the line if they manage to force a push-through somewhere."

"I don't think we will need combat controllers for this one anyway," Colonel Pace says. The air group commander, who is sitting across the table from me, has always been whippet lean, but after a few weeks of half rations, he looks positively gaunt. "The Shrikes won't have a long way to fly to reach the target zone. Hell, they'll barely have time to retract their landing gears."

"I'll have my platoons play backstop," I agree. "If the line starts to get thin, we'll be there to shore it up."

"That's going to be a logistical bench press no one's ever done before." The CAG strokes his chin with thumb and forefinger. "We land the infantry. Then we land the crew. And once that's done, we have to bring down all the ammo and fuel we can cram into the logistics and support birds."

"Can you pull it off?" Colonel Drake asks.

"We will fly and bring down ordnance as long as we can," Colonel Pace replies. "Keep enough ground clear for us to land a flight of drop ships, and we'll keep resupplying the infantry."

"Very well." Colonel Drake looks around at everyone. "Gentlemen, I know this isn't an ideal situation. But we're on a broken ship, in hostile space, without any effective weapons left at our disposal. The next seed ship that comes across us is going to finish us off without having to work for it. And that can happen at any time, so we need to move now. On the ground, we have a chance of holding out for a while. Up here, we have none. I am not willing to bet the lives of everyone on this ship on being able to steer clear of Lankies or hide."

"We can't get everyone off this ship," the CAG says. "Someone needs to keep things going while we get out what we can."

"The flight deck and supply crews leave last. I will stay up here and wind things down until we only have the bare essential personnel left. Then we'll keep things running until we've emptied out the ordnance magazines, or the Lankies show up. Whichever happens first," Colonel Drake says.

"If they show up before we are done, you may not get off this ship in time," Colonel Rigney cautions.

"We'll use the battlespace control squadron as our eyes and ears. They'll give us early warning if something's headed our way," Lieutenant

Colonel Campbell says. "If we get incoming, we can always take to the pods and abandon ship. We'll get the ship into stationary orbit above the city. Hell, we may even be able to give some fire support with the rail gun batteries from up here. They won't do anything to a seed ship, but they'll make a splash on the ground."

Colonel Drake looks around the room again.

"If anyone has misgivings, let's hear them now. I don't want to fall prey to tunnel vision because we have a need to hurry."

We look at each other for a moment. Then Colonel Rigney speaks up.

"It'll be a fight. But at least we'll be able to make it one. If we get blown out of space, all my troopers will die in their berths."

Colonel Pace nods his agreement.

"We brought all these planes and all this ordnance along. Might as well put everything to good use," he says.

They all look at me to hear my response.

"If I'm going to go out, I'd rather do it with a rifle in my hand," I say. "And I'm sure I speak for the whole STT on this one."

Colonel Drake nods and takes a deep breath.

"All right. Let's get off this ship and make ourselves a nuisance down there. We have one drive pod back online, but we're limited to thirty percent power output. You all have six hours before we're in orbit over Willoughby. Plan your deployments and prepare your units, gentlemen."

We all get out of our seats. I am closest to the door, so I unlock it and wait for the higher-ranking officers to leave the room. The last one to file out in front of me is Lieutenant Colonel Campbell.

"I'm pretty sure you told me yourself to steer clear of Medal of Honor shit," I say as I walk out behind her.

She turns her head to look at me and shrugs.

"I'm the executive officer of this ship, Major Grayson. I will not leave the skipper up here by himself and go hide in a bunker on the surface while this ship still needs to be in the action."

Then she cracks one of her dry smiles.

"But I have absolutely no intention or desire to be a hero. The second we spot a Lanky heading our way, I'm calling Abandon Ship, and then I'm running for the nearest escape pod."

CHAPTER 26

BASTION

*"Now hear this: We are approaching Willoughby orbit. All hands, stand
ready to execute battle plan Bastion. Repeat, all hands stand ready to execute
battle plan Bastion. T-minus thirty minutes."*

When the XO's announcement sounds, I'm in my berth, where I've
been trying and failing to get some sleep before the drop. I know that
this is going to be the last chance for quiet rest I'll get, but my brain
does not want to quiet down, and I don't want to dull my senses with
sedatives right before going into battle.

There's not much personal stuff in my locker. I've learned to travel
light and not get attached to possessions I can't afford to lose with the
ship, so I don't even have the few little mementos from my mother that
I used to carry around for the first few years of my career. They're now
safely on Earth with Halley, in a drawer in the kitchen of the little place
Chief Kopka has let us use as our home base for a long time now. The
only thing I have in this locker that wasn't issued to me by the Corps
is the antique M17 service pistol I keep in violation of regulations, a
going-away present from the Lazarus Brigades that has been my good-
luck charm for a while. I take the gun and its modular holster with the

spare magazines and close the sliding door on the locker. Nothing else in there has any value to me.

I sit down at the little desk one more time and activate the terminal. For a minute, I look at the picture of Halley and bring my heart rate under control with deep, slow, deliberate breaths. Then I close the terminal screen and walk out of my berth, keenly aware that it's probably the last time I'll ever see it.

———————————

The flight deck is the busiest it's ever been. Drop ships and support craft are lined up almost wingtip to wingtip, and ordnance racks are filling up the spaces between the ships. Spaceborne Infantry troopers are lined up in the assembly zones behind the drop ships, waiting for the word to board. On the far end of the flight deck, the ground-attack Shrikes are getting loaded up with missiles and cluster bomb dispensers. With all the flight deck personnel seemingly at work at the same time, the activity makes even the huge open space seem a little crowded. In several spots on the deck lining and the ceiling, I can see patches that the damage control crews have welded onto the holes left by Lanky penetrators, and scorch marks from extinguished fires.

The STT's Blackflies are lined up in their usual spot on the deck. All the team's platoons are already grouping up in the assembly zone, out of the way of the ordnance and fuel handlers who are busy getting the drop ships ready for action.

When I walk up to our assembly area, Captain Harper detaches himself from the gaggle of SEALs he's standing with and comes over to meet me halfway, just out of earshot of the closest team members.

"I didn't know medical had cleared you for combat drops, sir," he says.

"They didn't," I reply. "I'm violating the regs, so if you want to report me to the CO, go ahead."

"I think the skipper has other worries right now," Captain Harper says. "I would say it's your head to risk, sir. But you've had a head injury."

"And you think that may affect my command ability," I say, a statement of fact rather than a question. Harper just nods.

"I'm just an extra rifleman once we get down there, Captain. We are keeping the teams together by platoon. Every platoon leader will be in charge of their own squads. No need to mix and match for this mission."

"Which platoon are you joining?"

"I'll be going with the combat controllers. We lost Lieutenant Ellis, so second squad needs a new leader."

"I lost half my squads," Captain Harper says. "My section NCO and my second-in-command are both gone. I have eight men left."

"I know, Captain. And I'd go back to that moon and trade myself for them if I could. The best we can do right now is make ourselves worthy of what they did for us."

He gives me the barest of nods and turns around to rejoin his SEALs. From his facial expression and the length of his stride, I can tell that it wouldn't break his heart at all if I hit my head on the drop ship's hull on the way down and died of a brain bleed before we even get to the surface.

I walk into the assembly area, and the conversations cease as the troopers turn to face me and shuffle around in the limited space to form a rough semicircle.

"STT, listen up," I say. I wait a few moments until the final smatters of chitchat have died down. I haven't seen many of these troopers since the last time I did a pre-mission briefing here on this spot. There are gaps in their ranks now, faces I'll never see again, and I wonder how many of the men and women in front of me will be gone forever after the battle we are about to fight.

"Our mission is simple," I tell them when all eyes are on me. "We're killing Lankies. The SI will establish a perimeter in Willoughby City. They will hold the ground and defend the city while the drop ships bring down crew members and supplies. We will land at the airfield and act as an emergency fire brigade. If a section of the line needs reinforcement, or a breakthrough needs to be plugged, we will be there and relieve the pressure on the infantry."

I pause and look at the faces around me.

"This will not be a complex battle plan. We don't need to run recon or remain stealthy. We jump in and do whatever needs doing, and we kill every Lanky we see with whatever weapons we have at hand. The flyboys have assured us they'll take care of the ammo resupply. That's a colonial settlement down there. We'll have plenty of cover. Most of those buildings are prefab concrete domes, and all of them have subfloor shelters. Platoons will stay together as a unit. Forget special tactics. Today we're all infantry."

I look down onto the nonskid deck flooring and scuff it with the toe of my armored boot.

"When we leave this ship, we can't come back. There will be no higher ground, no fallback position. We stand and we fight, and we hold the line, or we're all gone. It's that simple."

To our left, a hundred meters down the flight deck from our assembly point, one of the SI's heavy-weapons platoons is walking their combat exoskeletons to the ramp of their drop ship to secure them for the drop. Some of the STT troopers look over at the noise of the heavy exos stomping from the flight deck onto the steel ramp. The PACS, power-augmented combat systems, have become an integral part of the SI battalions since I first got to test one four years ago on the flight deck of a different Avenger-class carrier. Every SI company now has a heavy-weapons platoon with four PACS for fire support. They're excellent force multipliers, and the morale boost they provide is almost as valuable as their firepower.

"I got to test-drive one of these once," I say. "On a different flight deck, four years ago."

The troopers who were looking over at the exos redirect their attention to me again.

"Some of you may have been there. New Svalbard. We had to defend the colony town against a Lanky rush. While airlifting the colonists to the carrier. They sent down the PACS we had on board for trials. Most of them were driven by the civvie techs because the grunts didn't have any training on them yet. They held the line until we had all the civilians off that rock, and then they covered our retreat. Sixteen of them, with no air support."

I nod over at the spot where the SI troopers are walking their PACS into the drop ship.

"Now they have four of them in every heavy-weapons platoon. Thirty-two for the whole regiment. And we'll have the entire air and space wing in support. We will hold the line."

There's no cheering or fist pumping, just a general murmur of agreement and nodding of heads.

"I was there when the Lankies first arrived," I continue. "Thirteen years ago, right here at Willoughby. They came in and wiped out almost every human on this planet in just a few days. No warning, no chance to get away, no time to prepare. Over a thousand colonists. Men, women, children. We arrived a few days later just in time to rescue a few survivors and count a lot of bodies from the air."

I have their undivided attention now. None of them were in the Corps when Willoughby happened, and I doubt that more than a handful have ever met someone who was there from the start because so many of us have died over the thirteen years in the meat grinder that followed.

"We will hold the line until the relief force arrives. That may be days, or weeks, or months. Doesn't matter. And whatever else happens—today we take the city back, and they'll have to fight us for every meter of it."

Overhead, the sound for all-hands announcements comes over the ship's crew address system.

"Now hear this: Bastion, Bastion, Bastion. Execute battle plan. Good luck and Godspeed," the XO announces.

There's a moment of silence, as if everyone on the flight deck is taking a collective breath. Then the din of activity swells again. On the far end of the flight deck, alerts blare and orange warning lights start flashing as the first Shrike ground attack craft are getting shuttled into launch position.

"Let's get to work, people. Board your ships and prepare for combat drop. I will see you on the surface," I say.

My STT troopers do their usual motivational *oo-rah* and turn to board their respective drop ships. I watch them file up the ramps in their battle armor suits. For this engagement we won't need bug suits. The regular battle armor is better for a stand-up fight because it can hold more ammo and offers more protection, and we have no need for the stealth the bug suits afford us. Once we land, the Lankies will know where we are, and they will come to us sooner or later.

I look around the hangar deck of the ship that has sustained us and brought us back from the rogue planetary system at the cost of itself. I salute the ship's seal on the hangar's forward bulkhead and follow my troopers up the ramp into my designated Blackfly.

———

The STT drop ships are usually the first ships out of the clamps on a planetary assault drop because we have all the pathfinder and air support control specialists in our ranks. On this drop, we're going in only after both SI battalions are on the ground, to cram as much heavy combat power as possible into the city right away. When we are finally out of the clamps and on the way to the surface, I tap into the external view.

When I first saw Willoughby with Halley thirteen years ago, it was a starkly beautiful world from space, with vast, barren continents and oceans that glistened in the sunlight. Now it looks like any other Lanky world, covered in a thick blanket of clouds that shrouds the surface from view. I look back at *Washington* through the lenses of the Blackfly's stern array, and the sight makes me amazed and thankful that she held together to get us to Willoughby. The damage to the underside is much more extensive than the limited view I had gotten from the circling drop ship with its wide-angle lens had made it seem. The carrier is still trailing frozen air and debris even as she has settled in her parking orbit, over six hours after the collision that wrecked her. The sight reminds me how fragile our species is, and how mad and reckless we are to be hurtling between the stars in little air-filled steel bubbles that can be broken beyond repair so easily.

I usually hate the nausea-inducing flight profile of a combat descent, but today I welcome it because it will put us on the ground much faster than a standard approach. When we break out of the cloud cover above Willoughby City, we're only a few hundred meters above the ground, and the airspace above the settlement is swarming with drop ships and attack craft. Our pilot pulls out of the corkscrew dive and makes a low pass over the city. Down in the streets between the moss-covered colonial buildings, I can see Spaceborne Infantry troopers setting up their fighting positions and PACS units stomping down the main thoroughfares toward their designated defensive sectors. There are over a thousand troopers in the Fifth Spaceborne Infantry Regiment, but the city is several kilometers across, so we have to be selective when it comes to our defensive perimeter because we'd need four regiments to cover the entire perimeter of the city effectively.

Our Blackfly swoops in low over the central plaza and lines up to land in front of the long-abandoned admin building. When I walk down the tail ramp and step onto the dirty, broken concrete, it occurs to me that I am probably the only human alive who has been to this planet three times since the Lankies took it over.

Outside, the cloud cover is complete, but it's the middle of the planetary day on this hemisphere, and just seeing a world illuminated by the light of a nearby sun is an almost religious experience after all these weeks in the darkness. If I could, I'd take off my helmet and turn my bare face toward the sunlight even though it's diffused by the clouds. This world has color, drab and dirty as it is here in this spot, and the moss-flecked concrete building in front of me is one of the most beautiful things I've seen in weeks.

In front of the admin building, the combat engineers of the SI regiment are already busy clearing the rubble piles in front of the main access vestibule. The thick double steel doors of the building's primary entrance are hanging askew in the opening, bent and pushed out of shape by the explosive charges our raid team used a month and a half ago when we went into the place to retrieve their data modules from the network center in the basement.

I look around at the buildings surrounding the plaza. This was the hub of the colony, and the center of most of the civil and commercial activity. One of the undamaged structures looks like it was a bar or a diner. I decide that it will make as fitting a headquarters for the STT as anything else we're likely to find, and it's close to the admin center in case we need to scramble for hard shelter.

"Over there." I point and mark the spot on the tactical display at the same time. "Sergeant O'Farrell, with me. We're securing that building. Everyone else, start unloading the supplies."

O'Farrell follows me across the plaza to the place I've spotted. There's a decorative neon sign affixed to the front of the building above the entrance, something that's usually frowned upon as a waste of electricity but tolerated and even expected for a colony's watering holes. The sign is long dark and partially covered by the moss that's encroaching on it, but as we walk up, I can make out the name of the place: **BAD CALLS**.

The bar's thick polyplast windows are still in place, so the building's interior wasn't subjected to the elements for the last thirteen years. It is merely dark and covered in concrete dust, not overgrown or rotted. As we clear the bar room by room, I expect to find dead bodies like we did at the admin center, but it looks like nobody stayed around for a last drink when the colony's alarms went off, and there are only some personal items strewn about in the booths and on the countertop in the main room. The desk in the back office has an overturned chair in front of it, and there's a green plastic plate with an unidentifiable serving of food sitting next to a stack of printouts that have fused into a big, moldy lump. Everything is structurally sound, and the auxiliary power connectors in the utility room are undamaged.

"Second squad, listen up," I say when I step out of the front door again. "We're going to set up shop in here. Get the mobile power cell and hook it into the aux in the back room. Let's get the supplies in. And start emptying out the armory. MARS rockets and rifle ammo first, then spare weapons."

"Contact north. Six LHOs out in the open, approaching from 358 degrees. Engaging," a voice on the command channel calls out.

We're halfway through emptying the Blackfly's armory when the first gunfire sounds in the distance, the unmistakable angry zipper sound of a Shrike's automatic cannon pouring out seventy rounds per second onto some hapless target. I put down the ammo container I've been hauling toward the bar and check my tactical screen to get a view of the situation. A little over a kilometer in front of the SI positions in the northern quadrant of the town, half a dozen Lanky icons have appeared on the map. As I watch their slightly staggered line advance toward the town, two of them blink out of existence before the echoes of the Shrike's gunfire have faded. The attack craft makes another pass, then a third, each one punctuated by another burst from the cannon. Then the Lanky icons are gone. The lead Lanky never made it inside of a kilometer.

"That's a good start," Sergeant O'Farrell says as he passes me with another ammunition container. "That air support is going to chew them up before they can get close enough for the grunts."

"That was just a probe," I reply. "They'll be back. And there'll be a lot more of them. Now that they know we're here."

The small plaza in front of the admin building is now packed with equipment and personnel. The combat engineers have cleared the rubble piles from the front of the entrance and managed to wrench the steel double doors open most of the way. Several mobile power units are sitting along the walls to the left and right of the entrance vestibule, multiple thick power leads snaking from their modular connectors into the building. Off to the side, away from the flow of personnel that is steadily pouring in from the airfield, there's now a grim stack of military body bags, the decade-old remains of the admin center personnel who were in the building when the Lanky nerve gas overwhelmed the filtration system and killed everyone inside.

I am about to pick up my ammunition container again when I see a familiar science vacsuit in the stream of people coming in from the airfield, white with orange trim. I walk across the plaza to reach Elin before she disappears in the admin building with the rest of the crew members that have just arrived from *Washington*.

"Andrew," she says when I walk up to her. She steps out of the way of the people coming up behind her. "It's good to see you."

"This must seem like a bad flashback to you," I say and nod at the admin building. "We were just here a month and a half ago."

"I'm just happy to be on solid ground again," she says. "They had to shut down half the remaining decks on the ship to save power and air. It started to get a little claustrophobic up there."

"Please tell me you brought all those samples and the colony's data modules with you. Otherwise, both our little field trips were for nothing," I say.

"Of course. That's about the only thing I brought from the ship."

She looks over at the pile of body bags containing the colonists' corpses that's just barely visible around the far corner of the admin building.

"We're going to hold out as long as we can," I say. "But if things go bad . . ."

"If things go bad, I am stashing everything at the bottom of that building along with all my notes," she says. "Someone else will find it and put it to good use in the future. We did *not* do all of this for nothing, Andrew. Whatever happens."

Behind me, there's a low electric hum. I turn around to see the lights turn on inside the bar where we set up shop, and the neon light above the entrance is flickering to life, segment by segment, until everything is lit up in red and green except for one section of a single letter. My troopers have successfully connected the external power cell we brought to the auxiliary power port of the building.

"Our temporary command post," I explain.

"Very nice," Elin says. "Let me know if you find any leftover booze in there somewhere. Because I am going to be good and ready for a drink after all of this."

In the distance over by the spaceport, a new burst of gunfire rings out, this time the slow thunder of a drop ship's hull-mounted heavy autocannons. The echoes roll across the town and reverberate among the concrete structures all around us. Elin looks in that direction and back to me, and I can see a flicker of fearful concern in her face.

"That building has been standing for thirteen years," I say. "The walls are a few meters thick. It's the safest place on this planet. You'll be all right."

She nods and shrugs her shoulders to reposition the straps of the bags she is carrying.

"Good luck, Andrew," she says.

"And to you. See you when it's over."

She rejoins the stream of crew members that are heading for the entrance of the admin building. Everyone is moving with a bit more urgency now. Overhead, two drop ships are flying toward the airfield at low altitude, their pylons bristling with ordnance. As I watch, one of them fires a heavy antiarmor missile, which drops from its pylon and streaks off into the distance on a bright jet of propellant in the blink of an eye. I look back toward Elin and see that she's already in the vestibule. Then she's safely inside, along with everything my team bled and died for since we arrived in Capella for our quick little special forces raid.

I turn and walk back to pick up the ammo box I put down earlier. There's cannon fire coming from two directions now, the spaceport and the northern perimeter. I check the tactical map as I carry the ammo container into the bar. The Lankies have resumed their probing of our defenses, two groups of five or six individuals each, approaching from different directions.

This is going to be a very long day, I think, and briefly curse my trauma-addled brain for not letting me sleep earlier when I had the chance. But now the die is cast, and we will have to deal with whatever score comes up because we won't get a second throw. All I can do right now is to bring in more ammo and stack more guns, and I hope it helps to shift the odds in our favor just a little bit with every trip I make. I'll get to rest when it's done, one way or another.

CHAPTER 27

——— SUPPLY AND DEMAND ———

"Group of twelve, in the open, bearing zero-five-zero, eight hundred meters."

"Close air inbound to target reference point. Missiles away."

"Good kill, good kill on four. MARS gunners, hold until they're inside five hundred. Don't waste rockets."

"Here they come! Seven—eight—nine hostiles, sector fourteen, bearing one-seven-four, one thousand and closing fast."

The planetary day on Willoughby is six standard Earth days long, so I have no way to gauge the passage of time by sunset or sunrise down here. The day has gone on for so long now that it feels we ought to have seen the sun go down and rise again at least twice. But the mission timer says we've been on the ground for only thirty-eight hours, and I haven't rested for more than ten minutes at a time in any of them.

The gunfire that started in just one or two sectors of our defensive circle is all around us now, swelling and ebbing in certain spots as the Lankies focus their efforts on different parts of the defensive line. The SI companies have set up ammo stashes at main intersections just a short distance away from the perimeter line, and my STT squad has been helping with the resupply for the last few hours, hauling cases full of grenades and magazines back from the dwindling main depot at the airfield. My suit's servos have been running so hard that I'm on the third battery pack since we landed. Overhead, the stream of drop ships and Shrikes coming in for strafing and missile runs is getting thinner as the fight goes on. The supply drop ships are hauling ammunition and ordnance down from the carrier as quickly as they can refuel and load up. But the attack drop ships and Shrikes are going through the fuel supply at a profligate rate; those ships are the only thing keeping the ever-increasing numbers of Lankies that hurl themselves against our defenses at bay.

"What is wrong with these fucking things?" Lieutenant Evans pants next to me as we add our delivery to the stack that doesn't seem to grow no matter how often we make the trip with the power assist of our armor suits at maximum. "We've killed hundreds of them. At what point do you stop giving yourself a bloody nose?"

"They don't think like we do, Evans," I say. When I turn around, an electric stab of pain shoots down my lower back and into my right leg, and I wince. A moment later, the armor's autodoc pricks me in the thigh with an injector, and the pain dissipates quickly, replaced by a general feeling of cool numbness that goes all the way from the right side of my waist to my ankles.

"It just seems unnatural," he says. He adds his fifty-kilo case of a trio of MARS rockets to the pile with a little grunt. "They gotta have some sense of self-preservation. Like any goddamn living thing."

"Lots of living things will play meat shield to save the hive," I say. "Bees. Ants. It's all about the group."

"Like I said, fucking unnatural," Lieutenant Evans replies. We've fallen back into a quick trot down the street back to the airfield, hopping over pushed-up concrete honeycomb and avoiding rain-filled potholes. Another Shrike thunders above our heads toward the perimeter, flying so low that it seems like I could make the armor jump on full power assist and touch one of the ordnance pods on its pylons. When the Shrike is almost directly overhead, the pilot launches a barrage of aerial rockets that shriek toward the unseen targets behind us like a swarm of angry little meteors. A few seconds later, the sounds of the explosions reach our helmet sensors, a rapid succession of overlapping thunderclaps, followed by the wailing of stricken Lankies.

"*Sector Three needs support,*" someone shouts on the command channel. We have fully reverted to radio communications now that the Lankies have found us, because it doesn't matter a damn at this point whether they can sense them or not. "*We're all out of MARS rockets. Nine hostiles inbound from nine-zero degrees, six hundred and closing.*"

Sector 3 is off to our left, down the road from the intersection we are about to pass. Sergeant Evans and I break into a run and take a left turn. On full power, the armor feels like it's mostly running itself, far faster than I could have sprinted even when I was in top shape. But when we come up to the perimeter, I still feel winded and bone tired.

In front of the platoon covering Sector 3, the gravel fields that reach up to the outskirts of town look like the seventh circle of hell. Countless Lanky bodies are strewn all over the landscape, whole and in pieces, and the sheer number of giant bodies is enough to force some of the new wave of attackers to climb over the smoking carcasses of their fallen brethren. The closest dead Lanky lies just a hundred meters in front of the platoon's firing line. Evans and I take up positions between the nearest pair of SI troopers and ready our rifles. A hundred meters to our left, a PACS unit opens up with its arm-mounted autocannon, firing single rounds at the incoming Lankies. The ones in the front of the attack lower their heads to present their heavily armored cranial shields to the cannon fire. One round clips the edge of a shield and sends chunks of it flying, and the Lanky rears up and wails just in time to catch the follow-up shots to the middle of its torso. It crashes to the ground, spraying gravel in huge gouts, and slides to a stop.

I check my tactical map for nearby air assets. The Shrike that just made a rocket run is in a wide left-hand turn back to the airfield. I open the TacAir channel and go into combat controller mode almost on autopilot.

"Shrike Six-Four, this is Tailpipe One. Request immediate close air support."

"Tailpipe One, copy," the pilot replies. *"I have no rockets left, and less than two hundred rounds of cannon ammo."*

"Six-Four, use it," I say. "On my mark, TRP Sierra. Lay down everything you have left immediately in front of it. Danger close."

"Copy, danger close on TRP Sierra," the pilot confirms.

The pitch of the engines in the distance changes as the pilot alters her course and continues her long turn to the left.

"Heads down," I shout on the local channel. "Close air incoming, danger close, danger close."

The Lankies are inside of two hundred meters when the Shrike opens up behind our firing line. The tracers from the rapid-fire autocannon reach out like a laser beam from an old Networks space adventure show and rake the line of Lankies from left to right. Amazingly, even some of the high-velocity armor-piercing rounds bounce off a cranial shield or two, sending ricochets up into the dark and cloudy sky. But the rate of fire is so rapid that there's no shelter for the Lankies from the storm of shells. The front row falls with piercing wails and flailing limbs. One of the Lankies coming up behind them takes a shell to the left arm, and the appendage tears off and careens through the air, sending the Lanky stumbling and crashing to the ground. When the gunfire stops two seconds later, only two Lankies from this wave are left standing.

"PACS from the rear," someone shouts. "Keep your heads down."

From the direction of the ammo dump we just resupplied, another PACS exoskeleton steps into the gap between the buildings directly behind us. The exo's pilot raises his right arm, which has an automatic MARS launcher mounted to it. He fires his four rockets in two-second intervals. One hits the lead Lanky square in the chest, and the second one hits the torso fifty centimeters lower. The Lanky crumples and drops to the ground like battle armor that has slid off a rack by accident. The third rocket misses the other Lanky's head by mere centimeters. The fourth tears into its leg just above what would be the knee joint on a human body. The Lanky falters with a shriek but keeps up its advance.

The SI riflemen open fire seemingly all at once. Lieutenant Evans and I add our own fire to the fusillade, and hundreds of rounds pepper the creature as it draws near. The combined weight of our fire finishes what the MARS rocket started. The Lanky falls without coordination and hits the surface with a resounding concussion that shakes the ground under my boots. My range finder shows eighty-seven meters to the spot where it fell.

"That was too fucking close," Lieutenant Evans says.

"The re-arming turnarounds are going to kill us," I reply. "They're in the air for two minutes and then on the ground again for fifteen."

The SI platoon leader comes trotting up to us from the left, reloading his rifle as he goes.

"Thanks for the assist," he says. "Do you have a TacAir controller to spare? This is getting to be the weak point on the east side. I'd like to have someone here who can call down the thunder without me having to pass it up the line first."

"Lieutenant Evans will stay with you and take over TacAir for Sector Three," I tell the SI lieutenant. "We just refreshed the MARS stock at the ammo point, so you may want to top off your gunners."

"Thank you, sir," the other lieutenant says. "We're holding them off. But things are starting to stretch a little thin down here."

"I hear you, Lieutenant. I'll see what I can shake loose for you from the STT."

"Evans, you have TacAir control for this sector now," I tell the combat controller lieutenant. "I'll try to rotate you out as soon as I can. You've been on your feet for a while."

"We all have," Evans says. "That's what stims are for, right?"

"I'm going to see what things look like back at the airfield," I say. "If they don't get the birds in the air a lot faster, we won't have much to direct before too long."

―――――――――

I trot back toward the airfield and check the tactical situation on the way. After the rush on Sector 3, there seems to be a general lull in the Lanky push. I don't know whether they just ran out of fresh bodies and are waiting for reinforcements, or whether they got temporarily discouraged and are now figuring out new tactics, but I decide that it doesn't matter. We needed a break in the relentless waves of probing attacks, and I am determined to enjoy the breather while I can. We've been on the ground for less than forty hours, but we have no reserves or reinforcements, and that sort of pace can grind the best combat unit down in a hurry. My headache has returned with a vengeance, and not even the armor's autodoc can keep it at bay for long before it burns through the painkillers.

Not even forty hours, I think as I reach the outer edge of the airfield apron. *We won't be able to hold on for weeks. We'll be lucky to make it another day or two.*

The airfield is a bustling hive of activity. The facility is meant for a handful of atmospheric puddle jumpers, not for an entire carrier air and space wing. Drop ships are landing and departing in thirty-second intervals, disgorging more personnel or ordnance. The deck hands and ammunition handlers are carting pallets of cannon ammo and racks of antiarmor missiles out of the cargo holds of just-arrived drop ships and wheeling them straight over to waiting Shrikes and assault drop ships.

The flight ops supervisor is in the reactivated control tower, which is now powered by several external power cells. The consoles in the control room are dark and dusty, useless to the military even if they worked. Instead, the Fleet air traffic controllers are directing the stream of incoming and outgoing drop ships from their portable control decks, using the tower only for its elevated vantage point. Out in the open past the airfield, dozens of shattered Lanky bodies are dotting a landscape that's scarred by many impact craters from high-explosive munitions.

"We have got to turn those Shrikes around faster," I tell the lieutenant colonel in charge of flight ops. "The last push got inside of a hundred yards of the line. Shrike Six-Four beat it back with his last two hundred rounds."

"If I could re-arm those birds with a wave of my magic wand, I'd do it," the ops officer says. "The good news is that we have plenty of fuel. The underground tanks were left almost full. The bad news is that we're short on ordnance. I can put everything in the air but they won't have anything to shoot."

"We're running low on MARS rockets and autocannon rounds for the PACS, too," I say.

"With the airlift capacity we have right now, we can't keep up. We're trying to haul both and we're falling short on both. But we have most of the crew down, so I'll have more drop ships on deck soon to send up for bullets."

"How long is that going to take?"

"Half an hour until the flight is on the deck. Then refueling and return, loading ordnance, and another drop. Figure three hours," the lieutenant colonel says. "It's the best I can tell you."

"The Shrikes are what's keeping us alive right now."

"I *know*, Major. I know. We're doing what we can."

It may not be enough, I think. But instead of voicing that thought, I just nod at the flight ops supervisor and leave the tower to let him do his job.

The ammo depot is set up in one of the undamaged hangars on the airfield. It's a hardened ferroconcrete structure, with walls almost as thick as those of the admin center. When I walk into the hangar, the pile of ammo containers and MARS rocket tubes is a lot smaller than it was when I picked up the last load of rifle magazines twenty minutes ago. I grab two of the remaining MARS rocket canisters, three rounds apiece, fifty kilos for each of my servo-assisted arms.

On the apron outside, another drop ship lands close to the flight line. The tail ramp opens as soon as the skids touch the ground. Ordnance handlers rush up to the new arrival and start hauling ammo racks off the cargo deck at once. The drop ship is loaded with aerial rocket pods, but the number of racks is nowhere near enough to arm every pylon on every assault ship on the flight line. I trot off with my load of infantry rockets, six more rounds that will be gone in twelve seconds if one of the PACS jocks uses them to fill up the autoloader of their MARS launcher.

"Willoughby ground forces, this is Washington *Actual."* The voice of Colonel Drake comes over the command channel, and I stop in my tracks and set down the ammo canisters.

"We have an incoming Lanky seed ship. I repeat, incoming enemy ship. They are less than ten minutes out, and they're on an intercept heading."

The sudden wave of despair I feel almost makes me sink to my knees. I take a deep breath and let it out with an angry scream that I don't broadcast to anyone. The effort makes the pain in my head feel like my skull is fracturing all over again.

"We are launching the remaining drop ships we have on deck. There is no time for the CIC crew to make it to the flight deck. Once the last drop ship is away, all remaining personnel will abandon ship and take to the life pods. Well fought, everyone, and we will see you on the other side. This will be this ship's last transmission. This is Colonel Paul Drake, commanding officer, NACS Washington, *signing off."*

It takes me a few seconds to collect myself and get my emotions back under control. Then I pick up the MARS containers and carry them back to the ammo depot, where I return them to the remaining little stockpile. This is what we have, and we won't get any more except for what's coming on the drop ships that are about to leave the carrier for the last time.

I think of the CIC crew and the distance from the CIC to the nearest life pod. The Combat Information Center is deep inside the ship's hull, in the most protected part of the carrier, and the escape pods in that section have the longest route to travel to get clear of the ship in an emergency. It will be a faster way off *Washington* than trying to make it all the way to the flight deck and then initiating a drop ship launch sequence, but the pods will come down on the surface of the planet mostly uncontrolled in the current atmosphere because they only have a small cluster of computer-controlled maneuvering thrusters. And wherever they put down, the Lankies will be drawn to the automated emergency messages they broadcast to let rescue ships know where they are.

I look over at the STT's Blackflies, which are parked near the end of the flight line in an area that's as far out of the way of the refueling and re-arming bustle as possible. Without external ordnance, they are not very useful as fighting assets, but they are still mostly fueled, and they have the best sensor packages of any of the Fleet's drop ships.

I run back to the control tower and take the stairs three and four at a time. When I return to the control room, the flight ops supervisor looks at me with something like mild exasperation. He's in the middle of a radio conversation on his headset, and when I skid to a stop in front of him, he holds up a hand to stop me from opening my mouth. I let him finish his communication and wait until he holds a hand over the boom mike of his set.

"You heard the news on the command channel," the flight ops boss says. "Ship's out of the picture. We have one more flight coming in, and half of it is people, not rockets. I'm afraid we will have to use up what we have and hope for the best."

"Where's the carrier right now?" I ask.

"Keeping station above our heads," the lieutenant colonel says, in a tone that makes it clear he thinks I'm a bit of an imbecile. "Geosynchronous orbit above the city. Shortest flight path for the drop ships."

"So where are the pods going to come down?"

"Wherever gravity and the atmosphere decide they're going to drop," he says. "Who knows with these winds. Could be anywhere in a three-hundred klick radius. Maybe five hundred. Why?"

"Someone has to pick them up before the Lankies home in on those emergency transmitters. I have five Blackflies sitting out there without ordnance on the pylons. But they're fueled up."

The flight ops supervisor gives me a long look.

"Do you really think they'd be better off back here than out there?"

I shake my head. "Doesn't matter what I think. Where do you think the skipper would want to be in the end?"

There are a few heartbeats of silence between us. Through the thick polyplast windows, I can hear the ramjet engines of another Shrike spooling up for takeoff in the distance. Then the lieutenant colonel shakes his head lightly and shrugs.

"You got me there, Major. If the skipper had a choice, he'd be on one of the drop ships that is going to set down out there in twenty minutes," he says. "If you're volunteering your STT birds to make the pickup, go ahead. I'm giving you clearance. We don't have any missiles left for them anyway."

"Thank you, sir," I say. "I'll bring everything back in one piece."

"Don't make promises that aren't entirely in your power to keep, Major," he says as I turn to leave.

CHAPTER 28

PODS AND RODS

"Flight section, this is Dagger Actual. Do you read?"

"Dagger Actual, Flight. Loud and clear, sir," Captain Prince replies.

"Spin up the birds," I say as I run along the flight line, weaving every now and then to avoid flight deck personnel hurrying to their own business. "Dustoff as soon as I get there."

"Copy that. Lighting engines now. What's our target?"

"We are going to pick up the skipper and the rest of the crew once their crash pods hit the dirt," I reply.

"Solid copy," Captain Prince says. *"That beats the hell out of sitting around on this apron. Makes me feel worse than useless."*

The cargo hold of the Blackflies is smaller than the one on a Dragonfly or Wasp, but devoid of troops or cargo, it looks cavernous as I trot up the ramp of Blackfly 05. I hit the ramp switch on the way in and take my seat at the command station on the forward bulkhead.

"Flight, I'm in. Dustoff at your discretion."

"What heading?" Captain Prince wants to know.

"Just get her into the air and above the cloud ceiling. We'll track the pods on active as they come down," I say.

"We're using radar? No EMCON?"

"I think the cat's pretty much out of the bag, Captain. A few dozen kilowatts aren't going to make any difference at this point. The life pod transmitters are going to make noise anyway."

"*Roger that,*" Captain Prince says. "*If we spread the flight out to twenty or thirty klicks per ship, we can maximize coverage. Since we're throwing EM discipline out the window.*"

"Go ahead," I reply. "Flick whatever switches let us reach those pods as soon as they hit the dirt."

"*Affirmative,*" Captain Prince replies.

The Blackfly throttles up and lifts off from the airfield's concrete apron with effortless speed, unencumbered by the usual weight of cargo or thirty-plus grunts with guns and heavy armor. I turn toward the bulkhead, lock the seat into position, and activate the screens on the command-and-control console. A few minutes later, we are in the clouds and bouncing on the currents as the ship ascends at a much steeper angle than usual. In our wake, the other four Blackflies are clawing their way up into the Willoughby sky with us. When we pop out of the clouds ten bone-jarring minutes later, the trailing ships of our flight peel off and disappear to the left and right of Blackfly 05 to assume their positions in the line-abreast formation that will span a hundred and fifty kilometers.

"*Dagger Flight, go hot on active sensors,*" Captain Prince sends.

The situational display on my command console comes to life with a flood of new information. With the radar active, the ship has eyes that can see hundreds of kilometers in all directions, cut through the cloud coverage, and map the ground below in fine detail. The sky above Willoughby City is the busiest place on the plot by far, with a dozen or more drop ships and Shrikes circling overhead in search of targets.

The carrier's escape pods are already in the upper atmosphere, carving their way through the air on their ballistic trajectory from orbit. The networked radar arrays of the five Blackflies pick up the echoes bouncing back from the steel-and-alloy hulls of the pods from hundreds of kilometers out.

"There they are," Captain Prince sends from the cockpit. *"Tracking multiple radar contacts, bearing two ninety, distance three hundred. Looks like four pods."*

Four pods, I think, and do the math in my head. Each pod has space for ten people. The flight deck personnel would have crammed into the last drop ships to leave the deck, which can hold forty people comfortably and a hundred if they don't mind sitting cheek to jowl. Four pods could be enough to have gotten the CIC team and the rest of the skeleton crew out, but pod launches are risky by nature, and I have no idea how big of a crew they needed to run the bare essential functions of the ship.

I hope you didn't pull any stupid Medal of Honor shit, Sophie Campbell.

I train the cameras of the ship's sensor dome at the spot in the sky three hundred kilometers away where the carrier's escape pods are falling toward the planet base first in long, steady arcs. With the magnification cranked up to maximum, I have no trouble picking up the fiery trails they carve across the sky as the atmospheric friction heats up the air around them, streaming orange and red plasma flames in their wake. I let the drop ship's computer project their trajectories and see that all four pods will land within eighty klicks of each other on the surface, on a small plateau almost four hundred kilometers away from Willoughby City.

"Dagger Flight, this is Dagger Lead," Captain Prince says on the tactical channel. *"Mark your targets. One ship per pod. Follow them in and make sure their LZ is sterile when they're on the chute. Then land as close as you can as soon as they're in the dirt. Dagger Zero-Three will provide overhead coverage."*

The pilots of the other ships send their acknowledgments. I watch on the plot as each of them marks their assigned pod.

"Let's kick it into burn," Captain Prince says.

Our ship throttles up and enters its calculated intercept trajectory for our target pod. As we dip back into the clouds a few minutes later, I try to imagine the people strapped into the seats on that pod, knowing they're in free fall toward the planet, and hoping that the pod will reach the ground. When the crew of *Versailles* bailed out of the ship over this planet twelve years ago, several of the escape pods had parachute failures and smashed into the ground, obliterating their occupants in an instant. *Versailles* was an old ship, and the pod chutes were probably overdue for replacement well before the ship made that final trip to Capella. But I've done enough bio-pod landings on Lanky worlds to know that even the knowledge of brand-new equipment wouldn't make the experience any less terrifying.

"*Tracking Pod Four. Twenty thousand, falling like a rock,*" Captain Prince says. "*Four minutes to splashdown. Make sure you're strapped in good and snug, Major. It's going to get a little choppy for a bit.*"

I toggle back my wordless confirmation. Our descent through the clouds at high speed is the most jarring one I've experienced in a long time, a teeth-rattling ride that feels like we're navigating a piece of driftwood through a hazardous stretch of river rapids. Unbidden, the memory of Halley taking me for the same ride thirteen years ago pops into my head with amazing clarity, right down to the sight of the rain streaking the polyplast panes of the cockpit, and Halley's expression of tightly controlled fear and absolute focus behind the stick.

Then we're out of the clouds, and the shaking and jolting subsides. In front of us, the life pods are now at slightly different altitudes and separated by tens of kilometers.

"*Altitude now ten thousand,*" Captain Prince says. "*Range fifty klicks. Three minutes to splashdown. Here comes the chute.*"

The forward camera is tracking the falling pod, and I watch the parachute stream from the top of the pod on its bundle of lines and deploy into a bright orange canopy a moment later. Captain Prince puts the Blackfly into a steeper dive and rushes ahead toward the projected splashdown area. We're less than a thousand meters above the ground now, and the barren landscape unrolls itself below the ship at breakneck speed.

"I have eyes on a pair of hostiles," Captain Prince announces matter-of-factly, and the comprehension of what he just said jolts me like a burst of electric current.

"I don't see 'em," I send back. My forward view is still locked on the descending pod that's now thirty kilometers away, so I unlock the array and reset the magnification.

"Thirty degrees off our port-side bow, five klicks," Captain Prince calls out. He puts the ship into a left turn to bring us toward the threat. I see the Lankies as soon as he has straightened out the turn—two individuals, striding across the plateau in their usual unhurried-looking pace, kicking up little plumes of dust with every step.

"They're not heading for the splash site," Captain Prince says.

"Yet," I reply.

"Your call, Major. We have no missiles on the racks but I have a full cassette for the cannons."

"I'm not taking any chances today," I say. "Hose 'em down."

"Affirmative," Captain Prince says.

He opens fire with the heavy autocannons at two thousand meters. The Lankies are aware that a threat is nearby because I see them changing course at the last moment and heading for the cover of a nearby ravine, but the armor-piercing shells cover the distance in a second and a half, three times faster than the sound of the blasts coming from the muzzles. The stream of shells hits the ground a hundred meters in front of them, and Captain Prince walks the burst onto the target with a minute correction of our flight path. The fountains of dirt and gravel kicked up by the cannon rounds wander over to the Lankies and then erupt all around them until both creatures are obscured by the clouds of debris from the impacts of the heavy armor-piercing shells with their secondary payload of high explosives. When we pass over the spot where the Lankies were walking just a moment ago, the draft from the drop ship diffuses the dust, and I see that both are sprawled on the ground, limbs contorted in ways that look unnatural even for their strange and unsettling anatomy.

"Splash two," Captain Prince says. He brings the ship back onto course for the landing site, where the orange canopy of the life pod is now just a few hundred meters above the ground.

The Blackfly puts down on the plateau just thirty seconds after the pod touches down, a scant hundred meters away. I unfasten my harness and run through the cargo hold to the tail ramp to open it.

"Neighborhood is clear right now, but I wouldn't dawdle," Captain Prince sends. *"Where there's two, there's more."*

"Don't I know it," I reply.

I step out onto the plateau and rush over to the life pod that has settled in textbook fashion on its flat heat shield. There are no windows on the pod, just an egress hatch. When I am halfway to the pod, there's a dull crack, and the hatch flies off the pod and thuds onto the rocky ground, kicking up a small cloud of brown dust. Then someone's helmeted head pops up in the opening and looks over at the drop ship that's standing nearby with running engines.

"Someone order a ride?" I shout, and the head turns toward me. Even from fifty meters away, I recognize the face behind the transparent shield instantly.

"You have *got* to be kidding me," *Washington*'s executive officer says when she spots me. She turns around and shouts something to the other people in the pod that I can't make out over the noise of the drop ship engines. Then she climbs out of the pod and drops to the ground. One by one, the rest of the CIC crew follow her out of the rescue vehicle: Lieutenant Cole, Captain Steadman, Lieutenant Lawrence, and the two enlisted helmsmen. The last one out is Colonel Drake, whose scruffy red beard makes him obvious. The relief I feel manages to suppress even the pain in the right side of my head for a few moments, and I laugh out loud.

"That was a shit experience," Lieutenant Colonel Campbell says when she walks up to me. "Next time I have to do this, I think I'll just go down with the ship instead."

———

We're in the air again just a few minutes later, with the CIC personnel strapped into the jump seats near the forward bulkhead. Everybody looks pale and shaken by the experience. Nobody is injured except for a few bumps and scrapes here and there, but I still chide myself for forgetting to bring along one of the STT's Spaceborne Rescue specialists who are all trained combat medics.

"How's the situation on the ground?" Colonel Drake asks when we have climbed through the clouds and the ship no longer sounds and feels like it's going to shake itself apart.

"Not ideal," I say. "Grunts are running out of rockets. Shrikes are running out of missiles. We have plenty of fuel but we're short on all kinds of ammo. They just throw themselves against the perimeter. We've killed hundreds at this point, and they keep coming."

"Shit." Lieutenant Colonel Campbell smacks the back of her helmet into the padded wall behind her a few times. "If that Lanky ship had given us just twelve more hours. We barely got a quarter of our ordnance ferried down."

"It was a big risk," the CO says. "We knew that from the start. But getting off the ship was the only option."

"Anything at all from the Fleet?" I ask. The XO just shakes her head in response.

"Not ideal," I say again.

"No, Major Grayson," Colonel Drake says. "It isn't."

The elation I felt at the successful rescue earlier has now been shunted aside by a dark sense of foreboding. Without all the supplies from *Washington*, we won't be able to keep up the fight much longer, and without enough food to keep three thousand people alive, we won't survive for long in the admin center even if the engineers have the building's air filtration system and the oxygen generators working again by now. We've made a huge effort to get ourselves from one dead end into another, and now we are about to run out of road. I feel a deep and profound tiredness, as if all the events of the last six weeks are catching up with me at once in this place and moment.

"So what do we do next?" Lieutenant Cole asks.

"We go back and fight, Lieutenant," I say. "That's all that's left to do. We fight until we run out of bullets or bad guys, whichever comes first."

"Five minutes to the airfield," Captain Prince announces a little while later. *"Prepare for turbulence."*

We dive back into the swirling cloud layer that blankets the planet, and the roller coaster starts anew. When I was a green private in the Territorial Army, I used to try to divine what was going on with the ship by the sounds that were coming from the hull, or the ways the wingtips were flexing and bouncing in the atmospheric currents, but I learned very quickly that I don't have the first clue about what keeps drop ships in the air, and that there's no reason to panic if the pilot is still calm.

When we pass through the bottom of the clouds and emerge a thousand meters above the ground, I hear Captain Prince say something in a low voice that gives me the first genuine scare of the day.

"Oh, shit."

I bring up the view from the forward array. We are a few kilometers from Willoughby City, and the ground below us is crawling with Lankies.

They're advancing in bigger groups than I've seen since we first engaged them—twenty, thirty at a time, moving in the direction of the city. When I change the field of view and look across the settlement to the north, I see that the advance is coming from the north as well, hundreds of Lankies pushing in on the perimeter from two sides, and I know that whatever we have stockpiled in the intersections and the hard shelter at the airfield isn't nearly enough to stop this tide. I can see from the air that the SI troopers have already shortened the defensive line at the airfield to consolidate their firepower, but now the perimeter cuts through the runway the Shrikes need for a loaded atmospheric takeoff. Drop ships are swarming overhead, pouring cannon fire into the advancing Lankies at long range. I see MARS rockets launching all over the defensive line in the south, angry fireflies that rush into the horde and fell Lankies with every hit, but the gaps they tear into the ranks get filled up almost right away. Despite their immense size, they have never looked as much like warrior ants as they do now, determined as they seem to get obliterated just to pave the way for the next wave.

"Going in," Captain Prince says curtly.

He puts the drop ship in a shallow dive and unloads his cannons into the stream of Lankies below us. There's no need to adjust aim the way he did when he gunned down the two Lankies near the splash zone of the life pod. Almost every cannon shell finds its mark, tearing through a body or ripping off a limb, sending bits and pieces of cranial shields and skulls flying. The Blackfly's guns pour out a stream of death and dismemberment, carving wide gaps into the ranks of the Lankies. Then we're crossing the SI's defensive line, and Captain Prince pivots the ship and swings the tail around to face the oncoming mass of eggshell-colored bodies. He shoots in controlled bursts, five and ten rounds at a time, blowing Lankies apart wherever the heavy shells hit.

And then the ammunition cassette in the hull is empty, and the only sound I hear over the roar of the engines is the whirring noise of the feed mechanism trying to shovel nonexistent shells into the breeches of the autocannons.

High up in the sky above Willoughby City, an explosion lights up the clouds from above, like a small sun trying to burn through the gray funeral shroud that covers this place. I change the angle of the forward array upward and see a bright spot spread across the clouds and expand.

"That was orbital," Captain Prince says from the cockpit. "The ship just went up."

It's the perfect closing act to the cosmic tragedy that's unfolding below us, and I almost want to applaud whatever entity had such a great taste for awful timing, showing us the destruction of the ship that got us across an unfathomable gulf of space and back again, right before our ultimate defeat.

Now I know what the end of the world looks like, I think.

"That doesn't look right," Captain Steadman says. "That's not a fusion bottle losing containment."

"What the hell else would it be?" the XO asks, defeat in her voice.

Steadman looks at the image from the sensor. The light from above the clouds is fading slowly in intensity, but it's still bright enough to turn the gloomy skies above the colony town into something akin to bright daylight.

"That's a superheated hull blowing up," Steadman replies in a tone of mild wonder. "Looks like someone just got creamed by a particle-gun salvo."

"The fuck did the Lankies get their hands on one of those," Lieutenant Colonel Campbell says.

"I really don't think they did," Colonel Drake replies.

"NAC ground forces, NAC ground forces. This is Battle Group Pacific. Hold fast. Kinetic strike inbound two klicks north and south of your perimeter. Clear all airspace over the target zone immediately. I repeat: hold fast."

The voice on the NAC guard channel is speaking in slightly accented English, in a clipped and businesslike cadence. I have no idea who or what constitutes Battle Group Pacific, but I know that I've just heard the best radio message I've ever received, and that I want to meet the speaker and pledge my undying loyalty. I look around at the other officers in the cargo hold. Everyone is either cheering or grinning, and even Lieutenant Colonel Campbell has a big, unalloyed smile on her face.

There's a sound in the air like a giant bedsheet getting ripped in half, and two kilometers in front of the southern perimeter line, at least fifty Lankies disappear in a geyser of dirt and shattered rock that blooms a hundred meters high. A second one follows, then a third and fourth, hammer blows from the sky that split the surface and pulverize everything they touch. I switch to the stern array and see that a similar row of impacts is plowing the ground to the north, throwing up a curtain of billowing dust, unleashing all the energy of a small tactical nuke without the radiation. Someone is firing rail-gun rounds at our engagement zone with surgical precision, sending Lanky body parts into low orbit with every shot. We watch from our elevated vantage point as the impacts shift to the west and east and back to north and south, until the ground two kilometers away in every direction from the colony outskirts is plowed and cratered many times over. When the barrage lifts, there are still Lankies left in the inner zone between the kinetic strikes and the outer edge of our defenses, but the rail-gun fire has whittled their numbers down to a fraction of the vast horde it was just a few minutes ago.

"You're not going to believe what I am seeing on radar," Captain Prince says. *"It's like I'm hallucinating. If I am, please don't shake me out of it."*

I swap the rear camera view with the tactical display. There's a steady line of radar contacts on the screen, dropping into the lower atmosphere from orbit, dozens of ships that are flying in textbook surface-attack formation. The sight of it fills me with wild, furious joy. Whoever these people are, they are allies, and they are coming to deliver death and destruction to the Lankies that were about to overrun us. I count the contacts on the screen and conclude that there's at least one Avenger with a full task force in orbit, maybe even a pair of them.

When the first attack craft streak down from the clouds and across our field of vision, they don't look like Shrikes at all. They're sleeker, more elegant, with curves instead of angles and bluntness, but no less deadly. The pair of attack ships makes a low pass over the Lankies to the south, dispensing munitions from underbelly canisters that are ejected in a rippling front-to-back cascade of igniting rocket motors. The payload rains down on the Lankies and buries them in a carpet of bright explosions. Another pair of ships follows in the wake of the first and repeats the process. The remaining Lankies finally seem to have found their sense of self-preservation. They turn away from the fire of our defensive line and the relentless bombardment from above and stride south toward the devastated strip of ground that has been worked over by the kinetic strike. But our new allies have no intention of allowing the Lankies to call a time-out. We watch with grim satisfaction as more flights of those sleek attack craft descend on the runners, disgorging their submunitions and taking out Lankies with every pass. Fifteen minutes after the first kinetic strike, there's not a Lanky alive within the zone that was bookended by the rail-gun hits.

"I think you can put the bird on the ground now," I tell Captain Prince over the ship comms.

The four ships that land in the middle of the airfield's apron a little while later are clearly drop ships, but they're not a make or model I recognize. The only thing that's like our Dragonflies or Wasps other than the general shape and obvious functionality is the color scheme, white with orange markings. When the strange drop ships settle on their skids and wind down their engines, I read the markings on the vertical stabilizer fins: **CVB-72 SEOUL**.

The deckhands and maintenance crews on the apron have all ceased their activities and are watching the scene that's unfolding in front of them. Colonel Drake and his XO are walking over from the Blackfly to greet the new arrivals, and the rest of us follow the skipper at a distance because things just got way too interesting.

"What the fuck," Captain Prince says next to me when he sees the unit markings on the new birds.

"Seoul?" I ask.

"CVB-72. That's one of the new Mark III Avengers. For the Pacific Alliance."

"I didn't know they were in service already," I say.

Captain Prince looks at me and grins without any humor.

"That's the thing. They're not. They just started construction on those three months ago."

"What the fuck," I echo.

"Exactly," he says.

The tail ramps of the new arrivals open, and troopers in unfamiliar armor walk down the ramps and gather on the apron. They have the Pacific Alliance flag on one shoulder and the Korean flag on the other. Following them down the ramp are two officers, one Korean and one NAC. The Commonwealth officer wears flag rank, brigadier general, and Colonel Drake salutes him as he steps off the ramp. The general returns the salute.

"Colonel Drake, NACS *Washington*," the skipper says. "My XO, Lieutenant Colonel Campbell."

"I know who you are, Colonel," the general says. "Everyone in the Corps knows who you are."

The general holds out his hand, and Colonel Drake shakes it almost reflexively. Colonel Drake exchanges salutes with the Korean colonel.

"General Waters, commodore of Battle Group Pacific" the flag officer says. "This is Colonel Jeong, Pacific Alliance. I don't know how it happened, but you have no idea how much pleasure it brings me to see you alive and well. We thought we had lost all of you."

"The crash buoy made it home," Lieutenant Colonel Campbell says.

"It did," General Waters replies. "Half the Fleet is on the way here. We were just the closest task force. Sorry for not announcing our arrival earlier. We've been in the system for half a day, but we couldn't broadcast to announce ourselves while we were sneaking up on the Lanky in orbit. We heard all your radio traffic."

"We are glad you arrived when you did, General. It was touch and go. We have quite the story to tell, sir," Colonel Drake says. "It's been a very rough six weeks since we left."

The general looks from the skipper to the deckhands watching from a distance, and then to the rest of us standing nearby. Something in his face tells me that I may not like what he is going to say next, and that ugly feeling of dark premonition kindles itself in a back corner of my brain again.

"Six weeks," the general repeats. He clears his throat and looks at his armored boots, clearly taken aback by what Colonel Drake just said.

"There's no easy way to break this to you, so forgive me if this comes as a shock," the general says when he looks up again. "Colonel, your ship disappeared from the Capella system over *three years* ago."

CHAPTER 29

BOOTS IN THE DUST

I walk around in a sort of daze for a while as swarms of the Pacific Alliance drop ships descend on Willoughby City, and the new attack ships circle overhead to take over the protection of the colony. The drop ships land in two-minute intervals and disgorge Pacific Alliance marines who immediately deploy toward the defensive perimeter, lots of fresh troops in brand-new armor. A short time later, the apron at the airfield is full of drop ships parked wingtip to wingtip, and the arriving ships have started to line up on the runway to unload their troops. Far off in the distance, I can hear the explosions of more cluster munitions and kinetic projectiles as the attack craft from the newly arrived task force expand the safe perimeter around the settlement.

"All STT units, this is Dagger Actual," I send to my team. "Reinforcements are inbound. Disengage and regroup at the STT assembly point back at the bar as the tactical situation permits. Dagger Actual out."

Another pair of drop ships comes in above the airfield and lands on the runway nearby. When the tail ramps have lowered, two squads of troops in PACS exos step out onto the weathered concrete and make their way up to the apron. They walk past me in neat formation, eight troopers piloting sleek exoskeletons that look more advanced than the ones we brought along. They're painted in a matte olive green that looks all business. The tactical markers stenciled onto the frames are familiar, but the Pacific Alliance uses a different regimental system and numbering scheme for their battalions and companies, and I have no idea to which unit those PACS belong.

When the PACS have trotted past the spot where I am standing, I walk over to the far end of the drop ship row to take a look at those sleek hulls, painted in the same martial green as the exos. One of the crew chiefs is standing in front of the tail ramp of his ship, which has **NACS WELLINGTON** and **CVB-70** stenciled on its vertical stabilizer. The chief is dressed in NAC battle armor and wearing the familiar rank insignia of a master sergeant.

"What model drop ship is this, Chief?" I ask.

He turns around at the sound of my voice on his proximity comms channel, and I can see him straightening up a little when he sees the rank on my armor.

"It's a Hayabusa, sir," he replies.

"I've never seen one of those."

"They're a new Pacific Alliance design. Came into service last year with *Tokyo.*"

"How many carriers are up there with your task force?" I ask.

"Two," he replies. "*Seoul* and *Wellington.* Plus support units. Fourteen ships in total."

"When did *Wellington* get launched?"

"Last year, same time as *Tokyo.* This is her second deployment. First one for *Seoul.*"

"Sorry if I sound a little slow, but I don't know what the current year is, Chief," I say.

The master sergeant gives me a long look, as if he is trying to figure out whether I am trying to pull his leg.

"It's 2124, sir," he replies. "April of 2124."

Even with the knowledge of the time gap since our disappearance, hearing the confirmation makes me a little light-headed. *Wellington* was supposed to be the last of the Mark II series to enter service—in early 2121, six months in the future, three years in the past, depending on personal perspective. We are three years behind the rest of the NAC, our lives put on freeze-frame in the world back home for over a third of a decade. I don't have a clue about the way the massive time dilation in the Lanky Alcubierre stream works. But while I know that I haven't really lost three years of my own life because only six weeks have passed for me, I am keenly and painfully aware that I have missed out on over three years of Halley's life.

"Thank you, Chief," I tell the master sergeant.

"Everything all right, sir?" he asks.

"It's been six weeks for us. We're all still in 2120 in our heads. Everyone who was on *Washington*."

"Are you serious?"

"Dead serious," I say. "We've lost more than three years."

"Holy shit." The crew chief shakes his head slowly. "That's fucked up, sir. No offense."

"It is fucked up," I agree. "I think it'll be a while before I'm all right."

I make my way back to the central plaza in front of the admin center. The streets of the settlement are bustling with troops now, Pacific Alliance marines going out toward the defensive line and tired, dust-caked SI troops from *Washington* coming back the other way.

At the repurposed bar we set up as the STT headquarters, the pile of ammo boxes in the middle of the main room has shrunk down to almost nothing, a marker of just how much of a close shave that rescue really was. Ten or fifteen minutes later, the Lankies would have overrun the defensive ring around the town in most places, and our coordinated efforts would have collapsed and devolved into hundreds of small-unit close-quarters engagements, with no supply lines or air support left.

I verify via TacLink that all my troopers are either at the HQ or on the way there. Every STT member who came down to the surface is still alive, and I am deeply thankful that I won't have to add any more names to the list of next-of-kin messages I'll have to send when we are back home. When everyone is assembled in front of the old colonial watering hole, I have them gather around me. We all look battered and exhausted after two days of constant mental and physical exertion.

"You've all seen the reinforcements and the new air support," I say. "There's a full Pacific Alliance task force in orbit, with two carriers. To say that they got here in the nick of time is probably the understatement of the century. You all know how close we just came to getting our clocks cleaned."

There's no disagreement in the ranks. I look around and see lots of sweaty faces behind dusty and scuffed helmet visors.

"You know we got our asses saved by the Pacific Alliance because their marines are all over the place. And I'm sure that most of you already know what I am about to tell you because the only two things that travel faster than light are a warship in Alcubierre and a rumor on the enlisted whisper network."

I pause for effect for a moment.

"We left Earth six weeks ago. While we were gone, three years have passed back home."

The fact that most of the STT troopers don't have a proportionate reaction to this revelation tells me that the enlisted intel network has already spread the news in the hour since the first Pacific Alliance drop ship landed. There's some cursing and tittering in the ranks, but nothing like the gut-punched reaction I had when I heard the revelation for the first time.

"Don't ask me how. I'd guess that it's something about time dilation in the Lanky pathways. We did travel nine hundred light-years twice. That's twenty times farther than anyone else has ever gone through Alcubierre. But I'd be talking out of my ass because I am not a scientist. We'll find out in due course. What matters right now is that we get to go home."

A hand goes up in the ranks. I recognize Sergeant Hill from my combat controller section, who was a classmate of Sergeant Mills at tech school.

"Question, sir?"

"What is it, Sergeant?" I ask.

"Does that mean we're going to get back pay and scheduled promotions for three-plus years, sir?"

There's laughter in the group now, a communal stress-relief valve that has finally been allowed to open. I grin and shake my head.

"Yes, I do believe that's how it works, Sergeant Hill. You'll be able to go on a monster bender once you're on leave."

I join in the bigger swell of laughter that follows. It feels good to see smiling faces and have a chance for levity again, and it makes some of my fatigue drop away.

"You have all done well," I continue. "You've done your duty as well as any podhead ever did. You held your ground even when the odds were stacked against us. Now we get to go home. But our job down here isn't quite done yet. We are making sure our crew gets onto the drop ships. We're bringing home the bodies of our colonists. We see off the SI platoons and make sure the last boots off the ground belong to the STT. And then we've all earned some rest. Let's get it done, people."

For the next hour, we evacuate the admin center and sort the Fleet personnel onto the many drop ships that are standing by to get them off this planet. When the *Washington* crew members and scientists are on their way to the ship, we line up on the airfield for roll call and final orders. There is nothing left for us to do here on Willoughby except to clear out the buildings and get the dead into body bags for the ride home and future identification, to give whatever relatives they still may have on Earth a sense of closure and something to bury. I'm beyond grateful when the Pacific Alliance marines take over the corpse sweep and the transport for us so the SI regiment and my exhausted STT troopers can leave this place and finally get showers, meals, and much-needed sleep. When the SI platoons start boarding the Fleet drop ships for their return trip to the carrier, my mission clock shows that we have been down here without rest or food for almost fifty hours.

The STT didn't get to be the first unit on the ground, but I make sure to fulfill my earlier directive that we'll be the last unit from NACS *Washington* to leave this place. Once the last SI troopers are in the air and on the way into orbit, I do a separate little roll call for the remaining members of my team. We have no colors to strike, no command to hand over. We just gather our things and walk up the ramps of the Blackflies that will ferry us off this planet. The Pacific Alliance marines are setting up a command post at the base of the control tower, and before I walk up the ramp to join my team for the ride home, I stand at attention and salute the Korean colonel who is standing nearby with several of his captains and majors. To my surprise, they all turn toward the Blackflies and return the salute in unison.

Then I walk off the soil of Willoughby and onto the ramp of the Blackfly, aware that this may be the last time my boots touch the surface of another planet.

CHAPTER 30

CONNECTIONS

Our STT drop ships find refuge on NACS *Wellington*, where a decontamination station is taking up a good portion of the carrier's flight deck. Up here, I see the familiar shapes of Shrikes and Dragonflies, shiny new machines with fresh paint jobs lined up in neat rows on the deck, all looking like someone hasn't even removed the plastic protectors from the factory yet. All the craft on the deck carry the seal of the Oceanian Defense Corps. For the first time I feel like I really have traveled forward in time, and I'm sure it's far from the last.

The idea behind the Mark II and Mark III Avengers was to have the other military alliances on Earth finance their construction and staff the ships under NAC flag and technical supervision, to gain the experience in deep-space military ops the smaller alliances have lacked until now. But those plans had just been put into place when we left, and the Avenger-class *Johannesburg* that made up the other half of our two-carrier strike force was the first allied-crewed ship to deploy under that plan. Now all the Mark IIIs are in the Fleet as well, bringing the total number of battle-ready Avengers to twelve after the presumed loss of our *Washington*. The battlecarrier force has quadrupled since we left, and we missed all of it. We are relics now, leftovers from what's practically another epoch in military tech and tactics development. The drop ships and assault craft on the deck are the same basic models as the ones from *Washington*, but they're just different enough to make it feel like we've arrived in a parallel universe, and the non-NAC markings on the tailfins only enhance the effect.

I endure the wait and the half-hour procedure for the decontamination and follow my crewmates down the passageways of the brand-new carrier to the noncom mess hall, which seems to have been reserved explicitly to segregate us from the rest of the ship's crew for now. But there's fresh food and drink, and I am breathing something other than canned air from my armor for the first time in days, so I go along with it and grab a meal with my comrades even though all I want right now is to get to a MilNet terminal and look up my wife. I don't even care if we really did end up in a parallel universe if she is in it as well.

After we eat and get a chance to use proper sanitary facilities again, some heavy NAC brass come into the room, two colonels and the brigadier general who broke the news to us earlier on Willoughby, accompanied by a whole pack of lieutenants and captains who have Military Intelligence and JAG written all over them.

"The Capella system is now an active combat zone again," the general says when I've called the room to attention and exchanged military formalities as the ranking officer in the group. "We have another task force inbound. *Seoul* has already splashed two seed ships since we've arrived. Turns out it really helps to know the exact location of their transition node."

"They'll start to wonder why none of their ships are returning," I say. General Waters shrugs.

"Sooner or later. But for the time being, we'll use the chance to keep swatting whatever comes through. That won't matter to you and your men, though. You're going to get out of this system and back to Earth as quickly as possible."

"Give us a bit of downtime and we can help with the mop-up operations down there," I say, even though there's nothing I'd rather do than to get back to Earth right now.

"You and your team have done enough," General Waters says. "The PacAlliance regiments have everything under control on the surface. They've come a long way in the last few years. We have a fast troop ship in the task force that will get your entire crew home and out of harm's way. The best way for you to help right now is to share your intel with Corps Command and our allies. It won't do anyone any good if things get hot in Capella and we lose you after all."

"How soon are you sending us off?" I ask.

"NACS *Greyhound* is already alongside and docked," one of the Fleet colonels next to the general says. "Personnel transfer is in progress. It should be your team's turn within the hour. Have a safe journey home. And get some rest. You've earned it."

I don't have any objections at all. We have done our part, and now I want to go home and see how much of my old life is still there. The war is moving on without me for now, and I hope that the world hasn't done the same thing while we were missing and presumed lost.

The troop ship is a new thing, a fast transport that is basically a floating barracks in space, built for the purpose of shuttling troops to garrison planets by the regiment without having to stack grunts in tiny berths or quarter them in reconfigured cargo compartments. Compared to the shipboard accommodations I've experienced in the past, the troop ship is a luxury barge, complete with a small but well-stocked RecFac to give the troops something to do other than push-ups during those long transitions to far-off garrison moons. The enlisted get to sleep four to a berth instead of eight or twelve, the NCOs get to share two-man berths, and the officers get their own staterooms. I have nothing left to put into the lockers and drawers in my berth. The M17 wouldn't have passed the security lock after decontamination that sniffs for forgotten ammunition or explosives, so I unloaded it on the way up to the carrier, threw the ammunition into the refuse chute of the Blackfly, and left the gun on the small-arms rack in the drop ship's armory for some Fleet armorer to wonder about. It was my combat talisman for a long time, but it has done its job, and I don't think I'll have any more need for handguns or deployment good-luck charms in the future.

We leave for the Alcubierre chute with a fast cruiser as escort. On the six-hour trip, I manage to talk the Neural Networks administrator of the troop ship into giving me access to the ship's local MilNet with a temporary authorization by getting friendly with her over my original navy job as network jockey. She lets me use the terminal in her office, and when I sit down in front of it, I know that I must look like a drug addict about to receive a fix.

The database on the ship is synchronized before every Alcubierre transition to have current data that can be passed on to colony computers. The data in the troop ship's system is only two days old. I search the Fleet's personnel database for HALLEY, D. (LTC). The system returns the query in less than a second. Her entry is there, but it's labeled INACTIVE. I bring up the message client and try to find her in the list of valid recipients just to double-check, but nothing comes up when I type in her name and rank. She no longer has a drop on the Corps-wide messaging system.

Knowing that her file is inactive without knowing the reason for the marker is worse than not having checked the MilNet records at all. There are a handful of reasons why a personnel file would be marked INACTIVE, and they would be buried inside the file and inaccessible for anyone without the proper access rights. Inactive files are usually either retired, medically discharged, or they've resigned. The last possibility, and one that I don't even want to begin to entertain, is that the owner of the file has been killed on duty.

I want to tear the screen off the terminal and throw it against the nearest bulkhead in frustration. But the ship's Neural Networks administrator was nice enough to stretch the regs for me a little, so I swallow my frustration and politely thank her for the access as I leave her office.

Thirteen hours later, we're back home.

The troop ship transitions into the solar system alone, leaving the fast cruiser behind in Capella. I've spent most of the journey until now sleeping in short, restless, drug-assisted naps, each no longer than half an hour, and each seeming to leave me more tired than I was before. There's a limit to the physical function of a human body, but there's also one on the mind, and I found that when the stress level gets high enough to override even the strongest of sleep aids and CNS depressants, it wears a person down as quickly as any physical hardship.

This time I don't have to sweet-talk someone into letting me borrow a terminal. The crew supervisors, aware of the restless buzz that has been going through the ship since we transitioned back into network range, have our MilNet IDs restored as fast as the comms lag to the nearest node allows. Two hours after we're back in our home system, I sit down in my berth and open the terminal screen with shaking hands. We can send comms requests for nodes on the civilian network, and the Fleet usually allows a handful of high-bandwidth sessions per year to stay in touch with family members. I haven't sent a request like that since my mother died because the only other person in my life has been Halley, and her military node allowed for unrestricted links as long as available bandwidth allows.

The query for the civilian comms nodes isn't instant because it has to travel to Earth and back, and there's a comms delay of almost an hour between the ship and there right now. I send my query and wait two agonizing hours for the result to pop up on my screen. There are half a dozen possible hits, but the right one jumps out at me immediately: HALLEY DIANA NMI>NAC/NA/VT/LF8029283917.

I type the connection request as quickly as my fingertips can tap the data fields on the terminal screen. Then I send it off with a tap that's so forceful that it makes the screen wobble on its hinges.

The return message comes two and a half hours later, during which I have not moved from my spot for more than thirty seconds for fear of missing an incoming connection somehow, even though I can't make the signal travel faster than the speed of light just by sheer willpower.

INCOMING CONNECTION REQUEST <HALLEY DIANA/NAC/NA/VT/ LF8029283917>

I let out a shaky breath and tap the Answer button. The obligatory security screen pops up that lets me know I am about to talk to an unsecured civilian node on a five-second censorship delay, and I acknowledge the screen impatiently.

Then I see the face of my wife in almost real life for the first time in what is absolutely the longest six weeks anyone has ever lived through.

Halley's cheeks are streaked with tears, and the sight of her wet eyes makes my own tears well up, and for the first ten seconds of our precious high-bandwidth vidcall time, we just sniffle and blubber at each other. She has long hair for the first time I've known her, pulled back into a tidy ponytail.

"Hey, you," I say. "You grew out your hair."

We both laugh at the inanity of my statement. She doesn't even try to stop the tears that are coming freely.

"I never mourned you," she says, and in the middle of that short sentence she starts crying so hard that the last word sounds like it's coming out of the mouth of a drowning person. I wait and wipe my eyes as she composes herself.

"I never mourned you," she repeats. "I never wanted to say you were dead. I never stopped hoping you were still out there."

"I was," I say. "And thinking about you every day."

"Am I just having a really cruel dream?" she asks. "How are you back? What happened out there?"

"I can't tell you yet," I say. "They've threatened to court-martial us if we blab. You know the military secrecy shit."

She nods and wipes her face with the sleeve of the light jacket she's wearing.

"Doesn't matter. As long as you're back, and it's really you. Tell me you're not some asshole alien impersonating my husband."

"I'm not some asshole alien impersonating your husband," I say. "Ask me something only I would know."

"What do I get my mother for her birthday every year?"

"Not a goddamn thing," I say, and we both laugh. It feels like all the pressure that has been trying to squeeze my spirit into a singularity for the last few weeks has been released at once.

"You look like it's been a rough trip all the way to the end," she says. "What happened to your eye?"

I reach up and touch the medical patch lightly.

"Helmet broke. The eye's still there, but I think my marksman days are over. And I picked up some new scars."

"They'll heal," she says. "Where are you?"

"Military secrecy shit," I say. "It's a censored line. You know the drill. If I try to tell you, they'll cut the link. We need to get debriefed by the intel brass first. But I will see you soon. Why are you inactive on MilNet?"

"I left the Corps," she says. "A year after you disappeared. I turned in my commission and took the payout. They finally approved yours as well, last year. I didn't want to take it because it would have been like admitting you're gone. But the chief talked some sense into me."

"How's the chief?"

"He's good," she says and wipes her eyes again. "He's good. I'll have to run over there and tell him. He'll lose his shit."

"You're not upstairs in our hideout?"

She shakes her head.

"No, I got a new place. You bought it for me. I mean, your bonus did." She laughs shakily through her tears. "Oh, shit. The Corps is going to want that money back now."

"No, they won't," I say. "They owe me three years' back pay and leave time anyway."

"They owe us a lot more than that," she says. "Look at what they took from us. All this time. All these days together."

"I never thought I'd see the day when you gave up the stick," I say. "I thought for sure I'd have to drag your ass out of the cockpit when you're fifty-five and you've refused general stars five times just so you can keep flying."

"I do miss it," she says. "The flying. Not all the other shit that came with it."

"What have you been doing with your days?"

She smiles and wipes her cheeks with the back of her hand.

"When I left, I started helping the chief out," she says. "The stuff your mom used to do. But I've been busy with other things in the last year."

"Other things," I repeat. "Like what?"

"Well." She looks away from the camera for a moment and bites her lower lip. "I filed the application two years after you had gone," she says. "They approved it last year."

"Application for what?" I say, but a slow realization is making my spine tingle even before she replies.

"Remember the thing we did together the year after Mars? When we were on leave over the winter holidays? At the Fleet medical center down in Bethesda?"

She looks at me evenly, waiting for my reaction.

309

"You did not," I say. "Really?"

"I got approval to use the embryo we had cryoed. That was always what it was for, wasn't it? To have a piece of each other just in case?"

"And it worked out?"

She nods with a smile, fresh tears welling up in her eyes.

"Well, Andrew Grayson, I hate to break it to you over vidcall, but you've been a father for ten months now."

I stare at the screen, dumbfounded, trying to process the wave of emotions that are washing over me like a raging river current over a rock. Halley watches me as I run my hands through my stubble with a long, shaky exhalation.

"Of all the things," I say. "Of all the things to miss out on. I wasn't there for it."

"But you are now," Halley says. "This little project of ours is just getting started. She is not even walking yet."

"*She*," I repeat.

"Your daughter," Halley says. "Our daughter. Phoebe Grayson-Halley. Ten months old next week."

I laugh even as I feel fresh tears running down the corners of my eyes.

"You named her after my mother," I say.

"Well, I sure as shit wasn't going to name her after mine," she says, and we laugh again.

"I'd get her in front of the camera, but she's asleep right now," Halley says.

"Let her sleep," I say. "I want to meet her in person for the first time. Not over vidcall."

"All right," Halley replies with a smile. "All right. Come on home. We will be there when you get here."

As if on cue, the console flashes its thirty-second warning to let me know that I'm about to hit the five-minute bandwidth allowance for this twenty-four-hour period.

"The Fleet is going to cut us off in thirty," I tell Halley.

"Three years, and they only let me have you back for five minutes," she says. "Fucking Corps."

"I'll send another request tomorrow," I say. "And the day after. And so on."

"I'll be here."

I kiss the tips of my fingers and touch them to the screen, and she does the same. We smile at each other and keep our hands on our terminal displays like that until the Fleet's comms link drops and my screen goes black again.

CHAPTER 31

—————— LEAVE-TAKING ——————

The fast troop transport reaches Earth orbit five days later, three days faster than I've ever made the trip past Mars before. I sit in the RecFac with a drink as we slot into the traffic pattern for Gateway Station. The old military orbital facility has been expanded and improved since I was here last, and I have that strange parallel-universe feeling again at the sight of a familiar space station that has changed so much in appearance since I was here only six weeks ago in my version of reality.

At Gateway, the Corps has shuttles waiting to take us down to Earth. There are fifteen hundred *Washington* crew members and a thousand Spaceborne Infantry grunts on the troop ship, and even with Gateway's enormous amount of shuttle docks, it takes a while to ferry everyone down to the surface. I suspect that the Fleet isn't terribly upset about the bottleneck because it breaks up the crew and keeps us from staging a large-scale mutiny at the prospect of being sent to a Corps base for several days of debriefing.

We spend the next two days down on Earth in isolation, on a NACDC base at Goose Bay in northeastern Canada, far off from any cities or towns that may have Network news stations with camera drones or platoons of investigative reporters. They give us thorough medical checkups and debriefings that feel like interrogations on occasion. I do what's expected of me and retell the same stories a few dozen times until I can reel them off from memory again and again, answering the same questions and drawing the same diagrams over and over. I don't need the admonition from the Corps legal officers to keep military secrecy and never talk to a reporter about what happened because I never intend to talk about it again with anyone who wasn't there, except Halley because she deserves to know. After two days of debriefings, the Corps has a few petabytes of testimony and data from the STT, and we are all tired and want to go home. Eventually, the Corps relents and releases us back into the wild when they can tell that we are squeezed dry of information and patience.

"You look like I feel," Sophie Campbell says to me in the officers' mess where the *Washington*'s command section has gathered for a last meal before we all go on our separate ways. I've just taken a seat across the table from her, with a plate that's loaded with all the starch and sugar I couldn't get for over six weeks.

"I don't doubt it," I say. "Doc says I have to gain ten kilos just to get back to normal. And the scars will need a good Fleet cosmetic surgeon."

"They will give you a first-class makeover. We're celebrities now. The civvie networks picked up the chatter. By now the whole planet knows we made it back."

"Just what I need," I say. "Public attention. All I want to do is to go home and take walks under a blue sky for a while."

"Blue sky," she repeats. "Not going home to the PRC, then."

"That hasn't been home since I was twenty-one. We found a place up north that would have us. In the Green Mountains. Clean air, real trees. The snow stays white when it falls."

"Nice. I think I've just about forgotten what a blue sky looks like. Been inside warships and space stations for too long."

"Good chance to hang it up, don't you think?"

She takes a sip of her coffee and shakes her head.

"I've been doing this for so long. I wouldn't know what the hell else to do. I guess I'll work toward getting my first own shitty little frigate."

"And she'll be glorious," I say, and she smiles.

"I have no doubt. What about you?" Lieutenant Colonel Campbell asks. "What are you going to do when you get home?"

"I think my podhead days are over," I say. "I feel like the battery is empty. And I'm a father now. My wife used our cryo egg when she thought I was gone for good."

"No kidding?" Sophie says.

"Not even a little."

"Well, congratulations. Boy or girl?"

"Girl," I say. "She named her Phoebe. After my mother."

The XO chuckles and takes a bite of her food.

"Oh, man. You are so screwed. I'm the XO of a battlecarrier. Second in command of a quarter-million tons of warship. Twenty-four nukes, fifteen hundred personnel. And let me tell you that I don't think *I'm* cut out for that responsibility. Being totally in charge of a child's development."

"I'm sure she'll turn out fine. Her mom is the most capable person I know. And I figured I'll learn on the job. Even if she does have a ten-month head start."

"Just keep that daughter of yours away from any recruiting offices when she turns eighteen," Sophie Campbell says.

"Oh, don't you worry about that," I reply. "She has two field-grade officers for parents. I think we've done more than our share for the Corps and the Commonwealth. Let her have a life without vacsuits. One where she doesn't have to memorize the route to the nearest escape pod."

"So, are you going to quit? Turn in your stars and call it a career?" she asks.

I shrug. "I don't want to have to do it anymore. Vacsuits and escape pods, I mean. Not after all of this. I thought I'd never get home again. I don't think I can put it all on the line again."

She looks at me over the rim of her coffee cup for a moment. Then she sips from it and puts it down on the table.

"There's an old saying. 'Those who can, do. Those who can't, teach.' Every time I've heard someone say it, they meant to talk some clever shit about teachers. But that's not what it means at all. It just means that the people in the village who have aged out of their jobs still have something to contribute to the common good. They can pass down their knowledge. God knows you've earned yours the hard way. You can always stay on and get an academy billet. Become an instructor. Make sure those new kids learn how it's done the right way. How to stay alive out there."

"It's an idea," I say.

"Well, think about it. You're a good small-unit leader. Be a shame to let all that experience go to waste. Stay on, collect your full pension, keep your access to Corps medical. Just a thought."

"I'll consider it."

We eat our meals in silence for a while. All around us, the mess hall is alive with noise, people chatting over their food, silverware clinking on plates, orderlies stacking trays and plates in the galley nearby. As much as I have hated so many things about the military life, I know that this is one of the things I will miss—the camaraderie, the small enjoyments after shared hardships, the gallows humor in tough situations, the trust in the troop next to you when you're in a battle line and facing dangers together that would drive a civilian to the brink of madness. Nobody who hasn't held that line can ever fully understand what it's like, the kinship that comes with going through such things together and coming out alive at the end.

When she is finished with her food, Lieutenant Colonel Campbell pushes back from the table and picks up her tray as she gets up.

"I'm going to collect what's left of my gear and get out of here. Now that they officially let us off the leash."

"I'm right behind you," I say.

"I was wrong about you. You did earn that rank. Forget the stuff I said to you when you came aboard. And our gym sessions kept me sane. If you end up staying in, look me up. Maybe we'll end up on the same tub together again somehow."

"Same goes the other way," I say. "If you ever decide you've had your fill of the Fleet, or you're on leave and don't know where to go, stop by in Vermont. There's a place in my town where we can get a good dram of ancient bourbon. It's stupid expensive, but I may even be able to buy us a round with my back pay."

"I'd like that," the XO says. "Stay out of trouble, Andrew."

"You too, Sophie."

———

I have another task to do before I leave, one that is best done in the privacy of a nearly empty Corps facility on Earth that has a hardwired zero-latency connection to the comms network.

There's a list I made on the way from the Alcubierre node to Earth, and as I walk back to my quarters, I take it out of the chest pocket of my loaner Fleet overalls and unfold it. There are twelve names on it, listed in alphabetical order.

I open the terminal in my quarters and send comms requests for twelve private node connections. In the text box labeled JUSTIFICATION FOR REQUEST, I enter the same text in every one of them.

I send the list of requests into the system. Three minutes later, they all return approved.

For the next few hours, I place calls to the relatives on record for my dead STT troopers, the ones we had to leave behind on the dark Lanky moon. The Fleet can't bring the bodies back to the families for funerals, but I can call them and give them the respect of letting them know how their loved ones died, and why. It's the hardest thing I've ever had to do as an officer, and every minute of it makes my stomach clench. But I take it on anyway because it's my task, my penance, something I cannot delegate to someone else or leave to an impersonal printout delivered in the mail.

Some of the relatives have node addresses that are no longer valid, or they don't answer the call even after I try the connection half a dozen times. Nine of the twelve nodes have a person answering, someone who knew and loved the trooper whose name is listed next to the node number I called.

A few of them curse at me or disconnect the call. Some show gratitude, and others burst into tears and vent their grief for the duration of my call. I keep the connection open when they do, so they can have someone to be aware of their grief and share in it. We all process loss in our own way, and I know that the calls I make are life changing for every party that answers, that they will always remember this day as one of the worst days of their lives.

The hardest call to make is the one to Sergeant Mills's family. It drives home how young she really was when I see that her parents are not much older than I am. They hold each other and cry quietly, and her mother thanks me for letting them know their daughter's fate before ending the call.

When I am done with the last call, I am mentally drained and shaken to my core by the flood of emotions that I just let wash over me again and again. But it's only when I have crossed off every name on the list and tucked it back into my chest pocket that I am ready to leave the base and go home.

CHAPTER 32

—— CENTERS OF GRAVITY ——

I take a shuttle from the airfield at Goose Bay down to HDAS Burlington, the Homeworld Defense airfield that's fifteen minutes by maglev train from Liberty Falls, where my wife and child are waiting for me. On the flight, I am struck by the beauty of the view that had been so familiar to me for so long. I used to nap on the shuttles whenever I had to go up to Gateway on deployment or back down to Earth on leave. But now I take in every little sight, from the way the sunlight glistens on the ocean to the snowcapped peaks of the mountains that are visible through gaps in the cloud coverage above the Northeast. Everything is new and vivid to my eyes, and I decide that something has changed, that I really am in a slightly different reality now, but that I don't mind it at all.

When I land in Burlington, I walk out of the base and into the maglev station just outside of the front gate, and then I am on the last leg of my journey, the fifteen-minute ride to Liberty Falls, and the gratitude I feel for being allowed to be here and now in this space and time is almost overwhelming.

————————

Halley is waiting for me at the entrance of the transit station when I walk into the atrium in the uniform they insisted on issuing me for the trip instead of letting me make it in the loaner overalls I got on NACS *Wellington*. She looks different in her civilian clothes and with her long hair falling loosely onto her shoulders, but I'd still recognize her from a kilometer away just from her posture and the presence she exudes. She doesn't run to meet me like a character in a cheesy Network romance. Instead, she looks at me as I walk up to her, and the smile she has on her face is just like the one in the picture of her I have memorized. The baby girl she is carrying in the crook of her arm is looking around with wide-eyed curiosity. She has Halley's hair, both in color and texture, soft wavy curls that I am seeing on my wife for the first time, the woman who has kept her hair short for as long as I have known her, to better fit it under a flight helmet. It's another one of the parallel-universe changes my brain insists have happened, but I don't mind this one, either.

"Hey, you," she says when I am standing in front of them.

"Hey, you," I reply.

"Still kicking?" she asks.

"Still kicking," I confirm.

"Meet your daughter," she says. "Phoebe, Daddy. Daddy, Phoebe."

Our daughter looks at me with her wide, curious eyes. They're the same color as mine. I can see Halley in her features, but I can also see my own face looking back at me, and that of my mother. I smile at her and she replies with an unsure little flicker of a smile in response.

"Hi, Phoebe," I say.

"Bee," she says.

"That's right," Halley says.

I embrace them both with a wide, careful hug. Halley's eyes well up with tears when I wrap my arm around her and touch my cheek to hers.

"If you think I am ever going to let you set foot on a spaceship again, you're out of your mind," Halley whispers.

I kiss my daughter on the forehead, and she turns her face and presses it against Halley's side. Her hair smells clean and pure. It smells like life.

"Let's go home," Halley says. I hold my embrace for a few moments longer, unwilling to relinquish the sensation of their warm bodies against mine. Then I release them and take half a step back.

"Let's go home," I agree.

Outside, the sun is shining through a break in the cloud cover, and the leaves are rustling on the trees in front of the station. The plaza is still exactly as it was when I came here with my mother, and she walked around to touch the tree trunks and make footsteps in clean snow for the first time in her life. So much has changed since then, and that day now feels like it happened a lifetime ago. But one thing has remained a constant throughout it all: the woman who has been a part of me since we met on the first day of boot camp.

We walk out of the atrium into the sun, and I stop and look up to enjoy the feeling of the warm sunshine on my face.

"Everything okay?" Halley asks.

"It is now," I say.

She smiles a knowing smile. Then she switches Phoebe to the crook of her left arm and holds out her free hand for me to take.

We walk down the stairs and onto the grass, joined in a snug little cluster, and my world clicks back into place, and I know that the fulcrum around which my universe turns is right here by my side.

───ACKNOWLEDGMENTS───

I started what would become the first book in the Frontlines series right before I applied to the Viable Paradise SF/F workshop in the summer of 2008. In hindsight, that seems like a lifetime ago. (It was an actual lifetime ago for my daughter, who was barely a year old when I wrote the first chapter of *Terms of Enlistment*, and who is now about to turn fifteen. But that's the sort of math I shouldn't be doing too often because it reminds me that I've logged those years as well since then.)

Back then, I had the whole thing planned out as a trilogy. But this particular story grew in the telling, as they say, and I enjoyed growing and expanding the Frontlines universe over the last fourteen years. I am profoundly grateful for the reader response the series has received over the years, which is the reason why it got to be eight books long to begin with.

Thank you to my agent, Evan Gregory, who found a home for the first two Frontlines books almost ten years ago and came up with the name for the series.

Thank you to my editor, Adrienne Procaccini, who has shepherded Frontlines through eight books (or rather, who has shepherded me through them).

Thanks are due to my developmental editor, Andrea Hurst, who has been on board from the first book to this one, and whose input has never failed to improve the final product.

Most writers hate writing acknowledgments. One immutable law of publishing is that even though the manuscript has been read dozens of times by the author, the editor, the developmental editor, the copyeditor, and several other people along the way, someone will open the finished book on release day and immediately find a typo that has survived the process, hiding under a chunky adverb and biding its time until the manuscript is finalized. Another one of those immutable laws is that you almost always forget people to thank when you write the acknowledgments, and that risk grows as the size of the acknowledgments page increases as the series grows.

There are so many people who have had a direct or indirect hand in the making of these eight novels, whether through beta reading, advice, moral support, technical know-how, or just by lending an ear and being a friend. Rather than trying to list everyone (and thereby setting myself up for failure once again and mortally offending the people whose names I invariably forget), I will simply thank you all: the fabulous 47North crew, the Viable Paradise staff and alumni, the Wild Carders, the Launchpad people, the Royal Manticoran Navy, all my friends and family, everyone who has staffed or attended a con where I was a guest, and especially everyone who has ever bought, borrowed, read, reviewed, or recommended a book of mine. I get to do this for a living because of all of you, and I am deeply thankful for that privilege.

Marko Kloos
Enfield, April 2022

ABOUT THE AUTHOR

 Marko Kloos is the author of two military science fiction series: The Palladium Wars, which includes *Aftershocks* and *Ballistic*, and the Frontlines series, which includes *Orders of Battle* and, most recently, *Centers of Gravity*. Born in Germany and raised in and around the city of Münster, Marko was previously a soldier, bookseller, freight dockworker, and corporate IT administrator before deciding that he wasn't cut out for anything except making stuff up for fun and profit. A member of George R. R. Martin's Wild Cards consortium, Marko writes primarily science fiction and fantasy—his first genre loves ever since his youth, when he spent his allowance on German SF pulp serials. He likes bookstores, kind people, October in New England, fountain pens, and wristwatches. Marko resides at Castle Frostbite in New Hampshire with his wife, two children, and roving pack of voracious dachshunds. For more information, visit www.markokloos.com.